\

THE SILVER RING

Jane Holland

Thimblerig Books

Thimblerig
Books

Published by Thimblerig Books 2023

PAPERBACK ISBN: 9798388484284
HARDBACK ISBN: 9798397371667

Imprint: Independently published
Cover Design: BookCoverZone

Other novels by Jane Holland

Contemporary Thrillers
GIRL NUMBER ONE (#1 UK Kindle Chart Bestseller)
LOCK THE DOOR
FORGET HER NAME
ALL YOUR SECRETS
LAST BIRD SINGING
THE HIVE
DEAD SIS
KEEP ME CLOSE
TAKE MY PLACE (a short story)
SNIP SNAP

Cozy Mysteries
UNDER AN EVIL STAR (Stella Penhaligon Thrillers 1)
THE TENTH HOUSE MURDERS (Stella Penhaligon Thrillers 2)
THE PART OF DEATH (Stella Penhaligon Thrillers 3)

Historical Suspense
MIRANDA (WHY SHE RAN)
THE MANOR HOUSE
THE SILVER RING

Jane Holland also writes wartime sagas as BETTY WALKER

Jane Holland also writes charming contemporary romance as BETH GOOD, both full-length standalone romantic fiction and the *Oddest Little Shop* romcom series – try her festive Cornish-set stories!

'I love Beth Good's quirky style!' – Katie Fforde, bestselling author

CHAPTER ONE

Stoke Newington, London, September, present day

Stella was looking for something but couldn't put her finger on what exactly. More power? Greater emotional depth, perhaps? Or *vivacissimo*, faster and more lively?

Mentally, she went through the opening chords of the music one by one, testing each phrase for robustness, nuance, resonance; considering how and where to place more emphasis without destabilising the whole. The piece had to work as a unit, to remain true to its form. Yet there should still be freedom within that structure to interpret each individual note in her own way, to allow her identity to shine through.

Yes, that was it. *Freedom*. That was what she was looking for.

The train roared and rattled through the dark, snaking underworld of the London Tube network. Strip lighting flickered, casting a sickly sheen over the heads of the other commuters, bent over devices or reading material. Hunched over the mobile phone, she sat staring at her reflection opposite. She looked tense. Dark-haired, wide-eyed, thinner than she used to be too, her face almost gaunt. But that was hardly surprising. The world had changed; grown harder, less forgiving. It had been a difficult few years, not just for her but for everyone.

Her phone buzzed and she glanced down warily at the screen.

I'm at the flat. Where are you?

She swiped the message away, pretending she hadn't seen it. *Out of sight, out of mind.* One of her late grandmother's favourite sayings.

Gripping her violin case between her knees, on her way to a private pupil, Stella flicked through a few tunes on her music app until she found the track she wanted. A recording of herself from last summer, playing Tchaikovsky's Violin Concerto in D Major, Op 35, part of a music festival at a small London venue. It had been one of the most exhilarating and yet mentally and emotionally exhausting performances of her life. She'd been playing well last year, and practising hard too, many hours a day, but she suspected her form had dropped off in recent months, so was hunting for ways to retrieve that magic. Perhaps her bowing was no longer so bold and expressive…

But as she listened, her mind kept flicking uneasily back to that message.

I'm at the flat. Where are you?

She imagined Bruno waiting outside her front door, leaning against the wall, arms folded, ticking off the minutes until she came home. Her skin prickled. She ought to report him to the police. They'd only dated briefly yet he couldn't accept that it was over. His obsession with her had to be verging on harassment now.

She'd consulted a friend of hers who worked for a law firm, but he'd shaken his head. 'Nothing the police can do unless he makes a real nuisance of himself. I'm talking verbal intimidation, entering the flat without permission, physical assault. Has Bruno done anything like that?' he'd asked.

Of course not.

Bruno could be a little creepy but he was essentially harmless. He would send her texts or slip cryptic little notes under her door while she was out. Sometimes he hung about outside the flat, waiting for her to come home, but always left promptly and without protest when asked.

'Then there's nothing you can do,' her lawyer friend had said, shrugging. 'Not unless it escalates.'

Stella felt sure it wouldn't *escalate*, whatever that meant in real terms. The whole thing made her uncomfortable though. Bruno still had a key to her front door, despite claiming to have posted it back through the letterbox weeks ago. Ideally, she ought to get the locks changed. Yet when she'd asked for a quote from a locksmith, the price had been so exorbitant, she'd given up on the idea.

Bruno wasn't dangerous, and he would get over her eventually. Because what other choice did he have? She had to believe that.

Besides, her money issues were a more serious cause for concern. She'd lost several long-term private pupils in recent months, all citing money troubles of their own when cancelling their lessons. Everybody was cutting back these days. She either needed to find better-heeled clientele or another orchestra post, which were like gold dust and would mean having to audition, something she loathed doing. And playing in an orchestra was so competitive and unnerving, it bruised her spirits just thinking about it. But it was either that or get a proper job. She might have to work part-time in a shop, for instance...

With a squeal of brakes, the Tube train shuddered to a grinding halt, and the man next to her rose to leave. His discarded magazine lay open beside her on the vacant seat. Her restless gaze moved to the page he'd been reading and fixed there, riveted.

LOST HEIRLOOM DISCOVERED IN NEW YORK

Her senses still drowning in the rising swell of Russian music, Stella picked up the magazine and stared at the various large glossy photographs that accompanied the article.

One photo showed a silver ring with an eerily familiar design: two serpents' heads with forked tongues, hissing at each other, their sinuous bodies melded together as they became the ring.

> *The lost heirloom of the Cossentine silversmith family has been bought for an undisclosed sum from an antique dealer in New York. The ring, stolen in 1939, was discovered during a routine clear-out of premises and the original owners contacted.*
>
> *But the mystery remains... How did the Cossentine ring, fashioned in London in the mid-eighteenth century, come to be in America?*
>
> *Celeste Cossentine is rumoured to have been in possession of the ring when she fled her family's summer home, the Cornish manor of Black Rock Hall, on the same evening that her entire family were poisoned. Police tracked the silver heiress as far as London, but the trail went cold following the outbreak of World War Two.*

Numb with disbelief, Stella studied the close-up photograph of the ring. It looked exactly like the one her grandmother had described to her so many times. Her long-lost silver ring...

Her grandmother's name had been Esther though, not Celeste. And she'd never once mentioned being heiress to a fortune or that her entire family had been murdered. Forgetful though her grandmother might have been in her later years, Stella was sure that a mass poisoning would have come up in conversation at some point.

> *The estate, once valued at over twenty million, is reputed to have dwindled in recent years to a few million, their London properties and the family silversmith business having been sold back in the fifties. Following the death last year of the only known surviving member of the family, Maurice Cossentine, his sister Celeste and her descendants, if any, would now inherit the estate and are actively being sought.*
>
> *Meanwhile, their Cornish manor Black Rock Hall houses a murder mystery exhibition dedicated to the atrocity of 1939, launched by Maurice just prior to his death and still attracting a modest number of visitors every year.*

Her stunned gaze shifted to a photograph of a vast, tree-surrounded property, with high chimneys and a slate roof, the view half-hidden behind a large board advertising the Cossentine Murder Mystery Exhibition, with *Can You Solve The Family Riddle?* written beneath, beside an image of a magnifying glass and a large, curly black question mark.

Now and then, Esther had spoken wistfully of childhood summers spent on the idyllic Cornish coast, though she'd always strenuously resisted Stella's suggestions that they take a holiday there, blaming ill health or a lack of money for not going.

Could this be the real reason she'd never gone back to Cornwall?

Stella returned to the photograph of the ring, peering at it more closely. It certainly *looked* like the same ring her grandmother had been wearing in that old photo of her and Grandpa. Esther had described it as a "family ring," saying it had been handed down from generation to generation until Stella's mum had taken it to the States and lost it. Or sold it, more like.

'Otherwise, I would have gifted the silver ring to you in my Will,' her grandmother had insisted, on the rare occasion when she'd discussed her past. 'Maybe one day the ring will turn up again. If that happens, you may need to prove it's yours,' Esther had added mysteriously, along with some baffling comment like, 'Remember, the fighting serpents. And the inscription... on the inside of the ring.'

Apparently, her grandfather had added his wife's initials to the ring as a wedding anniversary gift, alongside the original inscription: two words in Latin. *Love forever*.'

Stella had dutifully memorised these details, fascinated.

Could her late grandmother have been this surviving family member, this Celeste Cossentine, masquerading under an entirely different name to avoid being blamed for the gruesome murder of her family? If so, that would make Stella the lost heir to that huge Cornish manor, which would be rather welcome in her impoverished state.

Briefly, she indulged a vision of herself escaping Bruno and the city – and her frankly terrifying money worries – for a life of peace and luxury in the countryside.

> *Following the death last year of Maurice Cossentine, the only known surviving member of the family, his missing sister Celeste and her descendants, if any, would now inherit the estate and are actively being sought.*

Stella rolled up the magazine and stuck it under her arm, grinning.

The whole thing was ridiculous; she wasn't that lucky. But there could be no harm in delving into her grandmother's old trunk when she had a spare hour or two, to see whether she could dig anything up about Esther's past…

CHAPTER TWO

Black Rock Hall, North Cornwall, June 1939

It was dark by the time the slow and solemn procession of cars that had set off from London that morning finally passed through the open gates of Black Rock Hall in Cornwall.

Celeste, jerked awake by a low rumble of thunder, sat up with a gasp, momentarily confused. It had grown chilly in the back of the car and her skin felt icy. Rain was spattering against the car windows and there was an ominous creaking far off in the darkness, like the groan of timbers on a sailing ship. Tall trees swaying in the wind, she guessed, staring out into pitch-black that revealed nothing.

Briefly, she caught a glimpse of what looked like a ruined tower among the trees, looming sinister under scudding clouds.

'Wh-What's happening? Where are we?' She put a hand to the cold, misted-up window. 'That tower...'

'We're at Black Rock Hall, you silly goose. And

that's the folly they've been building in the woods all year for Mother. Though I don't imagine it will be finished until after we've gone back to London, more's the pity.' Her sister Jolie rummaged in the carpet bag between them, producing a small green glass bottle which she passed to her sister. 'Here, better take your medication. Just in case you forget later.'

Celeste eyed the bottle with dislike. 'I d-d-don't want it.'

'I d-don't c-care what you want,' Jolie replied, cruelly mocking the stammer with which Celeste had been cursed. 'Mother's orders. The family doesn't need any more gossip about your "nervous condition". I still don't understand why Father didn't simply leave you in that asylum... But I suppose now you're eighteen, he's hoping some eligible man will take you off his hands within the year. Then you'll discover what an awful pain in the fundament it is to be pregnant and treated like an invalid when you're perfectly well.' Jolie smoothed her creased woollen jacket over a swollen belly and tidied her hair before reaching for her hat. 'Hurry up and take a swig, would you? We're nearly at the house.'

Celeste shuddered, clenching her fist around the small green-glass bottle.

She abhorred the bitter taste and smell of her medication. It always made her worse too, nauseous and off-balance, though it was true she usually enjoyed a deep and dreamless sleep after a large dose.

A scalding white flash lit up her sister's face and the interior of the car. The maid in the front seat jumped with a squeak and even the driver said something, glancing back at them through the glass partition.

'Oh Lord, a summer storm.' Jolie peered out, groaning, 'That's all we need. My dress will be ruined. I hope the servants thought to bring umbrellas.'

Rain began to blast against the windows, a violent side wind punching the car, sweeping in from the Atlantic Ocean, invisible beyond the great house.

'Celeste? What's the matter now?' Jolie pushed her back against the seat. 'Stop staring out of the window and take your medication. Or I'll tell Mama you've been causing me trouble and then you'll be for the high jump.'

'There's no sp-spoon.'

'Look, just drink some, would you?' Jolie was becoming impatient. 'One good swallow should do the trick.'

Reluctantly, Celeste unstoppered the medication bottle and drank straight from the cold glass neck. She hated the taste, reminded of past 'episodes' followed by the punishment of being locked in her room for days on end. Or worse, taken away in the hospital's small wagon with iron bars at the window. Nausea rose at once, her stomach heaving in waves. But she closed her mouth on the sickness, swallowed hard, and handed the bottle back to her sister, coughing on the fumes.

'Show me your tongue, Celly,' Jolie said suspiciously.

Grimacing, Celeste stuck out her tongue, no doubt still stained with the dark treacly substance the doctors had prescribed for her 'condition'.

Her sister nodded, satisfied.

The great house was in view now. High dark turrets and slanted roofs stood out, briefly outlined against a violet sky. Lights glowed and were lost between trees. The cars slowed for the grand front entrance with its stately sweep of steps and tall double doors, tyres crunching on gravel.

Placing a palm flat on the rattling glass, its pane streaked with shadowy water, Celeste tried to imagine how it would feel to be outside in this turmoil. The deep rumble of thunder was loud enough to hurt her ears. It was as though everything inside her head had escaped and was outside now, slamming against the car and trying to get back in.

The medicine had left her dizzy and confused. She sucked in a breath, blinking. Outside, lightning flared again. Jagged white streaks left a ghostly after-image on the black skies like a photographic negative, closely followed by another crack of thunder. Its low rumble could be felt deep in her bones, as though the storm were also raging inside her body, not merely out there over the turrets and windswept cliffs of Black Rock.

Celeste imagined an angry god bellowing at them to leave its sacred place. Bellowing at *her*.

'The storm must be right overhead,' she whispered, her face pressed up to the chill, rain-streaked glass as she began to shake uncontrollably...

She couldn't remember what happened next. It must have been another of those horrible blackouts where she lost time. All Celeste knew was that she was lying on the wet gravel drive, staring up at the open car door. People were standing about her, looking down in dismay. She tried but couldn't get up. It was like being at the seaside, her body shuddering, hands clawing at wet pebbles, the storm roaring in her ears like the ocean's deep currents. The dark night sky swung in and out of focus. Car headlights pulling up behind them cast long nightmarish shadows. Slowly, forcing back the darkness, she dragged her way back to reality.

'She's had one of her stupid fits, I suppose,' Jolie was explaining, somewhere far above her, only her shoes on Celeste's eye level. Neat, black, polished ankle boots with tiny buttons which her sister always wore for travelling long distances. 'I told Father I didn't want to travel with her, that I wasn't a nursemaid.' She sounded furious. 'But he insisted, of course, because of my condition. As though expecting a child is the same as being a *lunatic*.'

Celeste closed her eyes, nauseous again. She could still taste the medication at the back of her throat, burning into her flesh.

'Don't be vulgar, Jolie.' Her oldest sister Fenella had arrived on the scene, her tone disapproving. 'Well, she can't lie there with all the servants staring. Have you checked if she's conscious?'

'I'm not a doctor,' Jolie replied coldly.

A new voice cut in. 'Should I fetch Mr Cossentine, Miss? He's gone inside with Mrs Cossentine.' The man sounded young and Cornish, a slow burr in his voice. Presumably one of the local villagers who always came to help out at the hall while the family were in residence for the summer.

'Lord, no, my father would go spare if he saw her like this.' Fenella sounded horrified. 'We need to get her into the house without any fuss. Ah, here's your husband, Jolie.' A note of relief now. A man had arrived to sort out their problem. 'He'll know what to do.'

'Harold, darling,' Jolie said quickly, her voice

low and conspiratorial, 'we need a hand. She's done it again, as you can see. In front of all the servants, too.'

'Don't fret, Jolie, we'll soon deal with this. You there, lad, come here.' Jolie's husband, the capable Harold Fortescue, began directing one of the servants to help him 'deal' with her. 'You take her arms, and I'll take her legs.' Celeste moaned in protest as male hands seized her extremities, intrusive and not particularly gentle. 'That's the way. Now, on a count of three...'

'Thank you, Harold, but if you'd care to step aside, I'll carry her indoors myself,' a more familiar voice interrupted, young but crisp with authority. 'I am her brother, after all.'

The strangers' hands miraculously disappeared. Celeste breathed easier. Friendlier arms slid about her and then she was flying, but held tight, secure.

'Maurice...' she murmured, daring to open her eyes at last. 'What happened? What did I d-do this time?'

He surveyed her, his eyes dark, intense, fringed with long lashes. Maurice was her junior by two years, yet at times seemed centuries older than any of them. 'They're saying you blacked out again. Fell out of the car. Now, lie still and be quiet. Unless you want me to drop you?'

Celeste obeyed, blinking up into wet swirling darkness as Maurice crossed the broad expanse of gravel before the great house with easy strides. She caught a flash of high walls and all the front windows lit up, the curtains left open to light the drive. The storm was still raging above Black Rock Hall, cold fingertips of rain tapping at her face, her throat...

Her brother snapped at the man following them, 'Keep up with me, would you? Can't you see she's getting wet? Hold the umbrella higher.'

'Doing my best, sir.'

She stilled, surprised. It was the local again, only this time she was able to pinpoint the voice. Young Jeffrey, the cook's boy. He and Maurice were close in age and had been thick as thieves the previous summer. Now it sounded as though her brother wasn't too pleased to see him again...

Maurice carried her up the broad front steps. Bright lights dazzled her in the entrance hall. Voices exclaimed around them, high with concern. She heard her father's deep voice in the distance and closed her eyes again. Their London housekeeper, Mrs Benchley, clucked her tongue, trying to persuade her brother to put her down and let one of the servants carry her upstairs.

'No, I'll do it,' Maurice insisted. 'Which room is it? Her usual?'

'The little one at the far end of the landing, near the servants' stairs.' The housekeeper sounded flustered. 'Will she need the doctor called?'

'What my sister needs is sleep.'

'And should I come up with you, sir? In case you've forgotten the way?' Jeffrey again, close by, his slow Cornish accent thick as clotted cream.

'No,' Maurice told him curtly.

Too embarrassed to say a word, Celeste stared up at the ornate white ceiling mouldings as her brother carried her briskly upstairs. So much for not exciting any more gossip…

The familiar small bedroom with the sloping ceiling was dark and felt damp, as though it hadn't been aired properly since last summer. But the bedcovers looked clean at least, and she could smell roses and lily of the valley, so the chest of drawers had been freshened with pot pourri in their absence.

'I'm sorry,' she managed to say, blushing as Maurice set her down on the narrow bed. 'I'd taken my m-medication, I swear it.'

'You have nothing to apologise for, Celeste. You're not well, anyone can see that. How is that your fault?' He turned on the light and came back to chafe her hands, looking her over critically. 'You're freezing, too. I'll get someone to light a fire in here.'

'In summer?' She smiled up at him wanly. 'Change the government while you're at it, would you? If you've got that much p-power…'

Her brother grinned, suddenly years younger. 'How about extra blankets, then? I can have some sent up to you. With a cup of hot milk to help you sleep.'

'I don't want to be any trouble.'

'You're my favourite sister, Celly. You could never be any trouble.' Maurice straightened, slicking back dark hair with a restless hand. 'Anyway, it was a bloody long journey but you can relax, we're here now. And you always love spending the summer hols in Cornwall, so it was worth the agony.' He went to the door, adding softly, 'I'll see you in the morning.'

After his footsteps had receded, Celeste rolled over on the bed and hid her face in her hands.

One minute she'd been looking up at the storm, the next she'd found herself on wet gravel, lying there in the rain, without any idea what might have happened to her in those intervening moments.

Blackouts.

That's what her doctor in London called her episodes of dizziness and amnesia. 'Fits' was how her father referred to them, not bothering to hide his contempt, and the others tended to follow suit. But at least Father had not forced her to remain in that horrid asylum, allowing her home so long as she promised to keep taking her medication.

What had Jolie said in the car? Something about Father hoping *some man* would take her off his hands.

Was her father planning to marry her off this summer, now she was old enough to be of interest? Celeste buried her face in her hands. She didn't want to be married like her sisters, made the chattel of yet another man, and tied down with a child or two in the nursery. It was 1939, for goodness' sake, not 1839! She wanted to be a free and independent woman, able to make her own way in the world.

A knock at the door interrupted these dark thoughts. She sat up too rapidly and was almost overcome by dizziness again. Despondency swamped her. So much for being able to make her own way in the world...

'Come in,' she stammered.

It was Becky, the cook's fresh-faced, fair-haired daughter, her arms full of blankets. Her mother preferred a Cornish cook while they were summering in the West Country and always employed Mrs Dunn to manage the kitchens, who lived locally and, in turn, bought her son Jeffrey and daughter Becky to work at the hall too.

Becky couldn't be much older than fifteen yet was already taller than her and had filled out considerably since last summer, her once trim figure now comfortably plump. 'Master Maurice asked me to bring these blankets up for you, Miss.' There was sympathy in her bright blue eyes. 'I heard you had a fall, getting out of the car.'

A fall.

So that was to be the official story, was it?

'Yes.' Celeste got up to check her reflection in the mirror. Her hair was damp and looked quite wild. 'Clumsy me.'

'Oh no, Miss…' Cheerfully, Becky bustled across with the blankets and shook them out across the bed. 'I'm sure that's not true. It's a fearful long journey from London; I expect you was mortal tired, that's all.' She turned, meeting Celeste's gaze in the mirror, her smile encouraging. 'Should I turn down the covers for you, Miss?'

'No, thank you, I can do that for myself. Did you see my m-mother downstairs, Becky?'

'Mr and Mrs Cossentine are in the drawing room with your brothers and sisters. Mrs Benchley is fetching them tea and refreshments.' Becky was frowning. 'You all right, Miss?'

She had sagged, Celeste realised, and pulled herself up again, squaring her shoulders and turning to the maid with a false smile. 'I'm a little hungry, that's all. My brother mentioned something about hot milk?'

'Ah, that'll be it.' Becky beamed. 'Fair famished, you were, and come over faint. Well, don't you fret, Miss. I'll fetch some up straightaway.' She winked, adding, 'With a nice plate of bread and Cornish butter. That'll soon set you right.'

As the girl went out, Celeste stared round at the door, hearing the key turn in the lock.

'Becky?' Taken aback, she strode to the door

and rattled the handle. It wouldn't budge. 'Becky? Hello? You... You've locked me in.' She banged on the door but nobody came. She had thought Becky sympathetic to her situation, but now this...

Celeste stood there a while in sullen silence, her cheeks hot with fury. Had the servants been instructed to lock her in? Were they to be her jailors now? And for what reason? Because she'd reacted poorly to her medication in the car, which was not at all unusual. Yet still Father refused to ask the doctor to lower her dose of the filthy stuff, no doubt feeling it was better to keep her locked up and barely conscious than risk her behaving in ways he considered unsuitable for a young lady in her position.

It was *outrageous.*

Eventually, she gave up and went to the window instead, dragging the curtain back to peer out at the darkness. The summer storm had moved on at last but the roofs and guttering of Black Rock Hall were still dripping, a constant musical pitter-patter outside. She leant over to study the sheer treacherous drop to the lawn below, noting how far away the nearest drainpipe was – quite out of her reach, in fact. Dizziness assailed her again and, for a horrible moment, she feared she would be sick. But the moment passed.

What were they talking about downstairs in the drawing room, her rigidly proper parents and siblings and their various hangers-on?

Her, she had no doubt, and how the Cossentine family needed to prevent news of her "illness" leaking out before they'd found a suitable husband to take her on. All except for Maurice, of course, who never joined in such hateful discussions, much to her relief. But her youngest brother was almost a man now. He would be allowed to roam the house and grounds at will this summer, to spend his time however he liked and with whomever he liked, no questions asked.

Whereas she, aged eighteen, was a prisoner.

Her hand clenched on the curtain, crushing the fabric. 'I hate them,' Celeste whispered into the glistening dark, meaning every word with a venom she hadn't known she possessed until then. 'I hate them all and I won't be married off. Let them try...'

CHAPTER THREE

Stoke Newington, London, September, present day

Nestling her chin into the violin rest, Stella set bow lightly to string and began to play. The long-familiar music enveloped and swirled about her until she was lost in another age – the early twentieth century – and in another part of the country – Cornwall. It was a place she had never visited in her life, yet had often dreamt about, inspired by her grandmother's recollections of a childhood spent in that ancient, myth-swathed landscape. With the sweet, intense notes of Vaughan Williams' 'The Lark Ascending' infusing her entire being, it felt as though she were there at last, treading barefoot through lush Cornish meadows, sunlight on her upturned face, listening to a lark in the blue sky, too high to be seen.

Her grandmother Esther had loved this piece, playing it endlessly on her headphones as she sat in their flat looking out over the rainy, grey rooftops of London.

Tears came to her eyes and her bowing faltered briefly.

It was almost ten years since Esther, her only living relative, had died at the ripe old age of one hundred-and-one, though people had always said she looked younger than her years. As indeed she had.

'A wonderful character,' friends and acquaintances had called her grandmother, crowding the memorial service, and bringing flowers for the old lady, who had lived in the lively London district of Stoke Newington since the end of the Second World War. 'So sprightly and ever-young too...'

But time had caught up with her in the end.

Even after her husband's death, Esther had refused to leave London. By the time she'd tracked Stella down in the States, a child living in care after her mother had died, her home had been this modest two-bedroom flat. Stella had taken over the lease on her death, somehow unable to move on, as though the tatty furniture and familiar surroundings kept her close to her grandmother.

Esther had left a little money to Stella. But it had all run out now, and the lease was up for renewal at an astronomical sum she had no chance of affording. Soon, she would need to leave these few rooms she had shared with her grandmother and start again somewhere new.

Somewhere that wasn't home.

She thought again of that magazine article about the silver heirloom ring, but only with passing interest. The chances of her grandmother having been a member of the wealthy Cossentine, yet never claiming her inheritance nor admitting her true identity even to Stella were remote. Though it was also true that Esther had been notoriously close-mouthed about her past…

As she bowed the last note, she became aware of another presence nearby, someone applauding. 'Bravo,' a familiar voice said from the doorway to the lounge. 'That was beautiful.'

A large, shadowy figure came into the room and her vision slowly focused on his face: dark, expressive eyes, an aquiline nose, the beard she had tried to persuade him against growing.

With a huge effort, Stella dragged herself back from the sunlit countryside of her grandmother's youth to the present moment.

'Bruno,' she murmured, violin still tucked beneath her chin, the bow held loosely between long, supple fingers. 'I didn't hear you come in.' Frowning, she returned to reality, adding uneasily, 'How long have you been standing there?'

'Long enough to remember that you are the most gifted violinist I've ever had the pleasure to know.'

The slight emphasis on those last words and

the languorous way his eyes ran over her body left Stella in no doubt what Bruno meant.

'Thank you.' She managed a fixed smile in response. More of a grimace, in fact, but that would make no difference to him. However stoutly she rebuffed his advances, he seemed barely affected. 'Though you shouldn't be here, Bruno. We discussed this and you agreed to return my door key.' She lowered the bow but kept it in hand, holding it across her chest almost defensively. Not much of a weapon, perhaps. It made her feel better though, facing him alone. 'You can't keep wandering in and out of my apartment whenever you feel like it.'

'I knocked,' he said mildly, 'but there was no reply. I knew you must be in because Mrs Li said she hadn't seen you go out today.' His dark eyes searched her face, full of concern. 'You were so upset on the phone last night, I was seriously worried about your state of mind. I had to check on you.'

'I was upset because I've asked you to stop calling, yet you pay no attention. It can't go on, Bruno. What you're doing... Well, it's close to stalking.' She paused, her heart thumping at having dared make the accusation to his face, and then added breathlessly, 'If you don't stop, I'll have to report you to the police.'

'You don't mean that.'

Bruno came closer.

Again, she felt a tremor of fear. She'd broken up with him after only a few months when he'd begun to behave possessively, at first dictating what she wore on their dates, and later controlling her meals and even her sleep routine. Then had come the night when he'd struck her across the face for daring to speak to an old friend at a nightclub, a man she'd recognised from her university days. There had been nothing between them but Bruno hadn't believed her stammered explanation.

Even though she'd stopped seeing him after that incident, he had refused to accept that decision, insisting that he would 'never' give her up. Vague threats had followed about what would happen if she continued to shut him out. But Stella had stood firm, and for the past few weeks she'd thought he was finally getting the message.

Now Bruno was here again, letting himself into her flat as though he owned the place. And her with it. Though at least this proved her suspicions about the key he claimed to have posted back through the letterbox.

'May I have my key back, please?'

Bruno fished for the door key in his pocket. 'Here you go.' He placed it with a faint clink on the glass-topped coffee table. 'Happy now?'

'Have you made a copy?'

'Don't be ridiculous.' He came towards her and she backed instinctively, gripping her violin bow tightly. His brows snapped together. 'I'm not going to hurt you, Stella. I would never hurt you.'

She sucked in her breath, watching him closely.

'Ah, yes.' He shook his head, reading her expression accurately. 'I told you, what happened… It was a mistake. I was jealous, that's all.'

'I think you should leave.'

Bruno narrowed his eyes. 'But I've only just arrived. And look.' He withdrew a box from his pocket and opened it, turning it towards her. Inside was a thin silver ring. 'I saw this at the antique market yesterday and thought of you. It could be your grandmother's, don't you think?'

She'd told him about her grandmother's lost ring one night, and had seen how fascinated he was by the story. 'So romantic,' he'd said softly, kissing her hand. '*Bellissima*.'

Stella shivered, recalling the article she'd seen in the magazine. The last thing she wanted was for Bruno to start fantasising about her being a wealthy heiress. She would never get rid of him then.

'I doubt it. My mother sold that ring in America years ago.' She considered him uneasily. 'You didn't buy it for me, did you? Because you know I can't accept any gifts from you, Bruno. Especially such an expensive –'

'It's not a gift. It's a proposal,' Bruno interrupted her, still holding out the silver ring in its velvet-lined box. 'Will you marry me, Stella?'

Her heart hammered violently. Was the man mad? They had broken up months ago and now he was proposing marriage? Her nerves prickled. They were alone together, and with many of her neighbours out during the day she couldn't be sure anyone would come if she screamed for help.

Caution prompted her to say, 'That's very sweet of you, but –'

'I want you to be my wife. We were made for each other.'

'No,' she said instinctively. 'Absolutely *not*.'

'Think about it properly before giving me an answer. I'm in no hurry, Stella, I can wait.' Bruno snapped the box shut and slid it back into his jacket pocket, seeming unmoved by her refusal. 'Your lease is up soon, isn't it? I know you can't afford to renew it.'

'That's none of your business.'

'Don't wait to be left without a roof over your head. I'm offering you a comfortable home, right here in Stoke Newington. You wouldn't need to leave London and you would certainly never need to work again.' His gaze slid to the violin she was still holding. 'I hate to see you prostituting yourself for strangers, Stella.'

'I beg your pardon?"

'Playing for money. Your talent is worth so much more than that. As my wife, there'd be no need to give lessons or perform to strangers.'

Bruno moved closer, looking her in the eyes, his smile disturbing. 'You would only play for me, behind closed doors.'

Terrified by the look in his eyes, Stella took a hasty step backwards. 'Get out,' she whispered, frantically wishing she could put her violin down, somewhere out of harm's way. If it got broken...

'Stella,' he said huskily, reaching for her with both hands. His eyes glowed with intensity. 'I've missed you in my bed. I want you so much...'

'No,' she gasped.

On impulse, her hand whipped up and she struck him across the face with her violin bow. The fine wood snapped near the end, the strings sagging and trailing. He recoiled, swearing viciously in Italian, a hand to his cheek where a thin, angry lash-mark was already visible.

Shaken by what she'd done, Stella staggered back and collided with the heavily over-stacked bookcase. It shuddered, and several books and other items fell from the top, one striking her head. An old scrapbook of her grandmother's, she realised, wincing at the pain. It fell open at her feet, scattering black-and-white photos, pen-and-ink sketches and other mementoes across the floor.

He growled something in Italian – an expletive? – but didn't come any closer, still nursing his cut cheek.

'Get out,' she repeated loudly, raising the broken bow as though to strike him again. 'Before I call the police.'

Bruno threw her a contemptuous look but turned to leave. 'This isn't over,' he snarled over his shoulder before banging out of the flat. 'You'll be seeing me again, *bellissima*.'

Stella sank to the floor, cradling her broken bow and violin, shaking. She'd never struck anyone before in her life and still couldn't quite believe she'd had the nerve to do it. Or that it had worked and he'd left the flat.

As her heart rate slowed, her gaze shifted to the key on the coffee table, a new fear growing inside her. Bruno had handed over the key to her flat with surprising docility tonight. Was that because he'd already made a copy, despite his denials?

With that in mind, she hurried to lock the front door, securing it with the chain for extra peace of mind. Then, rueful, she returned to examine the snap in her bow; it was clean enough and could probably be glued for now, but at some point she would need a new bow.

She regretted having damaged her most prized possession. But if she was now finally rid of Bruno and his obsessive behaviour, the sacrifice would have been worth it.

You'll be seeing me again, bellissima.

She hoped he was bluffing about that. What

else could she do but hope? If she went to the police now, Bruno might counter-claim that she'd assaulted him first, the mark on his cheek as evidence. And without any proof herself of his threatening behaviour, she might be the one they arrested.

Wearily, stooping, Stella began to tidy up the scattered photos and other odds and ends that had fallen out of her scrapbook.

One photograph caught her eye and she paused to study it, curious. It was of her grandmother Esther, probably in her late teens or early twenties, photographed with another young woman. Both were wearing nursing uniforms and caps, arms about each other's shoulders, grinning fresh-faced into the camera. She thought they looked remarkably similar; they could almost have been sisters.

She turned the photograph over. There, in her grandmother's distinctive scribble, were the words *Esther and me, 1940*.

CHAPTER FOUR

Black Rock Hall, North Cornwall, July 1939

Celeste lowered the newspaper and looked down the breakfast table at her mother, dread in her heart. It was over a week since she had been allowed out of her room at last, for 'good behaviour,' and even permitted to accompany her family to a modest party at a neighbour's house. At that party, old Sir Oliver Gliddon had singled her out for particular attention, much to her embarrassment, and later had come calling at Black Rock Hall with an unexpected proposal of marriage.

She had said a prim, 'No, thank you,' to the portly Devon landowner, a man of very few teeth and whose sideburns were positively Victorian.

Yet today, her engagement was here in the Times, printed in black-and-white, for all the world to see. How on earth had that happened?

'I don't understand, Mama,' she began tentatively, fearing to be locked into her bedroom again if she made a scene over this. But perhaps it was a simple misunderstanding. She couldn't believe her parents would have been so cruel and high-handed as to place announce her betrothal in The Times without even consulting her first. 'How did this announcement reach The Times? I didn't accept his proposal. I clearly said *no*.'

'Ah, but you intended to say *yes*. Given time to consider your situation and his handsome offer. And that's what matters.' Pushing her plate aside, her mother dabbed at her mouth with a linen napkin and then turned her gaze to Celeste's face. 'Now don't get into one of your flaps, dear. Have you taken your medication this morning?'

'Yes, we need you sane and in control of yourself,' her sister Jolie agreed between mouthfuls, casting Celeste a disapproving look. 'Tonight's family gathering is to celebrate my twentieth birthday, please don't forget. I won't stand for my party being ruined by one of your stupid fits of madness.'

'I... I don't suffer from fits of m-madness,' Celeste struggled to say, her face flaring with heat, but they all ignored her.

'Jolie, dearest, don't make a fuss. I have a splendid idea... Your birthday dinner can be used to celebrate Celeste's engagement too. Yes, why not?' Ignoring Jolie's thin-lipped fury, their mother turned to summon Priddy, their London butler who still came down with them to Cornwall every summer, despite being well past seventy and doddery on his feet. 'Pen and paper, Priddy. I need to send a dinner invitation to Sir Oliver straightaway. John can drive it over there in the car.' She grimaced. 'I only hope it's not too short notice and Sir Oliver will be available to join us tonight.'

The butler bowed, with a faint sound of creaking, and disappeared. He was only slightly less ancient than her betrothed, Celeste thought despairingly.

'But what if I want to wait before m-marrying, Mama?' she asked, aware there no little point in refusing to agree with her mother's assessment of the situation. Saying an outright no would only be dismissed as another 'flap,' dooming her to incarceration and medication again. But perhaps she could delay a little longer. Perhaps even until they returned to London at the end of the summer, putting her neatly out of Sir Oliver's reach...

'There'll be no waiting,' her mother told her sharply, bursting her bubble. 'You're eighteen now and you're to be married to Sir Oliver Gliddon of Alfardisworthy. Everything has been discussed and arranged between your father and Sir Oliver. Is that not so, darling?' She glanced down the long table at Celeste's father, but he said nothing, frowning, intent on some bills. Giving up with a sigh, her mother turned back to Celeste. She studied her daughter's face critically. 'I'm concerned about your colour, which is high. Are you suffering from a fever? After breakfast, I want you to take your medication.'

'I already took it,' she said sullenly.

'Let's see.' Jacob, one of her older brothers, lunged across the breakfast table to pluck the newspaper from Celeste's hands. He read the engagement announcement aloud to himself, a malicious smile on his lips. 'You should be happy. Sir Oliver owns half the land around Truro.' He tossed the newspaper to their mother, and picked up his knife and fork again. 'I say, when's the wedding? Before the end of the summer, I hope, so we don't all have to come piling down again from London to witness the great event. High time we got shot of you anyway, Celly.' He gave her a wink, shovelling egg into his mouth. 'And I fully expect you to have a bun in the oven by Christmas time.'

Horrified, Celeste looked to her mother for support. But Mama had opened the newspaper herself and was engrossed in an article on the inside pages, holding it out at arms' length to see the small print without her reading glasses.

'Jacob, that's beastly.' Hot-cheeked, Celeste glanced towards their father. But he hadn't heard his son either, it seemed, not looking up.

'No, that's married life, Celly.' Her brother grinned, downing the last of his tea with a gulp and rattling the cup back into the saucer.

'Sebastian and I will be running a book on how long it takes old sobersides to get you in the family way. All bets taken.'

'Don't be so vulgar, Jacob,' Fenella told him repressively. The eldest of Celeste's sisters, she was twenty-five and had been married for five years without producing a child, much to Mama's annoyance. She shot a glance at her husband, seated beside her and intent on his plate of black pudding and eggs, and then looked swiftly away. 'Besides, I agree with Celeste. She's far too young to be married.'

'Her chum Laurel was married at seventeen,' Jacob growled back at her. 'I don't recall anyone belly-aching about that.'

'Laurel married her childhood sweetheart. It's not the same thing at all.' Fenella studied Celeste with a downturned mouth. 'Besides, Celly knows nothing about life. She skipped going to school for that appalling tutor instead. Mama chose not to launch her as a debutante. She doesn't ride, she doesn't dance, she barely speaks in company... And apart from our summer holidays here in Cornwall, she's never left London.'

'Yes, and you know perfectly well why,' their mother said without raising her head from the newspaper. 'Celeste was never well enough to travel or mix with others. Now her schooling is over, she needs to be kept quietly at home until she is married. The doctors have all agreed.'

'They didn't agree I should be kept locked in my room for hours every day,' Celeste pointed out, but they all ignored her.

'Not much of a bargain for Sir Oliver, is it?' Jacob said laconically. 'Getting a mad wife...' He fell silent under their mother's angry glare.

'Your youngest sister is not *mad*.' Her mother hesitated. 'She's... fragile. And Sir Oliver is well aware of her condition. Your father discussed it with him extensively before he made his proposal.'

'A proposal I didn't accept, if anyone's interested,' Celeste muttered.

'The material fact is that Sir Oliver is over three times her age.' Seated across the table from her, Maurice finally spoke up, always her champion. 'An excellent match for her, yes. But the age difference... It doesn't seem right, Mama.'

Celeste threw her brother a grateful smile, though she felt a little fearful for him too, speaking up for her so boldly. An unruly sixteen-year-old, the youngest son of the family was as much of a black sheep as she was and far more likely to risk a beating for impertinence, being a boy.

Like all the Cossentines, Maurice was tall for his age, dark-haired and sallow-skinned, though his eyes were closer to jet-black than Celeste's own soft hazel. It was his affectation to wear an embroidered silk waistcoat everywhere, and he had donned this even for breakfast today, worn unbuttoned over a loose white shirt, giving him the decadent air of an artist. He wore his hair longer than was fashionable, much to their parents' disapproval, so that it flopped into his eyes and had to be knocked back impatiently at intervals. He didn't get on with his many siblings or extended family, except perhaps for Celeste, whom he tolerated and occasionally protected, always gentle and considerate with her.

But even there, she wasn't entirely sure of his true feelings. Was Maurice genuinely sorry for her, picked on and scapegoated by the rest of the family, or was he merely using her as a weapon to get back against their parents?

'I know arithmetic isn't your strong suit, Maurice,' Jolie said coldly, reaching for the butter dish. 'But Sir Oliver cannot be more than fifty-five. Please don't exaggerate.'

Although only twenty herself, Jolie had been married the year previously, to a wealthy London businessman of forty-three, Harold Fortescue, who had breakfasted early today and was apparently now walking the grounds of their large Cornish summer home with his two spaniels, the boisterous animals having been brought down from London only the night before. Her bulky figure indicated her expectant status, a triumph of which she was inordinately proud, as this would be their parents' first grandchild, despite having so many adult children.

'I can add up well enough to know why you and Harold needed to marry so swiftly, Jolie,' Maurice shot back.

Bright spots of fury appeared in Jolie's cheeks and she slammed the butter knife back onto the dish with venom, glaring at him.

'Mama,' she said in a high-pitched voice that was one of her warning signs of impending hysteria, 'are you going to allow Mouldy Maurice to spread such vicious rumours about me?'

'Please don't call me that,' Maurice said softly.

'He's been telling all his horrid friends that Harold and I jumped the wedding ceremony and it's… it's simply not true,' Jolie continued heedless, tears springing to her eyes. 'Martha told me it's all the talk below stairs.'

'Then your maid ought to know better and needs to hold her foolish tongue,' their mother snapped.

'For God's sake,' their father thundered from the far end of the table, finally looking up from the documents he'd been studying and casting the room into deadening silence. 'I can barely hear myself think with all your pointless chatter. During the Great War… ' He glared at Jolie, who had snorted, as she often did whenever Papa launched into his tales of the Great War. 'You may laugh, Jolie, but I'll have you know you wouldn't be sitting here today without those of us who fought for this country in those few terrible years.'

'Forgive me, Papa,' Jolie said quietly.

'During the Great War,' he continued, ignoring her apology, 'I frequently had occasion to punish men under my command who could not behave in a reasonable manner. I would not wish to punish my own children in the same way. But do not test my patience.'

Nobody spoke for a moment, and then Fenella asked curiously, 'What kind of punishments did you give the men, Papa?'

'It's not a fit subject for your ears, Fenella,' he said shortly.

'Please, Papa?'

He studied his eldest daughter with unusual indulgence, and then his mouth twisted. 'Oh, very well. Some of them deserved a sound thrashing, that's all. But others… Well, some of the men had a nasty habit of turning on an officer they didn't like. Soon as we were in combat, they'd shoot the officer in the back, and then swear it was enemy fire.'

'What bounders!' Jacob exclaimed.

'The trick was to root out such vermin early on and get them up on a charge as soon as possible. Followed by summary execution.' Their father nodded slowly, staring into a distant past, his face hard. 'Firing squad. That kept the worst of the scum in line. Though if you couldn't get a charge to stick, you'd have to shoot them yourself, right there on the battlefield. Before the blighters could get *you*.'

'Darling, for goodness' sake... This is the breakfast table.' Their mother looked shocked.

Celeste's papa stirred, still lost in thought. 'Hmm?' He glanced about at their horrified faces and then cleared his throat. 'Quite so, my apologies.' He sat up, frowning. 'Jolie, stop squawking like a peahen and finish your breakfast. You're eating for two now, remember. Jacob, find your eldest brother and tell him I need to speak to him this morning in my study. About these blasted debts of his.' He held up several of the sheets he'd been reading, half-crumpled in his fist, before continuing, 'And Celeste, you will do as your mother bids you and marry Sir Oliver.'

'But, Papa – '

He held up a hand, interrupting her. 'His age is the very reason we chose Sir Oliver for you. You need the steadying influence of a wiser head than your own, for we all know what happens when you're left to your own devices.' He studied her broodingly. 'You would not wish to be certified lunatic and confined to a cell for the rest of your days, I'm sure.'

Celeste bit down hard on her lower lip, saying nothing.

Her father's gaze moved to his youngest son,

darkening as he inspected the boy's sullen face. 'As for you, Maurice...Well, the least said about you the better. You'll never make an officer, that's for certain.'

Maurice said nothing to this, his head turned away, his attention apparently fixed on a view of the gardens, sunlight pouring through south-facing windows behind them to pool on polished bare boards.

Celeste glanced over her shoulder, wondering what had caught his attention, but could only see young Jeffrey out there on the lawn, wandering about idly and smoking a cigarette, presumably on a break. Since indoors servants were forbidden the grounds, she imagined the local lad would be served his notice if caught, so turned back straightaway and pretended not to have seen him. She knew he and Maurice seemed to be chummy, and she wouldn't hurt her brother for the world.

It seemed Mama felt much the same.

'Oh, my dear, please don't be cruel to my little Maurice,' their mother began weakly, but was interrupted.

'Don't dare tell me what to do,' Papa thundered at her. 'Little Maurice? The boy's sixteen, not six. Just look at him... Molly-coddled his whole life and it's made him soft. He needs discipline if he ever wants to become a man.'

Maurice's face was impassive; he might almost have been deaf. But their mother dissolved into tears, reaching for a handkerchief.

'There, now your mother is weeping. That's my cue to retire to my study.' Their father stood up, gathered together his reading material and strode from the room, saying curtly over his shoulder, 'Jacob, I instructed you to find Sebastian for me. It's an urgent matter. Why are you still eating?'

'Sorry, Father.'

Jacob hurriedly swallowed his mouthful, dashed a napkin across his lips and chin, and almost ran from the breakfast room in their father's wake.

In the silence that followed, Celeste sat staring down at her cold, uneaten sausage and eggs. She hated people raising their voices to her, so usually gave in for a quiet life. But she didn't want to be married, either. She'd turned eighteen in February, it was true, but Sir Oliver was old and wrinkly and had a tuft of hair sprouting from a mole on his cheek.

Yet what could she do?

Unless she wanted to be confined to an asylum for the insane again, as had happened after one of her more violent fits last year, it would be impossible to escape this marriage.

She watched in silence as Maurice sloped off with his hands in his pockets, heading out through the open French windows into the garden, just as Priddy returned in his slow-footed, ponderous manner to set pen and paper before her mother.

'Celeste,' her mother said tearfully, 'go back to your room and rest. I want you to look your best tonight.'

'Yes, Mama.'

Sir Oliver would be coming to dinner, then, regardless of her feelings on the matter. She was not married to him yet though. And perhaps her ancient betrothed might be so unfortunate as to die before he could drag her to the altar.

One could always hope.

CHAPTER FIVE

Stella flicked through a few pages from one of her grandmother's journals, seated on the floor beside the trunk that contained all Esther's most treasured possessions. She had tried reading them once before but the handwriting was so small and cramped, it was hard to decipher and she'd soon given up. This time she persevered, determined to do some proper investigative work. The photograph of her grandmother with another similar-looking woman, both in nurses' uniforms, had piqued her interest. *Esther and me, 1940*, it had said on the back of the photograph. But she was certain that tiny scrawl had been her grandmother's handwriting. Which made no sense, unless…?

She couldn't pinpoint exactly what she was thinking. But she needed to find out more about her grandmother's past before jumping to conclusions. There were few dates, unfortunately, but among the words she'd been able to pick out were *Zeppelins, ration book, air-raid siren…* So, this journal must have been written during the Second World War.

Though the journal wasn't only about her wartime experiences. *I miss my brother*, Gran had written at one stage, after attending a friend's wedding. Apparently, the groom had reminded Esther of her brother. *Though my brother was not the marrying kind.*

What on earth did that mean?

At last, she found a more revealing entry dated February 24th, 1942. Her grandmother would have been in her mid-twenties at that point.

Today is my twentieth-first birthday. Nobody knows that, of course, and I dare not breathe a word to anyone. Happy Birthday to me! Though I feel a hundred years old, not twenty.

Stella frowned, doing the necessary calculations on her fingers. 1942. No, her grandmother would have been twenty-five years old that year. Not twenty-one. And Gran's birthday had been May 12th, not February 24th, which was closer to her own birthday on April 2nd.

Esther had surely known her own date of birth?

Stella read the words again, slowly and carefully, to be sure she had not misunderstood. But there was no mistake.

Today is my twentieth-first birthday.

Nobody lies in their own diary, she thought, running a fingertip lightly over the faded loops and upward strokes. So February 24th had to be her grandmother's *true* birthday. But that would mean Esther had lied about her age; even about the date of her birthday, pretending to be four years older than she really was. Yet why do such a thing? As a woman matured, she might lie about her age to seem younger, but not older.

It made no sense.

Unless, of course, her grandmother had not been born Esther Sharpe but someone completely different. A woman trying desperately to conceal their true identity by taking on someone else's.

The other nurse in the wartime photograph she'd found, presumably.

The 'real' Esther.

Rather shakily, Stella made herself a coffee, took the tatty notebook over to her desk, and sat down to read more methodically under the light of an Anglepoise lamp.

Turning back to the first few entries in the book, all undated, Stella strained to decipher the tightly written scrawl, no doubt to make the most of the space during paper rationing.

It seemed her grandmother had trained as a hospital nurse during the war, which tallied with what she herself had told Stella on the few occasions when she'd discussed her younger days. Times had been tough but she'd enjoyed the work. Then a note of panic... *Went back to the silver workshop on my day off, just to see if the place was still standing, and old Jacob was there, sweeping up rubble. I turned away at once and ran all the way back home but couldn't get it out of my mind. I'm such a coward.*

The Cossentine family had owned property in London before the war, hadn't they? Her heart thumped as she flicked through a dozen more pages and came across the name, Esther, again and again.

People keep mixing me up with Esther Sharpe; we look similar, I suppose, though she's four years older than me and a touch wider in the seat. She's awfully tough though, never lets anyone get the better of her. That's what comes of being an orphan, she's always saying. You learn to stand up for yourself early on.

Then halfway through the journal, which seemed to have been kept on and off, quite erratically and even skipping a full year at one time, recommencing in the early months of 1944, she came across a passage which left her shocked and barely able to breathe.

Esther died of influenza five days ago, God rest her soul. I still can't believe it. She was the closest thing I had to a friend. I was really sick with flu for a while myself but woke up yesterday feeling much better, and am now on the road to recovery. I'm not sure of God's purpose here but it seems I have been spared.

Before she died, Esther gave me her identity card and papers, and insisted I should go abroad, posing as her. The poor love knew how terrified I've been about M. finding me, and how sticky the authorities are getting over 'lost' identity cards these days, so who knows how much longer I can trot out that tired old excuse?

As soon as I'm on my feet again, I'll resign my post here and make my way down to Dover. From there, it should be easy enough to sign up at one of the bases as a registered nurse, using Esther's credentials, and ask to be posted overseas as soon as possible. And if anyone queries the age difference, I'll say I'm lucky to look young for my years.

Stella re-read that passage, frowning intently. *M.* The lone survivor of the murders at Black Rock Hall had been called Maurice Cossentine.

Could Maurice be *M*?

At the bottom of the page, in a squashed-up postscript note, her grandmother had added, *I only wish I'd been brave enough to tell Esther my real name and story. She died thinking M. was a cruel husband and I'd been trying to escape him. I'll never forgive myself for lying to my one true friend.*

Stella sat in stunned silence for a long while, re-reading that entry.

My real name…

Celeste Cossentine, by any chance?

But why change her name in the first place? Someone else had been tried and hanged for the murders. The cook, according to what she'd found on the internet. Was it possible that her grandmother had murdered her entire family and then run away, concealing her identity to escape the rope, and that another woman had been blamed in her place?

Gran, a multiple murderer?

She refused to believe it. And yet there was her journal as evidence and the old photograph too… *Esther and me, 1940.* The same handwriting.

She needed to discover the truth. But how?

Less than a week after reading her grandmother's wartime journal, Stella cancelled all her upcoming lessons and took the train down to Bodmin in mid-Cornwall. From there, she transferred to a cross-country bus headed for the seaside resort of Bude on the rugged north Cornish coast. The bus journey seemed to take forever, but on arriving in the small, cheerful town of Bude, she found a taxi to take her to the nearby village of West Pol. The western fringes of the village bordered the large Cossentine estate and there seemed little else in the area, least of all places to stay.

She felt a certain amount of trepidation at leaving London, never having done much solo travelling before. And Bruno would be sure to react violently once he realised she was no longer at home. But it should take him a while to work it out, and perhaps he would eventually lose interest in pursuing her when she never answered his calls or texts.

That was her hope, at any rate.

Besides, running away for a week or two was far less traumatic than having to report her ex to the police for stalking.

The sun had gone down by the time the taxi pulled up outside the only pub in the village, The Silversmiths' Arms, where she'd booked a room.

Before leaving London, she had located a telephone number for the Cossentine Murder Mystery Exhibition. But the call had simply rung out, unanswered. Continuing to search online, she had eventually stumbled across the details of a Mr Hardcastle, the Bude-based solicitor who dealt with estate matters.

Fearing the solicitor might put her off coming down to Cornwall, she had made a face-to-face appointment without telling him exactly what it was about, except that it was connected to the Cossentine estate. Some instinct had warned her against giving too much away at this early stage.

It was Hardcastle who had recommended the pub. 'If you're looking for somewhere to stay around West Pol,' the solicitor had told her on the phone, 'there's not much choice, I'm afraid. But you could try The Silversmiths' Arms.' He had sounded relatively friendly, which had encouraged her to trust his recommendation. 'They do a good Sunday roast too.'

The Silversmiths' Arms was set back from the rest of the village, standing alone on the shortest side of a triangle of uneven grass where several large trees loomed against a darkening sky.

Once the driver had pulled away in the soft October dusk, Stella stood there with her luggage, listening to the quiet.

She was used to the constant roar of the city, people and traffic on the streets even in the early hours of the morning. Astonished, she checked her phone; it was not even seven o'clock in the evening, and yet the tiny village was almost silent, the pub car park deserted. The pub sign swung gloomily above the saloon bar door, creaking faintly, like something out of an old horror film.

She was shown up to her room by the landlady, Mrs Hepley, a short, plump woman in her late fifties with unlikely blonde hair and dark roots, and a self-satisfied air.

'I've given you a nice room overlooking the park at Black Rock Hall. It's a double with ensuite.' Mrs Hepley threw open the door and snapped on the light to reveal a pretty, old-fashioned pine bed with pink duvet, framed water colours of Cornish landmarks on the walls, and a narrow ensuite bathroom gleaming with white tiles. 'Two weeks, did you say?'

'Probably, yes.'

'That's a good long stay, m'dear.' Mrs Hepley seemed pleased by this until she noticed Stella's violin case. 'What's that, then? Some kind of instrument?' She frowned. 'You don't mean to play it while you're here, I hope. We have a strict rule about noise in the bedrooms.'

Stella's heart sank but she kept smiling. 'If you'd rather I didn't, then of course I won't. I only brought it because… ' She hesitated. 'I'm a professional violinist, you see. I take my violin everywhere.'

'Is that so?' Far from impressed, Mrs Hepley merely raised her eyebrows. 'Myself, I've always thought a fiddle sounds like someone strangling a cat.' She bent to straighten the bed covers, missing Stella's horrified expression. 'Breakfast is strictly between eight and nine, m'dear. Any later and you've missed it. Towels are on the bed there. Meanwhile, if you need any help finding your way around the village, or want us to call a taxi for you, just come down to the bar and ask.'

'That's very kind, thank you.' Stella hesitated. 'I do hope to visit a few places in the area, as it happens. Like the big house at Black Rock,' she added on a whim. 'Do you know, is it open to visitors out of season?'

'Black Rock Hall?' Mrs Hepley had gone to the door but turned at this, staring back at her with sudden, narrow-eyed hostility. 'You'll be interested in the Cossentine murders, then?'

CHAPTER SIX

On her mother's orders, Celeste trailed back up to her room after breakfast, but found nobody waiting there to act as jailor. Normally it would be Becky, cheerful but apologetic, turning the key in her door, or sometimes the housekeeper, Mrs Benchley, impervious to her pleas. But no doubt the servants were too busy preparing for tonight's grand party and no one was available to lock up the lunatic.

Unable to believe her luck, she grabbed a shawl and dashed down the steep flight of back stairs, commonly used only by the servants, emerging into a maze of gloomy corridors. Letting herself out of the side door into the vegetable garden that sprawled under the kitchen windows, she hurried towards the bluebell wood before she could be seen.

Most of the bluebells had faded away, but the light there was still cool and dim, transfused by a soft fragrant haze, and the narrow path wove in and out of the crushed remains of flowers. She took about ten paces under the low trees and stopped, closing her eyes and breathing deep, enjoying the salt Cornish air and the distant whisper of the sea. Black Rock Hall stood close to the cliffs and on a still day it was possible to hear the tide break on the rocks and even the odd shout from passing fishermen on their boats.

Celeste walked through the shady wood, churning with fear over her impending engagement to Sir Oliver Gliddon.

Would she be able to face having such an old man paw her, as she had seen her sisters pawed by their own suitors, now their husbands? It seemed obscene. And yet she had to comply with her father's will. The alternative – refusing and being sent away, perhaps back to the asylum as her father had threatened – was unthinkable.

Perhaps marriage would not be so very bad. As a married woman, she would at least be mistress of her own home and no longer subject to her family's demands. Though her sisters didn't seem particularly happy in their marriages.

Her steps faltered and she tried not to cry, bending her head to hide her face. Tears would only be used against her as evidence of further mental instability. She might even be accused of suffering another 'episode'. Then the local doctor would be called to sedate her, and she would no longer be allowed to join the family for meals. The servants already looked at her sideways, as though she were somehow dangerous. The humiliation of being kept drugged and above stairs for her own good would be too much to bear.

She came to a stretch of neatly manicured lawn leading to a timbered, hexagonal summerhouse with a view of the rocky coast below. Here, the roar of the sea was louder and the sun struck her face.

Celeste loosened the shawl from her shoulders, its warmth unneeded under the fierce sunlight, and knotted it about her waist instead. Looking ahead, she let the sea breeze whip at her unbound hair, uncaring what her mother would say when she saw its disarray later. She could always ask Becky to help her tidy it before luncheon, assuming she would be allowed to eat with the family. *I want you to look your best tonight*, her mother had said after breakfast, sending her back to her room to rest. Perhaps Mama had intended her to remain safely in bed until the dinner party. Except there had been no servant on hand to lock her in.

'If only I could disappear and never be seen again,' Celeste whispered to herself, hugging her thin chest.

From her vantage point, she could just glimpse the top of the vast dark rock that jutted up out of the shore, an ancient, limpet-encrusted monolith, surrounded by deep water at high tide and then left stranded with seaweed as the tide ebbed.

The legendary black rock that gave its name both to the beach and to the hall itself.

The Cornish locals swore that jumping from the rock's peak at high tide could cure anything from a broken heart to infertility, though few had ever dared attempt such a terrifying feat.

Beyond it, the stark, dramatic summer blue of the ocean stretched away to the horizon, and not for the first time, she wished she could simply jump on a ship and sail away. Celeste imagined herself as a stowaway or working her passage, perhaps as a nanny or a lady's maid. Anywhere in the world would do, so long as she could be free of these chains, perhaps taking on a new name so that she could hide from her family forever...

Though with war in Europe looming, any kind of travel might soon be impossible. She was caught in a trap, she thought dully, from which there was no escape.

About to turn away, a high-pitched cry from the summerhouse made her stiffen. As she listened, raised voices drifted back on the wind. A man and woman arguing?

She recoiled in trepidation, recognising the man's voice. It was surely Sebastian, her eldest brother and her father's heir, already as arrogant and unpleasant as her father himself. He had been missing at breakfast, and her father had sent Jacob to find him.

What on earth could Sebastian be doing all the way out here?

A loud thud left her frozen.

The woman gave another cry that was hurriedly stifled. A cry for help, perhaps? She sounded afraid for her life.

Heart thumping, Celeste took a few steps closer, staring. The hexagonal summerhouse, built on a slight rise near the cliff edge, was hedged about by wind-bent trees and thorn bush clusters. Her brother must be in there with a woman. And by the cries and the high-pitching pleas to be let go, he was doing something unspeakable to the poor creature.

The door to the summerhouse burst open and a servant girl staggered out, her clothing ripped, dishevelled hair streaming over her shoulders as she gasped and sobbed...

It was Becky, the cook's young daughter.

'No, sir,' the girl moaned as Sebastian came after her, his own clothing also awry, a wild look in his flushed face. 'No more, please, sir... I can't...' He made a grab for her but she struggled free and ran barefoot across the lawn, making for a gravelled pathway into the formal gardens. 'Please, leave me be.'

Sebastian began to run after the girl, but checked abruptly, his gaze lifting to where Celeste stood motionless, shrouded in the mouth of the bluebell wood.

She shrank further into dim shade, her breath caught in her throat, heart pounding with fear.

Had Sebastian seen her?

Her brother glanced down, hurriedly adjusting his clothing, and Celeste turned, fleeing back through the wood.

She didn't stop running until she'd reached the safety of the house. Hurrying up to her bedroom, she flung herself inside, standing in shock in the middle of the room and listening for sounds of pursuit. But all she could hear was her own heart thumping.

Poor, poor Becky... Was she very badly hurt? What exactly had Sebastian done to her?

The very worst thing imaginable, she feared, while not truly knowing what that might be. The kind of horrors she might be expected to endure as a married woman, perhaps.

Something ought to be done. But what? Should she tell her parents what she had seen? Or confront Sebastian about his misdemeanours directly?

The mere thought had her shivering with fear. Her parents would more likely be furious with her rather than her brother. She was not even supposed to have left the confines of her room, let alone been roaming the grounds, and as for facing down Sebastian himself...

Glancing at her reflection in the mirror, Celeste realised how wild and flushed she appeared.

So much for looking her best for tonight's party. Shakily, she went to the corner sink and splashed water on her hot face, trying to make herself presentable again. But the noise of her return must have alerted her mother, who came hurrying along the corridor while she was still drying her face.

'Celeste?' her mother demanded, bustling into her room without knocking, her thin brows arched in surprise. 'What on earth's going on? And why was this door unlocked?' Her eyes widened, taking in Celeste's appearance. 'What a sight you look! There's mud on your shoes, girl. Have you been in the gardens? All on your own?'

'I was about to change my shoes when you came in.' Celeste knitted her hands together at her waist, wishing she had the courage to defy her mother's strict rules. 'I went for a short walk, that's all. We've been down here for ages and I haven't seen the sea yet.'

'You're in no fit state to be wandering the house, let alone taking a walk in the grounds, especially unsupervised. What if you'd had an attack of dizziness with nobody to help you? Or one of your dreadful blackouts. You could have fallen off the cliff, for goodness' sake. I've a good mind to –'

'I'm sorry, Mama,' Celeste interrupted, unable to bear the scolding a moment longer. 'I won't do it again. But there's something I need to tell you.' She wrung her hands. 'Something about Sebastian.'

Her mother looked uneasy. 'You can tell me later.'

'No, it's important. I saw him with –'

'No, I don't want to hear it.' Her mother went to the window and looked down into the sunlit grounds, her face frowning and distracted. 'I've had a reply from Sir Oliver. He's coming to dinner and wishes to discuss your wedding date.'

'But I… I don't want to… m-marry him.'

'Now, Celeste, don't make me lose my temper. You heard your father this morning. There's to be no debate about this. You will marry Sir Oliver Gliddon and be very happy with him. He's a very wealthy man with a generous estate over the border in Devon and will keep you in luxury. You really ought to be ecstatic to have such a match, especially given your unfortunate little… problem.' She turned for the door. 'Now, take your medication and get some beauty sleep.'

'Mama, please wait…' Celeste met her mother's eyes, a sudden bloom of heat in her face. 'Sebastian r-raped a girl today. In the summerhouse.'

'I beg your pardon?' Her mother's face was rigid.

'It was Becky, the cook's d-daughter. When I was out for my walk, I saw her crying and running away with her clothes torn. Sebastian went chasing after her and –'

Her mother slapped her face, a ringing blow that sent her staggering backwards. 'Silence,' her mother hissed, her blue eyes wide and glaring. 'You must never repeat a word of that disgusting accusation again. It's a complete farrago of nonsense and you're not to mention it again, do you hear?' She strode to the door which still stood ajar and stopped abruptly, seeing someone lurking there in the doorway. 'Who's there?'

Jeffrey emerged from the dim landing outside, his fair head bowed. 'Begging your pardon, Mrs Cossentine,' he said, soft-voiced as always, 'but you're needed downstairs. Mr Cossentine sent me to find you.'

Her mother looked flustered at having her furious tirade overheard by a servant but drew herself up, nodding. 'Very well.' She glared around at her. 'I mean it, Celeste. I want you to take your medication and lie down on your bed for a rest.'

'I've already taken my medication this morning.'

'Then take some more,' her mother snapped. 'I'm sure an extra dose won't do you any harm. I'll ask Mrs Benchley to send a maid up later to help you wash and dress for dinner.'

'I don't need any help getting dressed.'

'Of course you do. You're not a child anymore, Celeste, and if you want to make a good marriage, you must learn to look presentable in company.'

Her mother paused, her chest still heaving with agitation. 'Wear the cream linen dress I bought you, with your birthday pearls. That will do nicely.'

She left the room, pausing on the threshold to study the servant, who was still lurking outside. 'Jeffrey, isn't it? The cook's boy?'

'That's right, ma'am.'

Celeste bit her lip, flushing with mortification. Of course, she'd forgotten… Jeffrey was Becky's older brother. Had he overheard what she'd said about his sister and Sebastian?

Her mother hesitated, looking him over. 'What a lovely Cornish accent. You're a fine-looking young man too. Your mother's pride and joy, I'm sure. And I daresay you could make first footman one day, if you work hard enough.' She added with a conspiratorial smile, 'Jeffrey, I need you to watch Miss Celeste take her medication. After that, you must lock this door and leave the key in the lock. You may bring up some lunch on a tray for her, but my daughter is not to leave this room again until the dinner gong. Is that understood?'

'Yes, ma'am.'

I daresay you could make first footman one day, if you work hard enough.

Sickened, hugging herself, Celeste turned to stare out of the window in despair. It was clear that her mother was also concerned the boy might have overheard them talking about his sister's rape and was hoping to buy his silence with this suggestion.

She couldn't imagine what Becky had been forced to endure today, nor how the poor girl was coping in the aftermath of her brother's attack. But she very much feared she'd find out soon enough if her parents had their way and married her off to a man she loathed.

CHAPTER SEVEN

Stella knew perfectly well what the landlady of The Silversmiths' Arms meant when she referred to the 'Cossentine murders' but thought it better to pretend ignorance. If the silver ring turned out to be completely different to the one her grandmother had worn, she would only look foolish if she'd told too many people about her suspicions. The estate solicitor Hardcastle was the only person she intended to confide in for now.

'I'm sorry,' she told the landlady politely, 'I don't understand.'

'The whole Cossentine family was poisoned at dinner one night in 1939,' Mrs Hepley explained, her voice still hostile. 'You must have heard of it. There's a visitor exhibition up at the big house dedicated to their murders. But you're right, it's closed for the winter now. Won't reopen until mid-April.'

'I'd still like to visit the house, even if the exhibition is closed.' Stella cleared her throat, feeling awkward under the woman's fierce stare.

'The owner's dead, isn't he?'

'Mr Maurice, you mean? Yes, that old sod passed a few years back.' Mrs Hepley pulled a face. 'Good riddance to bad rubbish.'

Stella was taken aback by the vehemence in the landlady's voice. 'You obviously didn't think much of him.'

'I didn't, even though this place takes its name from the family business.' Her mouth pursed. 'Silversmiths, they were, the Cossentines. Rich as Croesus, once upon a time. Though Mr Maurice spent most of it on drinking and gambling, or so they say.'

'In that case, I'm surprised the hall hasn't been sold yet.'

'They're still looking for his heir, that's why.' Mrs Hepley made a snorting noise under her breath. 'And good luck to them with that fool's errand.'

'Excuse me?'

'Celeste Cossentine. She'll be long dead. Died in America, most likely. That's where they found the silver ring Miss Celeste took when she left, after all.' She paused, screwing up her face as though at a bad smell. 'Besides, that nasty old place is haunted.'

'*Haunted*?'

'So people have been saying in the newspapers lately. Psychics, you know... Seems nobody in their right mind would want to live there now.

Except the man they pay to run the museum. He lives in and doesn't seem to mind. But folk who spend their lives in museums expect to see the odd ghost, don't they? Part of the job, I imagine.'

'I guess so, yeah.' Stella peered through the curtains but it was already dark out there. It was frustrating, but no doubt the view in the morning would tell her more. 'All the same, do you know if there's anyone up at the big house who could show me around?'

'You still want to go?' Mrs Hepley stared at her, shaking her head. 'I don't know if the curator would let you in out of season. Anyway, why bother? Like I said, there ain't nothing to see up there but a load of old dust and cobwebs.'

'And the ghosts.'

'Hmm.' Mrs Hepley gave her a sharp look, as though suspicious Stella was mocking her, and then bustled away.

Stella unpacked her case, fixed herself a cup of powdery-tasting coffee, and then sat down to study the various print-outs she'd made from her online searches. Maps of the area, local landmarks, a history of the Black Rock Hall and estate, and some information about the initial launch, three years ago now, of the murder mystery exhibition.

A floorboard creaked outside her bedroom door, and she dropped the map she'd been studying and got up. 'Hello?'

There was a moment's silence, followed by another few creaks, like someone moving quietly away.

Stella went to the door and opened it, peering out into the dimly lit passageway. She could see nobody there.

From below, she heard music drifting up the stairs and a burst of laughter from the saloon bar, along with the clink of glasses and scrape of cutlery. Staring at the shadows at the far end of the landing, she thought she caught a movement there. But when she located the light switch and clicked it on, the corridor was empty.

'Okay, time to see what the bar's like,' she muttered to herself, and turned to get her purse.

Two gin and tonics on an empty stomach later, a packet of salted peanuts notwithstanding, Stella's nerves had settled down somewhat. There was a large television screen on the wall showing a twenty-four-news channel on mute, and light rock music playing from the speakers in each corner. Stella shared the bar area with two elderly gentlemen, who looked identical enough to be twins, and a tiny dog who spent the entire time at her feet, gazing up at her with a hopeful expression. Other people sat at tables about the pub, eating and drinking, a few even playing cards.

Eventually, she grew tired of the stares and

mutters from curious locals, and got up from the bar stool, gathering her things.

'Early night for you, is it?' Mr Hepley paused in his wiping down of the counter to look up at her. He was a large man in his sixties, his bald head gleaming under the bar spotlights, boasting a grey-streaked, Tolkienesque beard tied up under his chin with a jewelled cord. 'Got everything you need, Miss?'

'Yes, thank you.' But Stella hesitated, glancing at the door that led out into the car park. 'I might go for a stroll before bed, actually.'

'Best keep to the main road through the village, then. Easy to get lost away from the streetlights.' He stroked his beard thoughtfully, nodding to the window. 'Dark of the moon tonight, see?'

'Don't talk rubbish to the lady, Bernard.' Mrs Hepley came hurriedly across to remind her which key could be used to let herself into the pub after hours. 'It's the Yale. In case you're back late.'

'Thanks, but I'll only be ten minutes. I just need to stretch my legs.'

Mrs Hepley opened the door for her and, standing in the doorway, helpfully pointed out the road that ran about the village green. Sure enough, there were streetlights at intervals, though with deep pockets of shadow in between. By contrast, the triangular stretch of grass itself, with its clusters of trees, was gloomy and unlit.

'While I'm outside...' Mrs Hepley reached into

her cardigan pocket, producing a lighter and a packet of cigarillos, the same brand of slim cigars one of Stella's eccentric girlfriends had smoked in university. The landlady lit one, catching Stella's eye and grimacing. 'My one vice now I've given up drinking.' Pungent smoke filled the air. ' My husband hates them though, so…'

Stella smiled and left her to it.

The village lay quiet and still, apart from a breeze that rustled trees and bushes in the darkness, not an entirely comfortable sound.

Stella slung her handbag over her shoulder and set off along the lit roadway, as advised, but soon discovered that the road on that side of the village was little more than a single-track lane with no pavement. As it began to narrow, a few cars parked to the left-hand side, she chose to walk in the middle of the road, listening for traffic. But there was no sound except the wind in the trees and her own footsteps, of course.

As she reached the apex of the triangular green, she passed a strange-looking tree on her right. There was a single streetlamp at that end of the road, casting a soft glow over the tree.

Curious, she paused and then detoured slightly, taking a few steps across the damp grass to stand beneath the tree and look up into its ragged canopy. On closer inspection, what she'd taken for diseased and misshapen twigs were dozens of faded strips of fabric hanging from the branches, twisting and rustling in the breeze.

'A wish tree,' she said under her breath.

Ribbons were hung in a wish tree as prayers or hopes for a good outcome. She laid a hand on the damp, gnarled, ivy-thick trunk, peering up into a mass of dark, ribbon-hung branches, but turned abruptly, suddenly sure that someone was watching her.

There was a light on in the nearest house. Her gaze rose, narrowing. It was an old building, the garden overgrown with tall rustling pampas grasses near the gate, and there was a face at an upper window.

A woman, was her fleeting impression. Pale and dark-haired, staring down at her. Then a curtain dropped and the window was dark.

Stella shivered, hugging herself as she turned back towards the road. Her heeled boots were surprisingly noisy in the silence, and she found herself walking softly, noting the darkened windows of most of the other houses she was passing. Apart from those locals still in the pub, could the whole village be in bed already? Or perhaps many of these were second homes or empty holiday lets, and nobody was home. That would make better sense, since it couldn't be much later than ten o'clock.

Aware of the late hour, she glanced back to see how far she was from the pub and caught a movement behind one of the parked cars. A black Land Rover.

Her heart began to thud. What the hell...? Had someone just ducked down behind the Land Rover? Someone who'd been following her in the darkness, perhaps?

She continued walking, tensed for an attack. But none came.

After a few dozen steps, she stopped and looked around sharply. There was nobody to be seen. Mrs Hepley had long since gone back inside The Silversmiths' Arms. The village street was empty, the parked cars silent and still. And, in the distance, the pub sign creaked faintly in the breeze.

CHAPTER EIGHT

Sooks, her mother's maid, came upstairs in the early evening to help Celeste get dressed and to arrange her chestnut hair in smooth waves, ready to pass her mother's inspection at dinner. But no amount of discreet face powder could conceal eyes reddened by many hours' miserable weeping.

Celeste had been watching cars pull up the drive for the past half hour, family members arriving for the party, tyres crunching over the gravel, but hadn't been able to see who was in each vehicle. She'd heard some commotion from downstairs earlier too, men's voices raised in anger and doors slamming.

'What was all the shouting about earlier?' Celeste asked, watching in the mirror as the maid's expert hands worked their magic.

Sooks glanced at her briefly, then continued to arrange Celeste's hair, her mouth folded small. 'Some trouble with your brother, I heard.'

'Sebastian?'

'No, Miss.' Sooks reached for the hair tongs. 'It

was young Master Maurice.' She hesitated, and then bent forward, adding in a conspiratorial tone, 'There was some to-do between him and Mr Sebastian. That's what they were saying below stairs, at any rate.' She met Celeste's gaze in the mirror, her expression disapproving. 'I wouldn't like to say what it was about but it sounded like a nasty business to me.'

'A to-do?' Celeste stared at her, apprehension coiling inside her. 'They had a f-fight, you mean?'

But it seemed Sooks was already regretting her moment of gossip, her colour high, her mouth once more prim. 'Best sit still now, Miss, and face front.' She used the tongs with ruthless efficiency. 'And don't touch your hair until you're called to come down.'

Jeffrey came to fetch her half an hour later. By then, she had worked herself up into near-hysterics, wondering what was happening downstairs, how Maurice was after his fight with Sebastian, and if they'd come to blows over what had happened with Becky that morning. She kept remembering how she'd seen the serving girl run out of the summerhouse, her clothing torn, her face flushed and tearful, pursued by her brother Sebastian...

It was too horrid for words.

She half expected to find her brothers still at fisticuffs and the whole place in uproar when she went down for dinner. Yet the house was eerily quiet as she followed Jeffrey along the landing, her fingers plucking nervously at her evening gown.

'Where is everyone?' she asked Jeffrey, but haltingly, as the boy looked so grim, his usual smirk vanished.

'Your mother has gathered everyone for drinks in the blue room before the dinner gong, Miss.'

'Is that where we're going? The b-blue room?'

'No, Miss.' The servant hesitated, a gleam of sympathy in his eyes at last. 'Mrs Cossentine instructed me to escort you to the library first.'

'I see.' Celeste shivered, playing with the lace shawl draped about her shoulders. No doubt she would have to sit through a discussion between her father and Sir Oliver about their forthcoming marriage. 'I was so sorry about what happened to your sister,' she told him in a low voice. 'How is she?'

Jeffrey stopped, looking round at her. 'Resting,' he said with careful restraint.

'Has my mother been to see her yet?'

'I believe Mrs Cossentine visited my sister in her room earlier this evening,' he agreed in a clipped tone, 'but only to dismiss her from Black Rock Hall.'

Celeste stopped dead in the hallway, staring at him with her mouth dropping open. 'Mama d-dismissed her? There must be some mistake.'

'I don't think so, Miss.' The Cornish boy was

holding himself stiffly, with dignity. 'But I'm being allowed to remain on at the hall, to be trained as a footman. Your mother says I may be sent to London at the end of the summer,' he added bitterly, '*if* I show promise.'

'I'm so sorry,' she whispered, and bit her lip. 'And Maurice? He was in a fight with Sebastian, Sooks told me.' When he didn't reply, she said softly, 'I know you and he are friends. No, don't try to hide it. You're both about the same age, why shouldn't you be friends? You must have seen him since the fight. How is he?'

His face was a mask, rigidly controlled. 'None too good.' The shake in his voice betrayed him, and then he broke, bursting out with, 'They beat him, Miss.'

'*What*?'

'It was your father and Sebastian,' he hissed, 'and your sisters' husbands too. They birched him hard and took turns at it.' There were tears of rage in his eyes now, his face flushed. 'Then locked him in his room.'

'But why? I don't understand –'

'For defending my sister and saying the police should be called. Only Sebastian claimed it weren't no rape.' Jeffrey rubbed red eyes with his knuckles, gasping, 'He swore Becky was willing. He called her a… a whore.'

'Oh God, what a beast.'

Faint laughter reached her from below and

the chink of glasses. Celeste hugged herself, listening with only half her attention. She would be in serious trouble if she didn't go down straightaway to the library.

'Take me to him,' she urged the boy. 'I want to see Maurice.'

'I dare not. I'll lose my position. Becky's already lost hers, and our mother will be next.'

'Then wait for me here,' she told him, impatient to see her brother. 'You can always say I wasn't in my room when you came to find me.'

She ran along the corridor to the winding side stair, hidden by a tapestry curtain, that led up to the small tower room which Maurice always occupied when they were at Black Rock Hall. The old window glazing was cracked and let in the draughts, and the place had bare floors and was spartanly furnished, so nobody else ever went up there and Maurice was left alone.

The door was locked, just as Jeffrey had said, but the key was in the lock. She turned it and knocked. 'Maurice? It's Celly.' When there was no answer, she opened the door a crack and peered inside. 'I heard what happened… Oh!'

Her brother was seated by the tower window, bare-chested and in his underwear, smoking a cigarette. His back was a mess of red and blackening stripes. He turned as she came in, and she saw dark bruises welling on his jaw and cheek, his eye blacked and his lip split and puffy.

'Oh, Maurice, what have they done to you?' she cried, and burst into tears.

He threw his cigarette out of the window and came towards her, shaking his head. 'You shouldn't have come. You'll only get in trouble too.'

'I don't care about that.'

They stared at each other, a few feet apart. She badly wanted to hug him, to tell him everything would be all right. But she didn't believe that, and besides, hugging him would surely cause him considerable pain.

'You poor lamb,' she whispered, studying his ruined face. 'I hope they've sent for the doctor. Has Mama seen you?'

He winced. 'Yes.'

'And what did she say?'

'That I shouldn't have interfered in Sebastian's business,' he said grimly, 'and that it wasn't worth wrecking the family's good reputation for one unimportant local girl who was stupid enough to be alone with a man. She claimed Papa had already been told of his interest in Becky and had been planning to warn Sebastian to leave the girl alone,' he added bitterly, 'only he was nowhere to be found.'

'Yes, of course... I remember him telling Jacob to find Sebastian for him at breakfast.'

'If he'd managed to warn Sebastian off her,

all this might have been averted. As it is...' He made a noise under his breath. 'Anyway, I begged Mama to call the police, to do the right thing by Becky. Instead, she dismissed her. Jeffrey's to escort the girl home tomorrow morning and not a word said to anyone about what Sebastian did. Can you believe it?' His mouth twisted in a smile that clearly hurt him. 'Mama's afraid of Papa, of course. Of what he might do if she stood up to him for once.'

'That's m-monstrous.'

He nodded and reached for his packet of cigarettes, lighting another one, his shoulders hunched, every movement careful and executed gingerly. 'So that's that, I suppose. Well, my back will heal, but as for my face... I think my damn jaw's broken.' He was smoking with delicate, wincing little gestures, the cigarette barely touching his lips, suggesting immense pain. 'Still, looks aren't everything. Sebastian's always got by without them, hasn't he?' She didn't believe his flippancy, hearing the break in his voice. 'You shouldn't be here, Celly. How did you even get out of your room?'

'Have you forgotten? I'm to be married off to Sir Oliver Gliddon. Our wedding date is being announced at dinner tonight.'

'Oh Christ, of course. I'm sorry.' His brooding glance studied her face, then rose to the door, sharpening. 'Who's there?'

She looked around to see Jeffrey lurking in the doorway.

'He was taking me downstairs,' she explained.

'Sir Oliver will be wondering where you are, Miss,' Jeffrey said awkwardly, not looking at Maurice. 'He's still waiting for you in the library.'

'Oh, let him wait!' She took her brother's hand. 'I'll come back as soon as I can. They're brutes, but they can't keep us both locked up forever. Then we can talk properly.'

Maurice shook his head, pulling away. 'You'll never see me again after tonight.' His voice sounded odd.

'What do you mean?' She stared, confused.

'I mean life's a bloody mess, Celly.' His eyes met hers, and she saw the despair and unhappiness he'd been hiding under his show of bravado. 'It's vicious and unfair, and all most of us can do is avoid getting hit by the worst of it. But now and then someone has to take a stand. Do what's right.'

'I d-don't understand. Are you leaving?'

'You've always been such an innocent, Celly.' Fleetingly, he touched her cheek, and then his hand dropped. A darkness seemed to envelop him, his brows a black line. 'You want my advice? Tell Sir Oliver no. Refuse to attend the dinner party tonight. Go back to your room instead.' His words were like icicles, cold and pointed. 'Take a stand for once in your life. Do what's right.'

Her brother wouldn't leave Black Rock Hall and the family, she refused to believe it. He was only sixteen, scarcely out of childhood. He had always wished to attend university and would need Papa's financial backing for that. Despite the wicked beating he'd suffered, to leave now would be disastrous for his future.

Besides, he had nowhere to go.

'I can't. You know what they'll do if I defy them. Send me back to that awful bloody asylum and this time I'd n-never get out.' Celeste rubbed away a tear. 'Maurice… Please don't go. Don't leave me.'

But he merely shook his head, turning away to stare out of the tower window again, smoking his cigarette.

'Goodbye, little sis.'

CHAPTER NINE

Her phone alarm sounded at eight o'clock. Groping for it with eyes still closed, Stella yawned, then stumbled out of bed and dragged back the sickly pink curtains to stare out of the bedroom window at the Silversmiths' Arms.

The first thing that struck her about Cornwall was the light. This was not the cold grey light of glass, steel and chrome and endless streets of concrete and tarmac but a warm, vibrant, natural light that seemed to pulse across the landscape, a living thing. The thin blue line in the distance was the ocean, she realised with pleasure, reminded of seaside holidays on the Kentish coast with her grandmother. Between the village and the sea lay a patchwork of damp green hills and fields, punctuated by one broad road that wound through an avenue of trees toward barely glimpsed chimneys and roofs.

Black Rock Hall.

She'd seen photographs of the huge house and grounds online. But somehow it had not seemed real until this moment.

That afternoon, she had an appointment to speak to Mr Hardcastle, the estate solicitor, who had an office in Bude, the nearest town along the coast. It would be the first time she had admitted to anyone what she was thinking, what she suspected, and she fully expected the man to laugh in her face and then show her the door. Nerves bit deep, leaving her abruptly breathless at the audacity of it all, and her first instinct was to fling open her violin case and play… Play until the nerves had gone and she was lost in the music.

But she couldn't play her violin. Not here, not now. It was only just after eight in the morning and Mrs Hepley would be unhappy. While she might be prepared to face the landlady's disapproval on some other morning, she couldn't manage it today. Not feeling like she did right now, so taut, so wound-up, so ready either to explode or fall apart…

'Slow down,' Gran would have told her. 'Try to be patient.'

Stella shut her eyes and could almost feel her grandmother's hand on her arm, steadying her nerves, calming her down.

'Not everything is a battle, Stella. Not everything has to be resolved at once. Sometimes running away is the best thing you can do.'

Except she wasn't running away this time, was she?

She accepted a lift into Bude with Mrs Hepley late morning, who had some shopping to do in town, and so arrived about two hours early for her solicitor's appointment. To kill time, she wandered about the pretty seaside resort, peering into shop windows at Cornish souvenirs and testing her legs on the steep hills. Finally tiring of aimless walking, she drank a hot chocolate in a coffee shop above undulating, windswept sand dunes that dropped away abruptly to sea level. The light really was magnificent, she thought, watching dirty yellow sand clouds whisked up by the wind. It was obvious why so many artists came to Cornwall to be inspired. And indeed, she often thought music and art were so close, what inspired one could inspire the other. The light here on the coast was a wild symphony, sometimes discordant but harmonious too...

Mr Hardcastle's office was on the second floor of a stately Victorian building on Lansdown Road, a steep hill overlooking the river at Bude.

His assistant Tara was a young, fair-haired woman with a vaguely hostile stare. She offered Stella a drink, which she refused, and then showed her into a light and airy office.

'Your two o'clock appointment, Mr Hardcastle,' she announced, and then left them alone together.

Mr Hardcastle was a large man, his blue shirt

straining over a generous belly, with a thick, unkempt head of once-dark hair, now salt-and-pepper. He stood to shake her hand and then sank back behind a desk heaped with paperwork, which juddered as his knees knocked it, an ancient-looking desktop PC humming noisily beside him, its screen saver whirling in patterns of lurid green and blue.

'So, Miss... erm...' He was rifling through papers, not looking at her.

'Stella Ffoulds.'

'Yes, how can I help you?' He finally unearthed a pen and then a notepad, which he flicked open to a clean page, scribbling her name at the top. 'You mentioned it was something to do with the Cossentine estate?'

There was nothing for it but to be straightforward.

'That's right.' Stella opened her handbag and pulled out her file. From this, she carefully extracted the magazine article she'd seen on the Tube, laying the cutting before him on the desk. 'It's to do with this.' She tapped the photograph of the silver ring. 'Please don't think I'm crazy, but I might be the one you've been looking for.'

'Sorry, *the one*?'

'The heir to the estate.'

Mr Hardcastle stared at her, his look arrested. Then he picked up the cutting and gave it only the most cursory glance. 'All right.' He handed it back to her. 'Prove it.'

Her hands trembling, feeling under suspicion, she took out the photograph of her grandmother wearing the ring. 'Here, then.'

Mr Hardcastle took the photograph, his air impatient. He thought she was a time waster, she realised. And maybe she was.

'What am I looking at?'

His voice was so brusque, she had to wrestle the urge to get up and walk away. But where would she go? She had nothing else left. Only this. And didn't she owe it to her grandmother to do this properly?

'That's my late grandmother, soon after the end of the second world war. And that ring on her finger… I'm pretty certain that's the Cossentine ring. My mother ran away when she was a teenager and ended up in America, and I think she took the silver ring with her.' Stella took a deep breath, pushing through her nerves. 'Mum died over there. My grandmother brought me back as a child, but the ring was never recovered. Gran thought she might have sold it in New York.'

'Hmm.' He took a magnifying glass out of his desk drawer and used it to study the ring in the black and white photograph, which admittedly was quite blurry and hard to make out. 'I grant you, this ring does look similar. But I'm afraid that still doesn't prove you are any relation to the Cossentines.'

'My grandmother always said it was a family heirloom.'

Mr Hardcastle was studying her grandmother's face. 'What was her name?'

'Esther Ffoulds, nee Sharpe.'

'And there we have your problem.' He shrugged, putting away the magnifying glass. 'The name of the missing heir was Celeste Cossentine.'

'My grandmother was always very secretive about her past. In fact, I have reason to believe she was living under an assumed name when she met my grandfather. A name she stole from another girl during the war, along with her identity papers.'

'That's quite a story.' He handed her back the photograph. 'Do you have any paperwork to back it up? Her original birth certificate, perhaps?' When she shook her head repeatedly, he sighed. 'Do you have any kind of documentation at all?'

'I have her journals.'

He raised his eyebrows. 'And in these journals, she mentions that her name was assumed?'

'As a matter of fact...' She flicked through to the photos she'd taken of the relevant diary entries and passed across her phone. 'It's not a birth certificate. But does it get your interest, at least?'

He read through the journal entries in silence, and then returned the phone, his gaze on her face. 'I'm listening.'

'I do have another photograph.' She handed

him the wartime snap of the two nurses dated 1940. 'That's my grandmother on the right. I don't know who the other woman is. But the writing on the back is in my grandmother's handwriting, which you can verify by comparing it to her journal entries.' She watched as he turned the photograph over, studying it with a grave expression. 'You see what it says? *Esther and me.* If my grandmother Esther wrote that, shouldn't it be 'Me and… another name, whoever that is with her? Do you follow?'

'Yes,' he said, apparently taking her seriously.

'Lastly, there's something my grandmother told me when she was dying. I can't be sure that I've remembered it right. I was only a child and she never brought it up again.' She paused. 'I've not seen it mentioned in any of the articles I found online, so I thought it might be useful.'

'Go on.'

'She said there was an inscription on the inside of the ring.'

He was watching her intently. 'I see.' He picked up the pen and finally made a note on the pad, though she couldn't read his messy scrawl, especially upside-down. 'And did she tell you what it said, by any chance?'

'It was in Latin. I can't remember the exact wording but it meant something like, 'Love forever.' Or 'Forever loved,' I'm not one hundred percent sure. And my grandfather had Gran's initials added later. I suppose with a C for Celeste, but of course I'm not sure. Perhaps he didn't know Esther wasn't her real name.'

He sat in silence, his gaze on her face.

'Well, that's it. That's all the proof I've got.' Stella saw scepticism in his eyes and blundered on, embarrassed, 'I think Gran did try to tell me, towards the end. But I didn't understand what she meant. Not until recently, when I saw the magazine article and started to look through her belongings again. But some old photos and a few journal entries aren't real proof, are they? Not when there's so much at stake. That big house, all the land around it…'

Still he said nothing.

She felt so sure he was about to send her away with a few scathing remarks about having wasted his time, she hurriedly put away the article and photograph. 'Anyway, I'm sorry to have bothered you.' Stella stood up and held out her hand. 'Thank you for listening to my story, at least.'

'Hold on, where do you think you're going? We still have plenty to discuss.' Mr Hardcastle motioned her to sit down again. 'What can I get you? Tea? Coffee? Maybe a fruit juice?' He went to the door and asked Tara to cancel his four o'clock appointment and put the kettle on. When he came back, he was smiling. '*Amor aeturnus.*'

'Sorry?'

'The Latin inscription on the inside of the

Cossentine ring. It means *eternal love*. Or words to that effect.'

'So there really is an inscription?'

'There really is.'

She stared at him, dumbfounded. 'You believe me?'

'I believe you, Miss Ffoulds. To the best of my knowledge, that inscription has never been made public. Not even when the ring was restored to the Cossentine estate and put on display. So, you couldn't have got that information online. Especially not the initials, which were added after the ring had gone missing. They were CC, if you're interested.'

'So my grandfather must have known who she was all along?' She was amazed.

'One would assume.' Mr Hardcastle sat down heavily behind his desk. The whole thing shook at his clumsy descent, heaps of files and paperwork shuddering, a few loose sheets even slipping to the floor. 'Though I'm afraid you're right in one respect. You will have to prove your identity more officially.'

'All right. How?'

'A DNA sample would be the best way to go.'

She stared at him, confused.

'Maurice Cossentine was a lonely, eccentric old man,' Mr Hardcastle told her. 'A confirmed bachelor to his dying day. Never having met the right woman, I suppose, he had no heir. So he made arrangements for how his estate was to be distributed,' he explained, adding, 'but *only* in the event that, by the fifth anniversary of his death, no family descendant with a proveable claim had turned up to claim it.'

She considered that, frowning. 'He has an heir already lined up, in other words?'

'A default heir, yes.' Mr Hardcastle gave her an apologetic smile. 'Obviously, I'm not at liberty to discuss who that person is. But if your claim is proven, it won't matter. You will inherit the entirety of the estate.'

She grimaced. 'Sounds like I'll be putting someone's nose seriously out of joint.'

'I wouldn't worry about that. Maurice was a very determined and single-minded gentleman, and his key focus was to keep the estate within the Cossentine family, so by inheriting you would be fulfilling his final wishes. He was convinced that the missing heir would turn up eventually; either his sister Celeste or some descendant of hers.' When she stirred, he held up a warning finger. 'But...' The solicitor smiled faintly. 'But he also knew that might not happen until long after his death. As the last known surviving member of his bloodline, he had to find a way to prove his heir's provenance. Before his final illness, Maurice left behind samples of DNA, to be held in cold storage, specifically in the hope that an heir would present themselves. We can take a DNA sample from you and compare the two. I'll make a few phone calls this afternoon and arrange for that to happen.' He studied her face through narrowed eyes. 'If you're willing, that is?'

Stella gripped the edges of her chair, breathing fast and shallow. Partly to ensure she didn't jump up and flee the room. Partly to remind herself that this was reality and not another one of her crazy dreams.

She nodded calmly, as though a DNA sample was a perfectly normal request. 'Of course I'm willing. That's why I came here, Mr Hardcastle. To find out if my grandmother really was Celeste Cossentine.' She took a deep breath. 'I'll do whatever it takes.'

Stella's head was buzzing and she couldn't think straight. Stifled and restless on the bus journey back, she abandoned the bus just before Widemouth Bay and set off on foot to the village via the coastal path instead.

The narrow, single-track path wound close to the cool, glittering expanse of the Atlantic Ocean at times, and then moved away again, snaking through open land thick with gorse bushes and heather and rustling, feathery grasses. At Widemouth, the path almost disappeared among sand dunes as it passed the vast stretch of beach at Widemouth Bay, where surfers in wetsuits showed like black-headed seals, their gleaming dots bobbing through constant, on-rushing rollers. The wind blew sharp, that close to the ocean, whipping Stella's dark hair about her face and sand in her eyes. But she persevered, head down against the fiery light-storm, and eventually found herself looking down on Black Rock, a dog-walkers' beach lined with ribs of dark-seamed rocks. Bristling with limpets and barnacles, the rocks were strewn with shiny, glutinous strands of seaweed washed by the tide.

There was a café and a tourist complex set close to the shore. The sign above the car park said Black Rock.

Black Rock Beach, she discovered online, was named after the massive rock that rose out of the rocky sand. It looked intimidating, but apparently people often climbed it in summer.

Stella found a dry spot on sand dunes opposite the black rock, settled a pair of sunglasses on her nose, and consumed a sandwich and a packet of beetroot crisps she'd bought in Bude. Below her vantage point, people came and went, walking their dogs along the flat sands or jogging, some chatting together as they strolled along the frilly water's edge, still some distance away. The sun reflected off the water in a million points of sequinned light, constantly shifting as the tide edged ever higher up the beach.

Turning, she could just see the top of the big house from here, the rest of the estate hidden among trees a good half mile or so inland.

She imagined Gran walking down to the beach via a footpath from Black Rock Hall, alone or with her siblings. That would have been before the war, when Gran was still a child and going by her true name.

'Celeste Cossentine,' she said to herself, trying the name out loud.

A seagull burst out of the dunes behind her, screaming as it wheeled and soared overhead, and she jumped violently.

'For God's sake…'

Her phone buzzed with a text message. Stella dragged it from her pocket and checked the screen. It was from Mr Hardcastle.

DNA test arranged. See attached link for details. Results may take a while. Let me know if you need anything in the meantime.

She let out a long breath. The truth of her ancestry would soon be known. But what about the truth of why her grandmother left this idyllic place and went into hiding for the rest of her life, too scared even to admit who she was on her deathbed?

Was it because her grandmother really was the one who had gone mad and killed all those people back in the summer of 1939? Gran had let drop a few hints about trouble in her childhood, it was true, admitting she'd always been considered 'fragile' and had even been treated for mental instability as an adolescent.

But there was a big difference between being a 'fragile' teenager and murdering your entire family at dinner…

CHAPTER TEN

Jeffrey escorted Celeste downstairs, both of them silent and withdrawn. When they reached the library, he caught her arm, his face troubled. 'Will you do what Master Maurice asked of you, Miss?'

'That's none of your business,' she said stiffly, and glanced down at his hand on her arm.

He released her at once. 'Beg pardon,' he muttered, and threw open the library door, his expression once more wooden as he announced, 'Miss Celeste, sir.'

Sir Oliver was standing by one of the many bookshelves, turning over a leather-bound volume. Putting the book back on the shelf at her entrance, he greeted her with a bow in a stiff, old-fashioned way. 'Ah, Miss Celeste, at last. I feared you might have changed your mind about our engagement and would not be coming.' He straightened, studying her low-cut dress with approval. 'But you're here now and how lovely you look. It's very kind of you to favour me with a few minutes of your time.'

Her fiancé was tall and slightly stooped, with

thinning silver hair and watery blue eyes. His smile was pleasant enough, and she had certainly never known him to be rude or leering. But it was hard not to be mesmerised by the hairy mole near his mouth, especially given that once they were married, he would almost certainly expect to kiss her with that mouth.

Celeste repressed a shudder, standing rooted to the spot.

Sir Oliver waved Jeffrey away, and held out a hand to her as soon as the door had closed behind him. 'My dear...'

When she didn't move, he dropped his hand and she saw disappointment in his face. 'But we're engaged now, are we not? There's no hurry.' He came towards her, smiling. 'I was delighted to see the announcement in the Times, by the way. Your father tells me you have agreed on a date for the wedding.'

'Have I?'

His brows flicked upwards at her limp tone but he continued smiling, apparently undeterred. 'A date in August has been suggested and I've given it the nod, assuming you're equally keen, of course.' He waited but she said nothing, so he continued in the same tone, 'Personally, I think it an excellent notion to bring the wedding forward. I'm by no means a patient man, and I believe your parents hope an August date will allow most of your family to attend the ceremony before returning to London at summer's end.'

'Yes, I imagine she does.'

His smile broadened at this passive response. No doubt he took it as a sign of her compliance.

He reached for her hand, and Celeste could not find it in herself to resist, caught in the grip of something larger and more powerful than she could ever hope to be. This was to be her fate now, she thought listlessly, and knew it would be better to accept the status quo rather than keep fighting. She'd spent three months last winter incarcerated in a cold, tiny cell on her doctor's orders, staring out through barred windows and kept heavily drugged to prevent her from protesting. Surely marriage, even to this old man for whom she felt nothing but repulsion, was a better prospect than being locked up for the rest of her life with only lunatics and other wretched women like herself for company?

'I'm so glad you felt able to accept my proposal at last,' Sir Oliver said softly, and raised her hand to his lips. This time, she couldn't quite stop herself from shuddering, and his eyes lifted to her face, becoming sharp. 'Cold, my dear?'

'I'm sorry… I may have caught a chill.'

His smile returned. 'You're unused to our changeable weather in the west, in fact. But of course not. A gently bred girl like yourself, you will have led a sheltered life in London's rarefied air, and rightly so. But once we are married, you will soon acclimatise. Riding, walking, even swimming in the summer... It's an outdoors life. My own mother used to swear by it.' His gaze held hers. 'Only a healthy woman can breed readily. And we shall soon get you healthy.'

Celeste did not know where to look, nor what to say.

'You are blushing. I have embarrassed you. My rude country manners...' Sir Oliver gave a laugh and patted her hand before releasing it. 'Though it's rather adorable to see colour in your cheeks. I forget how young you are.' His look was almost hungry.

To her relief, the door opened after a perfunctory knock, and her father stood there.

'Ah, excellent,' he said, and shook hands with Sir Oliver. 'Apologies for not being here sooner. I was speaking with the Cornish builder whose company is at work on our folly. Have you seen it there in the woods? Bit of a mess... My wife's idea, not mine, and only half-finished. But I'm assured it will be complete before the year is out.' He paused. 'Celeste, will you excuse us? I have some business to discuss with your intended before dinner.'

Thankfully, she gave Sir Oliver a brief smile before fleeing into the empty hallway. She passed her father's study, its door still ajar, and glanced that way, aware of somebody moving about in there. One of the servants drawing heavy curtains against the evening sunlight, by the sound of it. In the distance, the gong was struck to signify that dinner was ready to be served, and a door opened somewhere up ahead, a hubbub of voices rising as people moved through towards the dining room.

Celeste shrank back into the shadows, knowing that she ought to join her family as expected and yet wishing she could escape back up to the safety of her little bedroom instead.

Tonight, at Jolie's twentieth birthday dinner, they would announce her wedding date. Everyone would stare and congratulate her, and no doubt her brothers would make impertinent remarks and she would be left wishing the ground could swallow her up.

And then the ground did exactly that, rising to swallow her in a violent, unexpected welter of darkness…

An unearthly scream somewhere far off woke her, and she stirred in the gloom, her mouth dry, a deep throbbing ache at the back of her head. Barely able to open her eyes, Celeste tried to focus on what had happened. She recalled leaving the library at Papa's request so he could talk to Sir Oliver alone. Probably to discuss money, a marriage settlement. The dinner gong had sounded. She'd been standing just beyond the open doorway to her father's study. And then…

No, she couldn't remember anything beyond that. She must have suffered one of her maddening blackouts. All that worry she'd been feeling over Maurice's punishment and Sir Oliver's proposal, no doubt...

God, her head hurt so badly.

Struggling to her feet, Celeste blinked and swayed, momentarily unsure where she was. How long had she been unconscious?

With a moan, she put out a hand to prevent herself from falling and clutched something sturdy and wooden. Squinting through the pain in her head, she recognised the ornate scrollwork of her father's escritoire. There was a dark red Turkish rug under her feet and floor-length red velvet curtains at the windows, through which a strip of golden light was peeking, dazzling her.

This was her father's study.

How on earth had she got in here? Last thing she remembered was standing outside in the corridor. She could only assume she'd felt herself about to black out, so must have staggered in here looking for help, perhaps...

Glancing at the mantel clock, her vision still swimming, she was shocked to make out the time. She'd been out cold for nearly an hour.

Panic began to set in. The dinner party for Jolie's birthday! They would be finishing the meat course by now. There would be an empty seat at the table, intended for her but unoccupied.

Her mother would be cold with fury, her father incandescent at this latest act of disobedience. Her sisters would be disdainful and dismissive as ever. Her brothers would be snickering at her disgrace and making crude jokes in whispers about why she'd been detained. Though Maurice would not laugh. She could trust Maurice, at least...

Lurching towards the door, she dragged it open. The electric lights were not on in the hallway and the dimness soothed her eyes.

She stopped, shocked to hear raised voices and running feet. But the sound was muted, perhaps in another part of the house. People must have been sent to look for her, she guessed, her heart thumping in alarm at this thought.

Then she caught the faint noise of what sounded like a car engine starting outside, gravel spitting up as the car tore away at speed.

Celeste grew faint again, unsure whether to run and hide or hurry to the dining room to explain her late arrival as best she could. But what on earth could be going on? Had her father assumed she'd fled the house rather than face the announcement of her wedding date and sent out people to search the grounds for her, or maybe even fetch the police? They would never believe she'd fainted or had one of her strange fits. Though now she was beginning to wonder if someone could possibly have come up behind her, hit her on the head and knocked her out, then dragged her out of sight. She could think of no other explanation for how she'd ended up in her father's private study with the door closed, a room she would never ordinarily enter without permission. Yet besides a tender swelling on the back of her head, she had no proof to back up such a fantastical story.

She paused at the bottom of the stairs, tempted to run up to her room and pretend she had been asleep or resting this whole time. She could hear more shouting now. The hoarse voices of servants, raised in fear and urgency.

For the first time, terror struck her and she stood frozen, listening without understanding.

None of the family could be in the house, otherwise the servants would never dare make so much noise. Yet why would the family leave partway through a dinner party? Not simply her parents and brothers and sisters, but all their spouses too, and her aunts and uncles, and any cousins who might also have motored down for Jolie's twentieth birthday party.

Had war been declared, perhaps?

For months now, tensions between Germany and England had been growing. The newspapers had been full of it. Perhaps war had finally been declared and all the men were rushing about outside in excited self-importance, declaring themselves ready to do battle for the honour of the nation, while the ladies looked on in speechless admiration. She could imagine that. But it still seemed fantastical and not at all likely.

Gingerly, Celeste tiptoed down the hall, heading for the grand dining room they only used for special occasions.

To her relief, the servants' voices and sounds of running feet had died away by the time she reached the corner, and the passageway ahead was empty.

She halted though, startled by the incongruous sight of a large silver tureen on the floor. It lay in the doorway to the dining room, tipped onto one side, its contents spilt out, staining the dark polished floorboards with what looked like Mulligatawny soup. One of the footmen must have dropped the tureen and then just left it lying there, which was a thing unheard of. Nobody had even returned to clean up the soup.

There was not a single sound from the grand dining room, though the double doors stood wide open.

'H-Hello?' she said in a cracked half-whisper, and then cleared her throat, trying again. 'I say, what's g-going on?' She edged past the spilt soup, fearful of staining her immaculate white silk pumps with the soup. 'Hello, where is everyone?'

Celeste peered round the door, and her breath stuck in her throat. The dining room with its red flock wallpaper and dark wood panelling was like a scene from hell. Every single member of her family was still there but unmoving, like waxworks, slumped in their seats or over the table, or fallen to the floor, their chairs tumbled backwards or sideways in a haphazard manner. Her despairing gaze flew about the room, seeking out each familiar face in turn, shocked to see old Sir Oliver among them, flitting back and forth between limp bodies, sure that one of them, that somebody at least, perhaps her pregnant sister Jolie or her commanding, authoritative papa, must still be alive...

The whole room seemed to crystalise in her vision, somehow distant and unreal, as though she were looking down at a miniature scene captured in a snow globe, every detail perfect and frozen in time, preserved there for all eternity.

'Oh dear God.' She gripped the door, her fingernails digging into the wood, staring so hard her eyes strained in horror and disbelief. 'No, no...'

Then she turned and fled, just as the servants had done.

CHAPTER ELEVEN

Having ordered lunch at the pub bar and treated herself to a gin and tonic, Stella chose a window seat that overlooked the village green. From her vantage point, she could see the wish tree with its faded, flapping ribbons tied to gnarled branches. It looked out of place in the daylight, as though its sacred presence on the green was better suited to the hours of darkness.

She studied the few cars still parked along the edge of the green and wondered if she'd imagined that someone had been out there while she was walking, watching her... maybe even following her. It all seemed so normal now, just a typical Cornish village. People out jogging or walking their dogs on the green, the postie delivering letters and parcels on foot, a cheery-looking woman in high-vis jacket and shorts despite the chilly weather. But night-time always cast a different complexion on a place...

Mrs Hepley brought over her order of Cheddar Ploughman's, setting it before her with a smile. 'What did you think of Bude?' she asked, an odd inflexion in her tone. 'Nice little town, isn't it?'

'Absolutely,' Stella agreed enthusiastically. 'Such a lovely spot.'

'Mad busy in summer though. Hard to park and the shops all crowded with holidaymakers. We try to avoid it between May and September.' She hesitated. 'Any sauces with that? Bit of mustard, maybe?'

'Please.'

Mrs Hepley brought over a wooden mini-trug of condiments. 'Now, don't think I was prying,' she said awkwardly, 'but when I was tidying your room just now, I had to move a few papers off your bed.'

Stella, about to bite into a forkful of Cheddar cheese, looked up at her, surprised. 'I'm sorry?'

'I didn't mean to but I couldn't help noticing... You've been to see Mr Hardcastle in Bude, is that right?'

Stella was stunned. 'Have you been reading my private correspondence?'

'I couldn't help it,' Mrs Hepley insisted, but she sounded more belligerent than apologetic now. 'It was only a quick glance but his name leapt out at me. And something about Black Rock Hall?' Her sharp gaze interrogated Stella. 'What's your connection there, then?

Astonished by this direct line of questioning, Stella said coldly, 'That's none of your business, Mrs Hepley, and I'd be grateful if you didn't touch my things again. In fact, please don't bother making up my room again while I'm staying here. I value my privacy, even if you don't.'

'Yes, that's all very well, but… Is it true you think you're descended from the Cossentines?'

'Excuse me?' Stella felt thoroughly ruffled, and didn't know whether she should get up and walk out or tell the woman to get knotted. 'As I said, it's none of your business.'

'Well, that's where you're wrong.' Flushed now, Mrs Hepley folded her arms across a heaving chest. 'This *is* my business. It's important to all of us here in West Pol, but especially to me.'

Mr Hepley had appeared at his wife's shoulder as though to back her up, and nodded at this comment. 'That's right,' he said deeply.

'I don't believe this.' Stella sat back and fixed the landlady with a straight look. 'All right, I'll bite. Why is it anything to do with you that I might be related to the Cossentine family?'

'Because my great-grandmother was the cook, Mrs Elsie Dunn. The woman they tried and hanged for the murders up at the big house.'

Digesting this information, Stella felt awful. Her gaze fell before the landlady's glare. 'I'm so sorry… I had no idea.'

'Why should you? But before you go thinking

I'm related to an evil murderess, you need to know that my great-grandmother was innocent. She never did it, see? She was *framed*.'

'Framed?" Stella studied her, frowning. 'Who would have done such a thing?'

'The true murderer, of course.' With a dramatic air, Mrs Hepley flung out an arm as though indicating the great house, unseen to the west behind the pub. 'I'm not saying it was Mr Maurice, though some think it might have been. But at least he made an effort to find out who done it, with that murder mystery exhibition of his. But the youngest daughter... the mad one, Celeste. She was never found, you know.' She appeared satisfied by Stella's suddenly wary expression, nodding. 'We don't believe Elsie Dunn poisoned all those people. And we won't rest until her name has been cleared.'

'That's right,' Mr Hepley repeated. He dragged a flier out of his jeans pocket, unfolded it and passed it to Stella. 'You should come along. See for yourself.'

Stella studied the flier. It was promoting a meeting at the pub in early November. JUSTICE FOR MRS ELSIE DUNN was written in bold letters along the top of the flier, followed by a few details about the Black Rock Hall murders and Mrs Dunn's trial, accompanied by a grim artistic impression of a woman hanging from the gallows. HELP US CLEAR HER NAME ran along the bottom of the flier, with a website address and a mobile number.

'I certainly wish you luck in clearing her name,' Stella told them. Several people at the bar were staring across at her now, listening without any shame to their conversation. 'But I'm not sure how it affects my own situation. You seem to think we're on opposite sides. Please believe me, we're not.'

Mrs Hepley gave a bark of contemptuous laughter. 'Don't you get it yet? This has always been about two sides. Rich and poor. The haves and the have nots. The Cossentines and the villagers.' She pursed her lips, glaring down at Stella. 'And we know which side you belong to, with your funny accent and your violin.'

'My funny accent, as you put it, is just London with the slightest hint of New York…. That's where I was born.'

'I told you she was a foreigner,' Mrs Hepley threw at her husband.

'That's right,' he agreed solemnly.

'But I can assure you, I'm not a have, I'm a have not. And yes, I play the violin. But that doesn't make me *posh*.' Stella ran a hand through her hair, struggling against the feeling that she was under attack. 'Look, do you mind? I'm trying to have my lunch.'

The landlord and landlord exchanged glances. Then Mr Hepley whispered something in his wife's ear. She pulled an angry face, but turned and walked away, disappearing back into the pub kitchen.

Mr Hepley cleared his throat. 'Sorry if the wife came over a bit strong just then. But she feels deeply about it, you know? She wants to see justice done.'

'I don't blame her,' Stella said, but picked up her knife and fork in a pointed manner.

Mr Hepley nodded, and retreated behind the bar.

Aware of many pairs of eyes staring at her, Stella attempted to eat her Ploughman's lunch, but had little appetite left after that nasty little spat with the landlady. She wished Mr Hardcastle had never recommended this place. Why on earth had he done it? He must know the landlady was a direct descendant of the cook hanged for the Cossentine murders and that her presence here would be inflammatory.

Then she recalled that, at the time of recommending this inn, the solicitor hadn't known why she was coming to talk to him. Or not in enough detail to realise there would be a clash.

And Mrs Hepley should never have rifled through her private papers. The more she dwelt on that thought, the angrier she became. It really wasn't right, a stranger invading her privacy like that...

'Excuse me. I'm sorry to disturb you while

you're eating, but are you Stella Ffoulds?'

Stella looked up, halfway through a mouthful of salad. A skinny, narrow-hipped woman with sleek black hair that fell to her shoulders, framing an angular face, had come to her table. Her simple white dress was sleeveless and ended just below the knee in a lace hem, exposing legs almost as white as the dress and open-toed sandals secured with leather thongs around her ankles. She wore no rings and no earrings either, but a large opal hung around her neck on a thin silver chain. Stella guessed her to be somewhere in her late thirties, though it was hard to be sure; she had an ageless face, wise and lined in places, yet somehow glowing with youth at the same time.

'Yes,' she said indistinctly, swallowing her food. Something about the woman's intent stare made her ask abruptly, 'You're not another descendant of Mrs Dunn, by any chance?'

But the woman smiled, shaking her head. 'No. But I couldn't help overhearing your argument with Mrs Hepley.' She gestured to the seat next to Stella. 'Do you mind if I join you?' She was carrying a large glass of red wine. 'I promise not to shout.'

Stella couldn't help laughing. 'Please,' she said, and nodded the woman to sit down. 'I could do with a friendly face, thank you. I seem to be persona non grata at the moment.'

'Oh, well, the natives, you know...' the woman

murmured, her dark eyes gleaming with sudden malicious humour.

'I'm sorry?'

'The Cornish. They don't like outsiders.'

'I like the Cornish. What I've seen of them so far.'

'Of course.'

Stella gave up on her half-eaten lunch, putting her knife and fork aside and reaching for her drink instead. 'All right, you know who I am, but I don't know who you are.' She frowned. 'How do you know who I am, by the way?'

'Village gossip. It doesn't take long in a place this small, especially when someone who works with Mr Hardcastle also happens to live here in West Pol.'

Stella felt uncomfortable, wondering what else people were saying about her. 'I see.'

The woman held out her hand. 'I'm Allison Friel.' Her eyes were almost as dark as her hair, almond-shaped, and her mouth curved with a faint sheen of pink lipstick. 'Nice to meet you.'

'Likewise.' They shook hands, rather awkwardly, over the table. 'Who's the snitch, then?' Seeing Allison's confusion, Stella elaborated. 'The person who works in the solicitor's office?'

'Oh, that would be telling.' Allison played with the opal around her neck, delicate little movements of her long, supple fingers to make sure it was hanging straight. 'I'm glad to have caught you, anyway. You see, I have an ulterior motive for wanting to meet you. I run a website, focused on local news and history, and I'd love to scoop an interview with you for my next post. You're obviously going to be the talk of the village once the news breaks officially.' She held up a camera and, before Stella could even protest or tidy her hair, snapped a candid photo of her. 'You don't mind, do you? It's to accompany the interview. I hate posed photographs. They're so tacky.'

Stella was annoyed. A casual chat in the bar was one thing but taking her photograph without permission? Her nerves prickling, she began to gather her things. 'Well, this has been nice. But I should probably go back to my room now.'

'Must you? So soon?'

'I need to practise.'

The woman's eyes widened, fixing on her face. 'Practise what?'

'I'm a violinist,' Stella explained briefly. 'That's my job. I play and teach the violin.'

'My goodness… How marvellous.'

'It can be.' Stella checked her phone before slipping it into her handbag. No messages. But she'd blocked Bruno's number, so that wasn't a huge surprise. 'I need to play every day though. To keep my bowing arm in.'

'And the landlady doesn't mind?'

'As a matter of fact, she does. It can be difficult to play quietly. So I'd better keep to only a short practice session today,' Stella muttered, glancing towards the bar. 'To avoid more bad feeling.'

'How about bringing your violin over to my house, instead? You can practise there for as long as you like. I adore listening to good violinists. Such a rare talent.' Allison pointed out of the pub window. 'I live on the far side of the green. By the wish tree.'

Stella hesitated. 'Are you sure? I don't want to intrude.'

'Nonsense. You're welcome anytime. Come over now, if you're in the mood to practise.'

It was hard to resist such an invitation. Her spirits lifted at the thought of playing freely without the worry that she might be disturbing someone with her music. Not everybody enjoyed the sound of a violin.

'I'd love to,' she admitted. 'Thank you.'

'I'll wait for you outside then, shall I?' Allison finished her drink and stood up. She was quite striking with her pale skin and jet-black hair, Stella thought, and far more pleasant than she'd appeared at first glance. 'We can walk over together.'

There was that Land Rover again, she thought, spotting the vehicle with its black-tinted windows parked across the other side of the green. There seemed to be someone at the wheel today. But with the blacked-out windows it was impossible to be sure. They walked across the green in the direction of the wish tree. The grass was spongy underfoot and the air fresh and chilly after rain in the night.

As they passed under the wish tree, Stella glanced up at the hanging ribbons and saw Allison smile. 'Why is this here?' she asked the woman, smitten by curiosity. 'It seems an odd site for a wish tree.'

'Not at all.' Allison ran her long fingers through the dangling ribbons and twists of silver foil attached to the branches. 'With Black Rock Hall so close to the village, this place has long been a centre for spiritual activity. I moved here a few years back and tied the first prayer ribbon to its branches... And now look at it. I live right here, you see, beside the tree.' She indicated the house where Stella had seen a light on at an upper window when out walking. 'Before I came here, I worked in a hospice for ten years. It taught me so much about life and death, and the threshold between them... Now I'm a spiritualist. I run retreats and training courses for psychics, most of them held in my own home. So naturally my students gravitate here after a session, to relax and commune with the earth and its spirits. It's a place of peace.'

Inside, Allison showed her to a room where she

could play her violin, brought her a glass of water by request, and then left her to it.

Before leaving Stoke Newington, she had mended the snap in her bow with strong wood glue, and it had held well enough for a few trial bow strokes. But this was the first time she had really put it to the test with a prolonged session. So she began cautiously, one eye on that fine crack in the shaft, and gradually gained confidence, finding no difference in the bow's function, even when playing to the full length of the bow.

While Stella was playing, time held little meaning for her. It was not unknown for her to lose several hours without noticing while practising. But that was one of the beauties of playing, the ability to forget everything and simply melt into the music, become one with the melody. It was wonderful therapy, and all the more wonderful for being self-administered. She worked on simple exercises first to warm her bowing arm and find the right rhythm. Then she practised some more complex music she'd brought with her from London, propping the book of sheet music open on a cabinet and playing with complete concentration.

By the time Allison reappeared with a tray of coffee and biscuits, the skies were dark outside and Stella was exhausted, her mind in another place entirely...

Slowly, she put away her violin and bow, and

secured the case. Inside, she felt curiously blank, like a slate wiped clean. 'Thank you,' she said, flopping onto a chair, barely any energy left. 'That was fantastic. Just what I needed.'

'You're welcome. I loved every minute of it. I could hear you clearly from the room next door. Your range is extraordinary.' Allison pulled up a chair to sit beside her, her expression enquiring. 'You don't mind that I listened, I hope?'

'Not at all.'

The spiritualist had brought a book with her. This, she signed with a flourish and handed it to Stella. 'One of my own creations. Keep it, in return for the lovely music.' Her smile was shy. 'Probably not your thing, but I'd be honoured if you'd read it.'

Surprised, Stella turned the book over in her hand. It was entitled *Speaking With Spirits*. 'For me? That's very kind of you.'

'It may open your eyes to another world. A world beyond this one.'

'I'll certainly give it a try.' Though Stella grimaced, thinking of all the ghosts Mrs Hepley claimed walked Black Rock Hall at dead of night…

'I'm sorry, I can see you're uncomfortable. And I'm not surprised, given you may be about to inherit a haunted house.' Allison held out a hand for the book. 'You don't need to force yourself.'

'No, really. I'm happy to read it. As you say, it could be useful.' She was joking but Allison took her seriously, nodding.'

'There were so many deaths at Black Rock Hall. People taken before their time. Deep trauma like that... Well, it leaves a mark on a house, in my opinion.' Her voice had dropped almost to a whisper. 'A dark stain on its psyche.'

'Can a house have a psyche?'

'Goodness, yes.' Allison looked away and shivered, as though speaking from personal experience. 'Have you been up to Black Rock Hall yet?'

Stella shook her head. 'It's closed 'till spring.'

'Oh, don't worry about that.' Allison smiled. 'I know the curator slightly. Walter Whitely. Of course, he's not a friend. In fact, we don't get on particularly well. But I could suggest he gives you an informal tour of the house and exhibition.' She quirked a thin eyebrow. 'It seems reasonable, given you may be taking over the place soon.'

'I don't know... I'm not even meant to talk about the inheritance until they're satisfied that I'm a genuine Cossentine. I don't think Mr Hardcastle would be very happy if he knew.'

'Judging by what I witnessed in the bar, the whole village will know you're the long-lost heir by tomorrow morning.'

'Oh God...'

'But if you prefer,' Allison said more carefully, 'I won't tell Walter about your claim on the property. I'll say you're a researcher, writing a paper about the murders. That will appeal to his vanity, trust me.' She shot Stella a quick look. 'Does that sound better?'

Although uncomfortable with the idea of lying, nonetheless Stella nodded, too keen to look inside Black Rock Hall to pass up the opportunity. 'Thank you.'

Allison leant forward for her phone and tapped out a quick text, then smiled. 'There, all done. Now, how about a few quick questions for the blog, since you're here? You don't mind being recorded, I trust?' Noticing Stella's wary expression, she finished softly, 'Look, I promise not to publish anything before your claim on the estate has been verified. You have my word.'

CHAPTER TWELVE

Tears streaming down her cheeks, half blinding her, Celeste dragged clothes out of drawers and chests, throwing them over her shoulder in haste, discarding far more than she chose. The modest travelling bag she always used to convey her personals to and from London would have to do; her trunk and larger cases were all in storage, and besides, she would be on foot and must only take what she could comfortably carry. Which meant essentials only, she decided, plus her jewellery and any money she could find, for she must not be destitute and on the streets. That would be too horrible a fate.

Her mind kept flashing back to what she had seen, but she shook the gory images away. All she could focus on was getting away from the house as soon as possible and never coming back.

Once the police arrived, they would want to know who had survived, who hadn't been at the dinner; and how could she explain what had happened, how she had been miraculously spared from the massacre of all her relatives?

Nobody would believe her story; she barely believed it herself. And her reputation would do the rest. The 'mad' one, the girl fresh out of an asylum cell, kept locked up in her room... except for tonight. She might sometimes have wished ill upon some of her family, but she refused to hang for something she had not done.

Her bag crammed and bulging, Celeste crept to the doorway, catching a glimpse of herself in the standing mirror opposite – white-faced and staring – and almost laughed out loud at her stupidity.

She wouldn't get far still dressed in her best frock with its slender straps and white satin pumps. Quite apart from freezing to death once night fell, she would be spotted the instant she ventured outside in that ridiculous get-up.

Gasping, she dropped her bag, kicked off her shoes, wrenched the feathered fascinator from her hair and began to wriggle out of her gown, tearing the fine linen in her hurry. There was a rough pair of trousers and an old shirt of Maurice's in the bottom drawer, she recalled, and dragged them out. Her younger brother had lent them to her once when they'd all gone out blackberrying and had never asked for them back. A pair of stout walking boots completed this outfit, and she felt sure only close inspection would reveal them to be women's and not men's boots.

The shirt was uncomfortably snug, her chest having developed somewhat since those days. But she knotted a baggy black shawl about her throat and draped it over her more female contours, pulled down the flat cap that had once kept her hair away from the brambles, and checked her reflection again with satisfaction.

Nobody would look twice at her. Or not once dusk had fallen.

She slipped out of her bedroom, suppressing a sob at the thought of her own dear Maurice among those dead in the dining room... and then stopped, suddenly still.

Face after face flashed before her, their stillness and awful contorted expressions... and Maurice's had not been among them.

Because he was still in the tower room, of course. Mother had insisted he be kept locked away from the others after his beating this afternoon.

Relief flooded through her. Her dearest brother Maurice was still alive. Did he even know of the carnage below? She almost ran to the tower stairs to tell him what had happened and to ask his advice...

Then a coldness invaded her heart, and she stopped dead, staring at nothing.

You'll never see me again after tonight... Now and then someone has to take a stand. Do what's right.

Had Maurice done this? Killed their entire family?

'Impossible,' she whispered.

But then she remembered the coldness in his eyes, his hard stare as he sent her away, the resolution in his voice...

You want my advice? Tell Sir Oliver no. Refuse to attend the dinner party tonight. Go back to your room instead.

He had been covertly warning her not to go downstairs with the others. Yet she had ignored that advice and gone down anyway. And what had happened? She had come to, lying on the floor in her father's study, and staggered out to find all her family dead – except for her and Maurice. A terrible suspicion crossed her mind. Perhaps she hadn't suffered a blackout but had been struck from behind as she stood in the hall, shrinking from her duty. Then dragged into the study so nobody would see her fallen body and raise the alarm before the wicked deed could be achieved. That would explain the dreadful aching throb at the back of her head that still pained her.

She hadn't locked Maurice's door on leaving him.

Had her brother come sneaking down from his quarters, seen her standing in the hall, knocked her out, and then concealed her unconscious body? And then somehow managed to kill everyone around the dinner table in a vicious act of revenge for his ill-treatment that day…

It seemed incredible. Yet somebody had murdered them all. And she felt sure that Maurice, young as he was, was capable of taking a life. There was no doubt in her mind about that. But so many lives? And their mama's too? Was he *that* cold-hearted?

Celeste shuddered and turned away from the tower stairs. If Maurice had done this terrible deed, he would not be up there, calmly awaiting his arrest for murder. And if he was innocent, he might well think she was the guilty party, and force her to await the arrival of the police.

Either way, her best and only option was to leave Black Rock Hall at once and never come back. Though it broke her heart to think he was right and they would never see each other again.

Guilty or not, Maurice was now her only surviving relative.

Before heading downstairs, she ran to her mother's bedroom, knowing that she must take more items to sell. Most of her own jewellery was paste. Mama's was silver and gold, some set with precious jewels. Without something to sell, she would be forced to live on the streets or in the back slums of London, and how long would she survive once winter came?

Averting her eyes from the stark emptiness of her mother's apartment, she chose the smallest but most expensive items, but felt a sudden qualm on reaching for the ornate silver ring that nestled in velvet at the back of her mother's jewellery case.

The silver ring was the oldest and most valuable single piece of silverwork the Cossentine family owned, purely because of its antique provenance and the fascinating legends attached to its history.

There was a Latin inscription on the inside of the ring. *Amor aeternus.* By tradition, it passed to the eldest daughter on the death of the mother, and was supposed to ensure a long and happy marriage. She had always assumed it would go to Fenella, or perhaps Jolie, if the worst happened and Fenella died young.

'I'm the eldest daughter now,' Celeste whispered to herself, and slid the ring onto her finger.

The silver ring flashed in the triptych dressing table mirrors, incongruous against the stained shirt and rough trousers. It was a tell-tale sign she was not the poor labourer she was pretending to be.

Reluctantly, she removed the ring, placing it in the button-down side-pocket of her travelling bag instead. She dared not risk drawing attention to herself by stupidly flaunting any jewellery, however precious to her.

Gingerly, avoiding the steps that creaked, she crept downstairs. Already, she could hear voices in the corridors again, and kept to the shadows, making for the garden room where she could slip unseen from the house and across the lawns. But as she crossed an echoing hallway, a voice stopped her in her tracks.

'Miss Celeste?'

She whirled to find a weeping, red-eyed Becky behind her. The cook's daughter was staring at her in disbelief.

'You're not dead,' Becky gasped, rubbing her eyes and whimpering as she tottered forward. 'Not like... Not like your dear Mama and sisters, and... and Mr Cossentine himself.'

The girl almost fell, sobbing, but Celeste caught her, holding her tight in an awkward embrace. 'Becky, hush, not so loud, please...'

She glanced swiftly up and down the passageway, but nobody else was about. In the distance, she could hear the roar of engines though as cars made their way at speed up the long drive. 'I wasn't at d-dinner. I was... Well, never mind.' She released the girl with a quick, reassuring squeeze of her shoulder. 'I'm sorry, I c-can't stay. I have to get away.'

Becky stared. 'Get away, Miss?'

'The police will think I d-did it. Don't you see that? They'll say I had one of my episodes and –'

She fell silent, listening as several cars pulled up noisily outside the entrance, spitting gravel, and a moment later men could be heard entering the house. Men in boots, calling out instructions, asking questions and the butler answering in a tremulous voice she barely recognised, old Priddy no doubt shaken to his core by what he had witnessed tonight.

'Becky, I need to get out of here,' Celeste whispered urgently. 'You know what they'll say about me. That I'm n-not right in my head.' She paused, remembering the hideous staring face of her fiancé, Sir Oliver, among the dead. This disaster would touch his family too, and the extended families of her sisters' husbands, also at that table tonight. They would all be after her. 'I'll be blamed for these murders, see if I'm not.'

Becky didn't seem to be listening. She merely shook her head, great tears rolling down her pale cheeks. 'They won't blame you, Miss. They'll say my mother done it. She's the cook, ain't she? She made the soup what done for 'em.'

'The soup?'

She had a sudden memory of coming across the spilt tureen in the passageway, perhaps dropped in horror by the servant bearing it away as the first victims began to die after drinking its contents…

'She'll hang for this,' Becky moaned, dragging on her sleeve, 'and I know she didn't do it. My mother wouldn't hurt a fly. She's innocent, Miss. Stay and speak for her. Please, I beg you.'

'I c-can't.' Horrified, Celeste shook her head. She could hear the men heading this way now. Fear fanned white-hot in her chest, burning out her nerves. 'Nobody would listen to me, Becky. Don't you realise that? I'm the m-mad one, remember? Even if they don't put me on trial for murder, they'll find a way to lock me up for life after this. Anyway, why on earth would anyone b-blame your mother? If the soup *was* poisoned, it must have been an accident or... or someone with a grudge...' She realised too late that she might be incriminating her brother Maurice and abruptly changed tack. 'Listen, I'm sorry about Sebastian. I saw you with him at the summerhouse and t-told my mother about it. But she wouldn't listen.'

Becky was staring. 'You were the one who told Mrs Cossentine about me and Sebastian?' Her lip was trembling. 'I would never have said nothing about that. I'm not stupid. You know that she dismissed me? Jeffrey's been told to take me home first thing tomorrow. No references, no pay.'

'I'm sorry, Becky. I didn't realise how she would react. I thought she might help you. I was wrong.' The raised voices were coming nearer. 'I have to g-go,' she whispered. 'Please don't tell anyone you saw me. Goodbye.'

The side door out of the garden room was mere yards away. The evening air was still as

Celeste slipped through it and walked as steadily as she could across the lawns towards the woods, bathed in the light of the setting sun.

She was trembling the whole way, barely able to stay upright, but reached the edge of the wood without being followed or hearing angry shouts for her to stop. Unable to resist though, she looked back once, and saw a dark figure in the uppermost window of the tower, watching her.

Maurice.

So he was still up there in the tower room. He hadn't run from the police. Tentatively, she raised a hand, still unsure if he was the murderer or if he knew nothing yet of what had occurred at dinner.

Her brother stared back at her without raising a hand in return, and then reached up to close the curtains, shutting her out of his sight.

You'll never see me again after tonight.

Her heart thumping, Celeste turned and disappeared into the shady wood, her face set towards the coastal path and freedom.

Before the sun had properly risen, having not slept at all, she had tramped the several miles to Bude Station on the outskirts of the small town. Keeping her hair tucked out of sight and her cap pulled down low, she had managed to secure a third-class seat to London.

A woman in her compartment had heard about the murders, having a second cousin working as a groundsman at the house, and to Celeste's horror spoke of little else for the first hour.

'The youngest girl, the mad one, it looks like she done for them. Slipped a ton of rat poison in the soup, I shouldn't be surprised. She was always an unnatural girl, they say... Born backwards with an addled brain. My ma saw one like that at a freak show once, you know. Crossed eyes and drooling.'

And the woman she was talking to at exclaimed at intervals or nodded sagely, as though nothing could be more obvious than that a mad girl would want to poison her entire family for absolutely no reason.

Celeste had shrunk further into her corner, cap covering her face, arms folded across tell-tale breasts, and did not move a muscle until the two women finally disembarked at Exeter.

Less conspicuous among the third-class newcomers at Exeter, mostly tradesmen or country women with children, she sat a little straighter and dared look out of the window. Steam puffed past the partially open windows, filling the carriage occasionally and making everyone cough, but beyond its grey clouds, she saw stretches of moorland and sunlit towers on green hills and canals dotted with barges and working men. Villages flashed by in the distance and towns passed more slowly as the train stopped to pick up more passengers.

It was late afternoon by the time she found herself peering out at the familiar, sooty outskirts of London.

Gathering her belongings with relief, Celeste stood on the busy platform, a little lost and wondering where to go next. But the sight of a policeman near the ticket barrier, studying new arrivals from the West Country, soon had her hurrying out of the station, head down and careful not to draw attention to herself.

The evening papers on the newsstand were full of the murders. She bought a copy and read the lurid details with a sense of despair, for the inspector in charge of the case had indeed suggested that the youngest daughter of the family – the reporter had misspelt her name – had fled soon after the grim discovery of the crime and was therefore their chief suspect.

Celeste wandered the streets aimlessly, her bag growing heavier and the warm summer evening more stifling.

At last, she found herself before a familiar door, and after some moments' agonised deliberation, she knocked softly.

The door opened and her old nurse, Peggy, stood there, staring at her, mouth open, eyes wide. 'Miss Celeste?'

'I didn't do it,' Celeste whispered, broken. 'I swear it. You must believe me, Peggy. I would never... It wasn't me.'

'Oh, my poor darling.' Peggy dragged her into a tight embrace and then pulled her inside, closing the door to shut out the smoky night. Then she shook her head at her outfit. 'What on earth are you wearing? Well, never mind that. You come into the kitchen and have supper with us.' Two young girls, both mirror images of their mother, were already at the kitchen table, but moved up silently to let Celeste sit on the bench between them. 'That's May and June, my twin girls. They won't say a word, don't you worry.'

Celeste dried her tears and tried to smile. 'Thank you, dearest Peggy. I knew I could rely on you. But what about your husband?'

It had to be at least six or seven years since Peggy had left them to get married after two decades' service with the family. After that, Mama had decided the youngest Cossentine children no longer needed a nursemaid; Celeste had been packed off to a special boarding school for girls with behavioural problems, while Maurice had gained a new tutor instead. But they had both missed dear old Peggy with her comfortable lap and old-fashioned curls.

'Gone to sea, my darling.' Peggy patted her hand.

'I need somewhere to stay,' Celeste told her in a small voice. 'Though not for long. I expect the police will be looking for me and I don't want to bring trouble to your door.'

Her old nurse nodded, passing along a glorious bowl of soup and plenty of fresh-baked bread and butter. But later, when she'd tucked her twin girls up in bed, Peggy admitted that she wasn't sure she could let her stay for long.

'One of my neighbours came round to tell me what was in the evening paper,' Peggy said as they shared a glass of after-dinner sherry. 'Your poor Mama, and your poor, dear sisters... Jolie was such a pretty girl, though spoilt to a fault. I can't believe they're all gone.' She dabbed her eyes with a handkerchief. 'I knew at once it wasn't you who did such a godless act. But the police will blame whoever's to hand.' Peggy paused, her voice turning awkward. 'The thing is, I take in seamstress work now, and I can't risk losing the money. If people knew...'

'I won't stay longer than a week or two, and I won't show my face outside,' Celeste promised her at once, though secretly she wished she could stay with dear old Peggy forever. 'First, I need to cut my hair, so I'm not so recognisable. And I need a job. It doesn't matter where and I'm not afraid of hard work. All I need is the promise of a steady wage so I can get a room in a boarding house.'

'I know someone who might have a room for you at a reasonable price. And there's always plenty of work in London. Though you'll have to give a false name and lie about where you come from.'

'That's the easy part,' Celeste assured her. 'I'm going to be Lizzie Brown from Devon. I thought it up on the train.' She paused. 'But what if I have to prove my identity. Could I say that I lost my papers in a fire?'

Peggy gave her a grim smile. 'Now listen, pet, don't you worry about that. War could be declared any day now, and if it's anything like the last show, there'll soon be plenty of people in London without papers.' She poured them both another generous glass of sherry, though Celeste's head was already woozy and spinning. 'Nobody will bother looking for a runaway girl once war breaks out. The boys in blue will be too busy signing up to fight Mr Hitler, you mark my words.'

Celeste could only hope she was right. Because the thought of being put on trial for murder made her blood run cold...

CHAPTER THIRTEEN

The following day, Stella came back to The Silversmiths' Arms after a long tramp through fields surrounding the village, once glimpsing the high walls of Black Rock Hall through the trees and stopping to study the house with interest. She was curious about the place; she couldn't deny that. And not simply because she might be about to inherit it. Black Rock Hall had been where her grandmother had once spent the idyllic Cornish summers she had often mentioned. But it was also where she had found her family murdered and had fled, fearing to be blamed. Stella had no doubt her gentle-mannered grandmother was innocent. But if the cook hadn't murdered the Cossentines, as Mrs Hepley and her supporters seemed to believe, then who had?

She scraped mud off her shoes at the side door – making a mental note to buy wellies as soon as possible – and let herself into the pub. But there was no chance of heading straight upstairs unseen, as Mrs Hepley had heard the door and was waiting for her in the narrow hallway.

'I'd like a word,' the landlady said abruptly, nodding her through into the busy saloon bar.

'I'm really quite tired. I just want to go upstairs and –'

'I'm not asking,' Mrs Hepley snapped, 'I'm telling. I want a word. In here now, if you please.'

Once again, there was a busy lunch crowd in the pub and speculative eyes had already turned their way. The woman's tone raised her hackles but she decided to hear her out; there might be a genuine reason for her antipathy this time, though Stella couldn't imagine what. And at least the saloon bar was warm, logs crackling on an open fire, a large hairy dog stretched flat out in front of the hearth, one eye opening as she came in.

'Yes, what can I help you with?' she asked the landlady, her smile strained.

'Yesterday, you tried to pretend you didn't know what I was talking about. But it's all around the village now that you're Celeste Cossentine's granddaughter, and you hope to prove that and inherit Black Rock Hall.' The landlady tapped the side of her nose. 'We've got our sources. So don't bother to deny it.'

'I don't see how it's any of your business.' Stella saw the landlady's mouth open and jumped in quickly ahead of her, adding, 'I'm sorry about the cook, of course. You're descended from her, I know. But her guilty verdict was nothing to do with me.'

'Oh, is that right?' The landlady jabbed a finger at her. 'I've been speaking to my *own* lawyer today. And she says, we can sue for compensation. For a miscarriage of justice. Unlawful hanging.'

'Sue who, exactly?' Stella wrinkled her nose, puzzled. 'The police? The courts? Or the justice system itself?'

'Maybe, yes, all of them.' The landlady's face grew crafty. 'But the family too. We can sue the Cossentines.'

'How do you figure that?'

'Your great-uncle, Maurice… He gave evidence at the trial. Evidence that may have helped sway the judge against Elsie Dunn. Maurice Cossentine said she might have been angry about what happened to her daughter.' The landlady fixed her with a cold stare. 'Becky was still only a child at the time, fifteen years old, and she was raped by one of the Cossentine boys. The very same day as the poisoning. It was all in her testimony to the court.' Mrs Hepley crossed her arms, her chest heaving with righteous indignation. 'Becky was served her notice to Mr and Mrs Cossentine because of what happened to her.'

'Victim-shaming,' Mr Hepley muttered from behind the bar.

'That's right. Classic victim-shaming.' His wife nodded, her small mouth pursed up. 'And that's why the judge came down against the cook. To my mind, the Cossentines owe my family *compensation.*'

'But for what, exactly?'

'For Elsie's hanging and decades of public shame... Do you have any idea how it feels to belong to a family where one of you's been found guilty of so many murders? The Dunns haven't been able to hold their heads up in public for years. Elsie Dunn was an innocent woman hanged for a crime she never did.'

'She was a scapegoat.' Mr Hepley again.

His wife pointed to him without looking round. 'That's right. A scapegoat. So the real perpetrator could get away with their murders scot-free.'

'I see.' Stella felt many eyes on her; it seemed everyone in the pub was listening to their altercation. She felt anger bubbling up inside her and clamped her hands together, struggling for control. 'And who was this "real perpetrator," in your opinion? Or shouldn't I ask?'

'Your grandmother left Black Rock Hall that night and was never seen again. Bit fishy, isn't it? If she was *innocent.*'

'My grandmother was not a murderer.'

'Neither was Elsie Dunn.'

They were glaring at each other, the air prickling with tension.

'I don't think this is going to work, is it, Mrs Hepley?' Stella bit out, nettled and off-balance. 'I'd better pay what I owe you and leave. I expect I'll be able to find somewhere to stay in Bude easily enough.'

'There's no need to go that far,' the landlord said uneasily, stepping between them. 'You can stay if you like. I don't want people saying we threw you out or anything unpleasant like that.'

'Speak for yourself,' his wife muttered.

'No, thank you, Mr Hepley.' Losing her cool, Stella marched towards the door marked Accommodation. 'I'm going upstairs to pack. Maybe you could have the bill ready by the time I came down.'

'Hey, just you wait a minute…' Making a grab for her arm, Mrs Hepley dragged her back. 'I haven't finished with you. Typical bloody American,' she spat out, 'city girl, thinking you can come in here and lord it over us Cornish.'

'How dare you? Get your hands off me.' Stella was trembling now, breathless with fury, her face hot. 'My grandmother didn't murder her family. And yes, maybe that means Elsie Dunn did kill them. Or perhaps Becky herself did it. Had you even considered that possibility? After what happened to her – '

With a gasp, Mrs Hepley slapped her about the face.

There was an awful silence.

Mr Hepley hurried forward, pulling his wife away and apologising profusely. 'I'm so sorry about that, Miss Ffoulds, my wife's not herself at the moment. She's been under a lot of strain, what with the campaign and all. She's not been sleeping well.'

Cerainly, the landlady seemed almost as stunned by what she'd done as Stella was, standing wide-eyed and silent.

Her husband opened the Accommodation door for Stella, saying soothingly, 'You'd better go on up and pack, Miss. We won't charge you for your stay.' Mrs Hepley stirred then, blinking at him, and he repeated firmly, 'There'll be no bill to pay. It's on the house, see? For the inconvenience.'

So that she wouldn't report Mrs Hepley to the police for assault, more like, Stella thought indignantly, her cheek still smarting.

But she nodded. 'Very well.'

Upstairs, she threw everything into her case with shaking hands, angry and upset by that unexpected confrontation with the pub owners.

It had seemed so easy back in London; turn up, present her case, maybe inherit something, maybe get sent away empty-handed.

Now she saw how much more complicated the situation was. And the reality of the history involved was shocking too. Not mere characters in an historical account, but real people facing real consequences.

The police needed a scapegoat to hide the real culprit, someone had written in an online forum she'd stumbled across on a website dedicated to historic unsolved murder cases, castigating the slipshod police investigation and claiming that Mrs Elsie Dunn was innocent all along. The anonymous writer could have been Mr or Mrs Hepley or one of their supporters.

Perhaps they were right.

She returned to the bar, lugging her heavy bags down the steep and narrow stairs, and found Mr Hepley waiting to show her out.

'I'm sorry about what happened,' he said awkwardly, but she shook her head at his apology.

'It's all forgotten.'

'That's the spirit.' The pub landlord seemed relieved. 'Least said soonest mended.' He took her suitcase and carried it out into the chilly afternoon for her. 'Would you like me to call you a taxi?'

'No, thanks.'

But in fact Stella had not thought much beyond leaving the premises as quickly as possible. Now she chewed her lip, weighing up her options. Her finances were a bit thin, but she could catch the bus into Bude and try to find a cheap bed-and-breakfast place there. The town seemed to have quite a few still open, and they couldn't all be full this late in the year.

As Mr Hepley turned away, she became aware of someone watching her from the pub entrance. A man in a long dark jacket, a mobile phone in his hand. She glanced that way, curious. He was a stranger but there was something vaguely familiar about him. She had a feeling he might have been one of the people drinking at the bar when she came back from Bude yesterday.

A local then, perhaps. He could even be one of Mrs Hepley's fervent supporters, she thought, eyeing him apprehensively.

The man headed towards her, his gaze steady on her face.

'Yes, can I help you?' she demanded, immediately on the defensive.

'It's more the other way around,' the man said calmly. 'I couldn't help overhearing what happened earlier, and I wondered if you'd like a lift into Bude.' He paused, raising his brows. 'I'm parked right outside, and since I'm headed that way anyway...'

It was a tempting suggestion. Taxi fares were exorbitant and the bus wouldn't be easy to negotiate with so much luggage. But she needed to be certain he wasn't on Mrs Hepley's team. The last thing she needed right now was more trouble.

'You were eavesdropping on my conversation?'

'Actually, I was eating lunch in the snug,' he admitted. She had popped her head into the small room adjacent to the saloon bar yesterday, curious to see what was in there, and had found a narrow space with only two tables and a quiz machine. 'But it's a small pub and raised voices carry... It was hard not to hear the whole thing. And I do admit to seeing the slap.' He studied her face. 'How's the cheek?'

His smile was rather charming, which made her suspicious. But she could do with a lift into town. And it was only a few miles, after all.

'Fine,' she said shortly. 'Look, it's very kind of you,' she continued, but he shook his head.

'Happy to help. This all your luggage?' Before she could say anything, he had stooped and collected her two heaviest bags, his gaze flicking curiously to the violin case. 'If you're ready to go?'

She sighed, giving up. 'More than ready.'

Heavy clouds had been gradually rolling in from the sea, and it now looked as though rain was imminent. A good time to be getting a lift rather than struggling with her cases at the village bus stop, she thought, glancing up at darkening skies with a sense of misgiving.

A movement across the village green caught her eye. Someone drifting out of sight behind the wish tree. She caught a glimpse of floaty white fabric and wondered if it was the spiritualist again, Allison Friel... A strange woman, unusual and other-worldly. But she could become a friend, Stella sensed.

'Which one is your car?' she asked.

'It's not in the car park. I went for a walk before lunch so I parked it down the road, about a hundred yards away.' He turned his head as though to check how much she was carrying. 'Can you manage?'

'Of course.'

Now that she was less distracted by the awkwardness of her departure, Stella took a moment to study her rescuer more closely.

In the shade of the pub, she'd thought him younger than her, somewhere in his mid-twenties; in cold autumnal sunlight, she could see that he was a few years older, early thirties at least. His hair was dark, clipped very short to his head, almost a buzz cut, and he had the straight-backed bearing of a military man. His build could best be described as tall and muscular, with broad shoulders and an even broader chest, and he strode rather than walked. Black jeans, white open-necked shirt, black longline jacket, sturdy boots.

He struck her as capable, determined, no-nonsense. Absolutely everything she loathed and distrusted in a man, in other words. Though given her abysmal record with men, and especially how her most recent fling had turned out – Bruno had turned out to be a control freak who constantly suspected her of seeing other men behind his back – perhaps going for those dreamy, creative types was not exactly working for her.

'Here we are,' he said, and she heard the soft beep of his remote and saw the lights flash on a dusty, black Land Rover.

'This is your car?'

'Yes.' His head turned and his eyes narrowed on her face, and she had the oddest feeling he could read her thoughts. 'Why?'

Stella shook her head, reluctantly handing him her precious violin case as he deposited the rest of her luggage in the back. 'No reason.' Pushing paranoia aside, she climbed into the passenger seat. 'Forget it.'

CHAPTER FOURTEEN

Central London, October 1940

Celeste woke in the dark to the eerie wail of an air-raid siren for the fourth night running. Jostled by the other girls in her dorm, she struggled down the narrow stairs to the basement shelter, clutching a blanket and pillow, and found a corner where she could make herself comfortable again. Or as comfortable as could be expected in a cold, damp basement where the lights often went out, plunging them all into darkness for hours, and dust fell into their eyes and mouths every time the ground above shook with the force of a nearby detonation. There was always a collective intake of breath from those sheltering whenever that happened, then a gasp of relief as they realised it had not been a direct hit, that they were still alive.

'I'll be glad to be back on shift at the hospital,'

her friend Esther grumbled, wiping dust from her cheeks. 'Rather takes your mind off these damn bombs, doesn't it? Looking after the wounded… Except when it makes you fear you might be next in line. To be wounded, I mean.' She shook her head and more powdery-white dust showered the shoulders of her red flannel dressing gown. 'Oh… fudge!'

Celeste snorted with laughter.

Esther Sharpe had been her first real friend in London, apart from dear Peggy. They looked quite similar – both had similar shades of chestnut hair, both had dark eyes and cupid-bow mouths, and were roughly the same height and build – but Esther was older. Four years older, to be precise, and that seemed to make all the difference. That, and the horrid fact that Esther's parents had drowned in a boating accident when she was barely twelve years old, and she'd been left to fend for herself, sweeping out her uncle's grocery shop for a few pennies a week, plus board and lodging, and graduated to helping out behind the counter. At twenty-one, she'd managed to get herself on a nursing course, and was now a registered nurse, while Celeste was too young to be admitted to an official training course. Nonetheless, although far superior to Celeste in terms of experience and knowledge, she never gave herself airs and graces like the other trained nurses, and was always quick to help when Celeste didn't know what to do.

Of course, Esther had no idea that her real name was Celeste. To her friend, and to everyone she ever met, she was Lizzie Brown.

Lizzie Brown was the name she'd used when identity cards were introduced, and to her amazement had not been asked to prove her identity. A few months later, a ration book in the same name had also been issued to her. But, as Peggy had predicted, everyone's attention was on the war by then, and not the minor botheration of a few lost documents.

So now she was Lizzie Brown, and although she would face serious issues if she ever needed a passport, her identity card and ration book seemed to satisfy most requirements.

Thanks to a wartime scheme allowing unqualified nurses to seek work at the larger London hospitals, she had been granted permission to learn on the job by assisting registered nurses. And Esther had been her first mentor.

'Oh yes, have a good laugh. No dust on you, I notice, Nurse Brown.' Esther peered up at the low ceiling with an accusing stare as another bomb shook the foundations of the building and yet more dust trickled down onto her hair. 'Whereas I appear to be sitting in Dust Central.'

'Do you want to swop places?' Celeste asked meekly.

'I wouldn't ordinarily pull rank, but in this instance... ' Esther grinned. 'Yes, please.'

Both on hands and knees, they somehow managed to squeeze past each other in the narrow space, and settle down again in each other's places.

'Peace at last,' Esther said.

The ceiling shook with a tremendous thundering quake, and dust poured down on bother their heads.

'Oh, for goodness' sake!' Esther moaned, covered in white dust and looked for all the world like a ghost.

'Sibyl, might I have that newspaper, please? If you've finished reading it, that is. Thanks ever so.' On receiving the newspaper, Celeste quickly divided it into two halves. With a few practised flicks and twists, she fashioned both halves into admirals' hats, tossing one across to Esther and placing the other paper hat on her own head. 'There. Better?'

'Oh my God, Lizzie, you absolute genius.' Esther pulled hers down on dark wavy hair, like a nurse's cap, and they both bowed to each other gravely, while the other girls fell about giggling. 'I feel quite the thing in this.' She took a spare sheet from the newspaper, rolled it up to make a pretend telescope, and set it to her eye. 'Ready to report for duty on the high seas, sailor?'

'Aye, aye, Cap'n!' Celeste cried, saluting her.

'Oh please, can't you see I'm an admiral?'

A bomb hit somewhere above them; the ceiling lights shook violently, showering them with yet more dust, and blinked out.

'To be honest, Admiral, I can't see much of anything at the moment,' Celeste said, and they all roared with laughter.

Celeste laughed too as the game went on, becoming ever more ridiculous and far-fetched, but inside she was terrified, so terrified she could scarcely breathe. She was scared by the constant bombardment and the near misses and the uncertainty of everything. Scared that at any moment a bomb would hit and she would simply cease to be, obliterated into a million pieces that some poor sod would be forced to scrape together in a bucket and put a label on it. The last mortal remains of...

Except it wouldn't even be her real name she was buried under. She would die Lizzie Brown from a made-up village in Devon, a girl who had never really existed, except on the cover of a ration book.

But it was laugh or cry these days, and like all the other nurses, she only cried when nobody could see her, curled up in bed, blankets dragged over her head in case anyone was watching. Then, and only then, would she let the fear and the unhappiness pour out of her soul as she shook with silent sobs...

But whenever she was with other people, her patients at the hospital or her fellow nurses, or the nice one-armed man on the newsstand who always stopped to exchange some banter with her in the mornings, or the crowds of people crushed together in the underground stations, she smiled and laughed, and kept on pretending she wasn't afraid.

And then some nights, usually when there was a death on the wards, she would remember that evening at Black Rock Hall, peering into the dining room with all those dead faces staring back at her...

'I'm Lizzie Brown,' she would say under her breath, swinging her legs out of bed. 'Plain Lizzie Brown from Devon, that's me.'

Maybe one day she would believe it.

The all-clear sounded at last, and the nurses all gathered their things together and trudged wearily back to bed, though it was almost dawn.

'You're still wearing your admiral's hat,' Esther pointed out as Celeste nipped to the convenience before getting back into bed.

'Oops,' Celeste said with a grin, and marched into the loo without removing it. On coming out afterwards to wash her hands, she stared at herself in the dark cracked mirror above the sink. Her smile had gone and her eyes were empty. How many hours' sleep had she managed? Two? Maybe less?

She snatched the paper hat from her head and was about to toss it into the bin when her eye was caught by a single word among the newsprint, crumpled and upside-down, but nonetheless recognisable and jarring to her already shredded senses.

Mrs Elsie Dunn.

Every nerve in her body burnt-out and singing like a wire, she smoothed out the newspaper and stared down at the headline.

COOK HANGS FOR MASS MURDER

Horror crept along her skin as she scanned the first few paragraphs of the article, a sick taste in her mouth at the deliberately sensational note of the reporting.

It seemed there had been a lengthy investigation of the murders at Black Rock Hall, delayed because of the war and a shortage of man-power, plus the many post-mortems, testimonies and examination of evidence that had to take place. Eventually, the prosecution had presented its case, a trial had taken place at which Maurice had testified, and Mrs Dunn had been found guilty by a jury of her peers. Sentence had been passed by the judge, after consideration, and a few days ago, she had faced the hangman.

Poor, poor Becky... How the cook's daughter must have suffered, hearing the grim details of her rape paraded mercilessly through the courtroom, and then watching her mother go through hell and unable to do a thing about it. She remembered how Becky had even grabbed at her sleeve that night, trying to stop her from leaving. *Please, Miss... They'll say my mother done it. She's the cook. She made the soup what done for them...*

Abruptly, she bent her head and retched violently into the sink. She slid to her knees, then collapsed onto the chill linoleum and lay there in the grey half-light of pre-dawn, her throat choked, her head spinning.

Time passed. Light grew brighter outside the frosted glass window. Soon the other nurses would be getting up to wash and have breakfast. She couldn't be found in here, cowering like a wounded animal. Celeste sat up and dried her tears, and tried to screw her courage back together, ready to face a new day.

Slowly and carefully, she re-read the newspaper article, and this time focused on the final paragraph, which she hadn't reached before throwing up.

The cook's three children still insist, even after their mother's guilty verdict and execution, that the widowed Mrs Dunn did not murder the Cossentine family. They point instead to the disappearance that night of the youngest daughter, Miss Celeste Cossentine, whose whereabouts are still unknown, claiming that she committed the murders. Miss Celeste's fiancé, Sir Oliver Gliddon, was also among the dead, and some have speculated that their engagement had been forced upon her by her father. Judge Barrow QC, in his summing up, had directed the jury to pay no credence to such baseless speculation. Nonetheless, this reporter believes only the reappearance and testimony of the missing daughter can lay such rumours to rest forever.

Celeste shivered and closed her eyes. She couldn't bear to read any more.

Maurice had testified at the cook's trial, the report said.

She wondered what he'd said and if his evidence had damned the cook. She wondered if he'd been served his papers yet. He must be old enough now to do his basic training.

But no, she was kidding herself if she thought this verdict meant it was safe to return to her old life as Celeste Cossentine.

She didn't believe for a moment that the cook did it. Mrs Dunn had not been that kind of woman, however strong or compelling the circumstantial evidence against her. The cook had always had a soft spot for Jolie and been indulgent towards her, often fetching her special titbits to tempt her appetite, especially once she was expecting a baby. No, Mrs Dunn had not poisoned the soup that night. She had been a kind, generous, warm-hearted mother of three herself; she would never have murdered a pregnant woman, however much hatred she might have felt towards Sebastian and Papa for their callous treatment of her own daughter.

Which only left Maurice.

What was it Becky had said about Maurice that night? *Locked up for bad behaviour, the Master said, and not to come to dinner with the rest.* He'd been confined to his room as a punishment. But a punishment for what?

And had it made him angry enough to kill?

While Maurice was still alive, she could never go home. He had always been her favourite brother, the one she was closest to.

Now she couldn't think of his dark, sullen face without imagining him breaking out of his room, sneaking into the kitchen where the food was kept on the hot plate ready for serving, lifting the vast silver lid of the soup tureen and tipping in just enough poison to send them all to hell...

CHAPTER FIFTEEN

Sitting in the front passenger seat of the black Land Rover, Stella felt her phone buzz and took it out of her jacket pocket. It was a text message but she didn't know the phone number it came from.

I believe you'd like a tour of the Black Rock Hall exhibition. I'm available now, if you wish to come to the house. Walter Whitely

She stared down at the message, utterly bemused.

What on earth?

'You play the violin, then?' the man asked her, starting the engine. He checked in his rear-view mirror, beginning to reverse out of the space.

'Sorry? Oh, yeah…' Stella perused the message, trying to decide how to respond. 'I play professionally.'

'Seriously? That's amazing.' He glanced at her face. 'You okay?'

'I'm not sure.'

'Do you want to take a minute before we leave?' He hesitated, looking up and down the village road. His car was pointed towards the Bude road. 'Where in town am I dropping you, by the way?'

She studied the message again, frowning. Walter Whitely, the curator of the Black Rock Hall murder mystery exhibition, was messaging her. Allison Friel had taken her mobile number and said she would pass it onto the curator to see whether a private tour could be arranged. She knew the man 'slightly,' the spiritualist had said with a sour look. But if this invitation was entirely down to Allison, it seemed Walter liked her rather better than she liked him.

'Do you know Black Rock Hall?'

'Of course. Everyone knows it around here, it's a famous local landmark. Open to the public during the summer season.' He looked at her, brows raised. 'Is that where you want to go?'

'Do you mind?'

'Not at all. Though the place is likely shut up at the moment. These tourist traps tend to close at the end of the summer.'

She held up her phone, showing him the screen. 'Not according to this. Walter Whitely is the curator.'

He read the message without comment, and then shrugged. 'Fair enough.' He turned his car around at the first opportunity and headed towards the coast, cross-country. 'Sounds like you've made one friend in Cornwall, at least.'

'Who says I'm not a local?'

He grinned. 'Sorry to disappoint you, but the accent is a dead giveaway. Besides, I overheard that spat between you and the landlady just now. She called you an American. City girl too, as I recall.' He glanced at her curiously. 'New York?'

'I was born in New York, but brought up in London, mostly. I'm sure I don't still have an accent. Or not an obvious one.' Stella gave up trying to be discreet. 'Look, this isn't very fair. You seem to know everything about me. But I know absolutely nothing about you. Except that you drive a Land Rover and like drinking in snugs.'

He took one hand off the wheel and held it out to her awkwardly. 'Lewis Carrol,' he said, and grinned at her as they shook hands. 'And yes, I've heard all the jokes. Carrol only has one l, and I'm not the Lewis Carroll who wrote *Alice in Wonderland*, okay?'

'I wasn't going to say anything. Honest.' She hesitated. 'But did you write the *Jabberwocky*?'

'Ha ha.'

Stella began to laugh too and then fell silent. The Cossentine estate was coming up fast. The road snaked around the periphery of the grounds, and then the Land Rover was slowing for the turn into the drive.

A huge billboard welcomed visitors to the Cossentine Murder Mystery Exhibition, draped with a banner stating CLOSED UNTIL EASTER. Beyond that, a meandering avenue of bare-leaved trees led them down towards the main house. Stella turned her head, watching fields and meadows and shady woodlands flash past, and then overgrown lawns and the glimpse of a dilapidated summerhouse in the distance, before the dramatic plunge of cliffs. At last, the avenue of trees widened into a large gravelled area, and she leant forward, straining against the seatbelt, eager to see the house for the first time.

Black Rock Hall was a Georgian building, a warm yellowing stone façade with long windows on two floors, and smaller attic windows above below a dark grey slate-tiled roof. The central section was embellished with a triangular recess at the top, while the two wings on either side formed broad columns, so the whole building appeared at first glance to be a classical temple, with stone steps and a gravelled area stretching away in front to meet the smooth sweep of the lawns. Once, it would have been an impressive sight, coming up this drive in a horse-drawn carriage, perhaps to an evening party, with flaming torches lighting the way. Now though, the lawns were overgrown and strewn with autumn leaves, while the house itself showed a deep crack running across the ring-hand wing, the left wing almost entirely taken over by ivy. But the windows were all still intact, and as she watched, the tall double doors at the top of the stone steps opened, and a man came out to wait for them.

'Our host, I presume,' Lewis murmured.

Stella shivered, also staring at the man. 'It can't be... He's been dead for years.' She caught his puzzled sideways look and realised with a flush of embarrassment that he had not been talking about Maurice Cossentine. 'Sorry, I misunderstood. Yes, that must be the curator.'

'Do you know him?'

'No, but I met a spiritualist in the village who said she might be able to wrangle me a tour of the place. And it seems she was right.'

'A spiritualist?' He sounded bemused.

'I know.' She smiled. 'She was nice though. And it takes all sorts to make a world.'

They came to a halt below the steps, and Stella climbed out of the Land Rover, shouldering her bag. She looked up, past the man waiting at the head of the steps, to study the house, and it took her breath away to think that she might have a claim on this vast house.

Lewis came round the vehicle to look up at the house too. 'Pretty impressive,' he said in her ear, 'if a little rundown. Do you want your bags out of the back?'

'Yes, I'd better let you get off. I'm sorry... I've dragged you all the way out here and you were headed for Bude.'

'I don't mind.' He glanced at the curator, who had not moved, and met her gaze significantly. 'You sure you'll be okay here? I can stick around if you want.'

'That's kind of you, but I came down to Cornwall specifically to see this place, so… Thanks, I'll call a taxi when I leave.'

Lewis helped her lift the heavy bags out of the back. 'It was nice meeting you,' he said, and got back into the car. 'Good luck.'

He turned the Land Rover in a very slow circle, as though she might yet change her mind, and then drove away.

'You brought luggage.'

She jumped, looking round in surprise. The man had come silently down the steps while she was watching Lewis leave, and was standing at her shoulder, his gaze on the violin case.

He was a short man in his early to mid-forties, vaguely rotund in appearance yet somehow not overweight. He wore thin, tortoiseshell-rimmed glasses, a pink shirt and tie, with old-fashioned tweed trousers and jacket. His shoes were black leather, highly polished. Even if she hadn't already known he was the curator, she could probably have guessed his line of work just by his clothes.

'Yes, I'm sorry about that.' She smiled nervously. 'You must be Mr Whitely. I'm Stella Ffoulds.'

'I know who you are. I'm glad you got my message and were able to come so soon.' He held out a hand and she shook it. His grip was firm and steady, and she instinctively trusted him. 'Allison Friel gave me a call to let me know you wanted a private tour of the house.' He hesitated. 'How do you know Allison?'

'I don't,' she admitted. 'I only met her today.'

'I see.' He seemed to relax, and Stella belatedly recalled that Allison had said the two didn't get on very well. 'Well, I'm afraid not all the house is in a fit state to be seen. But I'm happy to show you around the main rooms downstairs. Some kind of research into the Cossentine family, is it?'

'Something like that.' Stella felt awkward, seeing him stoop to pick up her suitcase. 'I feel awful about this, but would it be okay to bring my things inside while I'm looking around? I haven't got a place to stay anymore, you see, so I was forced to bring my luggage with me. I'm sorry about the inconvenience.'

'There's no inconvenience,' he insisted, smiling.

Walter had already started up the broad stone steps with her case, so she grabbed the other bags and followed after him.

'It's only until I've managed to sort out a new hotel room and called a taxi,' she said quickly. 'Then I'll be out of your hair.'

Walter Whitely led her through the large double doors and into a cool, dim hallway, floored with white and gold marble and dominated by a vast chandelier that clinked and jangled slightly in the breeze from outside. Portraits and landscapes in oils hung from the wood-panelled walls and a grand staircase stretched away into shadow on the first floor. A large white statue of a woman stood on a plinth partway up the stairs, holding aloft a lamp, presumably to light the way to bed, though the lamp was unlit and the woman's features were unclear.

Their footsteps echoing on the marbled floor, Stella followed him across the hall and came to a halt under the many-branched chandelier, staring up in wonder at its hundreds of perfect glass teardrops. She hadn't even known this kind of thing still existed outside royal palaces and stately homes. Though perhaps this place was a cross between the two.

More than ever, it felt as though she were caught up in a fairy tale, with her the lost princess, and this her enchanted castle...

'What do you think?' Walter asked, stopping beside her. He glanced up at the exquisite chandelier with a smile. 'Would you like me to turn it on?'

'It still works?'

'Of course. Though it costs an enormous amount to run these days.' The curator put down her suitcase and went to a panel of light switches at the base of the staircase; seconds later she was staring up into thousands of scintillating points of light that sent tessellated shadows spinning everywhere as the breeze caught the glass teardrops and shook them slightly, like leaves on a tree. 'Beautiful, isn't it?'

'My goodness, yes.'

'Shall we leave your bags here for now?' he suggested, pointing out an alcove to one side of the stairs. 'They should be quite safe.' He took her case across, watching with interest as she stowed her violin case with the others. 'You're a violinist.'

'That's right.' Still gripping her handbag, Stella turned on her heel, staring wide-eyed around the hall. She felt so over-awed by her surroundings, she felt almost faint and could barely speak. If there were such things as ghosts, she thought, her grandmother had to be looking down on her right now. 'Erm...' She cleared her throat. *Get a grip, Stella, for God's sake. The man will think you're mad.* 'This is very kind of you.'

'Not at all,' he said, with a quiet chuckle. 'It's boring when the whole place is shut up for the winter.' He turned off the chandelier and the hall darkened, somehow colder without all those gorgeous lights sparkling above their heads. 'I have so little to do out of season, though I try to keep busy, cataloguing books in the library here and, of course, writing my book.'

'What kind of book are you writing?'

'I'm compiling a history of this house and the

Cossentine family.' He eyed her speculatively. 'I wonder if our research overlaps.'

He must think she was a rival academic, she guessed, and hurriedly disabused him of the idea. 'Oh, I'm not really a researcher. Not for a book or anything. I'm just doing a little private digging. For my own interest. Though I may turn it into an article for online publication.'

'I see.' He sounded almost disappointed.

'I hope you don't think I'm here under false pretences?'

'Not at all,' he said politely.

She felt embarrassed, sure that he thought exactly that. But she could hardly tell him the truth. Or not yet, at any rate.

'I don't want to keep you from your work longer than necessary. So maybe just a quick look round, since I'm here now?' She studied the myriad of doors off the grand hallway with a growing sense that she had bitten off more than she could chew. This bloody enormous place couldn't possibly be hers. It was simply unthinkable. 'Where should we start?'

'Since you're a musician, perhaps we should begin in the music room.' Walter indicated a closed door across the hall, and she headed that way with him. 'As I said before, I'm afraid some parts of the house are in serious disarray. The roof has a tendency to leak, and there have been some structural issues... But most of the important public rooms downstairs are still in good order.'

The music room had natural wood floors that needed a little tender loving care, and threadbare, moth-eaten curtains at the windows that badly needed to be replaced. But it was a large room, perfect for a group recital with a small audience, and there were two pianos, not merely one. Folded music stands leant against the wall, and stacks of sheet music had been left on a desk to the back of the room, while the light in there was fantastic, the grain and knots of the bare floorboards lit up by sunlight pouring in through holes and gaps in the curtains.

'This must have been amazing, back in the day,' she said, wandering from one piano to the other. She tested a few notes. 'Both these need re-tuning.'

'Agreed,' he said, looking embarrassed. 'But the estate can't afford it. We can't really afford to keep the exhibition going much longer, to be honest. There was money put aside by Maurice Cossentine before he passed away, for the general upkeep of the house and the exhibition. But not nearly enough.'

She had turned to stare at him, disheartened by this news. 'Does that mean the exhibition will have to close?'

'Not if I can help it. I'm still in talks with the bank so we can reopen in the spring. But we don't get many visitors, all the way out here on the north coast. Not even at the height of the season. Tourists come to North Cornwall for the beaches and the cream teas, not to be intrigued by an old murder mystery from the thirties.'

'Such a shame.' She trailed a finger along the dusty top of one piano. 'I haven't even seen the exhibition yet.'

'Would you like to?' Walter's face seemed to light up. 'The exhibition isn't here in the main house. Mr Maurice wouldn't allow that. He wanted the house preserved exactly as it was in his youth. Instead, he had one of the larger outbuildings converted to house the exhibits.'

'You wouldn't mind? Even though it's closed until Easter?'

The curator hesitated. 'Well, it is a little irregular... But I don't see why not. I've been meaning to go over there to check everything is still secure. There was a bad storm a few days ago; sometimes these winds straight off the Atlantic can shatter a window. So I could show you around once I've checked the building.'

'Thank you.'

As they crossed the hall towards the double doors out into the grounds, Stella slowed and stopped. She lifted her head, staring up the broad sweep of stairs into shadow on the first floor.

'Is someone else in the house?' she asked, puzzled.

'No.' Walter stopped, looking back at her in

surprise. 'I live here alone, in a small apartment on the first floor. It's all part of my contract.' He too peered up the dim staircase, as though wondering what she'd seen. 'Why do you ask?'

'Sorry, I thought...' Stella gave an embarrassed laugh, feeling ridiculous. 'I can't hear anything now. But for a second, I could have sworn I heard...'

'What?'

'Music,' she finished reluctantly. 'I thought I heard somebody playing the violin up there.'

CHAPTER SIXTEEN

London, March 1944

Seated cross-legged on a bed in the basement of the nurses' home, draped in a shawl and shivering, her journal balanced on her knee, Celeste scribbled, head bent over the thin pages. She had been keeping a journal since the first months of the war, though sporadically, since paper and ink were scarce. But she could die at any moment and nobody would know anything about her. This journal, at least, would survive a gas attack, perhaps even a bomb blast, and then someone might pick it up and read a few pages, and know that she had lived and died, though not her true name. But these words were something to set against the darkness, both a private testimony to her fears and a way of staving them off.

'What... What are you writing, Lizzie?' Esther

croaked from the bed next to her, peering out of a mound of blankets, her face flushed and sweaty.

Three days ago, they had both been diagnosed with influenza, given a bottle of medication between them and confined to this tiny room in the basement, away from the other nurses but safe from the continuing German bombardment. A wise decision, given how contagious and debilitating the flu was.

A jug of fresh water and simple meals of bread and stew were left outside their door daily, and every now and then, a doctor would pay them a quick visit, his face masked to avoid catching the sickness. But it had been a boring and monotonous three days, and Celeste, who was already beginning to feel better, had nothing much to do except read a rather dreary romance that one of the girls had lent her and stare up at the pipes in the basement ceiling whenever it shook from an explosion above.

Esther, who appeared to be far sicker, could not seem to lift her head far from the pillow, and had to be fed her meals by hand. A bronchial infection in her childhood had left her with a weak chest, she'd told Celeste, and so she never coped well with coughs and colds.

'My journal.' Celeste grimaced. 'I haven't kept it in a while, so I thought I'd better catch up with my entries… Just in case, you know?'

'In case you die.'

Esther was not stupid, she thought, and flashed her a grateful look. 'Well, we are at war. And one of these days I expect a whopping great bomb is going to be dropped on the nurses' home or the hospital, and I'd like to leave something behind.' She chewed on her lip, turning the leather-bound journal over in her hand. 'Assuming this survives me.'

'You should... write home. Let your people know you've got the... the flu.' Esther sneezed violently and then shuddered, gripping the blankets closer about her neck. 'Oh God...'

Being an orphan, Esther had no family to write to, and was obsessed with the idea that Celeste must have people out there who were worried about her. It didn't matter how often Celeste told her usual fib that she was estranged from her family and didn't want to talk about them, let alone write to them, Esther seemed convinced that she couldn't possibly mean it.

'You're lucky,' Esther continued after a moment, her voice weak. 'To have a family, I mean.' When Celeste looked away, embarrassed that she had lied about her background, claiming to have a mother and father and siblings back home in Devon, her friend asked huskily, 'What is it, Lizzie? I know there's something else that stops you from writing home. Whatever it is, you can trust me; I won't tell another living soul, I swear.' She made a feeble gesture over her chest, the sign of the cross. 'Cross my heart and hope to die.'

'Don't,' Celeste said urgently.

'Just tell me what's troubling you, please.' Wearily, Esther lay back and closed her eyes. 'Oh, my head aches and my eyes are watering and I can barely breathe without choking.'

'Should I ask someone to fetch the doctor again?'

'What good would that do? There's no cure for influenza.' Esther lapsed into a lengthy paroxysm of coughing, and then gasped, 'We're best friends, aren't we?'

'Of course.'

'Then be a friend and tell me something to distract me.'

Closing her journal, Celeste took a deep breath. She couldn't possibly tell her friend the truth; it was too horrible, and she couldn't even think of that night without digging her nails deep into her palms and feeling sick. But she could make up a story to explain her situation and distract her friend from the terrible sickness consuming her body. She was good at making up stories, and she trusted Esther never to speak of it to anyone else. What harm could there be in it?

'I'm a married woman,' she lied, and saw Esther's head turn on her pillow, her eyes growing round with wonder and fascination. 'Yes, I know. A dreadful admission, isn't it? I haven't told a soul, let alone Matron. If she knew, she and Sister would run me out of the hospital so fast my feet wouldn't touch the ground.'

'But who is he?' Esther put a hand to her chest, struggling to speak. 'Is he a soldier? Has he gone to fight?'

'No, he's a… a doctor. With an inner ear condition. He was excused active service. So he works in a hospital in Devon.'

'Goodness.' With difficulty, Esther was struggling up onto her elbow to stare at her. 'I've heard you say a man's name in your sleep, you know. Once or twice. I didn't want to rag you about it. But maybe it was your husband you were dreaming about?'

Celeste was shocked. 'I say a man's name in my sleep? What… What was the name?'

'Maurice.'

Her cheeks flooded with heat. She was mortally afraid, and tried hard to conceal it, forcing a rigid smile to her lips. 'I really said his name in my sleep? Gosh, what an odd thing.'

'Is that your husband?' Esther was watching her keenly.

Her hands were shaking uncontrollably. She had not heard her brother's name spoken out loud in so long.

But her friend was watching her so closely, it was tempting to blurt it all out, make a clean breast of it, and then… She thought of poor Mrs Dunn, hanged for a crime she almost certainly did not commit, and her insides turned to ice water.

'Yes,' she whispered. 'That's his name. Maurice.' She put a hand to her mouth. 'Maurice... Brown.'

'But why are you not with him? I don't understand.'

'He beat me.'

'Oh no, that's awful!'

'I... I could barely walk afterwards, the first time.'

'He beat you more than once?'

'Oh yes, many times.' It was truly awful how easily the lies came to her, but she went on, lying barefaced to her best friend and suffering the shame of it deep down inside. But what else could she do? 'He's a very jealous man, you see. Every time a man so much as spoke to me, Maurice would claim I'd been giving him the glad eye and would hit me for it. With his slipper or belt, whatever came to hand first.'

She was thinking of her father, who had often taken a slipper or a belt to her as a child for some misdemeanour. It had only ever been a few sharp blows but the shame, the humiliation of it, outweighed even the pain in her memory...

'What a prize bastard.'

Celeste stared at her friend, shocked. It was the first time she had ever heard Esther use such a word. But she nodded, instinctively agreeing.

'Yes,' she gasped, and began to weep. The tears were real enough, even if the story was not.

'Maurice was a very difficult person to love.'

'He sounds it.' Esther gave a croaking sigh, watching her. 'But married to a doctor? I always knew you were too good for the rest of us. Not that you give yourself airs and graces, but you're so well-spoken and all those long words you know... I could tell you were a cut above the other girls.'

'How awful you make me sound. Esther, are you pulling my leg? I certainly never mean to put myself above anyone else.'

'Don't fret, you can't help it. Goodness, just imagine if Sister knew you were married to a doctor; she would bust a gut.'

'Please don't tell anyone,' Celeste said urgently.

'My lips are sealed.'

'It would be too dreadful if he were to find out where I am.'

'Honestly, I won't say a word, promise. Not even for the satisfaction of seeing Sister's face. But you must have loved your husband once or you would never have married him.' Esther saw her expression and stretched out a hand to her. 'Maybe you still love him a little bit, I think?'

'I don't know about that.' But Celeste took her hand, grateful for her friend's warmth and sympathy. She had rarely felt such support before in her life. Eventually, her panic abated and she was able to say more calmly, 'Anyway, that's why I never write home. My parents disapproved when

I left him. They said I had to go back to my husband, even if he was beating me. They said marriage is forever, and that I'd made my bed and had to lie in it.'

Esther was nodding. 'A different generation.'

'Exactly.' Celeste squeezed her hand thankfully. 'So I dare not let my family know where I am. They would tell Maurice straightaway, and he'd come here and force me to go home with him, and… It would be too horrible for words.'

'Poor, poor Lizzie.'

Guiltily, she said spontaneously, 'That's not even my real name, to tell you the truth. I dared not give my real name when I signed up for work here in case he tracked me down. I'm so sorry to have lied to you, Esther.'

'God, never apologise for doing whatever you need to survive.'

'My real name is –'

'No, don't tell me. Please don't… What if I should get delirious and tell someone else by accident?' Esther's smile put strength in her. 'Besides, you're my own dear Lizzie Brown, and always will be.'

'Thank you,' Celeste whispered, a tear rolling down her cheek as she realised this was the first time since leaving Peggy's home that she'd admitted out loud that she wasn't Lizzie Brown. 'I don't deserve to have you as a friend.'

'Oh, tosh!'

They both giggled and clung together for a while, and then Esther's grip slowly loosened, and Celeste saw that her friend had fallen asleep at last, though pale now and wheezing with every breath.

Softly, in case she disturbed Esther's sleep, she reopened her journal, and took out the newspaper cutting she'd tucked into the back cover.

Unfolding it, she felt again the strange shock of seeing her own face staring back at her. Or a grainy approximation of what she looked like.

She recognised the photograph. The original had been taken at a portrait sitting for her seventeenth birthday. Her mother had been pleased with it, saying it could be used in the newspaper when she made her debut. But her father had dismissed the idea, insisting she was still too fragile to be a debutante and would need to be married off behind closed doors.

Under the photograph, the newspaper advertisement read, *Have you seen Celeste Cossentine, missing heiress? Reward offered for good information. Contact Wetherby and Saunders Solicitors, Goodge Street, London.*

It was not the first time her brother had tried to track her down. A series of advertisements seeking information on her whereabouts had appeared last year, much to her consternation, with any information to be forwarded to Maurice Cossentine of Black Rock Hall.

But this was the first time he had used a photograph.

Fear squeezed her chest as she studied her black-and-white likeness. It was blurry but still recognisably her. But perhaps only because she knew she was looking at herself. Would anyone else make the connection between this unclear photograph of a missing heiress and Nurse Lizzie Brown?

She hoped fervently that they wouldn't. Her hair was very different now, chopped roughly and scraped back off her face, not the luscious tumbling dark locks of her seventeenth year. And her gaze had changed. Her eyes were harder now, more direct. More confident too. The blurry, unfocused stare of her days on medication was long gone.

But if they did, she was prepared to run again, if she must. She stared down at the advertisement, wishing she knew what Maurice wanted with her. He would have gone to war on reaching his majority, she felt sure. Yet he was still reaching out through his solicitors, looking for her. Unless he had been killed and she was now the only surviving heir.

A jolt of despair knocked the breath out of her. Maurice, dead? Her fingers tightened on the dirty newsprint. She couldn't even think such a thing. Besides, if he had been killed, she would have seen it in the lists of the dead or in a newspaper report, she felt sure. She still scanned the lists weekly, though she didn't know why. She couldn't believe the cook had killed their family in revenge for her daughter's violation. It had to have been Maurice. Sebastian had beaten him badly, and then the others had taken their turns lashing him too, teaching him a lesson about family loyalty first and foremost. He had been hurt and furious and just cold enough to do such a terrible deed.

You'll never see me again after tonight.

But it seemed he'd changed his mind. The thought of seeing him again filled her with strange delight and awful terror at the same time.

Carefully, she replaced the cutting in her journal. Later, she would burn it. But she would like to look at it again once more before destroying it. And remember...

Wrapping her shawl more tightly about her shoulders, she thought for a while, and then wrote, *Esther does not seem to be getting any better. I am very worried about her. But she's young and strong, and the next few days should see her turn a corner, God willing.* She hesitated, and then added carefully, *Esther tells me I've said M's name in my sleep a few times. So that horror follows me even into my dreams. What a terrifying prospect. There was another advertisement in the newspapers last week. Will I never be free of the past?*

CHAPTER
SEVENTEEN

North Cornwall, Present Day

The Cossentine Murder Mystery Exhibition was housed in the old stable block behind the main house, Stella discovered.

'These stables could accommodate up to twelve horses at a time,' the curator told her, throwing open the door and gesturing her inside. 'Plus three carriages, with a generous loft space above where the grooms and stable hands slept.' In a kiosk to one side of the door, he flicked a series of switches, and lighting came on through the building, along with faint music and a voice speaking somewhere at the other end. 'Now it houses a Murder Mystery Exhibition, dedicated to the last days of the Cossentine family.'

'Very impressive,' she said, shivering in the cool, musty space.

Walter Whitely handed her a small plastic bag

labelled a Murder Mystery Kit. 'In there, you'll find a pencil, a clue card, a notebook, and a pamphlet listing useful information... Potential suspects, for instance, and their likely motivation for murdering the family. The idea is, you follow the exhibition from room to room, filling in your clue card and notebook, until you reach the dining room...' He paused. 'Some visitors find the dining room reconstruction a bit gruesome, I'm afraid, but that's where the actual murders were committed. It's our key exhibit.'

'I'm fully prepared to be grossed out.'

'Excellent.' With an encouraging smile, Walter signalled her towards Room 1. 'Shall we, then? There's an audio guide but we won't bother with that. I can talk you through the exhibition myself.'

By the time they reached the final few rooms of the exhibition, Stella knew more than she could ever have needed to know about the members of the Cossentine family and their seething hatreds, secrets and obsessions, described in lurid detail over Rooms One through Seven. It seemed to her that any one of them could have murdered the rest, including her grandmother, whose treatment had been abominable. But of course only two members of the family had escaped the murders, so it was either one – or possibly both – of them, or someone not related to the family at all. One of the servants, for instance. A rival silversmith based in London was also among the listed suspects, though there was no evidence he'd been in Cornwall that summer.

Room Eight was devoted to various local myths and legends that had sprung up in the wake of the poisonings. There were blurry photographs of a 'woman in white' often seen walking the cliffs either at dawn or dusk in the vicinity of Black Rock Hall. This was held by some to be the ghost of Celeste Cossentine, in the assumption that she'd been the murderer and had died by her own hand soon afterwards. Others held it to be the ghost of Mrs Cossentine, seeking revenge for her death and that of nearly all her family. And a few claimed it must be the cook – for cooks traditionally wore white, as Walter pointed out – whose restless spirit could never be at peace until the true killer was uncovered.

Stella made no comment on these theories, especially the ones about her grandmother, but studied the boards politely.

There were tales of a spectral hound too, but no photographs, only vague sightings by visitors to the hall and the occasional dog-walker in the woods that surrounded the estate, catching a glimpse of a huge ghostly dog with flaming eyes running through the trees. There was no explanation for this, except that Mr Cossentine had owned several hunting hounds, and this was said to have been his favourite. Some speculated the faithful animal might even have lapped up some spilt soup and died alongside his master…

'Formed any suspicions yet?' Walter had talked her through the contents of each room, friendly and considerate, open to all the questions she'd asked and never once impatient to move on before she was ready.

'To be honest, no.' With an embarrassed smile, Stella flicked through the untidy scribblings in her notebook and studied her clue card. 'So far, everything does seem to point to Mrs Dunn.'

She felt guilty, saying so, after her row with the Hepleys. But really, it did seem to make the most sense, on the face of it.

He nodded. 'Yes, and that's precisely where the police investigation led in the early forties. To the door of the family cook. It was mostly hearsay and circumstantial evidence that brought about her conviction. But in those days, that was enough to seal Mrs Dunn's fate, especially for a crime of such staggering proportions where the Crown and the public urgently needed to see justice served. Which brings us to Room Nine.' He led her through the fake, wood-panelled doorway into the next part of the exhibition. '*Et voila*!'

There was a wall screen showing a sepia film, deliberately distressed to look like an old film reel, showed the silhouette of a woman, barefoot and in a prison issue gown, standing in front of a closed trapdoor. She was hooded and there was a noose about her neck. Beside her, a man in priest's garb stood, head bowed over a prayer book, intoning words of comfort.

A speaker, crackling slightly like an old radio, issued the sounds of the woman's breathing, alongside the words of the prayer.

'That's horrible.' Stella looked away, her skin crawling. She suddenly wished she hadn't agreed to come and look at the murder exhibition; it was bloody creepy and disturbing, and this whole place was going to give her nightmares.

'I take it you believe the cook was innocent?' Walter asked, noticing her discomfort.

'I didn't say that.'

'Ah, so you agree she was guilty, then? In which case, this was a deserved punishment, albeit a barbaric one. People are no longer hanged for murder in this country, and rightly so.'

Still not looking at the screen, Stella struggled to express what she was thinking. 'Before I came down to Cornwall, I thought the cook was the likeliest culprit. Not least because she was tried before a jury and found guilty. There must have been a good reason for that. But now...' She looked down at the clue card, flustered. 'I'm not sure there's enough evidence either way. Unless I'm missing something important.'

'Somebody poisoned the soup,' he reminded her patiently, ticking off points on his fingers.

She got the feeling he had said all this a thousand times before to other visitors to the exhibition. 'Someone angry enough to murder all those people in cold blood. Which suggests a close connection and a strong personal motive. Bad enough to enact this massacre at a family gathering, but one of the Cossentine women was pregnant. Jolie Fortescue, whose birthday they were celebrating that night.' He was watching the actors on screen with a sombre expression. 'A most heinous crime, wouldn't you agree, to knowingly poison a pregnant woman?'

'Of course I agree; I'm not a monster.' Stella forced herself to look at the mini-film again, though the sight of the noose around the woman's neck turned her stomach. 'But it all seems a little too convenient. I mean, you must know this stuff inside-out. Who do you think did it?'

'This is *your* murder mystery tour, Miss Ffoulds. It's up to you to decide her fate.'

Stella stared at him, shaken and bewildered. *This is your murder mystery tour.* For an awful moment, she thought he knew exactly who she was and why she was there.

'What do you mean?' she asked huskily, wishing she could leave without completing the tour. She had steeled herself to be faced with some unpleasant exhibits, but this re-enactment of the hanging was truly disturbing. She shivered, aware of the draughty echoing emptiness of the converted building, the faint whistle of the wind outside its walls. 'I don't get it.'

'Here, you can be both judge and jury.' Walter pointed out a control panel set in front of the screen, which had reset to the beginning and was now showing the images on repeat. There were two large buttons: one red and marked GUILTY; the other green and marked INNOCENT. 'Choose whichever verdict you believe is correct and press the corresponding button.'

'I don't believe in capital punishment, however terrible the crime. Like you said, *this* is barbaric. I'm glad the death penalty was abolished.'

'Death was still the punishment for murder back in the thirties. So, unless you believe she didn't do it, you must declare her guilty and press the red button.'

'Then I choose the opposite,' she said defiantly. 'I believe the cook was most probably a scapegoat,' she said, remembering what the Hepleys had said. 'The police couldn't solve the case but needed to make it seem as though they'd found the murderer, to silence public opinion and appear more competent.' She took a deep breath. 'I choose an innocent verdict for her.'

Pressing the green button marked INNOCENT, Stella watched as the screen changed. The priest removed the noose and plucked the hood from the woman's face to reveal a plump, fair-haired woman in her fifties, smiling tremulously into the camera lens. The sound of the prayer gave way to cheering and applause.

Celeste felt ludicrously relieved, as though she had genuinely saved the cook from her fate.

Ten seconds later, the video reset to the original image, with the woman standing hooded and bound beside the priest, waiting to be hanged. But she was sure, in those few seconds when the hood came off, that she recognised the woman in the film.

'Personally,' Walter remarked in the silence that followed, 'I think it more likely the cook *was* the guilty party. Her daughter Becky had been raped by Sebastian Cossentine and nobody was prepared to punish him for it. It's my belief the cook took matters into her own hands that night.'

'By murdering the whole Cossentine family? Rather disproportionate to the young man's crime, surely?'

'But let's not forget, the police investigation found that Mrs Dunn had both the means and the motive. It was her soup that poisoned them, prepared by her own hand, nobody else's. And the jury found the revenge motive a compelling argument at the time, as you can see from the trial coverage.' He pointed to a yellowing newspaper cutting displayed in a glass case beside the screen. The headline read, COOK HANGS FOR MASS MURDER. As Stella glanced that way, he pressed the red GUILTY button and stepped back to watch. 'As do many others to this day.'

The images changed again. This time, a deep male voice off-screen said, 'It's time,' and a hand slowly pushed the woman forward until she was standing directly on top of the closed trapdoor. The priest stepped back, still intoning his prayer. The woman's breathing became a kind of gasp as she could be heard whispering, 'Lord have mercy,' over and over under her breath.

The trapdoor opened and the hooded woman dropped straight through it, only to be caught up with a snap when the rope reached the end of its length. Her body jerked, her feet shook violently about, and then she was still, left hanging there like a ragdoll.

Stella turned away, sick to her stomach. 'Oh God.'

Walter was clearly surprised by her reaction. 'It's only a reconstruction,' he said mildly. 'The woman lives locally. The man playing the priest is her husband. They both volunteered to re-enact the hanging for this exhibition.' He looked at her, concern in his eyes. 'Nobody was actually harmed.'

'The Hepleys,' she muttered.

'Sorry?'

'The reenactors. They're the Hepleys. They run The Silversmiths' Arms, where I've been staying.' He was nodding but she pressed on, saying,

'You're wrong, though. The cook was harmed, wasn't she? She was hanged for real. Having seen this, I can understand why Mrs Hepley wants to highlight the injustice done to her family and clear Mrs Dunn's name. And I… I find things like that film disturbing,' she finished lamely, not sure how else to explain her visceral reaction.

'I'm sorry.' Walter hesitated, blinking in surprise. 'I had no idea you would be this upset or I would never have shown you that film.'

'FYI, that was a very realistic hanging.'

'Again, I can only say how sorry I am.' Walter took off his glasses, polishing them with his tie. 'The reconstructions are intended to feel realistic,' he explained laboriously, 'and more sensitive types can find them tough going. That's why we don't allow entry to under-sixteens. If you prefer to leave without seeing the final room, the murder scene reconstruction –'

'No,' she interrupted him, taking a deep breath. She'd come here to discover what her grandmother had seen that night, and she couldn't wimp out now. 'Let's get this over with, shall we?'

'Of course.' Walter settled the tortoiseshell-rimmed spectacles back on his nose. 'I have to say, you're a brave woman, Miss Ffoulds.' With an encouraging smile, he gestured her towards the final door. 'Time for dinner.'

CHAPTER EIGHTEEN

The hospital was on high alert, rife with rumours about a high-powered visitor due any day now for an inspection of the facilities.

Celeste, who had only been cleared for a return to duty that morning, was as excited as everyone else about special visitor, wondering who on earth it could be. A Member of Parliament, perhaps? Or perhaps one of the royal family? She had seen the princess Elizabeth in the street once, doing ambulance duty, and had been ridiculously moved by the sight of the sight of such a young woman – her own age, really – pulling her weight in this war like the rest of the populace. But nobody seemed to know who was coming to visit. Everything had to be deep cleaned, all the same, the wards made spick and span, and all the nurses looking at their best in immaculate, well-starched uniforms.

'I say, nurse,' one of the patients said, sitting up

in bed, a fresh-faced young soldier with a nasty shrapnel wound in his side. 'What if it's Churchill himself, coming round the wards? I'd wouldn't half like to shake his hand... The old British bulldog, eh?'

'Settle down, Private,' Celeste told him firmly, and bent to check his pulse.

The young man eyed her with a grin but to her relief did not make any insolent comments, as many of the soldiers did. Celeste thought she must have acquired that most difficult of things for a nurse to master, the 'voice of authority,' until she turned and found Matron behind her, looking stony-faced.

'Nurse Brown,' Matron barked.

'Matron,' she said nervously, wondering what on earth she could possibly have done to merit that hard stare, given that she had only just returned to work after being laid flat on her back for weeks with flu. But perhaps her uniform was not up to muster, especially with an inspection coming.

'You are relieved from duty,' Matron informed her, and signalled another young nurse to take Celeste's place on the ward. 'Follow me.'

Surprised, Celeste followed Matron into the corridor, her heart thumping. Once there, she checked her cap was straight, and then said hurriedly, 'I'm sorry, Matron, but –'

'I'm told Nurse Sharpe is in a poorly way,'

Matron interrupted her, 'and has been asking for you. Doctor Fairweather doesn't think it can wait until the end of your shift.' She nodded when Celeste merely stood there, stunned and speechless. 'Go on, then. No time to waste.'

Abruptly understanding what Matron was saying, Celeste turned without another word and ran, not caring if she got in trouble for it later.

In the stuffy basement room where they'd been sheltering together during their long bout of influenza, she found Esther being tended by a fellow nurse, masked and careful not to sit too close to the patient.

Lizzie flopped heavily onto the end of Esther's mattress, breathless and fatigued after running all the way down there. Perhaps she was not as fully recovered as she'd thought. 'Matron told me to come urgently. How is she, Rosa?' Her friend had her eyes closed and seemed to be resting, but uneasily, breath bubbling and rasping in her chest. 'I thought Esther was on the mend yesterday. She was sitting up in bed and smiling. Asking for soup, of all things!'

'How long have you been nursing?' With a deep sigh, Rosa gathered her things and got up to leave. 'You must know they often seem much better,' she whispered in Celeste's ear, 'right before the end.'

'*The end*?'

'Doctor Fairweather said she has maybe a few hours left. Maybe as much as a day, if she really battles.'

Celeste stared down at her friend, numb with disbelief.

'I'm very sorry.' Rosa touched her shoulder briefly. 'Look, you're here now. I have to get back to work. Esther doesn't have any family, does she?'

Silently, Celeste shook her head.

'In that case, may I leave you to sit with her? At least until…' Rosa looked away, suddenly awkward. 'Well, you know.'

Yes, she knew.

In the hospital, they called it *the death watch.*

Matron always insisted on setting a nurse to sit with a dying patient if they had no relatives who could be summoned to their bedside. The nurse would hold their hand and talk to them, set a cooling cloth to their forehead if they were over-heated or cover them with blankets if they were cold, keeping them clean and cared for until their last breath. That was why Matron had sent her here. Because she knew Celeste would be the best person to sit and care for Esther until the end.

'Yes, of course,' she said mechanically. 'I'll sit with her. You go, Rosa.' She moved to the chair next to the bed, and took her friend's hand. It was clammy to the touch, her pulse erratic. 'I'll do what's necessary.'

Once they were alone, Celeste let herself droop and gave in to tears. She cried until her eyes were sore, until suddenly she felt her fingers clutched tight and looked up to find Esther peering up at her with eyes that were surprising clear and lucid.

'Stop it,' Esther whispered.

'Oh, Esther… ' Celeste sobbed, and then gulped, trying to wrest back some kind of control over herself. 'I'm sorry, I know I shouldn't… But the doctor said…' No, she was being selfish. This was not about her, she thought fiercely. This was about Esther. 'Can I get you something, dearest? A drink of water, perhaps? Another blanket?'

Esther struggled for breath. Her eyes closed and she said nothing for a long while, wheezing rustily, deep in her tortured lungs, until at last she managed to say, 'No, I want to… give *you* something.'

'Me?'

She turned her head slightly on the pillow, gazing vaguely across the room. 'Over there.'

Celeste turned, unsure what she meant. 'Your handbag?'

Her friend jerked her head, still fighting to breathe. 'My identity card. My… my papers…'

'Sorry?'

But Esther did not seem able to hear her anymore. Her eyes closed, and soon after her face turned ashen, except for her lips, which were tinged with blue.

Hurriedly, Celeste fetched Esther's bag and scrabbled inside for her identity card and her papers, including her nursing credentials. These, she set carefully in a row on the bed.

'I have your papers,' she said close to her ear, and then took up her friend's hand again. 'Dearest, can you hear me?"

Esther's breath gurgled in her throat and her upper body heaved up and down with the effort to breathe.

'Look, I know it's hard, but I need you to fight,' Celeste said hoarsely. 'Keep battling this damn thing. If I made it, so can you.' She rubbed Esther's clammy hand against her cheek, trying to warm her up. 'Come on… You're my only true friend, the only one here that I trust. Please, darling, I can't lose you now. I couldn't bear it.'

For some time, Esther lay in a kind of stupor, only her chest still working laboriously, her breath wheezing and croaking.

Then, quite suddenly, she opened her eyes and stared up at Celeste. 'I want you to have them,' she said clearly.

'Have what, dearest?'

'My papers. When the… the war's over, pretend to be me. Use my papers to go abroad.' Esther's breath began to rattle in her chest, an awful sound that frightened Celeste more than her chilled skin and fading colour. 'That's what you've always wanted, isn't it?' she whispered, her voice a mere thread of sound. 'To escape your husband forever?'

They had often talked long into the night about their dreams, how Esther wished she could become an adventuress and travel the world, and how Celeste would love to find some quiet corner of a foreign land and live there in peace, far from the chance of ever being discovered by Maurice.

Celeste was weeping again. 'Yes,' she sobbed, nuzzling at her friend's hand. 'But if you get better, you can come with me. We could travel the world together. Wouldn't you like that?'

But Esther did not speak again.

'He isn't my husband,' Celeste moaned, tears pouring down her cheeks. 'He's my brother. I lied to you… I'm so sorry. I always meant to tell you the truth, but I thought there'd be plenty of time. Oh Esther, please don't go… Don't leave me.'

But her friend's hand lay limp in hers, and her chest no longer struggled to breathe, her whole body perfectly still.

CHAPTER NINETEEN

They'd reached Room Ten in the Cossentine Murder Mystery Exhibition and stopped, Walter looking at her expectantly, almost with pleasure. He was clearly very proud of the great work he and Maurice Cossentine had done in putting this together. 'Now for the chef oeuvre,' he murmured.'

Room Ten was dimly-lit, no doubt to increase the sense of horror, and it took Stella a moment to adjust to the low lighting. She groped her way into the chill, echoing space, vaguely aware of the curator moving away from her side. There was the musty smell she'd noticed throughout the exhibition, but also now a hint of something acrid and metallic on the air.

Almost like the scent of blood, she thought uneasily.

'This is where the infamous Cossentine murders actually took place,' he said, lost in thick shadow near what she guessed must be the exit from the exhibition. 'The grand dining room.'

A long dining table stood facing her, set for at least thirteen diners, each one with their own place card written in flowing italics on a white, black-bordered card: studying those nearest to her, she realised these featured the name of each victim, according to their position at the table. The gleaming wood table itself was dressed with ornate candelabras, silver cutlery, a large floral centrepiece, and white-and-gold chinaware bowls... the grim plastic yellow-brown substance in each was supposed to represent the poisoned soup, no doubt.

The candles flickered with a faint yellow light, clearly electric and not real flame, but provided just enough light to see by. On the far wall behind the table were three black-and-white police photographs of the murder scene, blown-up and framed; one glance told her that, with the exception of the place cards, the exhibition had faithfully reproduced the exact details of that night, down to the accurate positioning of the cutlery.

She looked down at the table again and shivered; the skin crawled on the back of her neck and goosebumps rose on her arms.

Slumped in their seats, with some fallen to the floor, were the victims of the poisoning. Most of them dark-haired, all immaculately dressed in evening suits and silken gowns, the women wearing make-up, their lips bright scarlet, a striking contrast to their pale skin.

For a few horrible seconds, Stella wondered if they were real people. More local actors, perhaps, like the cook and the priest from the hanging film in Room Nine. They looked so completely perfect, so indistinguishable from living people. But of course the exhibition was closed for the off-season; nobody would have been able to get here in time and into costume for an impromptu private tour. She almost laughed at loud at her own craziness. Her brain wasn't working properly, or she would never have thought such an insane thing. Besides, the longer she stood there, staring at them, the more their absolute stillness was an impossibility.

Nobody could hold their breath that long.

Her heart thumping, Stella reached out a hand to the nearest figure – a woman in an elegant green gown, positioned face-down on the table, her eyes wide and staring at nothing – wanting to touch her and yet not wanting to at the same time.

'Waxworks, the lot of them,' the curator said, still in the shadows. 'Good, aren't they?'

Stella jumped at the sound of his voice; she'd been so engrossed in the sight of these perfect dead bodies, she'd forgotten he was still there.

'Like you said, very… realistic.' She realised two

of the seats were empty, and not because the person sitting there had fallen to the floor. They had no occupants at all. Yet both seats had place cards. 'Who...?'

She edged closer to one of the empty seats, craning her neck to read the card. *Maurice Cossentine, youngest son, absent from dinner. Could he have been the murderer?*

'How strange.' Her voice was loud and intrusive in the silent room. 'Maurice okayed that caption? He didn't mind having his innocence questioned?'

Walter seemed to chuckle. 'Maurice was a good sport. Besides, it was always considered unlikely. He was only sixteen at the time and had argued with his brother Sebastian Cossentine earlier that evening. According to the servants, the row descended into a brawl, and young Maurice was no match for his big brother. His father punished him for brawling and confined him to his bedroom without supper. So he never partook of the poisoned soup.'

'Born under a lucky star,' she whispered, her gaze drawn to the empty seat. It was something her grandmother used to say about her. *Stella... born under a lucky star.*

'Perhaps.' The curator came forward into the light of the electric candles and stood over one of the fallen men, who appeared to have died clawing his way towards the door. 'This is

Sebastian. The eldest son and heir. He was the one whom the cook claimed had raped her daughter without facing any consequences. The girl was only fifteen at the time.'

Stella risked a glance at the back of the fallen waxwork's head. 'Sebastian doesn't sound very nice.'

'You think he deserved what he got?'

'God, no.' Stella thrust her clue card and pencil back into the kit bag, struggling to stay calm. But this place was getting to her. 'To be honest, I don't know what I think. Except that some of the family appear to have been particularly unpleasant people.' Her gaze skimmed over the obviously pregnant woman and she swallowed, looking away from the horrible scene of carnage. 'Sorry, all this emphasis on the macabre... I find it vile and upsetting. I take it you don't?'

'I find it fascinating, I'm afraid.' The curator hesitated, pulling a face. 'But it's different when you've been involved with a project like this over a number of years. I suppose I've grown a hard skin where the Cossentine murders are concerned.' He gave her an apologetic smile. 'Rest assured, if someone I knew was murdered in real life, I'd be just as shocked as you.'

'Is this any the less horrific for having happened a long time ago?' Stella wasn't sure. Before turning away, she peered at the place card beside the second empty seat to confirm what she already knew in her heart, and read it out loud. '*Celeste Cossentine, youngest daughter. Absent without explanation at the dinner and said to have fled soon afterwards, taking an heirloom ring with her.*'

Just saying her grandmother's name made her fidget with guilt, aware that she hadn't told him the whole truth.

'Why was Celeste never a serious suspect?' she asked him.

'Hard to say. Because she was a delicately raised girl of only eighteen and the police didn't believe her capable of such an horrific crime? The defence did suggest her as either the poisoner or an accomplice during the trial. She'd suffered poor health for years, spent some time in an asylum, and was seen fleeing the house that evening. But it was decided that Celeste must have run away out of fear and died before she could be found by the authorities, either by her own hand or simply by misadventure, her own health being so fragile. Ultimately, the cook was an easier candidate for the rope.' His eyebrows tugged together darkly. 'The working classes were always first to be blamed when a crime had been committed. As is still the case today, unfortunately.'

'So they never found Celeste?'

'No, never. Though they found the silver heirloom ring quite recently. In fact, it's on display just beyond this room. Maurice sought both Celeste and that ring for many years, never giving up... In part, that's why he created this exhibition. He always hoped it would lure his sister out of hiding, if she was still alive, and allow her at last to inherit her share of the estate. But alas, he never heard from her. So one has to assume Celeste Cossentine died long ago, possibly in America. That's where the ring was found.' He looked at her oddly. 'Is that the focus of your research interest? The youngest daughter?'

She flushed, hurriedly shouldering her handbag. 'Erm, she's part of it. I haven't really decided.' Coming round the table, she nearly fell over the prone waxwork figure of the father, his hands outstretched towards the door. Walter caught her as she stumbled. 'God, sorry, so sorry... I didn't see him there,' she gasped, and turned blindly away as he righted her. 'I'm ready to leave now.'

Immediately outside Room Ten was a glass display case. Inside, nestled on velvet, was the ring with the entwined serpents from her grandmother's photographs. An illustrated board related the history of the silver ring, and how the youngest daughter of the house had fled with it, seemingly overseas, as the ring had recently been found in New York and restored to the estate.

Stella stopped to read the story of the ring's journey from a pawn shop to a private collection, and thence to a big auction house following the owner's death. That was when its provenance had been uncovered by an assiduous investigation mounted by the auction house after an employee spotted the similarities between it and the lost Cossentine ring.

It was a fascinating account, but she dared not linger, aware of Walter's curious gaze on her face. Bad enough that a few of the villagers had uncovered her connection to Black Rock Hall; she wasn't ready to discuss it with the curator himself. Not yet, not while everything was still so raw and uncertain. Besides, he might not be amused that she had wrangled an invitation without being entirely honest with him.

On the wall opposite the exit was an enlarged black-and-white photograph, displayed under glass. She raised her eyes to the woman in the photograph and felt a faint dizzying shock. Those dark eyes, huge with emotion, the springing chestnut hair, the delicate chin...

'Celeste Cossentine,' Walter told her, following her gaze. 'Taken in London at a portrait photographer's studio when she was seventeen, the summer before tragedy struck. The police used this photograph after she ran away, hoping to jog people's memories. Maurice also had a copy taken for newspaper advertisements when he was trying to find her in later years, offering a reward for information.' He paused, glancing from Celeste's face to Stella's with gradually widening eyes. 'My goodness. You look amazingly like her.' He frowned, looking more closely. 'The resemblance is really quite uncanny. If I didn't know better –'

There was no point trying to conceal her identity anymore. The photograph shouted their relationship to the world, and given that he would soon hear the truth from the village grapevine anyway...

'Celeste was my grandmother,' she said flatly.

'Good God.'

'I'm sorry I lied to you, Mr Whitely, but I thought it better to be discreet.' She met his astonished gaze frankly. 'That's why I'm here. To claim my inheritance. Always assuming the bloodline can be proved.'

'Yes, I can understand that,' he said slowly, and led her out of the exhibition. 'But what an incredible thing.'

Outside, the October afternoon was surprisingly warm and bright; the clouds had rolled away while they were inside, and the overgrown lawns and gardens were bathed in autumnal sunshine.

'After all these years. I thought nobody would ever turn up to...' He was blinking. 'I have to admit, Miss Ffoulds, I'm staggered. I had no idea who you were.' He sounded genuinely winded by the revelation. 'If I'd known, believe me, I would have been far less...' He drew in a sharp breath. 'The exhibition... No wonder you were so disturbed. It must have felt brutal to you.'

'Yes,' she said simply.

'I'm so sorry. If only you had told me beforehand... Though I can see why you chose to conceal it, of course.' He rubbed a hand across his forehead, still looking stunned. 'I wish Maurice had lived to see this day. He would have been delighted to know his line continued. And to meet his great-niece at last.'

'I would have liked that too,' she admitted, her voice choking with emotion. 'Even though Maurice sounds like he was quite a difficult man, he would still have been family.'

'Yes, indeed,' he said gravely, and turned to lock up the exhibition. 'Look, you said you had to find a new hotel or bed-and-breakfast place. Why not stay at Black Rock Hall while you wait for your claim to be proved? There's a guest room I could let you have. I'm sure nobody would object.'

'Stay *here*?' Her voice came out squeaky; she was stunned and not quite sure what to think. It would certainly allow her to learn more about the place she might be going to inherit. 'That's incredibly kind of you. But I'm not sure if I should. It might all come to nothing, after all.'

'It's a big house, Miss Ffoulds, and not an easy place to be on your own, especially at night. I've been living there alone ever since Maurice passed.' Walter pocketed the key to the exhibition and gestured her back towards the house, his smile lopsided. 'To be honest, I'd welcome a little company.'

'Well, in that case...' Stella fell in beside him, glancing up at the old house. Its windows winked in the sunlight, seeming to look down on her with pleasure. For now, she couldn't decide if this unexpected bend in the path was a good or bad omen. Either way, she liked Walter Whitely and she was going to take a chance and accept his offer. 'Thank you.'

CHAPTER TWENTY

Bayeux, France, late June 1944

'Nurse! Nurse! Nurse!' The words were a slap in the mouth. 'What the bloody 'ell d'you think you're doing? Get back to the camp, come on, move it, move it!'

Celeste blinked, gasping, abruptly aware of her surroundings. It was pouring with rain and she was standing in the old, abandoned dugout with a grizzled-looking orderly bellowing in her face. The last thing she recalled was getting into bed last night and tumbling asleep almost as soon as her head hit the pillow, her body rigid with fatigue. Now she was fully clothed, outside, with two men staring at her from under sodden caps, their eyebrows dripping, faces running with rain.

'What's the matter with the silly little tart?' the older one continued, glancing at his companion. Then he yelled in her face again. 'Your ears not working, Nurse? I said, move it!'

'I... I...'

By the grey light, it was still early, and she was shivering with cold, she realised. Her uniform was drenched, heavy with rain, and her shoes and nylons were plastered with mud.

One of the men shoved her from behind, not waiting for her brain to catch up with her body, and she stumbled in the mud. Their hands grabbed at her, looping under her arms and shoulders. Together, they dragged her up a makeshift ladder and out of the dugout, and then she was being forced to run beside them, slipping and sliding in mud patches, splashing through oil-slick puddles up to her ankles, until she was left to stand, dripping and sodden, in the nurses' quarters, the roof of the tent drumming with rain above her, grey-white canvas walls billowing about her like the sail of a ship.

'Esther, what on earth...?' One of the other nurses came running up, dumped a blanket around her shoulders and began helping her strip, her movements swift and ruthless. 'My God, you're a complete mess. You need a hot wash.'

'What... What's the time?'

'Gone seven-thirty.'

'No time to wash... Late for my shift.' She dragged off the rest of her wet clothes and thrust them into the communal wash basket, scraped her wet hair into some semblance of neatness, and grabbed a fresh uniform and underthings from her bedside cabinet. 'Thanks, Ruth.'

'What were you doing out there in the rain?' Her face curious, Ruth helped to wipe her shoes clean of mud.

'I don't know.' She breathed through her nose, in and out, in and out, trying to calm the heaving anxiety in her chest. 'Sleepwalking, I think,' she lied. 'I used to suffer from it as a girl.' She'd blacked out again, hadn't she? Lost time, forgetting where and who she was. 'How do I look?'

Ruth looked her over critically but nodded. 'You'll do. It's been sheer bloody carnage out there all night anyway; nobody will give you a second look.'

The rainstorm passed as quickly as it had arrived, leaving muddy puddles shining in deep, oozing ruts left by army vehicles. The sky that had been gunmetal grey first thing now grew blue and almost serene as the clouds rolled away. Sunlight picked out ambulance windscreens and cap badges, glinting cheerfully. Clutching an armful of bandages, Celeste hurried from the supply tent to the makeshift hospital they had erected less than a week ago, the frontline constantly shifting ever further into the French hinterland as the occupying German forces were pushed back.

'You there, Nurse Sharpe, not so fast...' Doctor

Xavier called above the chaos in the Casualty Clearing Station. 'I need you over here, please.'

The Casualty Clearing Station was where the wounded soldiers were first brought in on stretchers from the battlefields and left there to be assessed and dispatched for treatment, according to the severity of their wounds. Sometimes the wounded were there only a few minutes before an orderly was called to convey them elsewhere. Sometimes they lay there for hours, steadily worsening, or died quietly while they were still waiting to be seen. But that was war, as she'd been told half a dozen times in her first shocking, catastrophic week there; in war, people died, and that was that.

Nurse Sharpe.

She almost passed the doctor without acknowledging his shout, stopping abruptly as she realised that 'Nurse Sharpe' was her.

Having spent the past few years being Lizzie Brown, it was still a shock to hear herself addressed by her friend Esther's name, whose paperwork she had used to join a military nursing unit and escape England. There seemed as much chance being killed in London by the German's indiscriminate bombing regime as here on the frontline in France, and at least here she was doing something useful with her time on earth. Saving people, preventing further deaths.

'Yes, doctor?'

Doctor Xavier was standing over an unconscious man on a raised stretcher; there was fresh blood on his hands and his white coat, but he seemed unaware of it, examining the man's chest wound with professional interest.

'Give those to one of the junior nurses,' he said curtly, indicating the stacks of laundered crepe bandages in her arms. 'I need the assistance of a skilled nurse here. These young girls are keen to help, and I applaud them for it, but most of them are too squeamish for this procedure.'

He waited impatiently while Celeste passed the bundle to Maria, a scared-looking girl in her early twenties, and directed her where to take them.

'Come on, nurse, hurry up.' He unslung the rubber stethoscope from about his neck. 'This chap is dying and making quite a racket about it. Try to keep him still while I check something.' He glanced up at an orderly. 'You there, help me lift him.'

Celeste held the patient as still as she could, watching without flinching as the doctor listened painstakingly to the man's lungs, a frown on his face.

Since sailing for France as a newly recruited member of the Queen Alexandria's Imperial Military Nursing Service, she had seen some truly dreadful things, moments that would haunt her forever. It was ironic that she was roughly the same age as Maria, the girl she'd dispatched with the bandages, and yet, as Nurse Esther Sharpe, her age was assumed to be four years older and her skills those of a registered and highly experienced nurse. Thankfully, she had read all Esther's training manuals before leaving London and learned a great deal about traumatic injuries during her time dealing with bomb victims, so it was with a dispassionate expression that she held the patient's weight on her own chest, ignoring the blood now staining her newly donned white apron. It would look far worse before the end of her shift, she thought grimly.

'Right, lay him down again. That's it, easy does it.'

Celeste caught a flailing arm and pinned it to the stretcher with difficulty. 'Doctor, I'm sorry but I can't make him lie still.' The man was struggling and straining against her hold, jerking his whole body up and down on the stretcher.

'I'm not surprised.' Doctor Xavier called for his tray of sterilised instruments. 'Poor fellow can't breathe. He's drowning in his own fluids.' He nodded to the patient's uniform. 'Get that jacket and shirt loosened, would you?'

'Yes, doctor.' Her fingers fumbled with the buttons of his torn and blood-spattered uniform; a task made even harder by the patient's increasingly erratic movements.

The doctor selected a thin scalpel and, putting a knee to the patient's upper body to hold him still, bent over the man as soon as she was clear. 'One small incision, and...' Delicately, the doctor inserted a straw-like tube in the hole he'd created, which connected to a bottle on the floor beside the stretcher. Almost at once, a thin cloudy liquid began to drip through the tube into the bottle. 'Hey presto!'

Celeste felt an enormous sense of relief as the man, who had been making a terrible noise and thrashing about, finally settled and lay still, his chest beginning to rise and fall on its own again.

'Oh, well done,' she could not help saying, and watched as the doctor swiftly fixed the drain in place using tape and bandages. 'Will he survive, doctor?'

'Probably not, to be honest. He's already lost a great deal of blood and I don't like his colour.' Job done, Doctor Xavier wiped his bloodied hands on a cloth, his gaze already seeking out other patients. 'But have him taken to B Ward and get his wounds sutured. He's a young chap. Might as well give him a fighting chance.'

Under Celeste's instructions, two orderlies bore the man away to B Ward, carefully keeping the chest drain in place, while she followed with his uniform jacket and the watch he'd been wearing, removed prior to treatment.

Celeste studied him anxiously, cleaning his wounds and setting careful sutures into his torn flesh while he was still unconscious.

He was a young man, not much older than herself, and handsome once the mud that had caked his face and hair had been cleaned away. Like too many of the soldiers who came their way, he was an enlisted man, a private, and, to judge by his wounds, he'd been in the thick of it today. She wondered if he had a wife or girlfriend back in England, or maybe just a mother praying for his safe return, and willed him to pull through and make it home again, to provide a little light at the end of a long, dark tunnel for those he'd left behind.

They had lost so many patients this past week, it had been a bloodbath out there, with the Germans putting up fierce resistance to the incoming Allied troops. The countryside had been heavily mined and although their side was working hard to clear safe passage, there were inevitably casualties. She had seen men blinded or almost blown apart, or with limbs missing, bravely clinging onto their last breath, agony in their eyes, crying out for Jesus or their mothers.

It all seemed so futile and such an appalling waste of life. And yet if they were to give up and let Hitler ride roughshod over the rest of the continent and even her own dear England…

No, that was unthinkable. So, the bloodshed had to continue, and all she and the other nurses could do was keep helping the wounded and trust their side would triumph in the end.

On finishing the sutures, Celeste got up to wash her hands at the sanitation unit, a few feet away.

For some reason, the foul bloodied water in the bowl made her think of the muddy dugout where they'd found her wandering at dawn. Thank God they were well behind the front line here; otherwise, she might have been shot by one side or the other or taken prisoner by the enemy, raped and murdered. The Allied nurses and auxiliary staff had all been warned about keeping within the limits of the camp.

Did she have a death wish? What on earth was wrong with her?

As if she didn't know ...

While she was gone, the young man she'd been working on stirred, making a choking noise.

She hurried back, drying her hands on a towel, and found him staring around himself vaguely, as though trying to work out where he was. That was common with those wounded who had lost consciousness during battle. One minute more alive than they'd ever been, fighting hand-to-hand or mounting an assault; the next in bed and in excruciating pain, like as not dying or near to it.

'You're in the field hospital at Bayeux,' she told him quickly. 'You're safe, all right?' She searched his face for signs of fever, always a danger after surgery, but saw none. 'I believe you and your party were caught in an ambush.'

He tried to speak, and instantly discovered that he couldn't. Celeste saw panic and distress in his face. He made a gurgling noise and raised a hand, groping for the tube in his chest, no doubt meaning to rip it out.

'No!' she cried and caught his hand. 'You mustn't.'

His gaze shifted to her face, and stopped there, his eyes narrowing, his mouth forming words he couldn't speak.

'That tube is keeping you alive,' she explained, still holding his hand. 'You need to leave it in place until the doctor says otherwise. Or I'll be forced to strap your arms to the bed. Do you understand? No, don't try to speak; you might dislodge the tube. Blink once for yes, two for no.'

He blinked once, and his arms sank back to his sides.

'Well done.' Celeste released his hand and drew a blanket up over his bandaged torso; she wanted him to sleep. 'Don't try to move. Don't try to do anything, in fact, except lie there and let your body heal.'

The young man glared up at her, clearly frustrated.

'I'm sorry, Private, I know this must be difficult for you. But please understand, we're trying to keep you alive.' She paused, pushing the lank fair hair away from his forehead. His skin felt cool, which was a relief. 'Be grateful and, for God's sake, don't pull your stitches. Understand?'

His lips twitched in a torturous smile, his gaze fixed on hers. Then he blinked again. Once for yes. There was something almost comical in his expression...

Even at death's door, wrapped up in bandages like an Egyptian mummy, he was rather charming. Celeste found herself smiling back at him without thinking.

Abruptly, she stopped and whisked away to check on the other patients in B Ward, putting that young soldier out of her mind.

She had sworn never to smile at a man like that in case it led to more than just friendship. As far as she was concerned, getting close to another human being would mean sharing *everything*. Total honesty. And she could never share the truth about herself with another living soul.

The wounded private's name was Daniel Ffoulds, Celeste had discovered, or 'Danny,' as he preferred to be called. He came from North London, he told her once the tube had been removed and he could speak. His mother was a well-to-do widow, his father having been killed in the Great War, and he was the youngest of three sons. His older brothers had joined up early in the war, and he'd been chafing at the bit for the past year, impatient to be old enough to enlist.

'I didn't want my brothers thinking I was a

coward,' he explained, pulling a wry face. 'Or Mother. She's always so proud of the other two, telling people what her eldest boys are up to. On campaign in the desert somewhere, last I heard.'

Only one of his injuries was still causing her serious worry, and that was the deep gash to his chest, the one that had nearly killed him. Several soldiers in his unit had been killed in an explosion, which Danny had only survived because one of the men in front had been blown back into him, shielding his body from the worst of it.

Before applying a fresh bandage, Celeste lightly dusted his chest wound with yellow Sulfa powder to keep it from becoming infected, and made a quick note on his chart about the colour, smell, and consistency of the injury. She felt confident the wound was slowly beginning to heal, despite its severity, but feared permanent damage had been done to his lungs. One thing was for sure; he would never be fit enough to fight for his country again, and she couldn't help feeling a little glad about that. It was awful to patch these boys up only to send them back out a week or so later, probably to their deaths.

'I hope this won't spoil my chances of getting a good job after all this nonsense is over,' he rattled on hoarsely, watching her with bright eyes. 'Both my brothers worked in the City before the war, you see. Bags of loot between 'em. Whereas I'm poor as a church mouse.'

'Do try to stay quiet, Private,' she told him, finishing her work and stooping to collect the old bandages.

'I jabber on too much, I know.' Danny caught at her hand as she moved away. 'I say, Esther, did I ever thank you properly? For saving my life, I mean?'

Celeste couldn't help smiling down at the long, supple fingers holding her wrist. She had discovered he was a year younger than she was, and he had such an open, trusting face, it was hard not to feel indulgent towards him.

'That's what we're here for. And you ought to be thanking the doctor, not me. I merely sewed you up afterwards. But please don't call me Esther.' He had asked what her name was a few days previously, and she had whispered it in his ear, though it was strictly forbidden to be on first name terms with the patients. 'You'll get me in trouble,' she added in a low voice, tugging against his grip.

'Sorry,' he said in his hoarse whisper, but then mouthed, 'Esther,' with a mischievous smile as he released her hand.

She couldn't help smiling back at him. 'You're incorrigible.'

'I'm trying to be.'

Celeste laughed, a sudden lightness in her heart.

One of the senior nurses on the ward must have heard, for she turned her head, looking their way with a disapproving frown.

Hurriedly, Celeste straightened. 'Better get some rest,' she told him briskly. 'I've heard you're due to be moved to the dispatch area soon.' The dispatch area was where they put the soldiers who were fit enough to return to their units or needed to be sent back home to England for rest and recovery. 'So close your eyes and get some proper sleep. Is that clear.'

'Yes, Nurse,' he whispered meekly, but winked after her, making her laugh again.

When she went back later that day to check on Danny's progress, unable to stay away, another patient was in his place, fast asleep. She asked a whistling orderly where the earlier patient had gone and he told her with a grin. Apparently, the doctor had seen Private Ffoulds at lunchtime and made the decision to ship him straight home to England.

Celeste thanked him and went about her usual duties, smiling as she moved between the rows of beds in B Ward. Nothing had changed. Yet she felt strangely unsettled.

She'd made friends with the young soldier during his time in the field hospital, listening to his funny anecdotes whenever she checked his vitals or changed his bandages, and she really ought to be pleased that Danny would be on his way home soon.

'Have you gone and fallen in love with that boy?' she asked herself during her break, sitting down alone with a mug of tea to watch new patients being carried out of the field ambulances and into the Casualty Clearing Station.

She blinked, thinking it must have started to rain, only then realising with a start that she was crying.

'Idiot,' she muttered.

At the end of her shift, she hurried to the dispatch area to wish him good luck on the long journey home, but the place was empty. The trucks carrying the wounded to the ships had already left.

Trudging wearily back to the nurses' quarters, she heard Ruth call after her. The other nurse came running up and pressed a scrap of paper into her hand. 'This is for you,' she said breathlessly, and gave her a wink. 'From one of the patients who got shipped out tonight. Looks like you've got an admirer.'

Celeste waited until she was alone on her bunk in in the nurses' quarters before unfolding the scrap of paper.

Dear Esther, I'm being sent home. If we win the war and you come back safe, I'd be honoured to stand you dinner. Address below, if it's not been blown to kingdom come by now. Yours ever, with undying gratitude, Danny Ffoulds.

Her heart beating stupidly fast, Celeste read the note several times, studied the North London address he'd given, and then reached under her bunk for the lidded tin where she kept her passport – made out in the name of Esther Sharpe – and other treasured possessions.

Silver glinted at the bottom of the tin, and for a few precious seconds, she cupped the ring in her palm once more. *Amor aeternus* was the inscription on the inside of the silver band. *Eternal love.* But that was not something she could ever expect to enjoy.

But still… Maybe after the war…

A group of nurses came laughing into the dorm, and she wiped away her tears, sitting up straight. Wrapping the silver ring in the folds of Danny's message, she clamped the lid back on the tin and put it away.

Out of sight, out of mind, she told herself firmly. But, in her heart, Celeste knew that she would never forget Danny Ffoulds.

CHAPTER TWENTY-ONE

There it was again. Someone playing the violin nearby. The faint opening strains of… Yet even as Stella thought she recognised the music, it broke off, and the great house lapsed once more into silence.

Stella, who had been on her way downstairs for a walk in the grounds, waited on the stairs, head cocked, listening in vain for more.

'Walter? Is that you?'

Frowning, she went slowly back up the stairs to peer through the window which overlooked the entrance steps and gravelled parking area at the front. Walter's car was still not there. She had heard him go out early that morning and he wasn't back yet, unless he had parked somewhere out of sight.

It was tempting simply to continue out of the house as planned, taking the kitchen passageway to the back door he had shown her yesterday and crossing the lawns to the woods and cliffs beyond. But she was curious now, and a little angry too. Even the faintest strains of a violin were instantly recognisable to her, a professional musician, and she knew she wasn't imagining things. While she was interested in the idea of the supernatural, she was not in any way superstitious or given to odd beliefs. If she had heard violin music, then either another violinist was in Black Rock Hall or someone was playing a recording. There was a distinct difference between live music and recorded, and last time she'd heard the violin, her ears had told her it was not being played live.

But why would somebody be randomly playing a recording of violin music, particularly when she was alone and there was no one else on hand to verify having heard it?

She knew only person who might do something like that, and he had no idea where she was.

Bruno.

A shudder ran through her, but she stiffened, more determined than ever to discover who was messing with her head. Bruno had a relentless streak, it was true. But he couldn't have found her. Not yet, at any rate.

Retracing her steps along the upper landing until she reached and passed the bedroom Walter had given her, she kept going, listening all the while…

A creaking sound turned her head, and she

followed it along a secondary landing into what felt like another wing of the house. It was shabbier here, deep scratches on door frames, wallpaper peeling in corners. The temperature dropped steeply as she came level with an alcove covered by a thick curtain lifting gently in a draught.

Pulling back the curtain, she found a cobwebby staircase behind it, leading up into shadow. From above the creaking sound came again. Could that be what she'd heard? Not a violin but a loose window or door creaking?

No, impossible. She knew what a violin sounded like. And yet she knew others might suggest it and look at her sideways if she continued to deny it.

'Hello?'

A rustling from the top of the stairs. The creaking again.

Stella closed her eyes. She was alone in a supposedly haunted house, seriously contemplating going up a dark stairway to investigate strange noises. But she didn't believe in ghosts, did she?

'I must be crazy,' she said under her breath, and pushed through the manky curtain.

At the top of the steep, winding stairs, a half-open door opened into a circular room. The tower room, she realised. In the exhibition, she had read that Maurice Cossentine had used this as his personal hang-out, and had supposedly been locked in during the night of the poisoning. That had been his main defence, in fact.

The room was cold and sparsely furnished, eerily festooned with cobwebs, like it had been unused for years. An ancient window with leaded glass had not been properly secured and the wind had been blowing the door gently back and forth, the high-pitched scraping sound uncannily like a violin's high notes played badly.

Oh, not spooky at all.

Stella crossed the room and pulled the window shut, staring out towards the Atlantic. There were the cliffs above Black Rock Bay, within easy walking distance; the sea felt so close, she could make out white flecks on the incoming rollers.

She shivered, hugging herself in the chill air as she walked around, studying the contents of the room.

There wasn't much to see.

Dirty bare floorboards. A single bed stood against one wall. A rusty iron bedstead, sagging mattress stripped bare. She looked down at it, feeling sick. The mattress was filthy too, spattered with dark flecks like dried blood. A short length of thin rope hung down from one side, secured to the iron frame, roughly halfway along. Frowning, she leant over the bed, careful not to make contact with the stained mattress. Sure enough, there was the same thin rope on the other side too, the fibres oddly discoloured. Blood?

Had someone been restrained up here?

Her phone buzzed and she jumped violently, heart thumping. 'Oh God.' Taking a deep breath, she fished out her phone and glanced at it. Unknown Caller. Perhaps someone at the solicitor's office trying to get in contact with her. She accepted the call, walking to the window and looking out, trying to calm her jagged nerves. 'Hello?'

There was a long silence. Then Bruno spoke into her ear. 'Enjoying Cornwall?'

Her hand tightened on the phone, her breath strangled in her chest.

'I'm coming to find you,' he continued, his voice deep and pleasant. 'You've had your fun, but it's time to come home.' He paused. 'I'm looking at you right now. You don't look happy.'

She spun, staring at the room behind her. Was he here? In Black Rock Hall itself? Her gaze flew from the bed to a broken mirror to a collection of dusty old crates. There was nobody in sight except her, fractured into a dozen mad jerking images by cracked glass. The door was still ajar. The dark stairs stood silent beyond.

Swiftly, she leant forward to stare out of the tower window instead. No new cars below. No sign of anyone on the lawn or in the formal gardens.

Her foot wobbled, standing on something soft but bulky. She raised her foot, staring down. It was an ancient, damp-stained cigarillo, only half-smoked and then crushed underfoot on the bare floorboards.

'I salute your taste, though,' Bruno continued in her ear. 'Such a charming place. I like the name too... The Silversmiths' Arms. Just don't get too comfortable there. I'll see you soon, Stella.'

Then he hung up.

The Silversmiths' Arms.

He thought she was still staying at the pub. Yet how could he even have known about that?

Abruptly, she remembered Allison Friel snapping a photo of her in the pub to accompany the interview. There had been a meal spinner on the table between them with the pub's name at the top. Allison must have published the interview online before the DNA tests had come back, despite promising not to.

Now Bruno knew where she was, and it was obvious he would soon be on his way down to Cornwall. If he wasn't already here.

Stella stared out across at the cliffs, her heart hammering, snatching at each chilly breath with difficulty.

Beyond the lawns and the wild gnarled woodlands, trees bent almost double by the prevailing winds, she could see a large wooden structure, surrounded by bushes. A summerhouse, it looked like. The same one mentioned in the exhibition? Surely it couldn't have survived all this time, out there on the exposed land near the cliffs. Or could it?

As she stared, a hooded figure in white slipped out of the summerhouse and darted away through thick bushes.

'What the hell…?'

Stella pressed against the cold cracked glass, her breath clouding up the window. The figure swam briefly, pale against green. Impatiently, she rubbed the milky glass with her fist, but whoever it was had vanished.

Had she just seen the 'woman in white'?

CHAPTER TWENTY-TWO

North London, spring 1946

Celeste crumpled up the scrap of paper in her fist, tears in her eyes, her chest tight with emotion. The North London address that Danny had given her when he left the field hospital at Bayeux was no longer there.

The building where he had lived was a complete shell, three storeys destroyed by a German bomb, to judge by the tall, elegant houses still standing on either side. The war had been over nearly a year, but although rebuilding was starting to take place in the centre of London, the clean-up on the outskirts was taking forever. Almost every street was punctuated again and again by these grim, empty spaces, like a decayed mouth with hardly any teeth left.

She stared about the place, struggling not to cry. Danny's house was a mess, like everywhere else these days. The burnt-out remains of an armchair lay on its side nearby, a broken toilet seat beside it balanced on a bed of rusty old springs and chinaware fragments. Rubble was strewn around these remnants, dust spiralling as a sharp wind blew through the London streets, lifting tattered shreds of wallpaper and lacy nets on window frames no longer attached to a house…

Celeste shivered and drew her coat closer. She stared into the remains of Number Seventeen, barely able to breathe, her spirits were plunged into such turmoil. For weeks now, since first deciding to take Danny up on his offer and visit his London home, she had been struggling against indecision, unsure whether to take a chance on the one man she had ever found truly interesting, knowing she could never tell him who she really was.

Now, she had finally galvanised herself to visit him, and this was what she had found. Emptiness and ruination…

'You all right, love?'

A wizened old woman in a shapeless frock had paused as she pushed a filthy pram full of bricks down the street and was looking across at Celeste in curious sympathy.

'I'm looking for Mr Danny Ffoulds. He was a Private in the war but came home wounded.' Celeste turned away from the ruined house and smoothed out the crumpled paper, showing the address to the woman. 'He used to live here. At Number Seventeen. But, as you can see, there's nothing much left of…'

Her voice broke on the horrible words, and she swallowed against a lump in her throat, almost too afraid to ask the obvious question, in case what she heard broke her heart. But she had no choice. Not now she had come all this way in search of him.

'Do… Do you know what happened to the family?'

'Course I do, dearie.' The old woman gave her an encouraging smile and turned, nodding further along the street. 'They got took in at Number Twelve, Railway Terrace, didn't they? Not far to walk, just a few blocks east.' Helpfully, she pointed the way. 'The widow and one of her sons, that's all that was left of the family when the bomb fell. Don't know his name. She had three grown boys, all done their duty, but only one come home from the war to her, poor soul. He might be the one you're looking for.' The old woman blinked, grimacing as dust blew down the windy street. 'Mrs Ffoulds has been taken sick, they say,' she added. 'I don't give much for her chances. Not wiv all the hospitals full.'

'Oh dear.'

'Whoever you're looking for, I wish you luck, dearie.'

Celeste rubbed away a tear. 'Thank you.'

The old woman grunted and continued down the street, the battered pram of bricks lurching from side to side as it hit obstacles.

Following the instructions to Railway Terrace, she eventually came to Number Twelve, a narrow, terraced house with dusty windows. She studied the building in silence, a dark foreboding in her heart. Railway Terrace was a comedown in the world from the larger property the Ffoulds had been living in before. But they weren't camped out on the streets, which was something, and had not been forced to move far. There was always a silver lining, wasn't there?

But perhaps she ought not to have come, purely on the strength of a few words scribbled on a scrap of paper. The world they had all known before the war had changed, and many people had changed too as their lives had been transformed. She might not be welcome now.

After a moment's hesitation, Celeste straightened her back and knocked at the door, steeling herself for the news that Danny had perhaps not made it, after all, and one of his brothers had survived instead. At least she would know...

The door opened.

It was Danny. Her knees almost wilted with relief. He was wearing a shirt with frayed cuffs and a mismatched tie, his trousers worn and patched at the knees. His fair hair was overdue for a cut and he didn't appear to have shaved that morning. But for all that, she thought him as handsome as ever.

'You probably won't remember me,' she began, her voice shaking.

'Esther?' Then he was grinning and pulling her into the house. 'Good God,' he kept saying. 'Good God, I never thought to see you again.' They shook hands awkwardly, and then he groaned and pulled her close for a kiss. 'I'm sorry,' he said afterwards.

'No, it's all right...' She laughed as he spun her around, breathless. 'More than all right.'

He was grinning too. 'I can't believe you found me after all this time. Did you see the old house?'

'Yes,' she agreed, her eyes locked with his, 'it broke my heart to look at it. You always spoke of your home with such pride. But your mother survived?'

He nodded, closing the front door. 'We were in the underground shelter that night, or we'd both have been flattened along with the building.' His face darkened, his eyes searching her face. 'Though my mother's not well, I'm afraid. I'm at my wit's end, to be honest.' He leant forward and whispered, '*Cancer*,' in her ear. 'They say she's only got a short time left.'

'Oh, Danny.' Her eyes filled with tears. 'I'm so sorry.'

'Yes, well…' He ran a hand through his flopping hair and looked away. 'Come and have a cup of tea. Since the bombing, we share the house with Mr and Mrs Arnold. Such good sports, they are, letting me and Mother stay until we can find fresh digs. Bloody Jerries, though… They've left London in a right old mess, don't you think?'

'Yes, it's awful,' she agreed, following him into the small back kitchen. 'Looking for work?' she asked without thinking, glancing at the newspaper he'd dropped on the table, several job vacancies ringed.

He flushed, putting the kettle on to boil, and she regretted her question. 'I'm sure I'll find something soon.' She saw him wince as he bent to light the gas stove and realised he must still be in pain from that chest injury. Perhaps it had not healed properly, or the scar tissue was irking him. 'I'll take any job that's going. They're looking for railroad workers, the paper says. Only a few minutes' walk to the station. Thought I'd better apply.'

Fetching down a tin of dusty-looking tea, he spooned a tiny amount into the pot. 'I'm awfully glad you've come to visit me, Esther.' Their eyes met. 'Seeing you again reminds me of happier days.' His expression became curiously intent. 'Do you know what I mean?'

Celeste sat down, her heart thudding as she gazed up into his smiling face. 'Yes, Danny,' she breathed. 'I do.'

'And how about you, Esther, what have you been doing since the war ended? Did your parents survive? Where was it you said you came from?' He saw her troubled expression and stopped. ' Sorry, I remember you never liked to talk about your family when we were at Bayeux. Bad memories and all that. Look, let's make a promise to each other, shall we? No looking back and no asking questions.'

Smiling with his usual optimism, Danny poured boiling water into the pot, for all the world like a druid peering into a cauldron as steam wreathed about his face and shaggy fair hair. '

'No asking questions,' she agreed with relief.

With slow and careful steps, Celeste carried a basin of warm water up the steep stairs to Mrs Ffoulds's bedroom. Danny's mother was sitting up against the pillows, but her eyes were closed and her skin was waxen. In the past few weeks, she had lost so much weight, she looked swamped by her white cotton nightgown, like a little girl in her mother's clothing. Celeste had never nursed someone with a wasting disease like cancer before, but she knew the signs of mortality and had warned Danny it could not be long now.

'I miss my boys,' Isabella said in a hoarse whisper, while Celeste gently washed and dried her parchment-thin skin. 'The two sons I lost to the war.' Her sharp eyes dwelt on Celeste's face. 'You love Danny, don't you?'

Embarrassed, Celeste nodded.

'You'll look after him when I'm gone? Danny can't look after himself. He needs a good woman.' Her bony hand crept out to grip Celeste's wrist. 'Are you a good woman?'

'I try to be.'

'Something about you, though.' The sharp eyes bored into her skull. 'Something not quite...' Isabella didn't finish, abruptly releasing Celeste's hand and sinking back onto her pillows. 'But you'll have to do. There's no time and nobody else.'

Danny had asked her to marry him soon after she'd arrived in London. 'Esther Sharpe,' he'd said, kneeling at her feet and clasping her hand, 'will you marry me? No need to answer straightaway.'

'Yes.'

He'd blinked. 'Yes?'

'Yes.'

'Oh dear Lord...' He'd bent to kiss her again, and Celeste had felt heat flood her face, experiencing real desire for the first time.

Ever since that day, she'd been fretting about marrying him as Esther Sharpe and not Celeste Cossentine. It felt wicked, lying in her vows before the altar. Yet how could she admit who she was?

She knew Maurice had survived the war and was still hunting for her, with rewards advertised in the newspapers from time to time, and she was simply terrified of him now. The more she thought about that night at Black Rock Hall, the more certain she was that Maurice had been the poisoner. Afterwards he must have asked Jeffrey to lock him back into his tower room and tell the police he couldn't possibly have done it, because he'd been a prisoner at the time. That had been Jeffrey's sworn testimony at the trial. She remembered reading about it in the newspaper and feeling suspicious, knowing they had left Maurice's door unlocked when she went downstairs to speak to Sir Oliver.

Despite the cook having been hanged for the murders, Maurice must know that she could still testify that his door had been unlocked that night, and if her brother was indeed a cold-hearted murderer, he could have no qualms in killing her as well to conceal the truth. Maybe Danny too, if he tried to get in Maurice's way. And she could never bear to be the cause of any harm to Danny; he was such a creature of light and joy…

But the truth was important between man and wife, wasn't it? What could be more important in a marriage than honesty?

'Danny,' she whispered urgently now, 'there are things about me you don't know. I haven't always been like this. Sometimes, when I was a child, I had… fits… episodes. My father would lock me in my room. He said –'

'Hush, darling,' Danny said, holding her tight. 'I don't care what your father said. Or what you did as a child. We agreed no questions and no looking back, didn't we?' He smiled at her, his brows lifting, open face aglow with emotion. 'You're the woman I love and am going to marry. That's all I need to know.'

So she closed her eyes and let him kiss her, and buried her need for the truth deep in her heart.

Isabella Ffoulds died in June 1946, but she lived to see her son married to Celeste in late May, and even managed to attend the simple ceremony. They had little spare money for fripperies, but the church was still decorated with summer flowers from two previous weddings that week, now sadly wilting. Celeste breathed in their sweet heady fragrance through her vows and held Danny's gaze as he slid the ring on her finger, tears in her own eyes. It was the happiest day of her life.

They had a two-night honeymoon in Hampstead, and then Danny returned to work on the railroad, where he was already popular for his gift of making people laugh. After his mother's death, the sale of her best jewellery – which Mrs Ffoulds had been hiding under the mattress against a rainy day – allowed them to rent their own place closer to the city. It was only a basement flat but, after sharing with another couple for so long, it was a little slice of paradise to them.

When Celeste discovered she was expecting a baby, she wandered about in a daze for weeks, speechless with joy and unable to believe her good fortune. To have walked away alive from her family's massacre had been the first great stroke of luck in her life. Then she had somehow come through the war unscathed, at least physically, and met the love of her life, Danny. But now, life had surely given her the greatest gift of all.

She knew then that, if God existed, she must have been forgiven for everything she'd done in the past, for all those dark, wicked secrets carved deep into her heart and never shared with anyone, not even her beloved Danny.

An innocent new life was growing inside her, and with it, the hope that she might one day live free of the terrible burden she carried, the guilt of having survived.

CHAPTER TWENTY-THREE

DNA swobs and a blood test were taken at the local clinic, all done within fifteen minutes, leaving Stella wondering why she had been so nervous about the process.

That afternoon, on returning to Black Rock Hall, she found a flyer pushed under the front door.

SÉANCE: WEST POL VILLAGE HALL.

The date of the séance was that evening. The glossy flyer featured a colour photo of Allison Friel looking suitably ethereal, pictured on the cliffs with a stormy ocean behind her, black hair flying, her eyes tinted to look bright sapphire.

SPEAK TO YOUR DEPARTED LOVED ONES. FREE ENTRY WITH THIS FLIER.

Stella crumpled the flier in her fist, closing her eyes on a wave of fury. The spiritualist had promised not to post her interview with Stella online until after the DNA results were confirmed. But she had done so anyway. Not only had Bruno used that post to track her down, but their impromptu interview in the pub had been presented in such a way that Stella came across as disturbed, if not downright barmy. *Heir to Black Rock Hall haunted by her murdered family*, was the deceptive subtitle, with all her comments quoted out of context to make it sound as though she'd swallowed every crackpot theory out there about the Black Rock Hall murders.

'For God's sake…'

Walter was in the library, halfway up a stepladder, poring over some archaic, leatherbound volumes. They had missed each other for the past few days, Walter frequently out at unspecified 'meetings' and Stella content to have more time to herself, feeling less visible here at Black Rock Hall. Bruno might be in Cornwall by now and searching for her around Bude and West Pol. But very few people knew she was staying at the hall itself. Which suited her just fine.

'This was pushed under the door,' she told him between gritted teeth, holding up the crumpled flier. 'Promoting a séance tonight at the village hall.'

'Let me see.' He came down the ladder to examine the flier, turning it over in his hand. 'Yes, that Friel woman is a nuisance. She litters the village with these fliers every month. The parish council has been trying to prevent her séances ever since she arrived, but without much success. It's a free country,' he added with a grimace, 'unfortunately.'

'Does anyone ever turn up?'

'Goodness, yes.' He peered at her over his glasses. 'They're immensely popular. People come from as far away as Bodmin, I believe.' Dismissively, he read aloud from the flier, '*Speak to your departed loved ones.* People are intrinsically gullible, I'm afraid.'

'Or desperate.' Stella hesitated, abruptly recalling the figure she'd seen from the tower window. The 'woman in white'. Though it didn't mean anything. It could have been anyone out walking the cliffs in a white outfit. She certainly wasn't going to mention it to Walter and see him look at her as though she were deluded…

'Here,' he said, handing the flier back. 'I'm sorry if it's upset you. But I can't control what people put through the door, more's the pity.'

About to crumple it up again, she changed her mind, folded the flier and pushed it into her back pocket instead. Perhaps if she walked over to the village hall tonight and confronted Allison publicly over that interview, she might be able to shame her into removing it from the website.

Meanwhile, she needed a way to calm her nerves. 'Do you mind if I play my violin? I need to practise.'

'You wish to use the music room? But of course,

be my guest.' Walter smiled, pushing his glasses up the bridge of his nose. 'It's been a long time since this old house heard the strains of a violin... I'm sure it will be pleased.'

He was speaking about the house as though it were a person, she realised, and hid her smile. Then, turning to go, something he'd said nagged at her. 'Wait, you said it's been a long time... Are you talking about Maurice?'

She recalled from one of the early rooms in the exhibition that her great-uncle had played the violin himself, and had thought it an unusual coincidence at the time. Though perhaps her grandmother had encouraged her to learn the instrument because it reminded her of her brother.

Maurice had been in his tower room at the time of the murders, he'd claimed in his testimony, and had not heard the servants screaming and shouting because he'd been practising his violin so enthusiastically. Which had struck her as unlikely. But apparently the police had swallowed this tale without question.

'Did he have a favourite piece of music?' she asked when he nodded. 'Perhaps I could play something in his memory?'

'Vaughan Williams' *The Lark Ascending* was what he invariably played in a melancholy mood.' He caught her jerk of surprise and misinterpreted it. 'He said it brought back memories of happier days. He suffered from depression in his later years, you know.'

'Poor man, how awful.' She struggled to hide her amazement. *The Lark Ascending* had been one of her grandmother's favourite pieces too. 'Though not surprising, given his difficult life story.' She hesitated, remembering the iron bedstead with the stained mattress and lengths of rope up in the tower. 'I went up to his room the other day,' she added slowly. 'I saw rope attached to his bed…'

He stared at her, suddenly very still. 'The tower room?' He blinked. 'I must admit, I've never been up there. When he took me on as curator of the exhibition, he was using the master bedroom at the top of the stairs. I believe he only ever used the tower room as a boy.' He frowned. 'Rope, you say?'

'Yes,' she said, embarrassed now, as though she'd been caught snooping. The DNA tests might prove inconclusive or even turn out negative, and then she would be leaving Black Rock Hall for good. It was asking for trouble, considering herself the heir to this place before anything had been formally announced. 'It probably dates back decades, then. Sorry, I ought never to have gone up there without permission.' She remembered the creaking noise she'd interpreted as faint violin music. 'Thing is, I thought I heard…'

His brows were raised. 'Yes?'

'Nothing.' She flashed back to that blog post

and its outrageous suggestion that she was obsessed with ghosts and hauntings. 'Don't let me disturb you.'

Hurrying away before he could press her for an explanation, Stella fetched her violin case from her bedroom and made her way back down to the music room.

Sunshine flooded across the polished floorboards, the panelled room warm and humming with light. Slipping off her jacket, she took her violin out of the case and checked it over. She had not played in days. Satisfied by the condition of the instrument, she then turned her attention to the strings, plucking them for the pitch and gently tightening the pegs, making sure the note was true. She did the same for her bow, applying resin generously to its long, silky strands, and then tightening it, checking the tension afterwards by inserting the tip of her little finger between stick and bow hair, which just fitted.

Carrying a dusty music stand to the centre of the room, she set it up and, having rummaged among the sheet music available in the room, soon found the music Walter had mentioned, though to be fair she knew the piece so well, she could easily play it without the music to hand. She played a few test notes, and then launched into *The Lark Ascending*.

The beautiful, haunting melody filled the room

and floated up the stairs, for the door was still ajar. The opening notes were to be played *cadenza* – interpreted freely – and she played the whole piece with emotion, strongly reminded of her grandmother and how she'd loved to sit in the long summer evenings, listening to Stella practise. Although she'd told Walter she would be honouring Maurice by playing this piece, it was in fact her grandmother to whom she silently dedicated the music.

As she played, she gradually became aware of what seemed like a faint echo of the music, and although she tried to ignore it, stretching with feeling for the final emotional notes, the echo became too much of a distraction…

She broke off and lowered her instrument, listening intently.

No, she was not imagining it. Someone else was playing a violin. Playing the same piece of music, almost in synch, now coming towards the end.

Striding to the door of the music room, Stella threw it open and listened, breathing hard. The music was fainter now, fading softly, but still seemed to be coming from upstairs.

'Walter?'

He came to the door of the library, book in hand, frowning in concern. 'Miss Ffoulds? Are you all right?'

'Don't tell me you can't hear that.'

'Sorry?' The curator looked at her blankly. 'Hear

what?'

Gripping the slender neck of her violin, her bow balanced in the same hand, Stella ran swiftly up the stairs and onto the first-floor landing, with its sombre rows of closed doors and huge urns bristling with dried flower arrangements below dark-spotted mirrors. She kept walking, making for the curtain that hung across the staircase up to the tower room.

'Hello?' The shadows ahead seemed to thicken at her approach. She dragged open the curtain and stared up into dusty spinning light, her ears on high alert. But the music had long since stopped. 'Who's there? Who's playing the violin?'

There was no answer. The air was still and silent, mocking her.

CHAPTER TWENTY-FOUR

North London, late March 1948

Celeste had been dreaming about Maurice again. She surfaced from sleep, recalling the dream in vague disjointed snatches before it could vanish forever. Maurice had been whispering a secret in her ear… She couldn't recall what the secret was, only that it was desperately important to keep it quiet. The scandal would kill their mother, he kept insisting. 'But Mother's already dead,' she told him in the dream. Then he turned away, and she realised with a shock it wasn't Maurice at all, but someone completely different… She ran after the man, needing to see his face, but he turned and thrust his fist deep into her belly, sending her writhing to the floor in agony.

The pain was what had woken her. And it was jarring now. Impossible to ignore any longer.

Danny must have felt her stiffen, because he

sat up, fumbling for the bedside lamp. 'Esther, are you all right? Are you crying?'

'N-No,' she managed to say, but with difficulty.

He peered at her, confused. 'Is it the sickness again? I thought you were past that stage now.' When she said nothing, he put an arm about her shoulders, saying softly, 'Talk to me, sweetheart. I can't help you if you won't talk to me. Are you feeling poorly?'

Celeste shook her head and put a hand to her belly, waiting for the sharp squeezing pain to come again. Slowly, she realised she'd been aware of it in the background for some hours, while dozing and dreaming, a rippling spasm that hadn't really begun to bother her until now.

Now she caught her breath as the pain returned, more intense than ever, and gave a low moan as it passed. Because she knew it was far too soon...

Danny was staring at her in the warm glow of the lamp. 'Esther, you're worrying me. Say something, for goodness' sake. What's the matter?'

'It's the b-baby,' she admitted and swung her legs out of bed, trying to stay calm though her heart was thumping and she felt light-headed and nauseous. She was stammering too, though it had been years since that old affliction had troubled her. 'I think something's wrong.' That was when she noticed a bright red trail of blood on the white sheets and her nightgown, and clasped her rounded belly in despair, desperate to protect the little life in there. 'You'd better get dressed. I need to see a d-doctor. Urgently.'

Everyone had been so kind, Celeste thought, staring at the curtain as it flapped dully in the spring sunshine. Danny had brought her flowers, and the neighbours had been in and out of their basement flat for two weeks, cooking meals for them both, bringing her cups of tea, even taking their laundry home and returning it a few days later, beautifully clean and ironed. But it was time for her to get out of bed and start living her life again. Start cleaning the house instead of watching friends do it for her, and take in more darning jobs, which she'd been doing during her pregnancy to earn extra money towards baby clothes, and make herself look pretty for Danny again.

Every time she thought about getting dressed and going downstairs though, she remembered that awful night at the hospital, how she had lain for hours between life and death, struggling and panting, only to watch her darling baby boy born without breath, so still and bloodied, it broke her heart even to let that memory in…

An hour passed like that as she lay in helpless torpor. Then her mind shifted to an earlier unjust death, and gradually her feelings began to change, hardening inside her, spurring her into action.

Slipping out of bed, Celeste knelt to hunt under the bed for the small woven bag where she kept her most precious and private belongings. Drawing out her journal, she flicked through a few pages, realising how long it had been since she last completed an entry. Somehow, she had fallen out of the habit of keeping a journal. With tears in her eyes, she re-read her entries around when Esther had died, and her regrets about having lied to her closest friend; she had died thinking Celeste was Lizzie Brown from Devon, a married woman fleeing an abusive husband. Did she really want to live and die with Danny by her side, allowing him to think she was orphaned Esther Sharpe? All these different names and identities...

And what if the worst happened and he somehow discovered the truth about her? It would surely destroy their marriage.

'I must tell him,' she told herself, and closed the journal, meaning to leave it on the bed to show her husband later. Despite this, she found herself replacing it in the bag. 'But not today,' she whispered. 'Not yet.'

There was something small and hard in a twist of fabric at the bottom of the bag. She drew it out, unknotted the fabric, and stared down at the silver ring. It fell into her palm, cold and bright.

'*Amor aeternus*,' she read out loud.

Some devil made her slip it onto her ring finger. It flashed as she turned her hand this way and that, admiring it. Somehow, just wearing the ring made her feel stronger, more able to face life again. It was a reminder that she was still a Cossentine, even now she was married and nobody knew her history. She could hide and erase her past with lies and make-believe, but she couldn't change her blood or her past. This ring was a visible symbol for who she was. Silver was what she had come from and she could never forget that.

She pushed the bag back under the bed, her face set and determined. Getting up, she washed briefly in cold water, and then dressed, pulling on gloves to hide the ring on her finger. There was nobody about when she left the basement flat and walked unsteadily along the road, her strength gradually increasing as spring sunshine warmed her face.

She took an underground train ride across the city, not meeting anyone's eyes. The carriage was noisy and dirty, people crowded in like cattle. Finally reaching her stop, she stumbled out and up the seemingly endless stairs, exhausted by the time she reached the top and fresh air again. Her body was not healed yet. But it was her mind that she was most occupied with; the rest would have to wait.

For an awful moment, standing outside the underground station, she swayed there, utterly disorientated by the bright sky and the unfamiliar rubble of bombed-out houses. Everything had changed since the war, she thought miserably, casting about for something she could recognise, like a hound trying to regain the scent of the fox.

She had come here once before, while working as a nurse, back in the days when people had still thought of her as Lizzie Brown from Devon, out of curiosity and a sudden wave of homesickness. But she had only seen one of the workshop staff, sweeping up outside, and had not dared speak to him or let herself be seen and possibly recognised.

A woman in a print headscarf bustled past, head down, clutching a wicker basket and intent on the shopping list in her hand.

'Excuse me,' Celeste called after her desperately, 'I'm looking for the old silver workshops… You wouldn't happen to know if any of them survived the bombing, would you?'

The woman looked her up and down, then said haltingly in a foreign accent, 'I don't know any silver workshops.' She looked ahead, and then pointed. 'Maybe ask those men?' With a nod, she hurried on.

Celeste shaded her eyes against the sun, trying to make out who she meant. There were two labourers with a works van ahead, digging a hole in the middle of the narrow street and causing havoc as other vehicles tried to thread past them. But nobody was complaining; at least some civic work was being done, even if it was inconvenient.

She walked towards them, struggling to spot which of these ruined buildings might once have been her family's silver workshop and warehouse. Some of the places missed by German shells were nonetheless unsafe to live or work in; these had been marked with red crosses for demolition, but nobody had found time to knock them down yet. London was still full of such areas, as the councils struggled with the massive demolition and rebuilding work required. Danny had said only the other day that some councillors were claiming the work wouldn't be finished for years. Meanwhile, ordinary Londoners had to live with the turmoil and devastation left behind by the war.

She enquired of the workmen, but they merely shrugged, glancing at her with disinterest, and continued digging.

Slowly, she walked on, weary and disappointed.

But another hundred yards down the street, she stopped dead, finally recognising one of the doors. Yellow paint, a large brass knocker. The faintest whiff of a memory struck her...

Passing this door, her sister Jolie holding her hand tightly, both of them breathless and excited by the unexpected promise of a treat...

She had rarely ever come here as a child; only the males of the family had been permitted in the silver workshop. But on a few special occasions, her father had permitted the girls to come and pick out a modest piece of jewellery for themselves, usually from the 'seconds' basket where they put items not good enough for sale, most of which would eventually be repurposed by the silversmiths.

After the yellow door house, which was sadly marked for demolition, was a dark, quasi-medieval alleyway, narrow and leaning. The next two buildings on the other side of the alley were still intact. Above one of their doors hung a familiar sign: Cossentine Silversmiths.

As she stood there, her heart bursting, memories flooding through her like water undammed, the door opened and someone came out.

It was Maurice.

CHAPTER TWENTY-FIVE

The village hall at West Pol was set back from the main road, off a tiny lane opposite the church and unlit graveyard. Hardly the most comforting view, Stella thought, getting out of the taxi and finding herself confronted with cracked, antique gravestones glimpsed through the church gate and the sinister shape of a yew tree looming out of the dark. She was a little late, having changed her mind about walking there when she saw how thick the dusk was, but the door to the village hall was still open and she could hear voices from inside, the buzz of a meeting just about to begin.

For a moment, Stella hesitated on the threshold, half tempted not to go inside but to call the taxi driver back, who was still performing a careful three-point turn in the narrow lane, and return to the house. Or perhaps head into Bude for the evening. There were lively pubs there and even a nightclub.

But she needed to confront Allison Friel about her wholly unethical behaviour in promising not to post that interview online until Stella gave her the green light, and then not only posting it early, but presenting Stella in such a deliberately misleading way that anyone reading it would come away with a deeply unfavourable impression of her. And she wouldn't be able to rest until she had Allison's agreement that she would remove the interview at once.

Inside the hall, she found a board signposting her towards Room 1 for the Séance Evening. The door was ajar, and inside she could see tables set at right angles to each other in a large rectangle, all the seats facing inwards, so that participants could see everyone else.

As she poked her head round the door, the room fell silent. Several people turned to stare at her and she looked back at them defiantly. The séance-goers were mostly women, with a few men here and there. As she moved further into the room, she met a cold glare and recognised the pub landlady, Mrs Hepley, sitting with her back to the door. Her eyes were fixed on Stella's face with undisguised malevolence.

Allison Friel, who was seated in the middle of one of the tables, her head bowed, looked up and smiled. 'Ah, Stella,' she said clearly, 'come in, please. We're just about to start. Everyone, this is Stella.'

Nobody said anything.

Stella came in, her heart thumping. She hated confrontation but sometimes it was necessary. And she was the one in the right here. 'Could I have a word with you first, Allison?' she asked clearly. 'It shouldn't take more than a few minutes. In private, please.'

'I'm afraid not.' Allison looked back at her serenely. 'I'm about to start my séance. But if you care to stay, we can talk afterwards.' She waved a hand. 'Get the lights, would you?'

Stella wrestled with the desire to have it out with her in front of all these people, and the knowledge that she'd be doing herself no favours with the local community if she openly attacked one of their idols. If she did turn out to be the heir to Black Rock Hall, she might have to live with these people for a long time. The Cossentine family already had a bad reputation in these parts and a public row with Allison wouldn't do much to dispel that.

There was a bank of light switches beside the door. Self-conscious, her nerves prickling, Stella flicked them off, one by one, until the room was in semi-darkness, lit only by the glow of a plug-in blue-white lamp that sat on the table in front of Allison.

The séance goers shuffled their chairs aside to make room for her and Stella found herself sitting across from Allison in the gloom.

The spiritualist was already speaking again, welcoming everyone to the séance in a matter-of-fact way, with a few business items to get through first – fire exits; coffee break contributions – as though it had been a regular knitting group or art class. And while she spoke, her thin, pale hands fluttered like butterflies, rising and falling, describing circles in the air...

'You may experience odd physical symptoms during this séance.' Allison placed her hands flat on the tabletop at last, fingers spread wide. 'You may hear strange things. You may feel the touch of a hand that isn't there or a cool breath on your cheek that you can't explain. You may find your mind drifting and forget where you are.' Her voice was monotonous but somehow soothing, like someone lulling a child to sleep. 'Don't be alarmed, these phenomena are perfectly normal. It's simply the other world trying to reach out to you, to break through the veil and call to your psyche.'

Listening to these words, Stella felt a cold creeping sensation at the base of her spine, like a chill draught.

The room had gone deathly still as Allison began to speak, and when the door abruptly opened, light came flooding in from the corridor and everyone jumped, several women crying out.

Stella looked round at the door, blinking and disorientated. How long had they been sitting there in the gloom?

There was a man in the doorway, a harsh light behind him. Black jacket, black jeans. He hesitated, staring in at them. 'Are you the psychic?' he asked Allison.

'Yes.' She sounded annoyed.

'Sorry if I startled you. Do you mind if I join in?' Without waiting for a reply, he shut the door and came edging around the table, though there wasn't much room. 'I promised my mother I'd come.'

Stella watched him, secretly amused. It was Lewis, the man who'd given her a lift to Black Rock Hall after she'd decamped from the pub the other day.

'Has your mother passed over?' one of the women asked him, her look sympathetic.

'No,' Lewis said, grinning. 'She had a clashing event. Bingo.' He squeezed in beside a heavy-set young woman with purple hair. 'She wants me to report back on the séance. Tell her if it's any good.'

Mrs Hepley was looking at him with dislike. Had she spotted Lewis picking her up after leaving the pub that day?

'When you're quite ready...' Allison said in deliberate, acid tones.

'Sorry,' he repeated.

Glancing his way, Stella shot him a quick, reassuring smile, but decided it was probably best not to say anything to him. There was also a niggling doubt at the back of her mind that he really was there on his mother's behalf, as he'd claimed. It didn't seem a likely explanation for his presence here tonight. But the suspicion in her mind was vague and unformed, so she let it go.

'I need you all to place your hands flat on the table, thus.' Allison demonstrated, and everyone copied her. 'Spread your fingers wide, like starfish, and make sure each little finger is touching the little finger of your nearest neighbour. Just so.' Again, she demonstrated, her little finger brushing that of the woman next to her on one side, and then doing the same with the man on the other side. He was a short man in a dark green jumper and flat tweed cap, who reacted with a nervous laugh, but nodded, trying to match what she was doing. 'Keep the hands flat and touching. They are your conduits for the spirits tonight. If you break contact, you break the circle, and those who listen will be unable to speak to us.' She checked that everyone was obeying her. 'Those on the end of a table, you may need to stretch out a little to make full contact. That's it.'

Briefly breaking contact herself, Allison dimmed the lamp. 'Silence now,' she told them in an emotionless voice, returning her hands to the table. 'Listen to the spirits as they gather.'

Oddly nervous, Stella closed her eyes and listened. She heard nothing but her neighbours breathing and, below that, a faint electric hum. She remembered a passage she'd read in Allison's book on speaking to the dead. *The Nether Realms are always open to us; all we need do is be silent and listen for whispers from beyond this world.* She remembered the graveyard opposite the village hall and shivered again, suddenly cold. But she'd felt cold as Lewis entered the room too; perhaps a draught had crept through with him from the entrance. The evening had been sharp and crisp as she got out of the taxi; they would soon be in November. There didn't have to be a supernatural explanation for what she was feeling.

Glancing surreptitiously around the table, Stella could only see hands in the dim blueish glow of the table lamp. Disembodied hands. No faces. Everything else was in shadow.

Now, *that* was creepy.

'Is there anybody there?' Allison waited, and then raised her voice, asking again, 'Is there anybody there?' Seconds later, a shudder seemed to run through her body and the spiritualist gave a melodramatic groan, tossing back her head. 'Oh, we hear you... Yes, we hear you... Welcome, spirit.'

Stella bit her lip to avoid smiling.

'Tell us your name, spirit.' There was a long, uncomfortable silence. 'If you won't tell us your name, then at least tell us if there is anybody here you wish to speak to.'

Stella's shoulders shook with suppressed laughter. She risked a glance at Lewis but could barely make out his face in the semi-darkness; only the gleam of his eyes, watching her.

'I hear you… I hear you, spirit.' Allison's voice was changing, becoming deeper, more like a man's. Then she said, in a voice that grated, low and harsh, making the short hairs on the back of Stella's neck stand up, 'I wish to speak to my heir.'

Stella's gaze shot to Allison's face, all laughter gone.

'My heir is in this room,' the deep, monotone voice continued. 'I can feel her presence.' The others were looking around the circle in surprise, some of them muttering under their breath. 'Speak, heir, and let me hear your name with your own lips.' Stella sat rooted in silence, staring fixedly at Allison. The spiritualist's head was bowed, her sleek hair falling over her face. 'Come, child, do not be shy. I have long been waiting for you. I am Maurice Cossentine of Black Rock Hall.'

One of the women said blankly, 'Oh my God.'

The man next to Allison stared to left and right, eyes wide; Stella could see his head turning from side to side in the gloom, like a deranged bird. 'I don't understand… Who's he talking about?'

'The lost heir to Black Rock Hall,' someone muttered.

The woman on his other side whispered urgently, 'Didn't you read Allison's interview with her? On the website?'

'Is that *her*?'

They were all looking at Stella now.

Mrs Hepley made a contemptuous noise under her breath. 'Yes, that's the one he wants to talk to.' She broke the circle, pushing back her chair and standing up to point straight at Stella. '*She* is the lost heir.'

Stella stood too, her chair scraping noisily, and battled a strong urge to flee. 'I'm Stella Ffoulds,' she told them. 'But I don't know for sure yet if I'm even related to the Cossentines.' She looked around at the pale ovals of their faces turned towards her in the semi-darkness. 'That's where I'm here in West Pol. They're doing a DNA test on me. But the results aren't back yet. So for all I know –'

'No, you're the one,' Mrs Hepley insisted coldly. 'Allison asked the spirits and confirmed it on the blog this morning. You're the one whose grandmother ran away and left my great-grandmother to hang for a crime she didn't commit.'

'No, that's not true... Even if she'd stayed to testify, there's no proof my grandmother could have helped Elsie Dunn avoid a guilty verdict. She ran away because she thought her life was in danger, you see...' Horrified, Stella stumbled over her denial, but nobody was listening to her now, talking excitedly amongst themselves instead.

She looked to Allison, but there was no help there.

The spiritualist had flopped forward when Mrs Hepley broke the circle, like a puppet whose strings had been cut. She lay face-down on the table now, unresponsive, her black hair a dark pool, one hand showing, fingers bent like a claw, ringless and still.

Lewis got up and turned on the fluorescent overhead lighting, which flickered, coming on with a sickly, humming glow. 'Is she all right, do you think?' he asked nobody in particular, studying Allison's motionless figure, and got out his mobile phone. 'Should I call an ambulance?'

'Don't be daft,' the young woman with purple hair said sharply, and batted at his phone. 'Put that away. You'll only annoy the spirits.'

'Allison will be all right,' Mrs Hepley said dismissively. 'She's always like that at the end of the séance.'

'That's right,' one of the men grunted, nodding his assent. 'I've known her be out for ten, even fifteen minutes, once the show's over.'

'Is that it for the night, then?' someone asked, sounding disappointed.

'You shouldn't have broken the circle,' the man in the tweed cap said nervously. 'Allison won't be pleased.'

'Nonsense, all she needs is a hot, sweet cup of tea,' a grey-haired woman announced. 'I'll make it for her, poor lamb. Meanwhile, if you're going home, please don't forget your donations.' Pointing to the small glass jar in the centre of the table, marked FOR THE PSYCHIC, she left the room, heading for the small kitchen opposite.

Stella looked at Allison's dark head, still resting on the table, and knew she'd been outmanoeuvred. She could hardly confront the spiritualist about their online interview now, could she? Not unless she was willing to wait until she'd finally come around and been given some reviving tea. And even then she doubted Allison would give her a direct answer.

Gathering her things, she turned away in frustration, only to find a young woman blocking her way. She vaguely recognised her. 'I know you, don't I?'

It was Tara, she realised, Mr Hardcastle's assistant in the solicitor's office.

'You've upset the spirits now,' Tara hissed. Without waiting for a response, she grabbed up a pink beret, settled it awkwardly on her head, and shoved her way noisily through a forest of chair legs to the door.

'Does your boss know you come to these séances?' Stella called after her, but Tara didn't look back.

Casting resentful looks in her direction, most of the others had begun to collect up their things too, pulling on coats and scarves. It seemed the meeting was breaking up early.

Lewis hesitated by the door, brows drawn together as he met Stella's eyes. 'You okay?' he mouthed at her.

She nodded, glad to have one supporter here at least, though she really didn't know him any better than these other strangers. Still, she felt shaken and very much under scrutiny, and anyone extending a hand in friendship, however randomly, was going to get her vote.

'Hey, where do you think you're going?' Mrs Hepley demanded from the other side of the table, where she'd been standing over Allison's prone figure, arguing in a low voice with the man in the tweed cap.

Immediately, one of the other women blocked Stella's way, a belligerent look on her face, her eyes small and bright.

'Back to...' Stella faltered, suddenly reluctant to explain that she had come from Black Rock Hall, 'the place where I'm staying.'

'Which is where, exactly?'

'That's not your business, Mrs Hepley,' Stella said coldly. 'I only came here tonight to speak to Allison. But it's clear she's in no fit state to speak to anyone, so I'm leaving.'

Stella tried to step around the woman in her way, but found herself caught in a ludicrous game, dodging to the left and then the right, the other woman shadowing her so she had no clear path to the door.

'For goodness' sake…' she gasped.

A hand shoved her from behind, and she stumbled, dropping her handbag.

'How dare you?' Flustered, Stella glanced over her shoulder but nobody was near enough to have touched her. 'Who did that?'

Nobody said a word.

For the first time, she felt frightened, knowing herself to be among enemies and completely outnumbered.

Her heart thumping, she bent and scrabbled for her handbag among the chair legs, and then straightened, deliberately barging into the woman in her way. 'Excuse me…' The woman, who was much larger than her, barely swayed but let her through, laughing contemptuously. Stella threw her a hard look. 'Thank you.'

Someone ahead was opening the door for her. It was Lewis, bless him. 'I'll come with you,' he said, and followed her out of the village hall, reassuringly close behind.

CHAPTER TWENTY-SIX

Celeste was frozen to the spot, staring at the man who had just come out of the silver workshop. She had not seen her brother in years, yet she knew him instantly. How could she not?

He was taller than she remembered, but that was hardly surprising; he had been a lanky, under-developed sixteen-year-old when she'd last seen him, with over-long black hair, eyes sharp as razors, and a tongue to match.

Now, he was in his twenties, a grown man. He wore a pinstripe suit with a white rosebud in the buttonhole and a dark blue fedora with a broad white band. His shoes were glossy black leather and the car waiting for him further down the street was large and expensive, a chauffeur in livery waiting with the back passenger door open, ready to usher him inside. Her brother looked confident and powerful and wealthy, looking straight ahead as he spoke to the shorter man who scampered beside him, nodding and taking notes.

But of course he was wealthy, she thought, lifting a trembling hand to her mouth. He had inherited everything. All the money, the houses, the silver business. After the murders, there had been nobody else left with a claim.

Nobody except her.

'Maurice,' she whispered under her breath, and almost died of fright when he stopped and looked over his shoulder, exactly as though he had heard that tiny sound. His gaze was narrowed and frowning, hunting through the passers-by to see who had spoken his name…

Celeste turned and fled.

Despite her physical frailty, she managed to find the strength to run for several blocks until she could saw the first brightly coloured stalls of a street market ahead, and stopped there, gasping for breath and bent over, clutching iron railings for support. After a moment, she was sufficiently recovered enough to look behind and check nobody had followed her.

To her relief, she could see nobody in pursuit, though those who passed her in the street glanced at her curiously, and one woman even paused to ask if she was all right.

'I'm… I'm fine, thank you,' she said unsteadily, and began to walk on, weaving her way through the street market without looking at the wares.

It took a few more blocks until she realised where she was, and ducked down into the next Underground station, tracing the map with a finger until she saw her desired destination.

On the train, she sat swaying with hands clasped tight about her bag, her face set and grim, her reflection in the dark glass opposite somehow unfamiliar.

Maurice was not only alive and well, she thought, but clearly enjoying his newfound wealth and power. And why not? He had worked hard for his position. He had risked everything. *A sign of God's mercy?* Celeste laughed out loud, her mouth wide open, head back, and saw the people around her stare and then carefully avert their eyes.

She had to be careful, she reminded herself, and sank back into silent obscurity, trying to make herself as small as possible in the dim, noisy space. But in her head, she was still running and running, her whole body shaking with the need to get away from him.

He killed them, she thought, and felt her heart beat faster as she let those terrible memories back in, even if just for a moment. *He killed them and got away with it.* There was no other explanation possible for what had happened that night. *Unless you did it.* Her eyes lifted to the pale, staring face reflected in the train window opposite and then squeezed shut in horror. *No, no, no, no, no...*

Part of her wished she had marched up to Maurice and confronted him. 'Did you kill our mother and father?' she ought to have demanded, right there in the public street, with everyone watching and listening, with that odd little man taking notes. 'Did you kill Jolie and her unborn child? And all the others?'

He would have lied, of course. Maurice had lied to the police. He had lied to the judge and jury. He had lied to everyone. Why would he not also lie to her?

Because he's my favourite brother, her mind shrieked. *Because I love him and he loves me. Because we were always the youngest, the two who were mocked and bullied, made to feel unimportant and invisible...*

Her stop came and she stumbled out, not really aware of where she was going until she found herself standing in front of the narrow house with the shuttered windows again. Something had changed since her last visit though. The shutters were falling apart and the once-shiny doorstep looked uncared-for, its red bricks chipped and dirty. A thin-ribbed, soot-black cat in the street paused in its meticulous grooming to watch as she knocked at the door, and then continued, uninterested.

She would find sanctuary here, she comforted herself. Even if it was only for half an hour while she recovered her nerve. Her old nurse would know what to do; she really ought to have visited before today, but she'd been too afraid to open that particular can of worms again. Now it seemed she might have no choice.

The door opened and Celeste looked up in hope, only to see an unfriendly and unfamiliar face. She took a step back, scared and uncertain.

A large, bald man looked her up and down impatiently.

'What d'you want?'

She licked her lips. 'Is... Is Peggy home?'

'Who?'

'Peggy.' She blinked. 'Margaret, I mean.'

'Nobody here by that name.' He began to close the door and then stopped, looking back at her. 'Wait... The previous tenant's wife... I think her name was Margaret.'

'They moved? Do you know where they went?'

The man pointed down the street. 'Cemetery,' he said shortly. 'She died in the war. Bomb, I think. Hit the factory where she was working. Then he died too, about a year after. Broken heart, the landlord said.' He saw her expression and hesitated. 'Sorry,' he finished gruffly, and shut the door in her face.

Celeste felt stunned, as though after a blow to the head. Peggy was dead? Grief swelled in her chest and tears pricked at her eyes as she remembered her old nurse's warm, comforting presence and how happy she'd been in her new life with her husband and children.

Her poor dear Peggy...

As she stumbled away, dragging a handkerchief from her sleeve, she caught the glint of silver on her finger and realised she was still wearing the ring.

The silver ring, the family heirloom, there for all to see on her right hand. Two serpents, entwined, and a Latin inscription. She turned it slowly on her ring finger, staring down at the immaculate silver, thinking how loosely it fitted now. She had lost weight... And with this fresh grief, she had lost her last tenuous link to her family.

By the time she got back to their basement flat, it was dark. She had been walking for hours, she realised, and her feet were sore. When she let herself back in, she found Danny waiting for her; he turned from pacing the tiny living room as she came in to stare at her, his expression almost savage.

She had never seen him like that, and was scared. For a moment, she almost turned and ran away again.

'Where the hell have you been?' he demanded, and then embraced her fiercely without waiting for an answer, dragging her close for a kiss so urgent and searching it took her breath away. 'My God, Esther... I thought...'

'What did you think?' she asked, closing her eyes against the accusation in his face.

'It doesn't matter. None of it matters.' He took a deep, shuddering breath. 'You're back now.' He drew her to the table where he had laid out some cold food for them, and eased her out of the jacket. She was shivering, she realised; her teeth were chattering too, even though it was really not that cold. Chafing her hands to take the evening chill off them, his gaze shifted to the silver ring on her finger, though all he said was, 'Sit down, and let me fetch you something warmer to wear. You're freezing.'

On his way back from the bedroom with a cardigan, Danny stooped to switch on the electric fire, and it began to glow, ticking noisily, both bars on at once. It was a wildly extravagant gesture, though she was glad of the extra warmth.

'There,' he told her cheerfully, 'you'll soon feel better once the room heats up.'

'We can't afford the electric fire,' she complained.

'Nonsense... Just for ten minutes.' He sat next to her and fed her as though she were a child. A slice of bread and butter with a smearing of raspberry jam on top, and a few spoonfuls of tinned peaches served with thin, long-life cream. 'That's the last tin of fruit in the cupboard, so enjoy it. No, you eat it. I had mine earlier.'

She caught his hand as he scraped the last of the cream up for her. 'Danny, I'm... I'm sorry,' she stammered, not quite able to meet his eyes. 'I should have left you a note. Explained where I was going. You must have been so worried.'

He didn't say anything for a moment but brought the spoon to her lips again. Then he said, almost dismissively, 'That's not important. Besides, you've been ill. I'm glad you're home safe.' His brows drew together, and he added huskily, 'I'm sorry about the baby. We can try again.'

She nodded, her heart breaking as she thought of the tiny baby clothes she had knitted so lovingly in preparation for the birth. It wouldn't put things right to fall pregnant again. Nothing could ever 'fix' their loss. But perhaps in time, if she had another baby to care for, she might begin to put this pain behind her...

The bowl now empty, his gaze dropped to the silver ring, and she saw surprise in his face. 'That ring... I've never seen it before.'

'No,' she agreed in a whisper.

His expression was neutral. 'Did you buy it today?'

'No, I've had it for years.'

'You kept it well hidden, then.' Danny's voice remained calm and level, devoid of any accusation. He lifted her right hand, examining the ring more closely. 'It's a beautiful ring, Esther, and very unusual. It looks expensive too, real silver.' His gaze rose to meet hers, suddenly intent. 'Is it?'

Silent and miserable, Celeste sat there like a rabbit, caught and only waiting for the killer blow. It was consuming her spirit, burning her soul down to ashes, this terrible deceit, the lie she had to live every day, every hour, every minute. Whatever the consequences, she couldn't go through with this charade any longer. But what would her husband think of her once he knew the truth?

'Esther,' he said softly when she didn't reply, 'I know we agreed no looking back and no asking questions... But is there something you need to tell me?'

CHAPTER TWENTY-SEVEN

They managed to get away from the village hall at West Pol without any further incidents. After what had just occurred at the séance, Stella found it disconcerting to walk right past the gate to the spooky churchyard on their way to his Land Rover. But no evil spirits jumped out on them, and she even saw a few hardy souls trudging in twos and threes through the churchyard on their way home from the séance, which settled her nerves somewhat. If the locals found the graves utterly banal, she ought to be able to do so too.

Lewis drove super-fast but competently through the narrow Cornish lanes, his headlights picking out a pair of bright eyes in the hedgerow. 'Rabbit,' he said, as though she couldn't have guessed on her own, and then gave a short laugh. 'What a complete fraud that Allison woman is. All that, 'Is anybody there?' nonsense was bad enough, but to put on a man's voice and then collapse...'

'Yes, that was startling.'

'I wasn't startled; it was pretty much what I expected when I walked in and saw her.' His hands tightened on the wheel. 'She knows her audience though. They were stuffing tenners in that glass jar of hers, did you see?'

'I didn't leave any money for her,' Stella said, almost guilty.

'Nor should you have to. You were her star turn, after all.'

'I beg your pardon?'

'That woman was ecstatic that you were there, it was obvious. *The lost heir...* Hence the lavish interview on her website. Yes, I read that too. Nothing like a local legend to bring in the punters. And those credulous idiots lapped it up, didn't they?' His tone grew even more sceptical. 'She must need throat lozenges after putting on that deep voice. No wonder she had to pretend to pass out. I doubt she had much more up her sleeve than a quick cameo appearance for Maurice Cossentine, followed by that face-first dive onto the table.'

'You didn't believe a word of what happened tonight?'

'Did you?'

'I asked first.'

He grinned. 'I think it was a carefully planned and calculated performance, designed to make the most money possible and ensure people will come back for more without her having to produce any real spirits.'

'If you're not a believer, why go to a séance in the first place? And please don't give me that "I was only there for my mother" angle, because I won't believe it.'

Lewis slowed down to take a sharp bend with more care than usual. He was looking straight ahead, his face intent. 'If you must know,' he said in the end, 'I was there tonight to write an article about spiritualism.'

'You're a reporter?'

He shrugged, neither confirming nor denying it.

'Who do you work for?' she asked, suspicious. 'One of the nationals? Or a local newspaper?'

'I'm freelance.' Lewis busied himself with turning up the heating. 'When the article's done, I'll probably flog it around the nationals. See who bites.'

Stella considered that explanation. 'Is that why you offered me a lift before, when I left the pub? And tonight, too.' She studied his profile, illuminated by the green glow of lights on the dashboard. 'Do you hope to get more information for your article out of me? You'll be disappointed if so. Allison may have interviewed me but I don't know much about psychics or the supernatural, I'm afraid.'

'Ah, but you're the lost heir.' He was mocking her, she thought. 'That's definitely worth writing about.'

'Yes, all right, I didn't tell you the truth about myself before. It turns out I may be related to the last owner of Black Rock Hall, and that's really why I'm down here in Cornwall. But again, there's nothing supernatural about that.'

He whistled softly. 'It's quite a big thing, though.'

'Tell me about it.'

'That bunch in the séance didn't strike me as terribly happy about the idea. I was worried for you there.' He frowned. 'I wonder why they've taken against you.'

As briefly as possible, she explained the whole story and how the cook who'd been hanged for the Cossentine murders was a direct ancestor of Mrs Hepley. 'She has it in for me, that's obvious. And, as you saw back there, she has some kick-ass friends willing to help her out. At least,' she added, with a twisted grin, 'they wanted to kick *my* ass.'

'Which would have been a shame, given what a nice ass it is.'

Stella sucked in her breath, surprised and wondering at first if she'd misheard him, especially when Lewis didn't so much as glance in her direction, his gaze fixed on the rear-view mirror instead.

'Erm, thank you, I guess.'

There were bright headlights reflected in the side mirror, dazzling her, but that wasn't what had made her look away from him. She found Lewis attractive. Something about him tugged at her in a way she could not ignore, and it was physical – *definitely* physical. But this wasn't a good time to be thinking about getting involved with someone new. Not least because she'd made such a terrible mistake with Bruno; her taste in men was a little suspect at the moment.

At that second, Lewis swerved violently, almost steering into the hedgerow, and she cried out, 'Careful!'

Shocked, gripping the door handle, Stella stared round at him. He was still looking in the rear-view mirror. That's when she realised the Land Rover was being overtaken by a large vehicle so close to the driver's side, Lewis had been forced onto the verge to avoid a collision.

'What the hell…?' She turned to stare at the other vehicle, which was unseen except for a flash of silver-grey and the twin beams of their headlights dancing across the road ahead as the two cars swayed back and forth, dangerously close in the narrow, winding lane. 'Is the driver insane? There's no room to overtake here… We'll be killed!'

Lewis said nothing, wrestling with the steering wheel as the car bounced over stones, fallen branches and other debris on the verge. Listening to the violent clunks and rending noises beneath the vehicle, she could only be thankful they were in a Land Rover and not an ordinary car.

He wasn't braking though, she realised. 'Lewis, what on earth do you think you're doing?' She hung on grimly to the overhead strap, swaying violently as they rounded a blind bend, the other vehicle still powering alongside them. 'Are you *racing* this idiot?'

He said nothing, gripping the wheel for dear life, his face a mask of determination, all his attention on not crashing.

Abruptly, it was over.

Rounding the blind corner, they came face to face with a third vehicle. All she saw were lights, blinding them both as the oncoming driver urgently flashed them, and then Lewis was swearing and braking hard.

The other car accelerated and slewed in front of them.

Lewis swung in behind and brought the Land Rover to a halt, just in time for the oncoming vehicle to scrape past with a blast on the horn. Stella caught a glimpse of an angry-looking man waving a fist at them through the windscreen, and then he too was gone.

In the blessed dark that followed, she sat there, breathing as hard as though she'd been running, her gaze fixed on the disappearing tail-lights of the car that had nearly run them off the road.

Lewis unsnapped his seat belt. 'I need to check for damage,' he muttered, and got out.

Slowly, she unfastened her own seat belt and stumbled out, feeling sick now that it was over. She took a few steps in the chill dark, not keen on moving too far away from the headlights of the car but aware of a need to test her legs, which felt a bit wobbly.

Dimly, she became aware of the sound of running water.

'What's that?'

Lewis straightened from checking the passenger side tyres and bodywork for damage. 'A stream in the valley below,' he said shortly. 'We're quite high up here. The road runs over the stream in about fifty yards.' He pointed ahead. 'See the wall of the bridge?'

Squinting, she could just see in the bright, moth-attracting front beam how narrow the road was becoming. There was a road sign just ahead, indicating that it was about to narrow to a single-track road. Beyond that, there was a gleam of something that could have been a drystone wall. The bridge, she presumed. It looked barely hip-high.

Her blood ran cold. This was basically the last point at which it would have been possible for the two cars to drive neck and neck. After this, Lewis's car would have been forced off the road and over that low wall into the valley below.

'Shouldn't you have stopped and just let him pass?'

'I couldn't be sure he wouldn't block the road ahead with his car, and then we'd have been in a difficult position.'

'You think he might have got out and… what? Attacked us?'

'I don't know.'

She thought about that. 'How far is the drop into the valley?' she asked quietly.

'Far enough.'

Stella shivered and got back into the car without another word. There was no point freezing outside while he completed his checks.

When Lewis got back in, his gaze was steady on her face, though she couldn't read his expression in the gloomy interior of the Land Rover.

'You okay?' he asked.

'Not really. Someone just tried to kill us,' she said, her voice not entirely steady. 'Did you recognise the car? Or the driver?'

'No.' He paused. 'You?'

She shook her head but couldn't help thinking of Bruno. He didn't own a car, as far as she knew, but could have hired one to drive down here. And if he'd seen her with another man, yes, maybe he was just crazy and possessive enough to consider violence.

'Stella?' He was frowning. 'What is it?'

'It's just… There's a bloke I know back in London. Bruno. We were seeing each other for a while but I broke it off. He didn't like that.'

'You think it was him?' He sounded puzzled.

'No,' she said, feeling ridiculous for even considering it. Then hesitated, adding, 'Maybe. I don't know.'

'Let's get you back to Black Rock Hall, shall we?' Lewis started the engine, driving on at a cautious, sedate pace. 'I wouldn't read too much into what just happened. I doubt it was this Bruno character. For a start, he wouldn't have the local knowledge for that crazy stunt he pulled. Probably some village kid messing about in his dad's car.' But he threw her a sideways glance. 'Still, if you want to take my mobile number, you're more than welcome to call me if he does turn up.'

The chance of Bruno travelling all the way down to Cornwall simply to harass her was beyond unlikely. He'd only been trying to make her feel uncomfortable, threatening that. All the same, she would feel stupidly relieved to have Lewis's phone number, just in case.

'Thank you,' she said shyly.

The lights were all off in the big house as they approached, and Stella wasn't sure whether to be relieved that she wouldn't have to speak to Walter or discomforted by the idea of groping about in the dark for light switches and so on. After exchanging mobile numbers, she directed Lewis to drive round to the side of the house where she had a key for the door, but he refused to leave without making sure she got in safely.

'I'll be fine,' she insisted as he got out and walked with her to the side door, though in fact she was glad not to be alone in the pitch-dark.

Lewis had brought a torch from the glove box and shone it ahead of them on the gravel path. 'Is that it?' He picked out a door in the torch beam. 'You've got your key ready?'

'Yes.' She fitted it into the lock, and it turned okay. 'Right… Well, good night and thank you.'

'For what? Not getting you killed just now?' His voice was dry, the torch beam lowered to the ground between them. 'Or for rescuing you from the mob with pitchforks at the village hall?"

'Both, actually.'

He laughed softly. 'Never a dull moment with you, is there?'

'That's what it'll say on my tombstone.'

He bent forward and kissed her lightly on the lips. Stella realised in the same instant that she was glad he'd kissed her, and that she very much wanted to kiss him back. And she would have done, except that the door had opened unnoticed while they were looking at each other.

'Walter!' Stella broke apart from Lewis, her heart thudding violently as she took in the short, balding man with glasses staring straight at them both. 'God, you gave me a shock. I mean… I'm sorry if we disturbed you.' She blinked, hurriedly checking the time on her phone. 'It's not that late though. I thought you must still be out yourself.'

'I've been working on the exhibition all evening. But the house alarm went off, so I came back.'

'Someone broke in?' Lewis's voice was crisp and urgent.

'No,' Walter said slowly, looking him up and down. 'False alarm. Sometimes it does that, especially when it's a windy night.' He stuck out a hand. 'I've seen you around, I think. But we've never met. I'm Walter Whitely.'

'Lewis Carroll.'

'Like the author?'

'More or less.' Lewis hesitated, and then smiled at her. 'Well, I've seen you safely back. I'd better head home myself.'

'And where do you live?' Walter asked at once, still studying him.

'Near Bude,' Lewis said vaguely, and snapped off the torch beam, leaving them in a glinting darkness lit only by the ghostly light of the moon, just emerging above the avenue of trees. 'Good to meet you., Walter.'

He touched Stella's arm, a fleeting contact that somehow said more than words could have done. 'You've got my number now. Call me if you need me, okay?'

She had no choice but to follow Walter into the house before the lights of Lewis's car had even disappeared down the drive. Rambling on about his precious exhibition, Walter flicked light switches and led her through the maze of corridors until she found herself in the main hallway again, facing the shadowy stairs to the first floor.

'Goodnight,' she said wearily, and headed for the stairs.

'A moment, please.' Walter gave her a worried smile. 'Forgive me, but that was the man who dropped you off here before. Is he a friend of yours?'

'Sort of.' Then she hesitated. 'I met him when I was staying at the pub, that's all. He's one of the locals.'

'He may be local but he's not a regular at the pub. I know most of the regulars and he's not one of them.'

'You said you'd seen him around.'

'I've seen him in Bude once or twice, that's all. Hanging around...' He frowned and adjusted his small round glasses as though they weren't a comfortable fit. 'Has this man attached himself to you, then? You should be careful.'

'About what?' She shouldered her bag, feeling impatient. 'Look, thanks for the warning, but

Lewis is the least of my worries right now. We had a bit of a scare on the way back from the village. Some maniac nearly ran us off the road.'

Walter seemed genuinely shocked. 'How dreadful… Are you all right?

'Just shaken.'

'Thank goodness you weren't hurt.' He studied her intently as though checking for injuries she might have omitted to mention. 'Like I said, you need to be careful, Stella.' His brow was furrowed. 'It would be too awful to lose the long-lost heir to Black Rock Hall after such a long wait. Trust me, we *need* you.'

CHAPTER TWENTY-EIGHT

For three long weeks after her confession, when she had poured out her whole history, unburdening herself of the truth at last, Danny said nothing, going about his daily business as usual. But he barely touched her and she could feel his distance, both physically and emotionally.

Eventually, he came home with a bunch of flowers and kissed her on the lips with his old cheerfulness. 'That smells good,' he said, peering into the bubbling pot on the stove. 'What's for dinner?'

'Stew,' Celeste said, sniffing the flowers, her uncertain gaze on his face. 'Hmm, they smell beautiful. Thank you so much.' She found the pretty jug that served them as a flower vase and arranged them as she'd been taught as a girl – one of the many useless skills she'd acquired in her days as a member of the wealthy Cossentine family – and placed it on the dinner table. 'I love flowers.'

'I know,' he said softly.

Something about his stillness made her nervous. 'Is… Is it a special occasion?'

'Perhaps.'

Confused, she turned away as though to check the stew wasn't burning, stirring it slowly before adding another sweetly fragrant pinch of dried herbs. 'What do you mean? It's not our anniversary. Or my birthday.'

'Ah, but which birthday? You used another woman's name to marry me.' He paused. 'I imagine you also used her birth date, rather than your own.'

She nodded, still not looking at him.

'I thought maybe today might be your real birthday,' he continued, his tone flippant. 'Or tomorrow. Or one day next week. So I brought you flowers just in case. When is your real birthday, by the way?'

'I'm sorry,' she whispered.

Celeste hated the sarcasm in his voice, yet she knew she deserved it. Danny had only recently discovered that his wife was not the woman he'd been led to believe. Most men might have struck their wives for such a deception; he had not lifted a hand or even his voice to her. She would have to accept some sarcasm, at least, for not trusting him sooner with the truth.

Carefully, she replaced the heavy lid on the

stew pan, her hand shaking. 'February 24th,' she whispered, and turned to find him watching her, his gaze intent.

'Not May 12th?'

She shook her head. 'That was Esther's birthday, so I had to adopt it, as it was on all her official paperwork. Now I've told you everything, so can we please drop the subject?'

'And in what year were you born?' How old are you?'

Celeste closed her eyes and buried her face in her hands, unable to bear the weight of his steady gaze any longer. 'What does it matter?'

'What does it matter?' His laugh was light and disbelieving. 'I prefer to know who I'm sharing my life with, and everything about her, not merely the lies she's fed me so far.'

'I'm twenty-seven,' she burst out from behind the heat and safety of her interlaced fingers. 'Cross my heart and hope to die,' she finished childishly.

He was silent for a moment, so that she finally dared peek through her fingers at him. 'Not thirty-one, then?'

'Esther was four years older than me,' she said quietly, and dropped her hands to her sides, feeling helpless now, chewing on her lip and unsure how to convince him that her love for him was real, even if some of the facts of her life had been made up…

'Before we were married, my mother joked once that I was saddling myself with an older woman, and was I sure it was what I wanted?' His voice wavered. 'Now you tell me you're only twenty-seven.'

She stared at him, blinking. 'I'm still older than you, Danny. You don't turn twenty-seven until September.'

His lips twitched in a grudging smile. 'I suppose.'

She studied his face, an old fear nagging at her. 'You won't tell anyone about me? You won't make me go to the police?'

Danny looked pained. 'Good Lord, darling, what do you take me? An ogre? You've told me what happened at Black Rock Hall and I believe you. As far as the police are concerned, I don't see how speaking to them could be helpful. Someone was already hanged for those crimes, don't forget.'

'But the money,' she whispered, staring at him. 'My inheritance…'

He rubbed his forehead, considering that. 'My love, if you prefer not to claim it, that's your choice. I can support us both on my wages, and if you're happy with the way we've been living, then that's an end to the matter. Money doesn't always make people happy, Esther. Look at my mother… She was stinking rich before the war and the most miserable woman you can possibly imagine. Nothing was ever good enough for her, and especially not me, her useless youngest son. If you ask me, losing everything in the war made her a better person.' He touched her arm in a gesture of reassurance. 'Of course, I still have a few questions of my own about your past. But they can wait.'

'Thank you.'

Grateful for his understanding, and hugely relieved that he would not insist she approach the family solicitor for her share of the estate, Celeste returned to stirring the stew, fearful it might be sticking to the bottom of the pan.

By the time they'd eaten dinner and Danny had laid aside the political pamphlet he'd been reading, stretching out his legs, she thought the argument had been forgotten. Instead, he said thoughtfully, as they moved to sit on the sofa together, 'I thought we might not have so long to try again for a baby, when I believed you were already in your thirties.' He paused. 'You know, I always thought you looked young for your age.' She heard satisfaction in his voice. 'Now I know why.'

Danny drew her close for the first time since before she'd lost the baby, and for a moment she stiffened, not sure she was ready for intimacy. But his kisses were gentle and undemanding, and eventually she began to relax. She turned her face into his chest and let him touch her, her eyes shut tight, her heart thudding against his. He was her husband, after all, and she did love him very much, even if things had been shaky between them since she'd admitted who she really was.

Cupping her cheek, he kissed her mouth deeply, and she gave a soft moan, her hands stroking his fair silky strands of hair.

'Oh, Danny,' she breathed.

'Esther…' He lifted his head to look down at her, and then bent to whisper in her ear. 'I can't think of you as Celeste. It doesn't seem to fit.' His lips found her throat, making her shiver. 'You're my dearest Esther and you always will be. Do you mind?'

She shook her head, not protesting even when he lay her down against the sofa cushions and his intentions became clear.

'And I want you to be a mother,' he said, slowly pushing up her skirt, his breath catching as he exposed her stocking tops. His gaze was sensual and full-lidded as he gazed down at her, his mouth curving into the smile she remembered from more carefree days. 'We've had enough darkness in our lives, you and I, what with that damn war and my mother's illness… But I want us to forget the past and move on. I want to love you and make you happy again. Make us both happy.' He bent to kiss her on the lips. 'May I?'

Celeste linked her arms about his neck. She wasn't sure what she had done to deserve such a gentle, forgiving man, especially given the darkness she had come from and the horrors of her early life. But she was so thankful.

'You may,' she whispered.

Celeste continued to find blood on the sheets, month after month, despite a concerted effort on Danny's part to conceive another child. At first, she despaired, but then gradually forced herself to get on with life, as Danny had suggested. Whether or not they had a child was not something they could control, besides trying their best to make it happen. Sometimes her monthly show was late, and she would count the days anxiously, marking them off in a little notebook she kept specially for that purpose. When it stretched to three weeks late, she allowed herself to hope... But the blood would come eventually, and she would feel her excitement deflate, her world suddenly flat and colourless once more. Oh, she would smile, for her husband's sake, and wave to the neighbours as though nothing was wrong, and even began an evening class to improve her cookery skills, which had not been brilliant at the start of her marriage. But inside she felt somehow monotone, and only the memory of seeing Maurice in London again, almost near enough to call his name and see his head turn towards her, had the power to spark life into her eyes and bring a blush to her cheeks.

Had her brother seen her, further down the street, watching him?

No, he couldn't have done.

But the fear remained, ludicrous and irrational, pecking at her like a bird until she thought she would go mad.

One evening around Christmas, she dared to go back there, to the same street, the same corner, using the excuse of Christmas shopping. But the workshop and small warehouse behind it were both in darkness, and nobody was about.

'Excuse me, do you know where the owner might be?' she asked a man closing up his jewellery shop nearby. 'Or when he'll be back?'

She had been feeling nostalgic again lately and wanted to peer into the workshop just once more, for old times' sake – maybe even see some familiar faces – but she couldn't risk bumping into Maurice.

The man followed the line of her pointing arm. 'The silversmiths' workshop, you mean? You won't find anyone there, Miss. The place has been sold.'

'Sold?' she repeated, stunned.

'It was the old Cossentine family business. You know, them as was all murdered a few months before the war.' When she said nothing, he squinted at her, frowning. 'Now, don't tell me you didn't see the newspapers at the time? Well, someone had it in for them, well and good. The cook, I think they said it was. The only surviving son took over the firm. Maurice Cossentine. Only he didn't have much of a head for business, see?' The man tapped his greying temples, grinning at her. 'Place went downhill after the old man died, and the war did the rest. So he sold up. Some toff took over the family business. Moved it up to Birmingham, I think, and rented these premises out to a grocery firm. So we'll have fresh veg and tinned beans on the street soon. Though they won't move in until after the new year, I daresay. Still renovating the place.'

'I see,' she said, unable to conceal her dismay.

Maurice had sold the silversmith business? But the Cossentines had been working silver for two centuries at least.

The man, seeing her downcast expression, hesitated in pulling down his shutters. 'Was there something I could help you with, Miss? I could let you have a quick look in the shop if you like. We sell a range of genuine silver items. Necklaces, earrings, brooches, and the like.'

'No, thank you. I... I've changed my mind.'

She walked hurriedly away, but she felt shattered. Her view of the world had been turned upside-down in a matter of seconds.

For as long as she could remember, the name of the Cossentines had been synonymous with silver. The family business had been her father's pride and joy. He might have struggled sometimes to keep turning a high enough profit, for the family had been large and all lived extravagantly, yet she'd never been in any doubt that Papa was a successful and respected businessman, not only here in London but across the Continent and even further afield.

Now the family business no longer existed, according to that jeweller. Maurice had sold both the firm and the premises.

Her head was in a whirl. How could her brother have done such a thing? Maybe the cost of materials since the war had brought the business to its knees. Or perhaps he had lost too many skilled workers to the battlefields of France. It seemed such a dreadful, disrespectful thing to have done, so he must have had a really good reason. It couldn't simply be because he had no idea how to run a business, as the shopkeeper had suggested. What a comedown for the family if that were the case. Her father would be turning in his grave...

She couldn't help wondering how her brother planned to pay for the upkeep of the London house now that he'd sold the business. But that was no longer her concern, she reminded herself. And no doubt Maurice had a plan.

Celeste trailed wearily home and tried to forget about it. Yet she found herself constantly looking out for mentions of Maurice's name in the newspapers that Danny brought home, cutting out any snippets she saw and pressing them between the pages of her old journals like wildflowers, as though desperate for news of home. It was her lack of a child, she told herself; if she had her own family, she would not be constantly harking back to the one she had lost – or which had been taken from her, more accurately.

She finally fell pregnant again three years later, and this time carried the baby only five months before losing it again.

'I can't go through this again,' she told Danny when she came home from the hospital, pale and wracked with pain. 'I can't bear it. Please let's stop trying.'

One morning, at the advanced age of forty-one, long after Celeste had given up all hope of conceiving, she got up as usual and only then realised the sheets were still clean and it had been some months since her last show of blood.

Was this the menopause come early, she wondered?

Not daring to consider the alternative possibility, she waited a few more weeks, and then finally went to see the doctor.

A few days later, the blood test came back positive.

She was not quite able to believe what the

doctor was saying to her, although she dutifully wrote down the date of her first appointment with the midwife and placed the brochures he gave her on pregnancy and childbirth into her handbag to be read later. Her head was spinning and she did not know what to think.

A baby? At her age?

The doctor had described her as 'geriatric' on her notes, a term which left her embarrassed and upset. She was in her forties, not her eighties. But he explained it was merely what they called mothers not in their twenties. His manner was very calm and reassuring, but she still worried what it would all mean, both for her and the baby already firmly entrenched inside her. She had miscarried too often now not to be in terror at the thought of enduring such pain and horror again.

She wept all the way home on the bus, though for joy as much as in fear, and wept again when she told Danny that night, tears streaming down her cheeks uncontrollably, sobs shaking her slender frame.

'You're pregnant?' Her husband held her in his arms, frowning. She couldn't tell what he was thinking. 'We must have been careless, I suppose,' he said eventually. 'But I'm not sorry, Esther. And I can't pretend I'm not overjoyed.' He brushed her tears with the back of his hand, asking tentatively, 'My dear, are you really so unhappy to be expecting a baby again?'

'Only because I'm much older now, and it's so risky. What if we lose this one like we lost the others?' Celeste did not dare to hope for a better outcome. She knew how bitter it was to see those hopes dashed.

But to her delight and eternal gratitude she didn't lose the baby. She carried her unexpected pregnancy to full term, giving birth to a healthy daughter with a thatch of sleek dark hair and a set of powerful lungs, who screamed the place down while she was weighed, inspected and cleaned before finally lapsing into a fretful, blinking sulkiness that made Celeste laugh.

'What are you planning to call her?' the midwife asked with an indulgent smile, placing the tightly swaddled baby into Celeste's arms.

Celeste glanced up at Danny, who had a permanent grin on his face now he was a father at long last. 'Darling?'

'How about Isabella after my mother?'

She gnawed on her lip, uneasy about the choice, but thought it best not to argue. Such decisions needed to be made jointly, after all, for the sake of a peaceful marriage. Besides, her own difficult relationship with his mother was in the past now. This baby was their future.

'Perfect,' she said, and bent to kiss her sleeping daughter's forehead. They had been through hell together and given up hope of a child years ago, and yet here they were, proud new parents of a beautiful baby girl. 'Welcome to the Ffoulds family, Isabella.'

CHAPTER TWENTY-NINE

Somehow, Stella had known the test results even before being called into Mr Hardcastle's offices. Every instinct in her body had already told her what the authorities needed a medical test to confirm. A formality, he'd assured her. Only it felt far from a formality. More like an ordeal by fire.

To her relief, she didn't see Tara in the reception area when she arrived, Mr Hardcastle himself ushering her through into his office. She had been uneasy at the thought of seeing the young woman again since spotting her at the séance and being faced with such unexpected hostility. But maybe it was her day off.

Sitting in his office, she took the letter from Mr Hardcastle and studied it in silence. The words and figures swam on the page, her vision blurring.

'We'll have to release a statement to the press at some point.' The solicitor loosened his neon-pink tie and sat back in his swivel chair, watching her. 'People are going to want to know about you.'

Her heart beat erratically and she found herself taking short, shallow breaths to stay calm, as though she were terrified or in shock. Maybe a bit of both.

'Why?'

'The public always feel they have a right to know things like this.' Mr Hardcastle waved the paper away when she tried to give it back to him. 'No, keep it. That's your copy.'

There was a knock at the door. His assistant came in at last, looking rather pale and apprehensive. Not her day off, then. She was carrying a tray that held three glasses and a bottle of champagne.

'Ah, Tara, I was beginning to wonder where you were. Thank you for sorting that out.' He glanced at Celeste, smiling. 'I hope you don't mind a bit of bubbly this early in the day but I thought this result called for a proper celebration.' He stood waiting as Tara popped the cork and poured out the fizzing wine. Then he took one of the glasses and handed it to Stella, who was still staring at the DNA results letter. 'I'd like to propose a toast. To Stella Cossentine, now officially heir to the Black Rock Hall estate.' He lifted his glass, smiling down at her. 'Congratulations.'

'To Stella,' Tara muttered, and knocked back her glass of champagne before nodding to Mr

Hardcastle and scurrying back into the other room.

'To me, I suppose,' Stella said faintly, sipping at the wine. Bubbles went up her nose and she sneezed, putting down the glass before she could spill it. 'You said, when I first came to your office, that there was someone else set to inherit. Can I be told who that is, now?'

'I'm afraid not, sorry. But as I said before, you don't need to worry.'

'But it's such a big house – '

'The person named as the default heir is wholly unaware of their presence in the Will. That information was only to be released on the fifth anniversary of Maurice Cossentine's death. And in the event that the true heir turned up, the information was to be suppressed, precisely to avoid bad feeling.' Hardcastle was smiling wryly. 'He was a wily old soul, Maurice. Such a pity he was so afflicted in his final few years.'

'Afflicted?'

'You didn't know?' Mr Hardcastle sighed. 'Dementia. Brought on quite suddenly by a stroke. It affected him physically as well as mentally. In fact, he was confined to bed for a long time before his actual death. Though he had excellent care. A nurse who lived in, and Walter was always there, of course.'

'How did he die?'

'I believe he was 'wandering' in the night, as

they call it when dementia patients feel the need to get up at odd hours and try to leave the house. It was the nurse's night off and the curator had taken a powerful sleeping pill, so nobody even knew he was out of bed before it was too late. He fell down the stairs in the dark. Broke his neck. It was a great tragedy.'

She shivered. 'Poor Maurice.'

'He's buried in one of the local churchyards. Along with the rest of the Cossentines. It's a grand old tomb, you can't miss it.' He scribbled down the name of the church and passed the note across to her. 'In case you want to pay your respects.'

'Yes, thank you.' She tucked the note into her bag. 'Well, I don't know what to say. Actually, I don't know what to *do*. What happens next?'

'As I said, this office will put out a press release. *Long-lost heir returns to Black Rock Hall...* Something along those lines. We can draft something on your behalf for the newspapers, both local and national.' He took a long swallow of champagne, seeming to relish the taste. 'By the way, if the BBC ask to interview you, what should we say?'

'No,' she said flatly.

'It's your call, of course. But you might want to reconsider.' He regarded her, head to one side. 'In particular, you don't want to give locals the impression that you're too important to bother giving your side of the story. Unless you're planning to sell up and go straight back to London?'

Stella hadn't even thought that far. 'I come here to escape London.' She thought of Bruno and his relentless pursuit. 'Though I'm not sure how long I'll stay in Cornwall.'

'That's not an answer.'

She ran a hand through her hair, rattled by his insistence. 'I have no plans right now. To be honest, I'm still reeling from the news that my grandmother really *was* Celeste Cossentine.'

'It must be a shock to have your suspicions confirmed, yes. What happened to your grandmother has been one of the biggest mysteries in British criminal history, and now it looks as though the puzzle has finally been solved. At least, you hold some of the pieces of that puzzle, even if you don't know you do.'

'Sorry?'

'Her journals, her papers…'

'Right.'

'I expect there'll be plenty of people eager to talk to you and discover whatever you know about her life after she left Cornwall… What she did immediately after the murders, for example, and why she never came back or admitted publicly who she was.' He paused. 'Plus, of course, whether she ever told you anything about that night.'

'She didn't tell me a damn thing.' Seeing his

surprise at her sharp tone, she added, 'Like I said, I mostly pieced it together from her journal entries and that photograph of her wearing the silver ring.'

'Ah yes, the silver ring.' Hardcastle nodded thoughtfully. 'Still an astonishing thing though. People will want to know the story, that's for sure.' His gaze steady on her face, the solicitor drained his glass of champagne, and then returned to the paperwork in front of him. 'Look, don't worry about any of this. Unless someone pops up to contest your inheritance, it's a done deal.'

'Is that likely?'

'I wouldn't have thought so. Legally though, there are a few documents and formalities we need to go through before I can hand you the keys.'

'I'm getting the keys to Black Rock Hall?'

'Eventually, yes.' He frowned, looking down at the paperwork. 'The curator holds the keys at the moment, of course. He not only runs the exhibition but lives in at the hall, and part of his job is to look after the premises and ensure repairs are carried out promptly. But once we've dotted all the i's and crossed all the t's, I'm sure Walter will hand the keys back, no problem.' Again, he hesitated. 'You'll have to make a decision about his future role, of course, whether you want to keep the exhibition running and who should curate it. But that's a conversation for another day.' He shot her a curious look. 'You're staying at the hall yourself, I've heard. Does Walter know who you are?'

She nodded, embarrassed.

'Inevitable, I suppose, given all the local interest. Must have been a shock for him. Still, Walter always knew it might happen one day, the heir turning up on the doorstep.' He rubbed a finger around his shirt collar, grimacing as though it were too tight. 'By the way, I heard what happened at the West Pol séance. Sounds like a lively evening.' When she stared at him, he smiled. 'This is a small place. I'm not saying we all live in each other's pockets but word tends to get around pretty quickly.'

'Tara?'

His mouth twisted. 'Yes,' he admitted, 'she was my source.'

'I think she may also have been telling people about my claim on the estate.' Briefly, she described how Allison Friel had already known about her when they met at the pub, claiming someone who worked for him had leaked the information. 'It's made things awkward for me.'

His look was grave. 'Are you sure it was Tara? Because I'd have to sack her, if so. Privileged information, and all that. You have proof?'

'Only what Allison told me. But look, I'd rather you didn't sack her. Life is difficult enough for me at the moment.'

'Very well.' He was frowning though. 'I'll have to put her on a warning though. It's a serious breach of confidentiality.'

Stella picked up her glass of champagne and downed its contents in one, ignoring the bubbles pricking at her nose. The alcohol warmed her and made her feel braver.

'Is there any actual money associated with the estate?' she asked tentatively, not wanting to get her hopes up. 'Or is it just the land and house?'

'There's only a small amount left in the kitty now, I'm afraid. Nothing to get too excited about. There was the upkeep of the estate to pay for, plus our own fees, but the firm has always tried to be as frugal as possible, just in case...' He flicked through a few sheets in his folder. 'Yes, there's about six hundred thousand pounds in cash.'

Stella felt winded. '*Six hundred thousand*?'

'Not a fortune, considering how much it costs to maintain the house and grounds on an annual basis. But there have been offers for various parcels of land over the years, so you might want to consider selling off parts of the estate to liquidate assets without having to sell the main house. The woodland folly, in particular, has been very popular.'

She sat up, excited. 'There's a folly? In the grounds?'

'Rather a tumbledown folly, I'm afraid. I think

a few corners were cut when it was built.' Hardcastle smiled, seeing her expression. 'You like follies?'

'I've never even seen one. But the idea of it… A folly is so romantic, isn't it?'

'If you say so.' He smoothed his straining shirt over his large belly, a slight frown on his face. 'Though Maurice would have agreed with you. Despite its poor condition, he absolutely refused to countenance any renovations. He told me it reminded him of his mother… Mrs Cossentine designed it, you know, though the building work wasn't finished until after her death. He was quite sentimental about the old place. Spent many an evening out there on his own, by all accounts, despite the folly not having any electricity. In fact,' he added with a shake of his head, 'he even left instructions in his will that the folly was to be kept with the estate even if his executor – that's me, by the way – needed to sell off any land parcels to pay estate costs. To be brutally frank, it ought to be knocked down before it falls on somebody. But that's a matter for you to consider later.'

He began talking about the offers for land purchase they'd had from local farmers and landowners looking to expand their portfolio, while she listened, trying to keep up with the enormous figures he was throwing out.

Feeling she ought to make an effort to

understand her newfound wealth, she scribbled a few disjointed notes in a little book she kept in her bag. But her brain really couldn't grapple with the idea of so much money, on top of that amazing, albeit ramshackle, house and grounds. She'd spent too many years scraping a living as a musician and living hand-to-mouth for that kind of money to seem anything but miraculous.

Thank you, Maurice, she thought secretly. Even if he was a murderer and a villain, as Gran had presumably thought, she was still very grateful for her unexpected inheritance.

Feeling extravagant after all that talk of money, Stella splashed out on a taxi from Bude back to Black Rock Hall. As they drove through the village of West Pol, she noticed a few people gathered on the green, a little distance from The Silversmiths' Arms. A police car was slewed at an angle across the entrance to the pub car park, blue lights flashing, and an ambulance stood nearby with its back doors open, as though waiting for a patient to be brought out of the pub.

The taxi driver glanced that way too. 'Wonder what's going on there,' he muttered and slowed slightly as they passed, craning his neck to see more.

Stella also wondered but decided against stopping in West Pol to join the ogling villagers. 'An accident, perhaps,' she replied, though the presence of a police car as well as an ambulance sent a chill of dread along her spine. But it was none of her business. 'I hope it's nothing serious.'

Once the taxi had reached the turn to Black Rock Hall, she asked the driver to drop her off at the head of the drive, having decided to walk a long loop on foot to the hall and see where the boundaries lay. The air was crisp and cold and rather delicious, perfect for a walk of exploration through the woods.

She was just beginning to regret her decision, boots soaked with the damp grass and undergrowth, an autumn chill striking through to her bones, when she saw something up ahead through the trees that made her stop and suck in her breath with awe.

It was the old folly Hardcastle had mentioned.

Once it must have been a bold and imposing building, a single tower rising out of a cluster of trees, a stone parapet at the top, edged with tooth-like battlements. Now though, one side of the tower had cracked from top to bottom, a few stones missing in places, and many crumbling. As she drew closer, she saw ivy creeping up the other side, thick and glossy, which seemed to be practically gluing the stonework together. Perfect for the faux medieval touch, she thought, though she doubted it had been designed like that. Maybe a random lightning strike had cracked the tower, bringing some stones down, or perhaps the foundations simply hadn't stood the test of time.

There was a low door at the base of the tower, made of thick, dark, studded wood, looking like something out of a gothic horror film. She assumed it must have been a Victorian project – Victorian landowners loved follies and eccentric buildings, didn't they? – but the date carved above the door was in Roman numerals, which meant she needed to work it out for herself.

'December MCMXXXIX,' Stella read out the deep-carved numerals. 'That's M for a thousand. C for one hundred, then M for another thousand.' She frowned, trying to make sense of it. 'No, wait, the C is before the M, which means minus, doesn't it? One century before two thousand, then.'

If she'd been hoping for help by speaking out loud, none came. The woodlands were quiet and unresponsive, the only sounds a faint rustling of animals in the undergrowth and calls from birds in the trees above. Also, in the distance, she could hear the steady soft roar of the Atlantic Ocean.

'So that's 1900, plus three tens, and IX, which is another ten, minus one. Which gives me... December 1939.' She took a step back, surprised. 'Oh.'

She stared up at the tower's height, feeling the familiar spin of vertigo she always suffered in high places or when faced with a tall building, then lowered her gaze to the Roman numerals again.

The folly had been completed in the same year that the family was poisoned.

She considered the studded door, but didn't feel comfortable about going inside, assuming the place was even unlocked, which she doubted.

Slowly, she began to walk around the base of the tower, stepping over fallen stones and the humped bulges of tree roots, drawn to this fascinating remnant of another age.

Before she'd walked even halfway around the tower, the sound of snarling brought her up in shock. She'd heard rustling in the undergrowth only minutes before and had thought nothing of it. Now a dog stood a short distance away among the trees, staring straight at her. Its teeth were bared, thick fur standing on end in a ridge along its back. It was huge and grey, perhaps some kind of mongrel, but massively built, stiff ears pricked towards her, its gaze fixed and malevolent.

'Oh, brilliant,' she muttered, not daring to move.

It was hard not to be reminded of the 'spectral hound' mentioned in the exhibition in connection with the Cossentine legend. A dog that roamed the grounds, appearing and disappearing at will, howling on dark nights as it mourned its murdered masters. Though this was no phantom but a flesh-and-blood animal.

She shivered, meeting its narrowed, hostile gaze. She'd never been good with dogs. 'Erm, nice doggy.' She glanced about anxiously for its owner but saw no one among the trees. Just the hound and its slavering jaws. 'Good boy… If you are a boy, that is.'

The dog snarled again, crouching lower as though about to spring, and Stella broke with a cry, turning and fleeing.

CHAPTER
THIRTY

From the beginning, Isabella was an astoundingly beautiful child. Eliciting gasps of admiration from passers-by as a delicate, porcelain-skinned baby, once she'd left her fifth birthday behind she grew more willowy and graceful with every year that passed. By age ten, she was considered the most striking and theatrical girl in her year, awarded the lead role in every school play with seeming effortlessness. Celeste adored and doted on her wonderful daughter, always ready to give into her demands, keen to supply whatever Isabella wanted.

'You're spoiling her,' Danny warned her.

Perhaps she was. But how could she say no to her miracle child, the daughter she had never dreamed would come along to brighten her middle age? For she was becoming middle-aged, Celeste realised in the early Seventies, noting her thickening waist and wrinkling skin with dismay, while Isabella by contrast grew ever more sleek and swan-like. Not that Celeste resented her beauty; far from it. She had never been a great beauty herself and it filled her heart with joy to see her daughter receiving the sort of admiration she'd been denied at the same age. She was determined that the shadows which had blighted her own life should never touch her perfect little girl.

It was when Isabella hit puberty that the real troubles started. Always self-involved, Isabella's sweet but unyielding nature hardened then into something worryingly like egotism. Concerned by her occasional tantrums, Danny began taking her for long walks most weekends, where he would talk to her about life, politics, and how the world had fallen into a disastrous second global war. His feeling was that Isabella's upbringing so far had been too narrow and inward-looking, and she simply needed to have her world view broadened and challenged.

Isabella listened politely enough, but when asked, admitted to finding his stories dreary and pointless.

'The here and now is what matters, Dad,' she told him candidly. 'Your generation is the past. It's our time now.'

Danny's interventions made no difference. Isabella was already the bane of her teachers' lives by the time she turned fourteen and Celeste lost count of the number of times she was called into school to collect and chastise her daughter.

'What on earth have you done now?' Celeste demanded after the latest summons, while Isabella stood unspeaking in the headmistress's office with folded arms and a mulish expression. 'Your father and I both begged you to behave yourself.' She bit down the urge to say more, burningly aware of the headmistress looking on. 'I really don't understand you, Isabella. It's almost as though you don't want an education.'

Isabella flashed her a furious look. 'Perhaps if you and Dad ever listened to me, you'd know I've done nothing wrong.'

'Now, Isabella,' the headmistress told her, rising to stand behind her desk in an intimidating manner, 'that's not true, is it? You slapped Sally Hinkley about the face and tore off her Head Girl badge.'

'Only because she deserved it,' Isabella muttered.

Mortified, Celeste clapped both hands to her cheeks, wishing she knew what to do about her extraordinarily difficult daughter. 'Why on earth would you do such a dreadful thing?'

'She used a bad word about me,' Isabella said sullenly.

'I seriously doubt that.' Mrs Pratt gave Celeste a self-satisfied smile. 'Sally Hinkley is from a very good family. Her behaviour is impeccable.'

Celeste blushed angrily, forcing herself not to snap back at the hateful, sneering woman.

But she knew exactly what Mrs Pratt meant by 'a very good family' and it wasn't one where the parents had to scrape and scrounge every penny they could to pay for the uniform and any extras the school demanded. Although if Mr and Mrs Hinkley were indeed so very wealthy, they would be sending their 'impeccable' daughter to a paying school, not this second-rate establishment off a side-street in the busy hub of Stoke Newington.

They had moved here from North London after Isabella's first expulsion from school two years ago, when she'd discovered how much fun it was to leave dead frogs in her science teacher's laboratory coat.

Dismissing her daughter's naughtiness as a childish prank, Celeste had settled into the new area with pleasure, finding her neighbours delightful and friendly, and the shops so much more interesting and cosmopolitan. To her relief, Danny had managed to find work better suited to his education and was now a manager on the rapidly expanding London Underground system. The extra money had been helpful for funding their purchase of a large two-bedroomed flat, but with a mortgage now to be paid every month, it had not quite stretched to cover all their other bills. Celeste had taken on work in a chic little boutique, mending and adjusting dresses for their wealthy customers, and sometimes designing and making exclusive one-off new outfits for sale in the shop, which she enjoyed immensely.

But then Isabella had tried to set fire to a classroom and been expelled for the second time, and it had taken an enormous effort to persuade this new school to take on such a problematic pupil. Now, out of the blue, Celeste had been summoned to the school to discuss this fresh outrage.

'What a whopper!' Isabella exclaimed. 'Sally Hinkley called me a filthy tinker and a...' Isabella used a word that made both Celeste and the headmistress wince.

'Language!' Mrs Pratt exclaimed, her brows shooting up in horror. 'Isabella, promise me you will never use that word again. *That*... is a word that should never be spoken by any refined young lady.'

'How am I supposed to tell you what word she said without using the word?' Isabella demanded, not unreasonably to Celeste's mind, but then spoiled everything by adding, 'Though of course you're going to take her side, because she's a toff and her dad's on the board of governors. I know he is, because she never stops mentioning it. It's all, *Daddy says this, Daddy says that*... Blah, blah, la-di-da. She's a right clever-clogs and teacher's

pet too. Honestly, I don't know why I bother…'
She made a rude gesture at Mrs Pratt, sticking up
two fingers. 'That's what I think of you and your
bloody school!'

'Isabella,' Celeste said, groaning inwardly, 'wait
for me outside, dear.'

Her daughter shrugged and strode defiantly to
the door, leaving it wide open behind her so that
the headmistress's prim-faced secretary, sitting
at a desk just outside her office, could be seen
peering forward curiously to hear what was going
on inside.

'Mrs Pratt – ' Celeste began, flustered, but was
interrupted.

'The time for discussion is over, Mrs Ffoulds.
I took Isabella despite her poor record in the
hope that our own strict standards of conduct
would bring her into line.' The headmistress sank
down behind her desk, two spots of colour in
her cheeks, her mouth pinched. 'But any school
would struggle with your daughter's appalling
behaviour. I'm afraid expulsion is the only choice
left open to me.'

'You can't throw her out. She needs to take her
O Levels next year.'

'In that case, might I suggest teaching her
yourself at home?'

Seething, Celeste stalked out of the
headmistress's office and slammed the door so
hard it shook in its frame. She felt a momentary

quiver of guilt, meeting the shocked gaze of the secretary, but then stuck her chin in the air.

'Come along, Isabella,' she told her daughter, and took her hand. 'Let's get out of this horrid place.'

Celeste cut down her work hours and stayed home to help her daughter through her O Levels, while Danny took on overtime to fund a tutor who called in twice a week. To Celeste's relief, Isabella seemed to settle down once removed from a school environment. 'She has problems with authority figures,' she told Danny. 'I've been reading about it in this book from the library.' She held up the hardback, though he barely glanced at it. 'It's a very common phase in adolescents, apparently. We just have to wait it out.'

But Danny didn't agree. 'Isabella has a problem with not getting her own way,' he said grimly. 'And that's largely down to you.'

'Me?' She was stunned. 'You're her parent too.'

'But you're the one she spends most time with,' he pointed out. 'And it's you who refuses to punish her when she's misbehaved. What kind of message does that give a child?'

But if they'd thought her school years had been challenging, those were nothing compared to the hell of what followed.

After finishing her O Levels, Isabella spent almost the next two years lying about the flat reading fashion magazines and playing loud music, and then eventually got a job in a dress shop after Danny put his foot down. But it was nothing like the exclusive boutique where Celeste still worked. This one catered to a much younger crowd; the clothes were outrageously skimpy, and the owner, a man in his early thirties who wore chunky gold jewellery and drove a lurid orange Ford Capri, blasted music out of the shop all day long and called Isabella 'doll' and 'sweetheart' in front of the customers, which she claimed not to mind.

Danny was horrified when he visited her workplace one Saturday afternoon and witnessed the shop owner ogling their eighteen-year-old daughter.

'Isabella, I don't want you working there anymore,' he told her that evening, his expression troubled. 'I don't like the way that man looks at you.'

Unmoved by his disapproval, Isabella lit up a cigarette. A cloud of thick fragrant smoke billowed above her head. 'Yeah, well,' she drawled, 'it's none of your beeswax, Dad.'

Celeste was shocked. 'Since when do you smoke?' she demanded.

'Since someone passed me a ciggie at a party and I liked the taste.' Isabella took another drag on her cigarette and blew sickly-sweet smoke in their faces. 'It's cool to smoke.' She giggled for no apparent reason. 'It makes me feel good.'

Danny was staring at her in horror. 'Is that marijuana you're smoking?'

'Grass, Dad. It's called grass. Christ, you're so out of touch, both of you. Nobody calls it marijuana these days. Except the fuzz, I suppose. And nobody cares what they think.' Wearing a tiny leather miniskirt, Isabella crossed her legs and leant back on the sofa, seeming to delight in their discomfort. 'Anyway, I'm not going to stop working there, okay? I love Sherlock and he loves me.'

Her father repeated blankly, '*Sherlock*?'

'You love him? The owner?' Celeste felt nauseous, and not merely because of the cannabis her daughter was smoking in their flat. 'Oh my God.'

'I'll need a passport, by the way,' Isabella said, ignoring her distress, and knocked ash carelessly onto the carpet with one scarlet-tipped finger. 'Sherlock's taking me to New York next time he flies there on a fashion buying trip. I've always wanted to go to America.'

They hadn't known what to say, except to forbid 'Sherlock' to visit the flat. But their daughter was eighteen now, no longer a child; they couldn't tell her what to do, only hope she would develop some restraint and common sense in time.

That hope was in vain. Two weeks later,

Isabella left the flat in Stoke Newington and moved in above the dress shop with her lover. Danny was incandescent with impotent fury. 'They're not even married, for God's sake,' he kept saying, staring at the empty seat at the dinner table. 'What will people think?'

But Celeste said nothing. She was less bothered by what other people might think and more concerned about her daughter in the clutches of a much older and more sophisticated man.

Isabella's first grand love affair didn't last, of course.

There was a knock at the door one evening and two police officers told them in a shockingly offhand way that Isabella was in the hospital. 'Looks like an overdose,' the older one explained as they hurried to fetch coats and keys. 'Her boyfriend gave us this address when the ambulance picked her up. He said it was over between them, but he felt sure you'd look after her.'

Isabella lay in a kind of coma-like state for the next two days, but eventually surfaced on the morning of the third day, ashen-faced and with dark circles under her eyes. By the time the hospital called them back in, she was sitting up in bed, sipping at a cup of weak tea, still looking fragile but alive, at least. When they came to her bedside in the ward, she stared at them both with something close to disgust.

'My poor darling girl,' Celeste said, her heart breaking as she bent to hug her daughter.

'Don't fuss, Mum.' Isabella shrank from her, her once-bright eyes dark and full of loathing. 'You know I hate it.' She peered past them at the double doors into the ward, plucking peevishly at the bedclothes. 'Why are you here, anyway? Where's Sherlock?' She chewed on a ragged fingernail that had been bitten down to almost nothing, her air fretful. 'I asked the nurse to ring the shop hours ago; he must have got my message by now. Why hasn't he come to see me?'

'Oh, Isabella, I'm sorry.' Danny tried to hold her hand but she dragged it away, averting her face.

'He's not coming, is he?' she whispered.

Celeste and Danny glanced at each other, unsure what to tell her.

'We'll look after you now, don't worry.' Celeste was relieved that their baby would be coming home again, at least. 'I haven't touched your bedroom since you left. Everything's exactly as it was.'

Once Isabella was ready to leave the hospital, they took her home and put her to bed in her old room, wincing over the purplish pinprick marks on her arms, which the doctor had explained were the signs of drug addiction. 'She'll require special care for a few weeks,' he had told them, prescribing sedatives to be administered while she recovered. 'You'll need to keep her clean.'

'Clean?' Celeste hadn't understood.

'Off the drugs,' the doctor had elaborated. 'It won't be easy.'

That had been the understatement of the century, they discovered. Once they began to wean her off the sedatives as instructed, Isabella's drowsy, acquiescent mood rapidly changed to something out of a nightmare. She screamed obscenities and threw things, and even wet the bed some nights, clawing at the sheets as she battled her addiction.

Celeste sat up with her daughter each night and assiduously changed her bed linen and night clothes every morning. She lied to the neighbours when they came around to complain about the noise, telling them Isabella had a fever that caused delirium, but that it wouldn't last. And Danny took a few weeks off work so he could take the early morning shift while Celeste caught up on her sleep.

Eventually, Isabella began sleeping through the nights on her own, and their lives were able to regain some semblance of normality. But it was clear she would never be their little girl again.

Isabella didn't bother looking for more work after that but stayed home for the next few months, brooding and smoking heavily, though Danny strictly forbade her to bring home any more marijuana cigarettes.

Instead, she started getting drunk during the day and once had to be dragged away from Sherlock's boutique, where a small crowd had gathered. The police had been called after she started screaming and shouting at him in the street, accusing him of forcing her to have an abortion, a fact that had left Celeste heartbroken and Danny grim-faced and silent.

Neither of them mentioned this awful revelation to Isabella afterwards. What would have been the point? But it preyed on Celeste's mind. She herself had tried so hard and so many times to get pregnant, to carry a child to term, and yet her own daughter…

She loved Isabella. She always would, no matter what. But she didn't have the language to do her feelings justice. All she had was this devastating pain.

A few days after they'd brought their daughter home from the incident outside the boutique, Celeste had another blackout.

She woke to find herself in the street, with Danny staring at her anxiously. It was the middle of the night and she was wearing her nightdress. She had no recollection of how she got there or what she might have done while walking about in an apparently unconscious state.

'You had your eyes open,' Danny told her, 'you were awake. But you couldn't seem to hear me. It was like a trance.'

'I used to do that as a child,' she admitted. 'They called it a blackout.' She shivered, realising she was barefoot, and let him lead her back into the building. 'I'm sorry.'

'You're done in, that's all, poor thing. Hardly surprising, all the worry and sleepless nights you've faced with Isabella. Here, get back into bed.' He tucked her under the sheets. 'I'll make up a hot water bottle for you. Your feet are like ice.'

'Wait…' She gripped the sleeve of his pyjamas, her teeth chattering uncontrollably. 'I haven't had a blackout in such a long time. Why now?'

He ran a hand through his silvering hair. 'I don't know, love.'

Danny was a good man, always there for her, never complaining. Yet she still feared what it all meant, this belated return to the mental disturbances of her childhood. Was she finally going mad, as the doctors had claimed she would, back when she was her daughter's age?

'Why didn't Isabella come to us when she fell pregnant?' She was still anguished, tormented by this question. 'We would have taken her back, helped her, no questions asked.' Everything hurt and she could barely breathe, clawing at her nightie, the high neckline and tiny buttons up the chest suddenly tight and constrictive. 'When I think of it… Oh God!'

'Darling, stop tormenting yourself.' Putting his arms about her, Danny held her tight. 'Forget it.

It's done.'

'But why, Danny? Why doesn't she trust us?'

There was no answer to that, of course, and she knew in her heart there never would be. Her miracle of a daughter, her beautiful only child, had become a closed book. And that was what hurt more deeply than anything else.

CHAPTER THIRTY-ONE

Running from the 'spectral hound' had been the worst thing she could have done. Stella knew that as soon as she moved. But her brain had no apparent control over her instincts, which had spurred her legs into action, so that she was tearing around the base of the tower with a huge grey dog snapping at her heels, the animal snarling and barking in the most blood-curdling, chilling way possible.

She could never make it back through the woods to the house. Not without this vicious creature taking a chunk out of her leg. Several chunks, probably.

The door to the folly wasn't locked. If it had been, she would have been in serious trouble. As it was, she forced it open – it was stiff and swollen in the frame – and flung herself inside, putting her whole weight against the door to keep the dog out, who had instantly leapt up to prevent her escape.

There was a brief tussle, then the door shut.

She stood there, panting and listening to the dog's muffled barking from outside, fearful the door might give way.

Thankfully, it held.

There was a narrow, circular stone staircase leading presumably to the top of the tower with its medieval battlements. Pale light and a chill draught came whistling down this stairway, sending shreds of gossamer cobwebs on the walls shivering and fluttering. Craning to look up, she saw daylight through a window slit further up, though the rest of the stair was in darkness.

'Well,' she thought out loud, 'I'm not going up there.'

Her voice echoed, bouncing off the stone walls, and outside the dog barked hysterically and launched itself against the door again.

Backing off, she resisted the urge to yell something at the animal. That would only antagonise it further. Besides, maybe its owner had caught up with it by now, and she would be horribly embarrassed to be heard yelling futile insults at a dog.

She followed the short passageway into a small circular room, lit by more window slits, the walls festooned with extravagant cobwebs. She didn't like to think where all the giant spiders were lurking who had spun these webs; she just kept to the centre of the room and hoped any creepy-crawlies would stay in their hiding places until she'd gone.

The interior walls showed cracks in places where the exterior had tumbled down, but someone had covered the worst damaged area with blue plastic sheeting, so ancient it was riddled with holes. Metal scaffolding poles had been used to brace the sagging wall in places. She recalled what Hardcastle had said about the folly needing to be knocked down before it tumbled down, which was worrying. 'Please don't fall down while I'm in here, okay?' she told the stones, her voice surprisingly loud in the musty space.

Outside, she heard a muffled bark. The dog responding to her voice again. So it hadn't gone away yet.

'Damn it,' she muttered.

Taking out her phone, she was relieved to find a signal. Only one bar, but that was enough.

She hesitated over Walter's number, then called Lewis instead, purely on impulse. She groaned inwardly when the call went straight to the ansaphone.

'Hello, Lewis? It's Stella. Look, I'm sorry to disturb you but I'm in the old folly in the woods at Black Rock Hall. There's some massive beast of a dog prowling around the tower. It chased me in here, basically, and I'm worried it's going to attack me if I go outside. I know it's a big ask, but if you're not busy, is there any chance you could come and... Well, rescue me?' She winced, embarrassed. She'd never been a damsel-in-distress type, despite Bruno's insistence that she needed to be protected. But on this occasion... 'Ring me back when you get this message, okay? Thanks.'

Walter would have been closer, if he was at Black Rock Hall right now. But she couldn't see the absent-minded curator facing down a large dog on her behalf. Besides, it wouldn't exactly be a hardship to see Lewis again so soon. Assuming he got her message before the dog grew bored and sloped off into the woods, that is. That would be awkward.

There was a rickety table and chair near the hearth, both filthy with age, the tabletop encrusted with what looked like the solid pooled remains of burnt-down candles. There was still half a candle left, with a packet of matches beside it.

Pulling a face, Stella rummaged for a travel pack of tissues in her handbag, wiped the seat of the chair, and then sat down to wait.

Although the tower was circular, the room was not perfectly round. One section jutted out randomly, as antique and cobwebby as the rest of the room. Possibly the site of a secondary door or maybe a chimney that had been bricked over decades ago. The blue plastic sheeting slightly overlapped that area, and that too had been braced with a metal pole.

There was a shallow pot set beneath this sheeting, with a few brown stalks hanging limply over its lip. A flower pot?

As she studied this, trying to figure out why on earth someone might have left a flower pot under an area of plastic sheeting in a disused tower, an enormous spider scuttled out from behind this pot and began to scale the wall with long, hairy legs. She watched in horror until it disappeared behind a mass of cobwebs high on the stone wall; she'd always been scared of spiders, however illogical it might be. They just looked so menacing. Especially when they were huge like that.

Stella rested her elbows on the table, listening for any further sounds of the dog from outside. She couldn't hear anything but decided to wait for Lewis either to ring her back or to arrive at the tower before bothering to get up and investigate.

It took her a while to realise that the odd squiggles on the tabletop were not the tracings of a long-dead snail but writing, cut into the wood with a thin, sharp instrument. The point of a penknife, perhaps.

She bent closer, frowning.

M.C.

She ran a finger along the carved initials. Who else could that be but Maurice Cossentine, her late great-uncle?

Why would someone so wealthy, with a beautiful country house a short walk away through the trees, want to spend time in this grim little room? Unless he were lonely and uncomfortable in that big house, rattling about on his own, no other living members of his family to talk to, to share a joke with…

Now that she had seen his initials, the tower seemed less threatening and more intimate. A place of refuge and peace for the traumatised survivor of a family massacre. She had seen her grandmother Esther struggle against depression and anxiety at times, and not really understood why until this year, finally learning her secret history.

No, not Esther.

Celeste.

A little lower, she made out more initials, cut at exactly the same slant as the other two. By the same hand?

J. D.

Maybe he had met someone out here, privately, away from prying eyes. M.C. and J.D. A married woman? A man, perhaps? Maurice had never married, after all.

'A confirmed bachelor to his dying day,' Mr Hardcastle had said. 'A lonely, eccentric old man. That's how I remember him.'

Then again, it wasn't a terribly comfortable

place for lovemaking. Not unless there was an upper room with a bed. Though she had no intention of climbing those crumbling, cobwebby stairs into darkness to find out.

Stella closed her eyes, listening to the silence, feeling the weight of all that stone above her. Maurice may simply have come out here to be alone and listen to the same silence. She could imagine him sitting here to write a journal or read a book undisturbed, perhaps with a glass of wine at his elbow…

Her phone rang, loud in the silence. Startled, she fumbled to answer it, only belatedly realising she hadn't checked the number.

Nobody spoke, but she could hear breathing on the other end.

'Lewis?'

'Who's Lewis?' Bruno asked, a deep suspicion in his voice. She caught her breath in horror and fumbled to end the call, 'Don't hang up on me, Stella. Don't you dare hang –'

His voice abruptly cut off.

Numbly, she stared down at the blank screen, heart thudding, brain scrabbling to catch up with what had just happened.

Then she fetched up the number that had just called her. She didn't recognise it and it wasn't listed in her known callers list. Bruno, her possessive ex, had got himself yet another new phone, it seemed. She tapped to block this new number, but not quickly enough. A follow-up text had already appeared at the top of the screen, as though to mock her slowness...

It read simply, *I knew where you are*, accompanied by a photograph. She clicked to enlarge it and found a shot of a sandy beach with a huge, barnacle-covered rock gleaming in the sunlight, waves breaking about its broad base.

Black Rock Beach.

Somehow, Bruno had managed to track her from The Silversmiths' Arms to Black Rock Hall. Though it looked like a stock photo of the beach, not one taken by Bruno himself on the ground. So, was he physically here in Cornwall or still taunting her from his home in London?

She threw the phone away from her in a burst of frustration. There was a crack as it hit the flagstone floor and she winced. A knee-jerk reaction and ludicrous too, she knew it. But she'd reached breaking point as far as her ex was concerned.

The door to the outside opened abruptly, scraping along the uneven stone floor. Her nerves prickling, Stella jumped to her feet.

'Stella?' The newcomer spoke, out of sight in the dusty antechamber, and she sagged with relief, recognising his voice. 'Are you there?'

'Lewis, thank God.' Jumping to her feet, she scooped up her phone, irritated to see she'd cracked the screen, and slipped it into her pocket before heading his way. 'Did you see that enormous bloody dog outside?'

'No... I guess it must have run off.' Lewis was standing at the foot of the winding staircase, looking stylishly rugged in black jeans and a thigh-length leather coat like a model from a men's magazine. 'Are you okay? Did it bite you?'

'No, but only because I shut myself in here.' She smiled up at him shyly. 'Thank you for coming to rescue me, by the way. You seem to be making a habit of that.'

'I do rather, don't I?' Lewis grinned. 'My pleasure.' His gaze shifted towards the dim-lit room she had just vacated, and he frowned. 'What is this place?'

'A folly, built just before the war. Intended to be decorative, I believe, rather than for any specific purpose. There's not much here,' she added, following as he wandered through into the not-quite circular room. Lewis prowled about the room, clearly intrigued by the old tower, eyeing the dusty table with its carved initials, and stopping to study the bulging wall with its plastic sheeting and scaffolding poles. 'Not much of a design aesthetic, is it? I guess it was meant to be admired from the outside rather than occupied. Though I have a sneaking suspicion my great-uncle Maurice used to come out here to be alone.'

'Yes,' he agreed, turning to look at the table again.

'Still, I can't believe he would have used it at this time of year.' She shivered. 'This place is like a meat locker.'

'A summer hideout, then.'

'Maybe.' Frowning, she laid a hand on the thick stone wall. It was cold to the touch. 'Though I doubt much heat ever gets through these stones. It must be chilly in here even at the height of summer.' She shifted uncomfortably. 'Come on, let's go. My feet are like blocks of ice.'

'Wait.' Coming after her through the passageway, Lewis stood close in the gloomy, narrow area behind the entrance door. 'I've got some rather bad news, I'm afraid.'

Something in his voice warned her...

'What... What is it?'

'It's Mrs Hepley, the landlady at The Silversmiths' Arms.' He hesitated. 'She was found dead this morning.'

Stella didn't know what to say. She tried to read his expression but it was too dark. 'I don't understand/ Dead? How? You mean, a... a heart attack or something?' She recalled the police car and ambulance outside the pub earlier, and the small crowd of onlookers. 'An accident?'

'They're not sure yet,' Lewis said slowly. 'But a friend of mine works for the police. Forensics. He told me, strictly off the record, that it looks like poison.'

'Suicide, you mean?' Stella couldn't believe it.

But he shook his head. 'Apparently, there was extensive bruising to her jaw and upper arms. My friend said the poison was administered *forcibly*.'

'Oh my God!'

'She was murdered, in other words.' His voice was grave. 'There's one other thing... The police want to speak to you, Stella. As soon as possible.'

After Stella had attended the police headquarters at Bodmin to be formally interviewed, Lewis drove her back to Black Rock Hall, listening in silence as she described the traumatic experience of being suspected of murder. Dusk was falling as they left the small mid-Cornwall town, and by the time they were halfway across the desolate moors, darkness had shrouded the tough, rolling landscape of granite outcrops and grasslands dotted with sheep and the occasional wild pony.

'They think *I* did it,' she kept saying, still as shocked and breathless as she had been when the police officer asked for her whereabouts that morning. 'Can you believe it? As if I could ever... I mean, what possible bloody motive...? Oh, I feel sick.' She lowered the car window, dragging the fresh Cornish air deep into her lungs. 'Sorry, I'm just ranting now, aren't I? And you've been so good, so patient with me. I shouldn't have involved you. And to have driven me all the way to Bodmin...'

'You don't have a car,' he pointed out.

'Yes, but I could have got a taxi. Or the bus.' Stella shook her head, trying to calm down, but her pulse was still racing after the three-hour interview they'd subjected her to. 'It's all because we had that row, you see, and Mrs Hepley slapped me in front of all those witnesses in the pub. Then she's found dead and everyone's like, oh, it *must* be that awful woman from London who killed her. The Cossentine heir. Because, you know... it's poison. So it must have been me, right? Celeste's granddaughter, carrying on the long-established family tradition of murdering people they disagree with.'

He slowed for a tight corner, his eyes on the dark road ahead. 'Let it all out, Stella, that's the spirit. No sense bottling it up.'

'You don't think I killed her too, do you? Because if so –' she began hotly, but he shook his head.

'Don't be ridiculous.' He glanced at her sideways, his eyes narrowed. 'I know it wasn't you. The real question is, who would have wanted to kill a pub landlady? As I understand it, most people are murdered by someone they know well. Like a partner or family member. But from what I've heard, her husband's alibi is watertight. He was in Bideford in North Devon all morning, visiting his mother at a care home. Drove up there first thing. Came back to open up the pub for the lunchtime crowd only to find Mrs Hepley on the floor in the kitchen, already dead.'

'And I suppose he was seen by dozens of people during this visit.'

'I'm afraid so. But you have an alibi too. You were in Bude this morning, weren't you? Seeing your solicitor, you said.'

'Yes, thank God. Otherwise, I'd be in serious trouble, wouldn't I?' She chewed on her lip, remembering what the police officer who'd interviewed her had said about timings. 'I took a taxi back. But unfortunately, on the way in, it was good weather, so I walked to the bus stop in West Pol. Apparently, it's just possible I could have snuck into the pub on my way to catch the bus, taken about thirty seconds to murder Mrs Hepley, and then gone on my merry way as though nothing had happened, unseen by any village residents.' She ran a hand across her face, trembling. 'They took my fingerprints and a DNA swab. If they can match any of those to the crime scene...'

'They won't.'

'But if they do, if for some reason...' she burst out, and then stopped, her fists clenched hard. 'I'm being totally paranoid, I know. But I can't stop thinking about Bruno.'

'The musician who's obsessed with you?'

'Did I say he was a musician?' She looked at him, surprised. He shrugged, his face impassive, lit up by the dashboard lights. 'But yes, him. I'm not saying Bruno would frame me for murder as revenge for being dumped. I don't think he's that mad or that calculating. But he could have done it by accident, perhaps, and that might incriminate me, simply by association.'

'I thought he was in London.'

Briefly, she explained about his phone calls and texts. 'I can't help wondering if he came down to Cornwall, maybe yesterday, maybe overnight, and went to the pub to find me. Only I wasn't there. And maybe he got into an argument with Mrs Hepley, and next thing he's murdering her...'

'With the poison he kept handy in his pocket?'

They had passed through West Pol several minutes before, the pub closed up and dark, and were fast approaching the turn to Black Rock Hall.

She drew a shaky breath. 'Yes, that part of the puzzle doesn't quite fit. But maybe it was rat poison and she already had it lying around the place. I don't know... I'm grasping at straws here.'

'Did you tell the police about Bruno?'

'Of course, I'm not an idiot. I showed them his texts and the photo he sent me of Black Rock Beach.'

He had been smiling at the 'I'm not an idiot,' comment, but his brows tugged together sharply at this. 'He sent you a photo of the *beach*? So he's definitely here in Cornwall, then?'

'I think it was just a photo he'd pinched off the internet. But he could be here, yes. I gave them his details, so I guess they'll be checking his alibi too.' She laughed humourlessly. 'Oh, to be a fly on the wall…'

They had reached the entrance to Black Rock Hall and he slowed to a stop, gazing at the lit-up front windows.

'Looks like Walter is at home,' he murmured, and glanced at her. 'Want me to come in? Check there are no strange men lurking in the shadows?'

His glimmering smile told her there was more to the question than a quick check of the house interior. Stella was tempted to say yes, but this really wasn't a good time to be complicating her life with a new relationship.

Reluctantly, she shook her head. 'Thanks, but I'll manage. Anyway, I'm just going to crash. I badly need some sleep.' She leant across to kiss him, and his hand came up to caress her cheek. 'I'll be in touch.'

'Goodnight, Stella,' he said softly, watching her get out. 'Sleep tight.'

CHAPTER
THIRTY-TWO

Stoke Newington, May 1981

'Mum, will you tell me about your family?' Isabella asked one day, out of the blue, and Celeste froze, unsure what to say. Her daughter was lying on the sofa in their flat, looking through Danny's old photograph album. She rarely left the flat during the daytime now, though was frequently gone all evening, returning in the early hours, drunken and glassy-eyed. But at least she didn't seem to be addicted to drugs these days, which gave Celeste hope for the future. 'You're always talking about Dad's mum, and that's okay, she sounds like a mad old bird. But I want to hear about *your* parents and what happened to them. Where did you live? Are any of your family still alive?'

'I'm an orphan, you know that.' Alarmed, Celeste automatically fell back on Esther's history, on the lies she'd told everyone else about her past. She put down the knitting she'd been working on. 'I lost my parents when I was young. I told you about the boating accident.'

'Yeah, but it's always just like, *I'm an orphan*, and that's it. Like there was no before or after the accident.' Languorous in a pale blue kaftan, her daughter threw the photo album to the floor and lit a cigarette. There was a speculative look on her face. 'You know, I told Sherlock about you once, and he said…'

'Oh, not Sherlock again.'

'Hush, that's all over, I know he was a dick. But he was smart too. He knew stuff.' Isabella blew a lazy smoke ring up into the air, watching it disintegrate. 'He thought you were lying about the whole orphan thing.' Her gaze slid to Celeste's face. 'Were you?'

'Don't be ridiculous. Why would I lie?' Averting her face, she got up to put away her knitting, uncomfortable under her daughter's gaze.

All her instincts warned her against telling Isabella who she really was, about Black Rock Hall and the murders, and her uncle Maurice. The girl wouldn't be content with simply hearing about the Cossentine fortune. Too thrilled to find herself proved 'special' at last, Isabella would never rest until she had made a claim on the estate, with all the publicity that would entail, and the thought of facing her brother again filled

Celeste with creeping dread.

The older she became, the more convinced she was that her brother had been the murderer. Once, she'd feared she herself might have done it, acting out some terrible unconscious desire during her blackout that evening. But now she suspected that Maurice had struck her from behind, dragged her into the study, and then taken his appalling revenge on the family. *You'll never see me again after tonight.* Perhaps he'd originally planned to disappear afterwards, leaving her to take the blame, but her departure had made that impossible. All she knew was that Maurice would never stop hunting for the one surviving relative who could testify he had *not* been locked in his room at the time of the murders, a lie that had allowed him to escape the noose.

No, she must not endanger both herself and Isabella by admitting her true heritage, knowing her daughter would immediately seek out her cold, calculating uncle.

'Okay, so did your parents leave you anything?' Isabella demanded.

'Sorry?'

'To remember them by. A keepsake or an heirloom. Like Dad's mum left him those awful Toby jugs.'

Celeste hesitated, slowly closing the lid of her knitting chest. 'As a matter of fact...' Her heart thumped, but she took a deep breath and turned with a smile. 'My mother did leave me one thing. A silver ring.'

Isabella sat up and swung her legs off the sofa, her face glowing, eyes bright with curiosity. 'Valuable?'

'Very,' she admitted, and instantly regretted it, seeing the look on her daughter's face. 'That's why I don't wear it. I'm too afraid of losing it.'

'What's the point of having a valuable piece of jewellery and not wearing it?' Isabella was dismissive of her caution. 'Jewellery is about public show. It's a way of wearing your wealth, showing people how much you're worth.'

'I'm not interested in proving my worth like that.' She looked pointedly at the photograph album. 'Remember to put that away, won't you?'

Isabella rolled her eyes but dutifully replaced the photograph album on the shelf where it was kept. 'Show me this ring?' she asked, her voice light and teasing. 'I'd love to try it on, see if it fits.'

'Maybe another time.'

But Isabella kept on at her for days afterwards, even dragging Danny into the argument. 'Dad, why don't you ask Mum to put on her ring? I bet she'd look beautiful wearing it.'

'She's beautiful now.' Danny smiled at Celeste across the dinner table.

'Ugh, please.' Isabella toyed with her food, her expression sulky. 'I've never even seen this ring. Which is pretty unfair as I'm your only daughter, so I'm going to inherit it when... You know, one day.' She looked at Celeste from under long, mascara-thickened lashes. 'At least tell me something about it. What does it look like? Does it have any markings?'

The room was too hot, Celeste thought. Pushing away her dinner plate, she went to open the window and the small flat filled with the sounds of evening traffic and passers-by in the busy London street below. The smell of cooking drifted up on the warm summer air from the restaurants and takeaways on their block.

'Let's not talk about it,' she begged Isabella.

'But what's the big secret?' Isabella glared at her. 'Why can't I *see* it? Or did you just make it up? Maybe Sherlock was right and everything you tell me is a lie.'

'Izzy, for God's sake...' Danny said uneasily. 'Leave your mother alone.'

But Celeste couldn't bear it any longer, this long-drawn-out needling inquisition. She went through into her bedroom, scrabbled in her bottom drawer for her ornate box of precious objects, removed the ring, and took it into the other room.

'There,' she said breathlessly, and half threw the ring at Isabella, her hands trembling. 'You wanted to see it. Take a good long look. And then give it back to me.'

Her daughter had caught the ring with both hands and now opened her palm to reveal the silver ring lying there. Her eyes grew wide. 'Wow, it's heavier than I thought it would be. It must be real silver.' She turned it over, spotting the inscription inside the ring. '*Amor aeternus*. What does that mean?'

'It's Latin,' Celeste said. 'It means… loving someone forever, so that even time can't take that away from you.'

Isabella slipped the ring onto her wedding finger, ignoring Celeste's instinctive protest. 'It fits me perfectly,' she said with satisfaction, and lifted her hand, turning it this way and that, seeming to enjoy the pale sheen of the silver on her finger. 'And it's worth a lot of money?'

'It's worth more than money to me,' Celeste told her quietly, and held out her hand. 'Now give it back.'

'Why, so you can chuck it back into some dark corner? It needs to be worn. It *wants* to be worn. Can't you see that?' Isabella admired the ring again, and then smiled sunnily at them both. 'It's mine now.'

'Isabella,' Danny said, his gaze on Celeste's face. 'That's not funny. You heard your mother. Give it back.'

'Why? She never wears it, and it's going to be mine in the end, anyway. Why not let me have it now, while I'm still young enough to show it off at parties?'

'That's enough,' Danny said sharply, and leant across the table, trying to grab Isabella's hand, but she jumped up and danced about the room, laughing and spinning around, her long hair flying everywhere, waving her hand in the air, the ring glinting.

'It's mine now,' she was saying, her mouth curved in a mocking smile. 'Boring old mums don't get to wear beautiful silver rings like this. It's a rule... or it ought to be!' She gurgled with laughter at Celeste's impotent attempts to catch her. 'Oh dear, too slow, poor old lady...'

'Give it back to me!' Celeste screamed, her face red, her whole body shaking, a pulse beating hard in her throat.

There was silence in the room.

Isabella had stopped her mad, foolish dance and was now staring at Celeste with her mouth open. Then her face twisted and contorted to a snarling grimace, as though the laughter had been nothing but a mask and she had ripped it off.

'Here, take it,' she spat, and dragging the ring off her finger, threw it hard at Celeste. 'I bet it was stolen, anyway. Why else hide it away all these years and refuse to show anyone?'

'It wasn't stolen,' Danny insisted, though his voice lacked conviction. 'Apologise to your mother at once. You could have hurt her.'

'I'm not going to apologise.' Isabella folded her

arms across her chest, indignant. 'She's the one who yelled, not me.'

'Only because you wouldn't give it b-back,' Celeste stammered, her eyes brimming with tears, torn between guilt and relief at getting the silver ring back. She held it in one fist, clenched so tight it cut into the tender skin of her palm, but the pain was welcome. It was a reminder of the things she had done, the lies she had told, the terrifying charade of her life…

'Well, you've got your precious bloody ring back now. So you can stop with the crocodile tears.' Isabella shook her head, her voice heavy with contempt. 'I hope to God I never end up like you, Mum. You're nothing but a liar and a thief. And now I know your dirty little secret.'

'I think you should go out for a few hours,' Danny told her, his voice colder than Celeste had ever heard it. 'Clear your head.'

Isabella glared at him too but didn't refuse, grabbing up her handbag and slamming out of the flat.

Danny came round to hold Celeste in his arms, letting her cry against his chest. 'It's okay, it's over now,' he said soothingly, stroking her hair.

'I'm sorry I shouted.'

'Good Lord, don't apologise. She deserved it. The way she behaved… Where did we go wrong with her? Sometimes I can't believe she's our daughter.'

'You think she's a changeling? That some bad fairy swapped her for our real child?'

He gave a hollow laugh. 'Something like that.' He kissed her forehead but he sounded shaken. 'But we can't go on like this. I'm going to ask her to move out.'

'Oh, no, no.' Celeste was horrified, staring up at him, the tears starting again. 'I know she's d-difficult. But it was my fault this time. I shouldn't have raised my voice to her.'

'For God's sake –'

'Isabella's not strong enough to live on her own. Look what happened last time. It would be disastrous. Please, Danny.'

He closed his eyes briefly but nodded. 'All right. To keep you happy.'

'Thank you.'

'You know,' he said after a moment, 'it's our wedding anniversary tomorrow. I only realised this morning. Thirty-five years.'

'Thirty-five years,' she breathed, staring up at him in wonder.

'I've treasured every minute of them.' Gently, he picked up the silver ring from her open palm and examined it thoughtfully. 'We should have a slap-up meal in the West End to celebrate. Take in a show afterwards. What do you say?'

'Sounds lovely.'

'And I wondered about having something new engraved on this old thing, as an anniversary present. Something to make the ring *yours*, not theirs.' He was talking about her family, of course. 'How about your initials?'

She stilled. 'I can't… It would be EF for Esther Ffoulds. I can't be Esther on the family ring.' She shook her head. 'It wouldn't be right.'

'CF, then?' He paused. 'Or CC… for Celeste Cossentine.'

She caught her breath. 'You'd do that? For me?'

'Of course.' Danny smoothed back her hair and kissed her gently on the lips. 'I married a woman of mystery and I'm proud of that. Most men have such dull wives… But I have you, my darling CC.' His mouth twisted in a lopsided smile. 'Even if I can never tell anyone who you really are.'

A few months later, Celeste got up as usual after Danny had gone to work to find her daughter's bedroom empty and a note taped to her dressing table mirror.

Gone to America. Time to grow up. Don't bother looking for me. Izzie x

She touched the back of her hand to the pillowcase and it was still warm, a single strand of dark hair lying across it.

Her whole body shaking, Celeste curled into a tight ball on her daughter's bed and wept into that pillow until she had no more tears left. Only emptiness and the bitter ache of loss inside her.

'Perhaps it's for the best,' Danny said when he

came home from work, but she saw the look in his eyes and knew he was devastated too.

However much pain she caused them, Isabella was still their only child, and they would both love and adore her forever.

Later, urged by some awful premonition, Celeste went to her drawer in the bedroom and scrabbled through the ornate little box where she kept her treasures.

The silver ring was gone.

Years went by and Isabella never once got in touch to tell them where she was and what she was doing. Celeste looked in the mirror every day, watching herself aging, and wondered where she'd gone wrong with her beautiful daughter, once the light of their lives. But at least she and Danny still had each other, still as deeply in love as the day they'd married back in the Forties. Sometimes she feared her daughter must be dead, the silence was so profound. Other times she hoped Isabella had found some joy in her life, perhaps a good man to look after her, and that was why she spared no thought for their feelings. That thought gave her comfort, so she clung to it and shut out the colder voices in her head...

Danny, who had never smoked a cigarette in his life, developed a cough in his mid-sixties, soon after he'd retired from the railways. Nothing much to worry about, Celeste thought, but the cough grew more frequent, and came even in the summer months, when it couldn't be explained away as a common cold.

'It's just from when I was at work,' Danny grumbled, tapping his chest. 'All the lads smoked. We were often stuck underground together for hours, with me breathing in their smoke. A touch of bronchitis or emphysema, that's all this is. No need to fret.'

But she did fret. And nagged him for months to visit the doctor, who no longer looked twelve, but almost grown-up. The doctor listened to his chest and was not reassuring. Danny was sent for a dizzying array of tests at the hospital, to which he insisted on going alone, and returned from an appointment one day with a dazed look.

'Cancer,' he said shortly. 'In the lung, and spreading.'

'Oh God, Danny.' Celeste clung to him, barely able to believe what she was hearing. That little cough? Lung cancer? 'But the doctors must be able to do something about it. What treatments did they offer you?'

'Nothing to be done, they said. It's just a question of time.' He coughed and swore under his breath. 'Never so much as lit up a cigarette. And I'm going to die of the smoker's disease. Funny old life, isn't it?'

'I refuse to believe it.' Celeste begged him to go back for a second opinion. 'There must be some medical trial you can join. Some experimental treatment. You read about them all the time in the newspapers.'

Reluctantly, he agreed to ask the doctors, and after some form-filling, was enrolled on an experimental treatment for end-stage lung cancer, to see if his life could be prolonged.

'No guarantees,' the doctors told them sombrely, explaining how it would work and what to expect by way of side-effects. 'And remember, this isn't a cure. It's just to see if we can give you more time.'

Danny dutifully followed the regime, which involved day-long treatments that left him sick and weary, and medications that seemed to do more harm than good some days. But the trial ended, and he was still alive, nearly fourteen months after his diagnosis.

'Still breathing,' he would joke, before going into one of his exhausting coughing fits.

'That's because you're the strongest man I know,' Celeste reassured him, though she was frightened by how thin and ashen faced he had become.

Two months after the medical trial had ended, early on a Tuesday morning when he was due for a check-up at the hospital, Celeste brought him a mug of tea in bed, drew back the curtains with a cheery, 'Good morning!' and turned to find her beloved husband sitting up dead against the pillows. He'd been sleeping in Isabella's old room for the past month, so as not to disturb her with his constant coughing and restlessness, and must have died some time during the night.

She knew at once that he was dead. She had seen enough dead people in her life not to be unsure.

Gently, she put the mug down on his bedside cabinet, tea slopping out as her hand shook. His digital alarm clock ticked through to a new minute with a loud click.

'Oh, Danny, no…' Bitter with grief, she sat next to him on the edge of the bed and stroked his cheek, his silvery hair, cupping his jaw, which was sagging, his mouth still open. 'My poor darling, my wonderful husband.'

She stayed there nearly an hour, holding his hand and weeping from time to time, telling him how much she loved him, and what a marvellous husband and father he'd been, how she could never have got through life without him by her side.

Then she stumbled downstairs to call the doctor, feeling very old and tired. It was a bright and chilly late December morning. Standing at the window, she looked down into the busy street with its criss-crossed displays of Christmas lights swaying in the breeze; she was waiting for someone to come and collect the body.

The poinsettias had wilted and would need

to be thrown out, she thought, fingering them vaguely.

It would be horrible, forced to bury her husband without Isabella there to mourn him. But she had no idea where their daughter was.

Somehow, she got through it all, the dreary and heart-breaking business of sorting out Danny's affairs and organising the funeral. The church was packed the day they buried him; neither of them had been churchgoers, but they'd made many friends in Stoke Newington over the years, and all Danny's old work mates were there to see him off.

Celeste, having wept and struggled for days, endured the funeral dry-eyed, but declined to get up and give the eulogy, leaving that to one of his oldest friends instead, a man who'd served with him during the war and later came to visit now and then. She knew she could not have kept herself composed in front of so many people; she was not used to being the centre of attention, always having preferred to melt into the background and let Danny do all the talking and socialising. She'd suggested a few things that his friend could mention about their life together in Stoke Newington, and had organised the order of service and the church flowers, but now that the terrible day had arrived at last, she was content simply to listen and let the words of the eulogy flow over her.

She had done everything that was proper and needful for her husband. Now all that remained was for her to let him go...

Back at the flat after the funeral, the wake over and everyone having finally said their goodbyes and gone home, Celeste sat on her own with a bottle of wine and toasted the photograph on the mantel: her and Danny on their thirty-fifth wedding anniversary, dining together in a local restaurant.

'I miss you so much, darling,' she whispered, and broke down at last, falling to her knees, unable to stop crying. 'Tell me, what am I supposed to do now?'

But there was no answer. Only silence.

'You've spoilt everything.' Sobbing, she knocked a glass of red wine flying; it spilt extravagantly across the cream rug. She didn't care. Her whole life was empty, everything was finished and she was alone, so what did it matter? 'How dare you do this to me? How could you?'

An old madness seemed to take hold of her brain, like a worm burrowing, and her body responded, turning on itself until she was lying on the floor, clawing at her hair, her cheek wet with tears.

'How the hell am I ever going to live *without you*? God, Danny, I can't do this. I swear I can't, I simply can't...'

CHAPTER THIRTY-THREE

After leaving her on tenterhooks for days, the police finally got in touch to say they would not be taking the matter any further, but she should let them know if she was planning on leaving the duchy at any point. Relieved beyond measure, she asked tentatively about Bruno, but hit a brick wall there. Sounding cagey, the police officer refused to discuss that with her, and rang off, additionally warning her not to speak to the newspapers about the case as their enquiries were still ongoing and confidential.

She texted Lewis, wishing to share the good news with someone.

I'm off the hook. No idea about Bruno yet though.

He didn't reply.

Disappointed by his silence, she kept checking her phone for several hours after sending the message and experiencing the same slightly desolate shock each time she found the screen blank.

She had to warn herself off getting too involved with Lewis. Yes, he was attractive and she enjoyed his company. But this was hardly the time to be indulging in a new love affair and, besides, she knew so little about him. Plunging into a relationship with Bruno too soon, swayed by his charming smile and love of music, had taught her to be cautious. She was determined never to be that stupid again.

Once her claim on the estate had been confirmed in writing by Mr Hardcastle, Stella wrangled the key to the exhibition from Walter with surprising ease. 'Of course,' the curator said with a warm smile, fetching it for her at once. 'Would you like me to guide you around again?'

'Thank you, but I'd prefer an informal wander through the rooms,' she told him politely. 'I didn't take it all in last time. Since I'm probably going to be spending a great deal of time here in future, I thought it might be a good idea to really get to grips with my family history.'

'An excellent idea! I'll be in the library if you need me.'

The Murder Mystery Exhibition lay in gloom, despite the chilly autumnal light outside. She flicked on the lights and began her slow journey through the series of 'Rooms,' studying the information boards, old photographs and artifacts in glass cases with far more care this time around.

She spent a long time in the room devoted to her grandmother, Miss Celeste Cossentine. There were some charming old photographs of her as a child, while the information board listed various theories as to why she had disappeared and where she had gone. A male servant's account bore witness to the fact that Celeste had been taken unwell that afternoon, having suffered one of her 'funny turns,' and had been recovering in her bedroom at the time of the murders. Something about the account struck a jarring note with her, though.

Shortly before the gong, I was sent to accompany Miss Celeste down to the dinner party, where her wedding date was due to be announced. But she refused to leave her room, claiming she was too unwell. This was not unusual, her being a most fragile young lady and prone to mental disorder. So I left her there and continued with my duties in another part of the house. After the murders had been discovered, I returned to her room to let Miss Celeste know what had happened, as I feared for the balance of her mind if she should stumble upon their corpses without warning. Unfortunately, her room was empty, and although we searched for some hours, along with the police, we were unable to find her anywhere in the house or grounds.

The servant, Jeffrey, was described as being a 'footman-in-training' and also the cook's son. This, she realised, made him brother to the serving girl, Becky, whom several witness statements singled out as key to the day's events.

Mrs Hepley had told her this story, Stella realised, frowning as she read the housekeeper's testimony. That same day, Becky had been assaulted by the oldest son of the family. Some witnesses claimed it was a rape, others that she was simply mauled about by Sebastian Cossentine and left distraught. The housekeeper's account merely said, *I was unable to get any sense out of the girl, for she was weeping and clearly distressed, but her clothing was torn and there was bruising to her upper arms. Later, I heard young Master Maurice in an altercation with his eldest brother Sebastian regarding this assault, after which Mr Cossentine and other senior members of the family inflicted some punishment on the young man for speaking out of turn.*

Following the assault, Becky had been summarily dismissed from the Cossentine's employ, and the butler – known as 'Priddy' – speculated in his own court testimony that this injustice might have caused the cook to take violent action.

Mrs Dunn, the Cornishwoman in charge of the kitchens at Black Rock Hall, often displayed an intemperate, ill-disciplined nature, and I frequently suspected her of drinking on duty. When her daughter Becky came into the servants' quarters that morning, complaining that Mr Sebastian had made improper advances to her, Mrs Dunn was most vocal against her employers. She made various threats against the Cossentines and would have the police called, which I plainly told her was not going to happen without proper evidence that anything untoward had occurred. This infuriated her. She shrieked so loudly, I had to order her to desist. If the cook did tip poison into the soup that night, it would not surprise me. I'm not saying she did, mind you. Only that it would not surprise me.

The clue board displayed a police photograph of a ripped dress under the words: WAS BECKY'S ASSAULT THE MOTIVE FOR THESE MURDERS?

On a separate display, true crime theorists speculated that Celeste was more likely the murderer, rather than the cook, and that was why she'd fled that night, unable to face her guilt. An alternative hypothesis was that, as a vulnerable young woman with mental health issues, Celeste had been so traumatised by the sight of her entire family dead at the dinner table, she'd completely blanked it out and wandered away in a state of amnesia, never to be remember her real name again.

Stella lingered over that display, struck by a sudden memory. 'My father put me in an asylum, you know,' Gran had blurted out once, fury in her face, when Stella had suffered anxiety attacks as a teen and was prescribed medication for a few months. 'After I was allowed home, I lived in abject fear of being sent back there. He used to hold that threat over my head to make me obey him, while the vile medication he insisted on kept me in the most horrific dream state. But then he and my mother died, of course. In a... a boating accident, like I told you. So I was free.' Laughing awkwardly, Gran had added in a more light-hearted way, 'Funny the things you remember.'

With hindsight, it was clear that Celeste had been hiding something from her. But that didn't make her guilty. Stella simply couldn't believe her sweet, funny and loving grandmother could have poisoned her own family. Still, they did say that poison was a woman's weapon, and perhaps under the influence of some psychotic, hallucination-inducing drug...

Becky's own testimony in court was simple. *Mr Sebastian laid hands upon me and did wrong things to me what I don't want to talk about. Master Maurice stood up for me though. He said his brother deserved to be punished for what he done. But I know he didn't poison nobody, for he was beaten and locked in his room the whole evening for taking my part, and my mother is innocent too, and I can prove it. After Mrs Cossentine gave me my notice, Mother brought me down and had me sit by her during dinner service, as I was weeping so hard. I never saw her put nothing in that soup but what was supposed to be there, and I had a bowl of it myself before the*

tureen left the kitchen, and I never died. So whatever
was put in that soup, I swear to God it weren't my
poor mother put it there.

But it seemed the judge laid little store by
Becky's biased testimony, for he later instructed
the jury to recall in their deliberations whose
daughter she was and what had happened to her
that day.

Eventually, Stella came to the room devoted to
Maurice, the youngest son and only male survivor
of the 1939 massacre.

Last time, Walter had steered her through this
room at speed, perhaps in a hurry to be elsewhere.
Now, she was able to take everything in without
interference. She studied the display of blown-
up photographs: Maurice as a young man with
his family before the killings, handsome and
unsmiling, and several more from later years,
such as when he sold the family silver business
in the sixties, and as an old man too, standing in
front of the folly, wearing a flat cap and wellies,
and leaning on a stick.

Her great-uncle didn't look much like a killer.
But there was certainly something unusual about
him. A hint of darkness.

One thing that struck her about the testimony
he gave to police in the immediate aftermath of
the murders was his 'alibi,' if it could be called
that.

'Papa had locked me in my bedroom that evening

as a punishment for fighting,' his statement read, '*and told me I was to miss dinner. I was bored so began practising my violin. In consequence, I wasn't able to hear anything from downstairs. In fact, I didn't know anything was wrong until Jeffrey, one of the servants, came up later to tell me what had happened and let me out of my room to speak to the police. I was very much shocked and sickened by what I saw, but I swear I had nothing to do with it and have no idea how it happened.*'

'In consequence' seemed a very formal turn of phrase for a sixteen-year-old. But he'd grown up in a wealthy, cultured family and this had been the thirties. Perhaps that had been his habitual way of speaking. But it did sound rather stilted.

The information board that accompanied the photographs also contained a further witness statement from Jeffrey, who had also described being sent to collect Celeste in the previous room.

'*There was a row between young Maurice and his older brother, Mr Sebastian. I'm not sure what it was over, but I think it was to do with some disrespect Mr Sebastian had given the cook's daughter, Becky. It was a nasty fight and Master Maurice's jaw was badly bruised, maybe even broken. Master Maurice was confined to his room and told to forfeit dinner as a punishment for fighting.*'

Jeffrey claimed that he had been instructed to lock Maurice in his room and had kept the key safe all evening. '*Nobody could have entered or left that room while I had the key,'* he concluded.

This vital evidence had helped clear Maurice's name.

Stella frowned. Maurice had heard nothing from below because he was practising his violin? And how on earth could he have done that *with a suspected broken jaw*? Given that the correct playing position for a violin was for it to be balanced between chin and shoulder blade, trying to achieve this with a broken jaw would have been, in her judgement as a professional violinist, physically impossible.

Wandering through the rest of the exhibition, she hunted through the various statements, but found no further reference to the broken jaw suffered by Maurice. The story appeared to have been accepted without question. But then, a violin-playing sixteen-year-old locked in his bedroom as a punishment would never have been the police's prime suspect for what was essentially a mass murder.

There was a photograph of a middle-aged Maurice playing the violin in the music room at the hall. Beneath it was a button. PRESS TO HEAR A RECORDING OF MAURICE PLAYING THE VIOLIN.

She pressed it, curious.

The faint, crackling strains of a violin broke the silence, sounding across the years.

It was a few bars from the same tune she

had heard that first day at Black Rock Hall, drifting down from the shadows of the first-floor landing. The same one her grandmother used to hum under her breath, and which she frequently requested Stella to play on her own violin... Vaughan Williams' *The Lark Ascending*.

As the brief recording came to an end, something creaked behind her in the empty exhibition space. It sounded like a door opening. Or maybe closing.

Stella turned, frowning. 'Hello?' She raised her voice. 'Walter? I'm in Room Five.'

There was no reply.

After a moment, hearing nothing more, she moved on through the rooms of the exhibition, passing hurriedly through the mock-up of the hanging, until she came again to Room Ten, the dining room, the scene of the murders.

This time, avoiding the fixed glassy stare of the waxworks around the table, she focused instead on the information boards, especially the one that listed who everyone was and why they had been there that evening.

Sir Oliver Gliddon was a wealthy local landowner and engaged to Miss Celeste, the youngest daughter of the family, whose absence the night of the murders has remained one of the great mysteries of this case. Celeste had suffered from severe anxiety for years and was on strong medication that summer, to control what one servant described as 'fits and starts'.

Perhaps she ran away that night because she didn't wish to marry Sir Oliver, and so escaped being poisoned, purely by chance. Or maybe she was shocked into flight by the awful sight of all those dead bodies. But some of those who insist the cook was innocent of this crime still believe that Celeste herself was the killer, and that she murdered her family after a violent row with her parents earlier that day.

All we know for sure is that young Miss Celeste was never seen nor heard of again after that fateful night. So, while choosing your murderer, remember to ask yourself, WHAT HAPPENED TO CELESTE?

She became Esther Ffoulds and married my grandfather, Stella thought, and was about to leave the dim horror of Room Ten when a final sepia-tinted photograph at the bottom of the display caught her eye.

It was a holiday snap – a beach party, pre-murder, with most of the Cossentine family in attendance, some seated on blankets on the beach, the older members sitting upright on chairs carried down by the servants, no doubt, who all stood in uniform on the periphery of the shot. All except for one young man in livery, stooping to talk to a teenage boy seated on a seaweed-strewn rock. Taking an order for cream tea, perhaps?

'Yes, sir,' she imagined the servant saying in a

wooden voice. 'At once, sir. Whatever sir desires.'

The teenager on the rock was Maurice, she was sure of it. And he was smiling up at the young man – the only time she'd ever seen him smile in a photograph – with a shy expression.

The lights went out.

Stella gasped inadvertently, and then froze, her hand on the doorway. Her heart thumped hard in the silence that followed, so loud it was all she could hear. Then she caught a soft shuffling... As though someone were walking through the exhibition towards Room Ten.

Using the torch app on her phone, she tiptoed through the doorway and into the final space where the silver ring was displayed. It gleamed there, nestling on velvet, the glass case reflecting her frightened face in the torchlight. The huge photograph of her grandmother as a young woman watched as she passed beneath. Beyond the case, she could see the metal turnstile that led to the exit and daylight.

Somewhere behind her, the strains of violin music rose sweet and clear. The long-dead Maurice, playing *The Lark Ascending*.

Logic told her it was somebody trying to frighten her, and that she ought to stay where she was and confront them. But as the violin played on, eerie and otherworldly in that dark, musty-smelling space, the memory of those waxworks around the dining table came back to haunt her, and fear and superstition took the place of logic.

Suddenly, she couldn't bear the smothering darkness all around her and bolted for the exit, gasping and scrabbling in her panic to get out, and emerged, blinking and thankful, into the first light spots of rain...

'Stella?'

She looked round sharply to find Walter standing a few feet away on the lawn, staring at her in surprise. 'Hello... Where did you come from?'

'The house,' he said blankly, and held out two letters. 'The post just came. This is for you.'

She took it. From the solicitor, by the look of the frank.

'Are you all right?' He was looking over her shoulder at the old stable block. 'Was there a problem?'

'The lights went out,' she said, 'while I was still going around the exhibition. So yes, you could say that.'

'That does happen occasionally. The lights are on a timer, connected to a motion sensor. If it doesn't detect any motion, after a certain amount of time the lights cut out.'

'And does the violin music play by itself what that happens?"

Walter's gaze returned to her face. He looked shaken. 'I beg your pardon?'

But she already regretted having said so much.

She didn't want him thinking she was losing her grip on reality. 'It doesn't matter.' She handed him back the key. 'I left the exhibition unlocked. Sorry, do you mind doing the honours for me?' She couldn't face going back to shut the place up properly, and besides, she was still suspicious it was nothing to do with the lights being on a timer switch. 'By the way,' she added on impulse, 'I'd like the silver ring.'

'But it's on display. Part of the exhibition.'

'It belongs to me though, doesn't it?'

Walter hesitated so long she thought he might not answer. Then he nodded. 'Of course.'

'Then could you release it from that glass case and let me have it? That's the Cossentine family ring, and it's high time one of us actually wore it. We can always have a copy made for the display case.' The silver had not been worked so delicately and beautifully into a ring only to be hidden away for years or imprisoned behind glass to be ogled by curious strangers. She was sure too that her grandmother would have approved. 'Look, I need some fresh air. I've not been down to see the black rock on the beach yet. The cliff path is that way, isn't it?'

'Yes, but it's quite a steep descent, and there are no handrails. It's really not safe.' Walter sounded almost panicked as she turned away. 'And it's starting to rain.'

'Then I guess I'll get wet,' she threw back at

him.

No doubt Walter Whitely meant well, but the man was so fussy and over-protective, he was driving her mad. She had to get away and clear her head. Something had happened in the exhibition, something frightening and significant, but her head felt stuffed with cotton wool and she couldn't focus.

Maybe the black rock that had so fascinated her grandmother as a girl would work some magic on her too…

CHAPTER THIRTY-FOUR

The tedium of rooting through her late husband's paperwork became worth it when Celeste's search turned up a valid life insurance policy. Astonished and deeply grateful to Danny for having thought of how she would cope after his death, she laboriously filled out all the forms and sent off her claim. Early the following year, she received a cheque in the post for such an eyewatering sum that it would allow her to live comfortably for many years to come, while also receiving Danny's generous work pension as his widow.

Hating the silence of their empty flat, she took on volunteer work for a local charity, took dancing and watercolour classes, and played bridge some evenings with friends. Despite this whirl of activity, she often felt lonely and spent long hours staring out of her window at the grey rooftops of London, wondering where Isabella was and what she was doing.

As the years passed and she grew more accustomed to being a widow, Celeste sometimes dared think about Maurice again. He and the Cossentine estate were mentioned in the newspapers occasionally, and she would devour these articles with nervous excitement, thrown back into the past for a few dizzying hours. The few photographs she saw shocked her. The strong, handsome boy she remembered was so old, his face lined, silver hair thinning. But then she was old too. It was such a strange thought; she couldn't bear it. Maurice had sold the last of their London properties and retired, living full-time in Cornwall. Now and then he would place another advertisement, still offering money in return for information about her, and once she even spotted something in the personal columns. *MC to CC. Come home, the black rock misses you.* These attempts to reach out to her only fuelled her terrible fear of discovery. She would shudder and sit alone with the curtains closed for days on end, shutting out the world. Only once the fear had subsided was she able to venture forth again, head held high, Mrs Esther Ffoulds, née Sharpe, a perfectly unremarkable woman in her seventies.

More than ten years after losing her beloved husband, Celeste was flicking through the Evening Standard when she spotted a piece about missing persons tracked down by a London firm of investigators. On impulse, she took the plunge and instructed them to discover if her daughter was still living in England or if she had indeed emigrated to America.

Though even if they did find her, she knew it was a hopeless fantasy. Isabella had only ever come home when she'd run out of money. What possible use could Celeste be to her daughter now? She was an old age pensioner with a little put by for emergencies, but not enough to tempt a woman of extravagant tastes.

For some years, she heard nothing, despite getting regular updates from the investigators boasting about some new lead which ultimately led nowhere. Then, one icy winter's day, on trudging home from a trip to the local shops, Celeste found a letter waiting for her on the mat. From the envelope, she could tell it was from the private investigators.

She stared at it while unwinding her scarf and pulling off her gloves, not allowing herself to get too excited. 'They probably want more money,' she muttered to herself, putting on the kettle. 'For nothing much in return, as usual.'

It was over a year since the investigators had last been in touch, to ask for additional funds to keep the search alive. On that occasion, they'd given her the news that Isabella had definitely arrived in America but there was no record that she'd ever come back. Or not come back to England, at any rate. They'd asked for extra money to pay for a transatlantic investigation, which she had reluctantly sent.

Perhaps they'd found some trace of her daughter in America, she thought, a faint hope springing inside her. Waiting for the tea to brew, she began to read the letter and howled in grief before she'd even reached the end of the first paragraph.

'Isabella,' she cried, and slumped against the wall, moaning in distress.

It was the worst possible news.

Her beloved daughter, her precious Isabella, was dead. And the most sordid of deaths too. A drug overdose in a motel room, where she had checked in under a false name and paid cash.

She'd been dead over a year. With no passport or other identification on her at the time of her death, Isabella had been labelled a Jane Doe and buried under a number. The only clues to her identity had been an eye-witness statement that she might have had an English accent and had been calling herself 'Bella'. There had also been a CCTV photograph of her checking into the motel, paying with cash and using a false name.

The private investigators were now offering to put Celeste in touch with the British authorities so Isabella's body could be formally identified and repatriated.

But there was more.

'I… I have a granddaughter?' Celeste sank onto the sofa, the letter crumpled in her hand, barely able to believe what it contained.

The investigator who had flown out to America on Celeste's behalf had not yet managed to trace her young child, who'd apparently been left with friends in a trailer park while Isabella went travelling. Unfortunately, the friends had moved before the investigators could catch up with them, taking the little girl with her.

They couldn't confirm the child's name or age, or even if she existed at all. It was all hearsay at this point. But the investigators were hopeful of getting a fresh lead soon. All they needed to make their next big breakthrough was more money upfront.

And they were sure Celeste would be willing to pay.

In 2002, at the dawn of a new century, Celeste flew to New York, armed with a folder of official-looking papers and permits that would allow her to repatriate her orphaned granddaughter. The private investigators had finally tracked the little girl down to a state orphanage in New Jersey and, with the joint aid of the British and American authorities, it had been agreed that she should return with her only known living relative to England; Isabella having been an 'illegal alien' as they put it, the US officials seemed only too happy to part with her offspring.

America was a revelation to Celeste. Vast towering skyscrapers, bumper-to-bumper traffic, pancake stacks with maple syrup and eggs for breakfast, and a pace of life that left her dizzy. Yet it was exhilarating too, and she began to understand why Isabella had never come back to London, making this fast-moving country her home instead.

She checked into a motel in New Jersey and, with some trepidation, took a cab to a state facility the next morning to meet her granddaughter for the first time.

'Who are you? You a social worker?' the child asked on being shown into the office, looking Celeste up and down with undisguised hostility. 'You look pretty old.'

'I am pretty old,' Celeste agreed with a short laugh, her gaze eagerly devouring this thin, dark-haired little girl with the huge eyes who looked so brutally like her darling Isabella. 'I'm... eighty-five.' She had almost said eighty-one but caught herself in time, remembering to give Esther's age rather than her own. 'But that doesn't mean I can't look after you.'

'I don't need no social worker.'

'I'm not a social worker. Quite the opposite, in fact. You see, I...' With a hurried glance towards the heavy-set, badged official behind the desk,

Celeste drew up a chair and sat down beside the girl. Her pulse was racing. 'I'm your grandma.'

The girl stared at her, uncomprehending. 'I don't got no grandma.'

'Well, you have one now.' Celeste kept smiling but her heart clenched as she wondered what Isabella had told the child. Nothing, presumably. Or perhaps she'd lied and said her parents were both dead. That would fit Isabella's desire to break with the past, however much pain it caused everyone around her. 'And I'd very much like for you to come and live with me, if you're willing.'

The girl's eyes widened, but she said nothing.

'Perhaps you're thinking we haven't been properly introduced. And you're quite right. You shouldn't talk to strangers.' Again, Celeste glanced at the man who had organised this meeting – the director of the facility where her granddaughter was currently being housed, after being removed from her latest set of foster parents – but he wasn't even looking their way, his attention on his computer screen instead. She tapped her chest. 'I'm Esther Ffoulds. And what's your name, dear?'

Celeste knew her name, of course. But she wanted the girl to feel she had some power here, that she wasn't simply a human parcel being handed from one caretaker to another.

'Stella.'

'What a lovely name.' Celeste meant that

sincerely. 'Stella… It's from the Latin *stellum*, their word for star.'

The girl sat up, her gaze suddenly intent. 'What's Latin?'

'It's the old language of the Roman Empire. Your mother didn't tell you what your name meant?' But Isabella had never been taught Latin, of course. 'It means you were born under a lucky star.'

Stella's face had darkened at the word, 'mother'. She bent her head, picking at the desk with her fingernail. 'Mom's dead.'

'Yes, I know. I'm so sorry.' Tentatively, Celeste stretched out to pat her hand, but Stella snatched it out of reach, her eyes flashing.

'Don't touch me.' The girl jumped up, her chair scraping noisily. 'I wanna go back to the dorm. I don't need you.' Her voice was decided, her mutinous little face turned towards the man behind the desk. 'Hey, d'you hear me? We're done.'

Mr Shaw finally dragged his gaze away from the computer screen. 'Is that so, kid?' He didn't strike her as very friendly, Celeste thought, watching the man with dislike. 'I'm sorry to say you don't have a choice. Mrs Ffoulds is your next of kin, and that makes her your legal guardian until you hit the age of majority. Which is a long way off, Stella, seeing as how you're only…' He checked the screen again. 'Six years old.'

Stella glared at them both, arms folded tight.

Her face was flushed and tears were brimming in her eyes, but she didn't actually cry.

'Seven,' she hissed. 'I just had my birthday.'

'Okay, my bad, so you're seven years old,' he carried on in the same easy, smirking tone, 'but I tell you what. See this paperwork on my desk? It's been approved by the government. All that's left for me to do is stamp and sign this release form, and then I can hand you over into your grandmother's care.' He smiled at her benignly, though it was clear he was glad to be rid of her. 'I hope you remembered to pack everything, little lady. Because we won't be forwarding any lost toys to England.'

'*England*?' Shocked at last, Stella turned to stare at Celeste. 'I'm American. You can't do that. I won't go.' Her lower lip wobbled. 'I… I *refuse*.'

Mr Shaw's face hardened. 'You're not allowed to refuse, sweetheart. You know what a visa is? Well, your mom's visa expired years ago, so she was living here illegally when you were born. Plus, we have no clue who your father was. Therefore, you are officially required to go back to your mother's country of birth. Which is England.' Mr Shaw stamped the document in front of him, signed it with a flourish, and handed it over to Celeste. 'Good luck with her, Mrs Ffoulds.'

'Thank you.' Forcing herself to face the fury and terror warring in the little girl's face, Celeste held out her hand. 'Shall we go, Stella?'

Stella swore at her with real vehemence, making a rude gesture.

'That's not very polite, is it?' Mr Shaw seemed unshocked by her response though. Perhaps he had seen it all before. He got up ponderously to direct them out of his office and into the cold, grey corridor. 'Off you go now to England, Stella. Happy travels, we'll miss you.'

Gripping the bulging rucksack that contained all her granddaughter's worldly possessions, Celeste looked down at her once they'd passed beyond the wire-fenced enclosure of the state facility and gave the girl a wink. 'I'm rather glad to be out of there, aren't you?' she whispered.

Stella said nothing but her look was mutinous.

'I've booked us a nice big room at an airport hotel tonight,' Celeste pressed on, ushering her granddaughter toward the waiting cab she'd booked to take them directly to the airport, 'with dinner and breakfast too, then we'll be flying out to London tomorrow lunchtime.' Smiling, she held out a hand but Stella thrust hers into her jeans pockets, her face averted.

It was hard not to feel dismayed by this cold greeting. She'd spent months in negotiations with the authorities, arranging this wonderful moment. In all that time, she had never once considered that her little orphaned granddaughter might not want to leave the States.

'Do you like ice cream?' Celeste asked as she climbed slowly into the cab after Stella, her arthritic knee giving her trouble again. 'How about ice cream and jelly? You can have whatever you want for dinner tonight.'

Stella stared coldly out of the cab window, but her lip was trembling, a tear trickling down her cheek.

'Oh my dear,' Celeste said, trying to hug her but was shoved away. 'Please don't cry. Everything will be all right. I promise.'

It wasn't the perfect start she'd hoped for. Young Stella had clearly seen and experienced things most other kids would never have to, and there might be worse behaviour than a few swear words to come as a result. But she'd managed to find Isabella's daughter and was taking her home at last. That triumph must be enough to sustain her for now.

It had been decades since she'd had to cope with a rebellious young Isabella, and back then, she'd had Danny at her back, ready to step in and take over whenever she was exhausted. She was in her eighties now, for goodness' sake. Was she too long in the tooth to deal with yet another difficult child, and on her own this time? Only time would tell.

But time was a commodity of which she had precious little left.

Much to her surprise and delight though, the rebellious little girl she brought home from the States blossomed after less than a year under her roof into a polite and smiling, if somewhat over-earnest child. Stella, it turned out, was nothing like her mother. Not on the surface, at least. Though, no doubt because of the precarious existence she'd led for her first seven years on this earth, there were hints, now and then, of a deeper darkness inside her. A sadness too. And a creative sensibility that reminded her of Maurice at times. Her features too, so sharp and yet delicate, were very like Maurice's at the same age.

It occurred to her, watching Stella listen with rapt attention to classical music, which she had never heard before coming to live with Celeste, that she ought to invest in a musical education for the child.

Thankfully, an excellent violinist lived in the next building and he agreed to give the child lessons twice a week. Stella rapidly became his star pupil, and was soon passing examinations and winning musical competitions with apparent ease. She practised for long hours, which didn't please the neighbours particularly, but Celeste tried to make sure she never played her violin too late at night. The girl's academic work was strong too, which pleased Celeste tremendously, as Isabella had never been much interested in school except as a way of meeting boys. But Stella seemed oblivious to such concerns, almost never bringing friends home or mentioning boys.

They rubbed along together well, even though Celeste was beginning to feel her age, having to keep up with such a lively, young person. At the same time, she felt younger at heart now than since Danny had passed away, as Stella was forever using new words and introducing her to new things, like laptops and the internet. Celeste had used a computer a few times in her voluntary work, slowly and with misgiving. The internet was still a mystery to her though, and she wasn't sure she entirely trusted it. But seeing the world through a child's eyes was giving her a brand-new perspective on life.

Sometimes she brought up the past, trying to break through Stella's reserve.

The couple who'd been looking after her sent her into a drugstore, aged five, to steal something, and that was how she first came to be in care.

It took nearly a year for her to be connected to the Jane Doe who'd been found dead in a seedy New Jersey motel room, and more time yet for the private investigators to track her down. Stella had been fostered out in the meantime though had been removed from that home after some incident, the circumstances of which were never made clear to Celeste.

All she knew was that her young granddaughter had not been loved or looked after properly in years, and she intended to make up for that with endless hugs and kisses – however poorly tolerated at first – plus plenty of good food, good clothes, and good people around her.

'Do you remember your mother?' she asked one day, while Stella was trying to teach herself chess on the internet. It was a question she had asked before but received no reply. She was not ready to give up just yet though.

'A little,' Stella said after a long pause, and then moved one of her pieces on the screen.

'Did Isabella ever talk to you about me? Or about her father? She might have called him your grandad or grandfather.'

'Not really, no.'

Celeste sucked in a sharp breath and closed her eyes, an old agony striking deep in her heart. Had they treated Isabella so badly that she had decided to erase them completely from her life when she escaped to America? They had brought her up in a loving way and done their best to help their troubled daughter through her difficulties. So why shut them out in this way, even refusing to mention their existence to her own daughter?

The injustice was almost more than she could bear...

Stella asked in a small voice, 'You okay, Gran?' and Celeste opened her eyes to find the girl staring at her fixedly, a frown in those familiar dark eyes. 'Are you hurting?'

'No, goodness, no. I'm perfectly fine, thank you.' Parched, Celeste took a cautious sip of tea, which always seemed too hot for her these days. 'Mmm. Thirsty, that's all.' She waited a moment, hoping to make her enquiry seem more casual. 'Maybe your mother meant to tell you about us when you were older, only she…' She hesitated. 'That is, you…' And stopped, finding herself in a quagmire.

'Only she died before she could come back for me,' Stella finished for her in a matter-of-fact voice. She deliberated and then moved another piece on the electronic board, watching anxiously as the computer responded. 'Oh, shoot! Checkmate.' She slumped in her chair. 'I'm rubbish at chess. I never see it coming.'

The 'world wide web' was not something Celeste entirely understood, but she could see how useful it was for children in particular.

'Win or lose,' she remarked, after another sip of too-hot tea, 'you still learn something new every time you play.'

'I guess.' Stella began to close down the computer, not looking at Celeste. 'Mom did say something about you, actually.'

Don't get too excited, Celeste warned herself, while her hand played restlessly with the handle of her tea mug.

'Is that so?'

'I'd forgotten until you asked. But it was so long ago... Must have been just before she went away that last time, when she left me with Tina and Joel.' Her mouth flattened to a thin line, her distaste obvious as she recalled those dark days in the trailer park. 'I was only little.'

Studying her profile, Celeste wondered if what was coming would be good or bad. 'Yes?' she prompted her gently.

'Mom showed me something she had in a box in her handbag.' Stella hesitated. 'Something real special. But she told me it was a secret. Said I mustn't tell anyone about it.' The girl was looking at her anxiously. 'She made me swear it. Cross my heart and hope to die.'

Celeste understood, then. Her heart began to thud; she put a hand to her chest, breathing fast and shallow. 'Dearest,' she whispered unsteadily, 'could it have been... Was it a ring?'

Stella's eyes widened. 'You know about the ring?'

'Of course I do. In fact, it used to be my ring,' Celeste explained, picking her way carefully through the facts; she didn't want to make an enemy of her granddaughter too by saying the wrong thing. 'Isabella... Your mother... She took it with her when she left for America. I always wondered what happened to it.'

'She sold it,' Stella said flatly.

'Oh.' Celeste closed her eyes, feeling faint. 'You

know that for sure?'

'Yeah, Mom told me she was planning to sell it. That's why she showed it to me before she went away. She said it would have been mine one day, only she needed the cash.' Stella shrugged, but there was disappointment in her voice. 'Typical Mom, I guess. She let me see the ring, even put it on my finger... Then took it away and sold it.'

'Can you remember what it looked like?'

'Um, it was silver, and there were snakes coiled round it. Real old-fashioned. I don't remember much else, sorry.'

'No, it's I who should be sorry, Stella. For stirring up such bad memories with my questions.' Celeste hugged her granddaughter, tears in her eyes. 'She had problems, your mother. Poor Isabella. She tried hard but it sounds like she never managed to solve them.'

'Demons,' Stella offered indistinctly, and Celeste released her.

'Demons?'

'Mom used to say there were demons in her head and she couldn't fight them.' Stella got down from the table, looking more cheerful. 'Gran, can we make pancakes for tea again? With maple syrup and ice cream? They're my favourite. I'll make the batter and you can toss the pancakes, okay?'

Celeste agreed, smiling, but it was hard to hide her dismay. Isabella had sold the silver ring to buy drugs. Her lovely silver ring that had been in the family for generations and which she had carried safely through the London Blitz to the battlefields of France and back again, all those years and not a scratch on it, perfect as the day she had lifted it from her own mother's jewellery box.

Perhaps this was fate though, teaching her a lesson. She had stolen a family heirloom from her own dead mother on the night of the murders, and Isabella had stolen it from her years later, only to sell it to a stranger.

Tears of grief filled her eyes but Celeste fought them back, responding mechanically as Stella chattered to her in the kitchen, eagerly fetching flour and eggs for the batter mix.

She would never see the silver ring again.

CHAPTER THIRTY-FIVE

The rainclouds thickened and darkened as Stella made her way down the meandering cliff path towards Black Rock Beach. The few drops she had felt up at the house were steadily gathering strength, the light growing violet overhead, while a vivid whitish-grey illuminated the ocean for miles, rain soon pouring down, soaking her in minutes. She came to a sharp bend in the path and saw the wide expanse of the beach below, emptied of ramblers and dog-walkers in such inhospitable weather. The black rock itself rose sleek and black above the ribs of barnacle-covered rock that laced the foreshore. The tide was far out, barely visible in the misty distance, so that what looked like acres of gleaming rock and sand lay exposed, frilly with seaweed, its glossy jumbled strands everywhere.

Somewhere out there was America, her birthplace. It had not been 'home' for several decades and yet there was still a tug inside her at the thought.

Stella crooked an arm against the rain to help her see better. 'O my America! my new-found-land,' she whispered, quoting a line from some half-forgotten poem. John Donne, the poet.

America the Brave. Her birthplace, yes, but also the place of her mother's death.

She stared across the ocean, as though her gaze could somehow pierce thousands of miles of water to reveal a dark, familiar coastline further out west. There was nothing to be seen but rain haze though, a gloomy mist that coated everything in fine wet spray, and nothing to hear but the thunder of waves in the distance, a faint, unceasing roar like the inside of a shell.

She ought to head back to the house. With all this heavy rain pounding on her head and shoulders, spattering the rough dirt track with raindrops large as hailstones, it was ridiculous to keep walking.

And yet she was already sodden, her boots dark with it, hair hanging about her face in wild, tangled tendrils. More rain could hardly make her wetter. Besides, she had heard that weather fronts often passed with astonishing swiftness here on the Cornish coast; tempest one minute, glorious sunshine the next. So perhaps if she simply put her head down and toughed it out…

So she kept on, lurching from side to side along

the narrow, zigzagging cliff path, thick gorse bushes to her right, a sheer, exhilarating drop to her left.

Sure enough, as Walter had warned her, there was no handrail or guard to protect the unwary rambler, though sometimes the path was carefully guided away from the crumbling edge, to give walkers a sporting chance of survival. It was certainly not designed to be taken in a thunderous rainstorm. And yet here she was. She blinked raindrops out of her eyes, skidding in places as the descent steepened, almost falling once, but just recovering her balance in time by grabbing at a spiny gorse bush, swearing loudly as thorns ripped her palm.

She thought she heard someone shouting, but couldn't be sure over the roar of the invisible sea and patter of rain everywhere.

Reaching the beach at last, she trudged through sand dunes as heavy and clinging as wet cement, boots sinking deep, until she hit the flatter sand within reach of the waterline and began heading for the black rock. The sky was livid, the air electric. As she came within the last few hundred yards of the rock, lightning flared out, a burst of light illuminating the misty grey of the beach, followed six or seven seconds later by a long, deep rumble of thunder.

'Great.'

Stella stopped dead, peering up at the sky, not

sure what to do for the best. Rain was one thing, a lightning storm quite another. She was right in the middle of the beach here, utterly exposed and vulnerable to a lightning strike. But perhaps in the shadow of the great rock, sheltering under one of its overhanging outcrops...

She began to run for the rock, which was not easy, as she was close to the edge of the ancient ribs that lay at its base, slippery with weed and punctuated with deep, salt-water pools. Reaching these knee-high rocks, she clambered up onto the first one, and then hopped – or slipped – from one gleaming rib to another, still blinded by the downpour, while lightning split the skies again and the answering thunder deafened her.

A loud PING caught her attention, and she half-turned in confusion, looking about. But the rain was too heavy, she couldn't see a thing.

She kept making for the black rock. A loud whine shaved the air near her ear, followed by another PING.

Was someone shooting at her, but missing and hitting the black rock? It was so impossible and insane an idea that she dismissed it as soon as it occurred to her, and yet...

The next whine was dangerously close to her ear.

She stopped and turned, staring back up the beach. A car park was situated beyond the dunes, tucked away behind vast tide defence blocks and half-hidden by windswept shrubs. There was only one vehicle in sight, a black Land Rover that had just torn into the car park at speed and slammed on the brakes at right angles to the beach. As she watched, the driver's door was flung open and a figure in black plunged down the dunes, staggered through the soft, hampering sand, and then came running across the beach towards her at full pelt, shouting and waving his arms…

It was Lewis, she realised, too stunned to react. What on earth…?

She took a few steps towards him. 'Lewis?'

'Get back to the car, come on,' he yelled as he reached her, and began to drag her back up the beach. 'Move, move, move!'

She obeyed, propelled by the urgency in his voice, but felt utterly bewildered. 'For God's sake, Lewis,' she gasped, running breathless by his side. 'What the hell's going on? I thought I heard someone shooting –'

Another whine, and Lewis cried out and stumbled, knocked sideways. She grabbed his arm, pulling him back to his feet. He was pale.

'Are you okay? What's wrong?'

'Keep going,' he said through gritted teeth, and swore, one hand clamped to his shoulder. 'Got to… reach… the car.'

'Oh my God, are you telling me someone really is shooting at us?' Stella hauled him up the dunes in the pouring rain, terrified and out of breath, yet somehow finding the strength. To her relief, there were no more gunshots. But she felt horribly exposed.

The driver's side was still open, but when she pushed Lewis towards it, he shook his head. 'Can't drive,' he said unsteadily, still clasping his shoulder. 'Keys in ignition... You can drive, can't you?'

'Theoretically.' She bundled him into the passenger seat and ran round to the driver's side, jumping in and starting her up. 'Where to?'

'Just drive,' he managed to gasp, and then slumped in the seat.

He'd passed out, she realised in horror.

There was no time to think. Slamming the Land Rover into reverse, Stella swung the car round much faster than intended and lurched out of the car park in embarrassing fits and starts, taken aback by the power under her foot. She'd taken her test along with some school friends at the age of seventeen, learning in a hatchback, but had never needed a car in London and so had not actually driven since the day she'd passed. But at least it was an automatic gearbox.

She was making for Black Rock Hall, the most obvious place to seek shelter. Wet hair was dripping in her eyes. She flung it back impatiently and glanced at Lewis, wishing he would recover consciousness and tell her exactly what had happened back there – someone shooting at people on the beach? That made no sense at all, unless there was a maniac at large. But he was ashen-faced and his eyes were closed.

'Oh no.' His hand had fallen from his shoulder when he fainted, bright red blood on his fingers. 'Lewis? You… You've been shot.'

But of course he'd been shot. The way he'd staggered sideways, and then behaved so oddly, stumbling around, unable to speak… These had all been giveaways. But she hadn't understood.

'I've never been shot at before,' she hissed at him, though she knew he couldn't hear her. 'Or seen someone shot. I mean, it happens in America all the time. But this is Cornwall. There's no shooting in Cornwall.' She stared ahead, her hands gripping the wheel in a stranglehold. 'What on earth is going on?'

They were nearly at the turn to the hall. The rain had intensified. It was a thick dark curtain of water, blasting down across the windscreen and metal roof, raindrops boiling on the bonnet, smoking in great swathes of mist that clouded everything around them. It was like driving inside a cave. She fumbled with the windscreen wipers, hunting for the fastest setting, but even that seemed to make little difference.

Then she realised a car was behind them.

It was only a dark shape in the rear view mirror at first, somewhere in the distance, but then she caught the roar of a straining engine, deep above the pelting rain, and a large black car was right on their tail, headlights on full beam, blinding her. She had an odd sensation of déjà vu, and instantly knew where she had seen that car before…

Beside her, Lewis groaned, coming round, and she could have screamed in relief.

'Lewis, thank God… There's a car behind us. I think it's the same driver who tried to run us off the road the other night. What should I do?'

He half-turned in his seat, wincing. 'Don't let them get ahead of us.'

'How exactly am I supposed to do that?' At that moment, the vehicle behind them veered wildly and began to creep up on her right. 'Here they come.'

'Put your foot down.'

A wild suspicion crossed her mind. Could it be Bruno in that car? Was he the maniac who'd tried to make them crash and was now shooting at them? Was Bruno capable of such reckless, murderous behaviour? She couldn't believe it. And yet who else could wish her harm?

Unless it was Lewis they were trying to kill.

'But who is it?' she hissed at him, fighting the wheel on the tight bends. 'And why were they shooting at us? Are they after you or me?'

He didn't reply but opened the passenger window, the rain soaking his face and hair. He reached for his phone and sat back, breathing roughly, eyes closing.

'Lewis? Don't pass out, please don't pass out.'

'Accelerate,' he gasped.

She put her foot down hard. Nonetheless, the car behind started inching past on the other side, and she flinched to the right as something smacked against their rear bumper.

'It's no good. He's coming level.' She glanced that way and caught a glint of something metallic. 'Lewis, I think he's planning to shoot again,' she said urgently.

'Go right, go right,' Lewis shouted.

She obeyed, flinging the wheel hard right, the Land Rover spinning off the driveway and through a gap between trees so narrow she closed her eyes at the last second, sure they would never make it. Then they were past it and heading over rough terrain into the wooded area where the huge dog had chased her. The Land Rover was jolted up and down but kept going, designed for off-roading, though perhaps not at this speed.

Lewis was shouting into the phone above the strained note of the engine. Then she saw blinding lights behind them again, followed by a tremendous crack.

'He's shooting at the rear window,' she yelled, her hands shaking on the wheel. They were going up a slight slope now, the trees clustered thickly ahead. She wasn't sure how long she could keep this pace up, not with so many obstacles, and the sky so dark with the storm, it could almost have been night.

'We need to lose him,' he told her urgently, pointing ahead through the trees. 'Go that way and try to put some distance between us. That's not an off-road vehicle. He may not be able to follow us.'

She spun the wheel violently, following his directions. But the tyres bounced and leapt over huge stones hidden in the coarse grasses, and the wheel was jerked out of her hands. Too late, through the dark and the driving rain, she saw the looming height of the folly rushing towards them and screamed.

CHAPTER THIRTY-SIX

Celeste finished writing her letter, hesitated a long while before signing it at the bottom, and then sat back to read it through. She read it three times before she was satisfied that this was the final draft; the previous drafts, now crushed white paper dotted with ink, lay scattered about her like snowballs. She had said all that was needful. All that she could say without giving too much away. There was still someone to protect, after all. Her beloved Isabella's daughter, her own flesh and blood, her dearest Stella.

Perhaps she ought to have told her granddaughter the truth. But she couldn't bear to think of young Stella being hurt by revelations of the past. Or perhaps more accurately, being disappointed in her grandmother, just as she'd already been disappointed in her mother.

Though Stella was not so very young anymore, was she? She was almost eighteen, the same age as Celeste herself when she'd set out alone from Black Rock Hall, the silver ring hidden in her luggage, the whole world before her...

'I never expected to live so long,' she admitted to herself, and lay back against the pillows, staring out of the hospice window. Her room looked out over a garden, a soft green oasis in the heart of London's traffic-choked city. There were bamboos and feathery pampas grasses, and a glimpse of some white stone deity set amongst pebbles, with a tinkling fountain somewhere out of sight. 'If I had, maybe I would have done some things differently. Been more careful. Or more careless. I can't decide.'

The nurse, who must have slipped in quietly to check her blood pressure and pulse, because Celeste had not even noticed her there, was smiling as she pushed the machine away. 'Feeling better today, Esther?' Her eye fell on the letter. 'You want me to post that for you?'

'Would you? That would be very kind.' Celeste reached for a scrap of paper, her hand shaking slightly. 'It's to an old friend. His name is Maurice Cossentine. This is his address: Black Rock Hall, West Pol, Cornwall.' Her hand fell sideways and she stopped, too exhausted to continue. 'I'm sorry, I... I don't know the postcode.'

'That's all right; I'll find it for you.'

'Please don't tell him where the letter came from,' she said urgently. 'No return address; I don't want Maurice to know where I am.'

The nurse eyed her strangely but nodded. 'Of course not.' She picked up the address and the letter and bore them both away.

Celeste lay back, too tired to care anymore. That was that, then. Her gaze slowly returned to the garden outside the window. To the stone statue among the bamboos and pampas grasses. A smooth, rounded shoulder and the upturned palm of a hand. Like a glimpse of someone seen from a distance, a mythical figure in white, drifting through green trees, never quite visible...

'Gran?' The voice was familiar and insistent. 'Are you okay, Gran?'

Celeste opened her eyes. 'Of course I'm okay,' she said with faint hauteur. 'Why wouldn't I be okay? They look after me very well. I can't complain.'

'You never complain, Gran.' Stella sat down at her bedside, her young, open face turned trustingly up to her. She knew nothing about the murders. She knew very little about Celeste's darker past. Oh, she knew there had been depression and upsets. That Isabella had been a miracle child after many sadnesses, losses that had broken her heart and almost her spirit too. But of the rest she knew nothing, and that was how it needed to stay.

Except that one day she might be free to go

there, to touch the past and not be burned by it. 'When he's dead,' she whispered, not realising she had spoken out loud.

'When who's dead?' Stella tilted her head to one side like a small bird, watching her with bright eyes. 'Gran?' She laughed. 'You do say the oddest things.'

'Oh, yes, it's the drugs they give me,' Celeste told her, dismissing what she'd said with a wave of her hand. 'My brain goes funny.'

'Lucky you.'

'Read to me, would you? Something easy.'

'I've got Cosmo.'

'If you like, dearest.' Celeste closed her eyes and pretended to listen as Stella read aloud from an article about finding the 'perfect man'. I already found him, she was thinking, trying not to smile. My darling Danny... Where is he these days? I never see him... Then she remembered that he was gone, and her heart sank. She opened her eyes again to find it was getting dark outside and Stella was putting away the magazine.

'I have to go now, Gran,' she was saying, 'but I'll come again tomorrow.'

'You're not lonely at the flat without me, are you?'

'Goodness, no. Don't worry about that. I have my friends. And the goldfish. And my violin.' Stella smiled shyly, holding her hand. 'I... I've got a place at music college. I start in the autumn. Do you remember me telling you?'

'Of course I remember. It's cancer. Not dementia.'

'Sorry.' Stella looked away, and Celeste could see she had been crying.

'Hey, what's this? Tears?'

'I wish you weren't so poorly, that's all. I wish you could come home with me. I could look after you at the flat.'

'I prefer it here.' She didn't want her young granddaughter burdened with looking after an old lady. 'Besides, I like looking out at the garden here. It's so peaceful. It reminds me of Cornwall. Of the house where we used to spend our summers when I was your age.' She smiled, wistful. 'The house had beautiful formal gardens, but it was right on the sea too, so we had coastal grasses and rough land by the cliff's edge. You could hear the sea all day and night, a constant roar, like London traffic behind glass. Smell it too, all that salt on the wind…'

'Where was it, exactly? You never said, Gran. I'd like to visit the house myself one day.'

Panic streaked through Celeste's heart and she pulled a face, wincing in pain. 'No, I… I forget the name. It doesn't matter anyway. But there is something I want you to remember. Something important.'

'Yes?'

'There's a special ring. A family ring.'

'You mean the one Mom took to America?' Stella sounded puzzled. 'I know about that already.'

'But I don't want you to forget. It's the ring I'm wearing in that framed photograph, back at the flat. And I mention it sometimes in my old journals. Remember that. I want you to have them after I die.' Celeste kept having to remind herself that Stella already knew about the ring; it was so hard to hold things straight in her head these days. The older she got, the longer she spent back in the past, and the more difficult it became to separate lies from truth. 'Isabella took the silver ring with her when she left. Stole it, I suppose you could say. Otherwise, I would have gifted it to you in my Will.' She squeezed Stella's hand, smiling faintly. 'Maybe one day the ring will turn up again. If that happens, you may need to prove it's yours. So keep that photograph safe and remember what the ring looks like, won't you? The fighting serpents, the family emblem. And never forget what's written on the inside of the ring.'

'There's something written on the inside of the ring?'

'Didn't I tell you? Your grandfather had my initials added to the ring as a surprise gift. But it also bears an original inscription.' Celeste felt the past overwhelm her, barely able to gasp, 'Two words in Latin. They mean… *Love forever*.' She put a hand to her chest, struggling to breathe. 'Don't forget, will you? One day… One day, you may need to remember that.'

Stella nodded, saying simply, 'I won't forget, Gran. Please don't upset yourself.' She turned to call the nurse, adding with a smile and a wink, 'Your secret is safe with me.'

Her secret.

Celeste had closed her eyes, still gasping for breath. Her heart fluttered anxiously If only the girl knew…

Though one day she would know, of course, and perhaps take steps to find out more. But with any luck it wouldn't be until Maurice was safely dead. Her brother had no offspring to inherit the Cossentine estate, she had checked that, and no wife either. But that hadn't surprised her, knowing him as she did. The past was no longer her concern, however. Only the future.

She had finally written to Maurice, to tell him she was dying, but that she had a young granddaughter. She'd made it clear the girl didn't know anything about the Cossentine family and Celeste wanted it to remain that way until he too was gone. It had been a brusque letter, no sentiment attached, only a few bare words from sister to brother, survivor to survivor.

You may find the silver ring in America, she had finished the letter. *I forgive you your trespasses, Maurice. As I hope you can forgive mine. Amor aeternus. C.*

Her brother would understand.

CHAPTER THIRTY-SEVEN

Stella came to with blood streaming down her temple, and the Land Rover ticking loudly, rain still pouring down, a cold draught in her face…

They had crashed into the folly. The side with the cracked, fallen stones, by the look of it, on the opposite side from the entrance door. The bonnet of the Land Rover was wedged into the wall of the folly, the engine silent at last. She had killed his car, she realised, and felt absurdly guilty at the thought.

Belatedly, she recalled the car that had been following them, the lunatic with the gun, and realised the danger they were in.

Could it really be Bruno?

Somehow, she couldn't imagine the urbane, smooth-talking Bruno losing his cool enough to chase after her in a car cross-country, shooting out of the window like a gangster. Unless he were so maddened by jealousy, he didn't care if he killed her too.

'Lewis,' she muttered, turning to find him slumped against the passenger door, barely conscious. 'Oh God… Wake up, we need to move.' She touched his cheek. 'Lewis?'

To her relief, his eyes fluttered open, and he grimaced. 'Shot,' he muttered.

'I know. Can you get out? We're not safe here… We should get into the folly.'

Lewis pushed himself up, nodding with gritted teeth, and she hurried round in the rain to help him out of the car. With painfully slow steps, she got him into the lower room of the folly, having to grope her way in the darkness. She listened for sounds of pursuit but could hear nothing through the loud pelt of rain against the tower.

When she returned, again feeling her way along the cold wall, she scrabbled for the box of matches she knew to be on the table and, after trying five damp matches without success, lit the half-burned candle with the fifth.

Lewis was slumped on the wooden chair beside her, his eyes closed, blood staining his shirt. She didn't like the grey look about his mouth.

'I've lost my phone. It must be in the car. Did you manage to make a call?' she asked, crouching beside him in the glimmering darkness.

His eyes opened but he seemed to be having trouble focusing. 'Dropped it in the crash… Back on the road though, I managed to send a text…

Hardcastle.'

'The solicitor?' Stella couldn't see how that would be helpful but it didn't seem like a good time to say so. 'Better than nothing, I suppose. Once I'm sure there's nobody about out there, I'll go back to the car for my phone and call the police.' She put a hand to his shoulder and he winced. 'And an ambulance for you.'

'I'm... fine,' he mumbled.

'Sure you are.' She stood, her nerves stretched thin, and looked about in the pale flickering glow from the candle. Where the Land Rover had crashed into the wall of the folly, a few stones had been dislodged. Wind and rain were beating through this gap, the plastic sheeting slapping violently against the wall. Lewis kept flinching at each loud snap and rustle.

'Maybe I can tie that down,' she said.

There was some rope wrapped about one of the scaffolding poles holding up this already fragile part of the wall. Reaching on tiptoe to unwind it, she struggled to make a loop with the frayed end, a noose that could be tightened around one corner of the loose flapping plastic to hold it still. Having done that, she began to wrestle her way backwards out of the damp plastic sheeting, aware of an odd rattling, crunching sound as she did so, then heard a loud snap on stepping back.

Stella glanced down, frowning. 'What on earth...?"

There appeared to be a human bone at her feet. Long and thin, it looked like a skeletal forearm with bits of dark fabric attached to it. On stepping on the bone, she'd accidentally snapped it, though it was still being held together by the fabric remnants.

Beside it on the ground, she realised, peering more closely, were four or five little grey lumps. Finger bones?

'Stella?' Lewis had stirred, craning round to look at her. 'What is it? What's the matter?'

'Hang on, I'm not sure…' Hurrying back for the candle, she carried it to where she'd stepped on the arm bone, a tiny rivulet of hot wax scalding her fingers.

Slowly, Stella pulled back the decayed plastic sheeting from the crumbling, broken masonry and saw a gap to one side where several stones had tumbled away. But instead of letting in rain, the gap beyond them was dark and still. *A cavity*? That would explain the odd, not quite perfectly circular shape of this room.

Holding up the candle flame to this dark gap, she peered inside and recoiled at the sight of a human skeleton, hanging in chains and clad in what looked like dusty, moth-eaten formalwear.

'Oh my God,' she cried, almost dropping the candle in horror.

'Stella, for God's sake…' He was struggling to his feet.

'No, stay where you are. It's okay, I'm coming back.' She returned to him shakily, thankful that she wasn't alone, and replaced the candle on the table. 'You're not going to believe this, but there's a skeleton chained to the wall over there. Looks like it was bricked up in a specially-made cavity.' She shuddered, her voice barely louder than a whisper. 'I think it's been here a very long time.'

Lewis began to say something but fell silent at the sound of a dog howling somewhere close by. His eyes met hers through the candlelight.

'You need to hide,' he said hoarsely. 'There's a room at the top of the folly. Run, get up there. Barricade yourself in.'

'I'm not leaving you,' she began, but the door to the folly grated open and the wind whistled through, a sudden gust extinguishing the candle flame…

Then she heard someone behind her, and half-turned, too late to protect herself from a violent blow to the back of her head.

Stella could see something pale in front of her eyes. Mistily white and rectangular, with black italics moving in and out of focus. Slowly, her vision steadied and she was able to see what it was. A place card, mere inches from her face, where she lay slumped across the table, her head aching horribly.

'*Celeste Cossentine, youngest daughter. Absent*

without explanation at the dinner and said to have fled soon afterwards, taking an heirloom ring with her.'

She looked further, meeting the glassy stare of a dead woman with a bulging, paper-white face, and sucked in her breath in sudden realisation. She was seated at the dining table in Room Ten of the Cossentine Murder Mystery Exhibition, the waxwork figures of the dead all around her.

'Ugh.' Swearing under her breath, she sat up, finding it awkward to move, and groaned in pain. 'Oh, my head.'

Someone had hit her from behind in the folly.

But who? And why?

Belatedly, she recalled that Lewis had been shot on the beach and needed an ambulance. Panic flooded her veins. How long had she been lying unconscious here? Struggling to get up, she realised that her wrists had both been tied to the table leg next to her thigh. Two hard, narrow plastic bands dug deep into her flesh, restraining her in place.

'Good God… Are you kidding me?' Furious, she looked about for her captor, half-expecting to find Bruno there, and saw Lewis instead.

On the opposite side of the table, where Maurice's empty seat had stood, Lewis lay slumped with his head on the table, motionless. The white tablecloth was stained with his blood.

'Oh my God, Bruno… What have you done to

Lewis?'

'Who's Bruno?'

She looked round, startled by that voice.

It was Walter Whitely.

'I haven't done anything to your friend yet,' Walter said calmly, moving behind her. He set a large, leather-bound bible and a long knife in the middle of the table. 'We had to sedate him. Rohypnol. Rather a large dose, I'm afraid. His wound is still bleeding, it's true. But he shouldn't cause us any more trouble.' He paused. 'I'll ask you again… Who is this Bruno?'

She was scared and bemused, watching him. Walter had tied her to the table? Walter had drugged Lewis and brought him here? But why?

And who was this 'we'?

Perhaps he was working with Bruno. But the two had no connection at all. None of this made sense.

'Nobody,' she said cautiously.

'Good, because I don't want any more complications. You've caused me enough of a headache as it is, and I'd rather just get on with this.' Walter glanced over his shoulder. 'Ready, darling?'

'Yes, Walter, dearest.'

Stella knew that voice too. Horrified, she twisted in her seat just in time to see Allison Friel come floating into Room Ten, a calm, superior expression on her face. The spiritualist was wearing a judge's black robes draped over a long white chiffon dress that fell to her ankles, a black cap balanced on her head. She looked absurd.

Walter Whitely, of all unlikely people, and Allison Friel were behind this? She could almost have laughed, except that Lewis could be bleeding to death over there.

'What the hell is this?' Stella demanded of them both, wrestling against the zip ties. 'I thought you two hated each other?'

Allison laughed. 'Silly girl. You believe everything you're told, don't you?' She blew a kiss to Walter, who smiled at her in return. It was sickening to watch them.

'Listen,' Stella said urgently, 'You've had your wacky fun, but enough is enough. You need to let me go, okay? And call an ambulance. Lewis was shot…He's losing blood. He may even die.'

'He's certainly going to die,' Walter agreed. 'But that's his own fault. I didn't want to shoot him. Hard enough to get rid of one body, but two is a nightmare.'

Stella had still been half-clinging to the idea that Bruno was involved. But this revelation threw her. 'You shot Lewis at the beach?' she whispered. '*You*? But that means you were trying to shoot *me*, too.' She stared. 'Why, for God's sake?'

'We had hoped to kill you outside. Less messy that way and easier to dispose of the evidence. Then everything went wrong and we had to improvise. But it doesn't matter,' he said, shrugging. 'Allison and I have come up with a better plan. And this way we get to hold a proper trial.'

'Yes, it's very pleasing. The spirits will be so happy.' Allison was making her way around to the opposite side of the table, squeezing past the waxwork figures of the Cossentines to stand beside Lewis. 'And after the trial, we'll frame your deaths as a murder-suicide.'

'So clever of you to think of that, darling. It's the perfect solution.' Walter bent to check Stella's ties, seeming satisfied. 'Then we'll burn this place to the ground, along with all its self-indulgent, over-privileged display, and they'll be lucky even to identify your bodies, let alone work out how you died.'

Cold fear clenched her stomach, but she refused to let them see it. 'Sorry… Wh-What exactly have I done to deserve this?'

'Murder.' The curator half-smiled at her protest. 'Oh, not you personally. You as a representative of the Cossentines.' He indicated the waxwork figures arranged about the table. 'You are all guilty here. It's the family curse, you see.'

'Oh, not that bloody curse again.' She pulled hard on the zip ties and the whole table jumped. Lewis's head lolled sideways. Empty plastic wine glasses toppled and candle flames flickered, the candelabras shaking. Even the waxwork figures shifted uneasily as though alive. 'You two are going to prison for a really long time.'

'Keep still.' Walter yanked her hair so hard, tears came to her eyes. 'You're wrong, I won't go to prison. Thanks to Allison's blog, everyone in the village knows you've lost your mind.' He grinned down into her face. 'Poor mad Stella, who thinks she's being haunted... Seeing a spectral hound and a ghostly white lady? Hearing violin music that isn't there?' He laughed. 'Have you never heard of a remotely controlled recording? You were so easy to manipulate. You're even reading a book on communicating with spirits.'

Stella gasped. 'Only because Allison gave it to me.'

'Of course. But how simple to make it look as though you shot your lover in a fit of madness and then stabbed yourself out of guilt.'

'But not before setting fire to the exhibition,' Allison added helpfully, 'because it was a reminder of the bad blood you come from. Don't worry, it will all be covered in your suicide note.'

'For God's sake,' Stella burst out, 'you must be mad. Nobody will believe that nonsense.'

Walter's brows rose. 'Actually, the police already still suspect you of murdering Mrs Hepley. Yes, you have a vague alibi for the time but it's not rock-solid. A nudge here, a quiet word there... The police are easy to influence and your suicide note will help convince them.' He nodded at her shocked expression. 'Besides, the coroner believed without question that Maurice Cossentine fell down the stairs and broke his neck. So yes, I'm sure they'll believe this too.'

Her chest had constricted with fear. 'You… *You* killed Mrs Hepley? You were the one who poisoned her? And Maurice's fall… That wasn't an accident?'

'I didn't kill either of them.' His smile was chilling. 'But Allison did.'

Stella stared at Allison, who smiled back at her benignly. Slowly, a memory came back, Allison speaking to her that first day, under the wish tree on the village green. *I worked in a hospice for ten years.* 'Of course… She was Maurice's nurse.'

'Well done.' He looked almost impressed.

'But why kill Mrs Hepley, of all people? What had she ever done to you?'

'Hepley was an evil woman,' he said with disdain. 'We shared a hatred for the Cossentines, so I put up with her at first. But she took her hate campaign too far for my liking. She was planning to make a claim for compensation against the estate. If she'd won her case, the damages might have run into hundreds of thousands.' Walter shook his head, looking disgusted. 'I couldn't allow that. I'd waited long enough to inherit as it was. Unfortunately, we couldn't move openly against her, because she'd found out about my little association with Allison. Then we came up with a genius solution. To poison Hepley, making it look as though *you* did it, and then dispose of you before you could deny it. Two birds with one stone.'

Her scalp crept with horror at this matter-of-fact lunacy. But she was still confused. 'You'd been *waiting to inherit*?' Then everything clicked into place. 'You're the default heir. The one who would have inherited if I hadn't come along.'

'Correct.'

'But Hardcastle told me the default heir didn't know anything about that clause.'

Walter laughed, seeming genuinely amused. 'Considering I was the one who persuaded dotty old Maurice to put that clause in his Will, I can assure you I knew about it. Unfortunately, I couldn't quite get him to drop his search for the true heir all together. But it seemed best to be able to feign ignorance, in case the real heir ever turned up and I was forced to act to protect my investment. Hence the need for the executor not to disclose the identity of the heir until the full five years were up.'

'It... It must have been annoying for you when I turned up.' She glanced at Lewis, playing for time while she kept Walter talking. She held out little hope of them being rescued. But perhaps she could eventually persuade Walter to let them go.

'Extremely,' he agreed. 'Especially when you kept poking around the house, asking awkward questions. Allison tried to get rid of you for good the other night, running you and Lewis off the road. When that didn't work, we both went out after you today… I had the gun and Allison did the driving. We made a good team, I felt.' Again, he and Allison smiled at each other. 'But you are irritatingly hard to dispose of, Miss Ffoulds.'

'Sorry about that.'

'Oh, I'm used to being patient with people I dislike. All those years I spent working with your imbecile of a great-uncle, putting together this preposterous exhibition, just so he could "prove" to any heir of his sister's that he wasn't the murderer… That's what he told me, you know. That he was sure Celeste had left a child behind, and he wanted to reach out to them, to show he could be trusted.' He shook his head. 'Maurice knew people thought Elsie Dunn's conviction was unsound. He was obsessed with proving his innocence through the exhibition, though anyone who knew him well could see he wasn't a killer. Maurice Cossentine might have been a wealthy man, but he was soft inside, weak and pathetic. Just another lonely old man by the time I came on board to curate the exhibition for him.'

Walter gave a contemptuous laugh, adding, 'I hated him by the end, and he knew it. Then he started rambling on about changing his will, leaving everything to charity after all. When I teamed up with Allison, she took care of it. Told everyone in the village he had dementia and kept the ancient old fool safely out the way until we were ready to get rid of him.'

Listening to this, Stella's eyes had widened. 'The tower room. The iron bedstead. You tied him to the bed.' She felt sick. 'God, that's horrible.' Belatedly, she recalled the stained cigarillo butt she'd seen on the floor. 'But Mrs Hepley worked out you'd been keeping him prisoner up there, didn't she? Was she blackmailing you?'

'It doesn't matter whether she was or not,' he hissed, 'because she's dead now. And you will be soon if you don't shut up. I could slit your throat here and now. Is that what you want? To be executed without even a trial?'

'No,' she whispered.

'Good.' He drew a shuddering breath, appearing to regain control, and nodded to Allison. 'It's time. Let's proceed with the trial.'

'Is the accused wearing the Cossentine ring?' Allison demanded.

'Of course.'

Her grandmother's silver ring was glinting on her right hand, Stella realised with a shock, glancing down. She hadn't even noticed. It was an odd sensation to be wearing the silver ring at last. It fitted perfectly too.

'Then we can begin.' Allison raised her arms as though in invocation, her pale face devoid of emotion, curtain of black hair hanging straight, not a strand out of place. 'Walter Whitely, do you swear to tell the truth, the whole truth and nothing but the truth, so help you God?'

Solemnly, Walter took up the bible and placed his hand on the cover. 'I do,' he swore.

CHAPTER THIRTY-EIGHT

'On the 10th day of March 1917, my great-grandfather Thomas Whitely was murdered by Ronald Cossentine in cold blood.' Walter glared at Stella, his hand still resting on the bible as he gave his 'testimony'. 'Your great-grandfather told his superior officers later that Thomas Whitely was a deserter and that was why he shot him. But eye-witness accounts at the time indicate this was nothing but a lie and a vile smear against a good man's reputation.'

'Says you,' Stella muttered rebelliously.

Walter threw her a silencing look. 'In fact, Thomas had argued with Ronald Cossentine two days beforehand over a game of cards, accusing him of cheating. Cossentine refused to admit this. Two days later, he shot my great-grandfather in the back. His report described it as the summary execution of a deserter. But others swore it was cold-blooded murder.'

'A wicked act,' Allison cried, 'and deserving of punishment.'

'Indeed.' His cold eye swept the table of waxworks. 'For three generations, my family has been soiled by this cowardly act, and their spirits have been unable to rest. We know this through Allison's séances. Her work has given the dead a voice, just as this trial gives them a knife to wield for justice.' Walter looked down at Stella. 'What do you, the accused, have to say to this charge?'

'I had nothing to do with –' Stella began hotly, but he cut her off.

'You cannot speak for the whole family.'

'Why not? You've accused me on behalf of the family and I'm entitled to defend myself. Besides,' she pointed out, 'what proof do you have that Thomas *wasn't* a deserter?'

'More lies, more Cossentine smears,' he spat furiously. 'The truth is, you're as guilty as the rest of them.'

'I wasn't there and neither was Celeste,' she said furiously. 'Come on, 1917? She hadn't even been born then.'

'Don't you know your scripture, Stella? *The sins of the fathers shall be visited upon the children.*' He turned to Allison, apparently dismissing Stella's protests as unimportant. 'Judge, what is your verdict?'

'That justice must be done.' Allison's strange, other-worldly gaze came to rest on his face. There was sympathy for him there, almost tenderness. 'You have suffered much, Walter Whitely, as have I, being sensitive to the torments of the dead. Tonight, that agony comes to an end for both of us.'

Walter was nodding eagerly, his relief palpable. 'So, how must justice be served? What do the spirits say?'

'That innocent blood was spilt.' Allison shifted her gaze to Stella's face, and now her eyes held malice. 'Now let this woman's blood be spilt in turn. An eye for an eye, a tooth for a tooth.'

'Yes,' Walter hissed.

'Stella Ffoulds,' Allison called out, her voice echoing about the high-roofed space, 'you stand in for your great-grandfather, Ronald Cossentine, who murdered Thomas Whitely in cold blood. You're also the descendant of mad Celeste Cossentine, whom we believe murdered her family for the sake of that silver ring you wear and to avenge certain wrongs done to her. Celeste's guilt is clear to this court from her lifelong refusal to return to the family home even after the cook, Elsie Dunn, an innocent woman, had been hanged for the murders she committed, and despite the many attempts her brother made in reaching out to her through advertisements and rewards. We cannot know all the details of what Celeste did, nor her motives, but we can pass sentence on her. This final Cossentine death will appease both Walter's great-grandfather and all those about this table who seek justice and cannot rest.'

'No, this is a kangaroo court. You're only killing me to get the Cossentine estate, admit it.' Stella shook the table so violently, one lit branch of candelabra was knocked over. 'Let me go, you frauds.' The candle flames began licking at the white tablecloth on the other side of the table. 'You're deranged, both of you.'

'On the contrary, we're the only sane ones,' Allison flashed back at her. 'Walter's ancestors cannot be at peace while you live. Their anger has *infected* him. Can't you see that?'

'If you mean they've driven him stark raving mad,' Stella snapped, one eye on the spreading flames, 'then yes, I can safely say I'd noticed that.'

'You don't know what you're talking about. It's made me physically sick, not being able to lay my great-grandfather's spirit to rest.' Walter's voice rose in anger. 'I've got cancer, if you must know. I'm in constant pain. I try to keep it hidden, but…' He was visibly shaking. 'Do you have any idea what the endless gnawing pain of cancer does to a person? It changes you from the inside out. But once justice has been done and I receive my reward of Black Rock Hall, I shall be cured of this dreadful disease.' He threw out a hand to his accomplice. 'Allison has foreseen it in the stars.'

'I bet she has,' Stella muttered.

There was a volley of muffled barks from outside, and Walter threw another glance at Allison, this time worried. 'Is that dog of yours locked up in the car?'

'Of course. Something must have spooked him.'

'So that's *your* dog?' Stella gave a gasp of furious laughter. 'Not a spectral hound after all... You were the white lady too, weren't you? The figure I kept seeing out on the cliffs.'

Allison smirked. 'Not my fault you're so suggestible.'

'Enough talk,' Walter snapped. It was clear the dog barking had rattled him. 'Let's carry out her sentence, here and now.'

As he leant forward for the long-handled knife, Stella shrank away from him, yanking desperately at her tether again and shaking the table. The flames had reached the sleeve of the nearest waxwork figure. It was the eldest of Maurice's sisters, her place card naming her as Fenella. The fine, dusty fabric caught light, and fire ran along her white wrist, and now the smell of burning intensified.

'Walter, wait...' Uneasily, Allison had been watching the waxwork burn, flames licking at the lacy bodice of its evening gown. Now she slapped at the flames with a napkin. There was a wall jutting out on her other side, next to Lewis's still unconscious figure, making escape that way problematic; her only clear route would take her past the burning figure. 'Perhaps we ought to put this fire out first. Is there a fire extinguisher?'

'It doesn't matter. We were going to burn it to the ground anyway. Let me kill her now,' he insisted, brutally dragging Stella backwards so he could plunge the knife into her chest. 'Then you can shoot him, and the spirits can rest in peace.'

'Hang on,' Stella cried out, struggling as hard as she could, 'What... What does Allison get in return for all this?'

'She serves the spirits.' Walter's smile was cold, assured. 'And she will be mistress of Black Rock Hall once the house has passed to me and we can finally marry.' He raised the knife ceremoniously. 'Now, die.'

'Wait, wait, you have to listen to me... When we crashed into the folly tonight, we found a corpse chained to the wall. It was so old, it was mummified.'

'A corpse? In the folly?' Walter's raised hand had frozen in the air, the reflected flames glinting off the blade. He seemed genuinely taken aback, staring down at her. 'What are you babbling about?'

Stella coughed, blinking in the smoke. 'I think it's connected to the... the Cossentine murders. Either way, you're wrong to blame my grandmother. *She didn't do it.*'

'Walter, for God's sake, shut up and get the fire extinguisher!' Allison shrieked, batting at the flames as they rose, fire already consuming Fenella Cossentine. The waxwork's glass eyes stared straight ahead as her trunk sizzled and her face began to melt, her mouth elongating to a crooked rictus, as though screaming silently.

'I'm stuck... I can't get past this bloody thing.' Allison stumbled as she attempted to shove her way through the flames, but only succeeded in toppling Fenella's roasting torso into the lap of Sir Oliver Gliddon. 'Walter... Help me!'

Sir Oliver lurched to one side, catching fire and spreading flames to the next waxwork figure along. Almost within seconds, or so it seemed to Stella, that whole side of the table was alight, and the flames were spreading greedily along the tablecloth, heading their way.

Walter dropped the knife on the table, staring. 'Allison?'

'I'm going to climb on the table and jump across to you.' Allison was already scrambling onto the table, though the whole thing was alight now. 'Catch me?'

'Yes, yes.' Dragging his great-grandfather's murderer out of his seat, Walter dumped the head of the Cossentine family unceremoniously on the floor. Then he climbed onto the seat and held out his arms. 'Walk towards me. Careful now. Watch your feet.'

Allison stepped unsteadily through the fire, giving little shrieks of pain. The long dining table wobbled, clearly not as sturdy as it looked. 'I can't…. My feet, my ankles… They're burning!'

The space was filling with thick smoke. Stella tried to hide her face in the crook of her arm but was soon coughing helplessly. Both her hands were still tied to the table leg. There was no way to get free.

The smoke alarm overhead began to beep, piercing in the enclosed space of Room Ten.

Walter had climbed onto the table now, holding out a hand to his accomplice across the flames. 'To me, darling,' he called urgently. 'Hurry, the heat is intense.'

But flame was already licking up the folds of her chiffon dress and judge's robes and catching at the hems of his trousers. The table collapsed with a crash, tipping both of them the other way, back into the inferno of roasting wax figures. Their screams and cries as they struggled to be free of the flames were horrific.

'Lewis?' As the table had collapsed, Lewis too had disappeared from view, but knocked the other way, thankfully away from the fire. 'Lewis, can you hear me?'

Dragged to the floor with the fallen table, her wrists still bound with zip ties to one table leg, Stella slid her wrists down until they cleared the end of the table leg.

The silver ring glinted in the flames.

She was free.

Coughing and covering her mouth as best she could with her top, Stella fought her way through melting waxworks to peer over the other end of the collapsed dining table. Lewis had fallen in a fire-free pocket of space, but she could hardly see him, the smoke was thickening so fast. Clambering over the table, she began to hoist him out, but it was no use. He was simply too heavy.

'Oh God, Lewis...' She was crying and screaming his name, choking on smoke, when a hand came down on her shoulder.

'Stand aside, let me.'

She spun to find the huge, imposing figure of Mr Hardcastle behind her, a dog jumping up around the solicitor and barking excitedly. It was the 'spectral hound' that had chased her into the folly.

'You...' She gaped at him. 'How did you...?'

'Never mind that now. Where's Walter?'

She pointed silently towards the heap of burning, smoking bodies, now molten with wax, where flames were greedily consuming the other end of the dining table.

'I see.' He hoisted Lewis over his broad shoulder and carried him out through the back of the exhibition, the dog trotting after him, still barking. She stopped to hold the back door open but Hardcastle gasped, 'No, Miss Ffoulds, get out of here before the whole place goes up.'

Outside, he lay Lewis gently on the grass and

sank down beside him, his breathing laboured. 'Remind me never to do that again.' He bent to examine the blood stains that had spread across Lewis's shoulder and chest. 'Christ...I see he wasn't pulling my leg. His text said he'd been shot.' He shook Lewis, who groaned slightly but didn't wake up. 'Has he been drugged?'

'Rohypnol.'

'Right.' Hardcastle wiped his brow, coughing. 'I called an ambulance as soon as I got the text, which I'm afraid wasn't immediately...I was in a confidential meeting. Phone was off for several hours. Then I drove over here like a madman. Ambulance should be on its way though. Police too. But I didn't know we'd need the fire brigade.' He dragged a mobile from his pocket and threw it to Stella before collapsing onto the grass, breathless. 'Do the honours, would you?'

'Mr Hardcastle,' Stella said, clutching the phone and feeling like she was going mad. 'You seem very calm about all this. Do you *know* Lewis?'

'It's a long story. But yes. In fact, I hired him.'

'To do what?'

'To keep an eye on you,' he said, and jerked his finger at the burning exhibition building. 'Now call the fire brigade.'

'That horrible place can burn down for all I care,' she cried, her head throbbing from where she'd been struck earlier. 'Mr Hardcastle, please, I don't understand...' Had everything between her and Lewis been an act, deliberately done to keep her close? 'You hired him to *watch* me?'

'Not to watch you, but to watch over you. Lewis has been your bodyguard,' the solicitor told her, exasperated. 'I was suspicious about Walter Whitely. I was sure he'd hastened Maurice's death, perhaps even killed him, but I couldn't prove it. When you first contacted me, I thought there might be trouble over your claim on the estate. I didn't want to worry you though, so I hired Lewis to keep you safe. But I instructed him to be discreet, not make it obvious why he was hanging around.' He saw her face and grimaced. 'Oh, I see… Like that, is it? Well, I've known him for years and he's a good man. And a tough one too. I'm sure he'll survive this.'

'You… talking about me?' It was Lewis, his eyes flickering open to stare up at them. His voice was slurred. 'What… What's going on?' He saw the exhibition on fire and his eyes widened. 'Christ.'

'Don't try to talk,' Stella said quickly, dropping to her knees beside him in the damp grass, phone in hand. She stabbed out the number for the emergency services and put the mobile to her ear. She could already hear sirens approaching along the driveway, bouncing headlights picking out the house through the darkness. 'You're going to be okay. They gave you a drug, that's all.' She saw his unfocused gaze move to the ring on her finger. 'Yes, it's the silver ring. My grandmother's ring. I'll tell you all about it soon, I promise.'

Lewis smiled muzzily, his gaze meeting hers, and her heart soared. She knew then it hadn't been an act, that feeling between them. He hadn't been pretending to like her simply in order to keep her close.

'Hello, yes...' Stella turned her attention back to the emergency services call handler, her voice choking with emotion. 'Fire brigade, please.' She couldn't take her eyes off him. 'I need to report a fire.'

EPILOGUE

Black Rock Hall, North Cornwall, present day

Stella closed her eyes, her spirit reaching for the last climactic seconds of the piece, the walls of the music room echoing with the strains of her grandmother's favourite melody. Sliding her bow slowly and extravagantly along the string for that final, long-drawn-out note, she sighed and bowed her head. *That was for you, Celeste*, she thought, and could almost feel her grandmother's approving eyes on her, watching from beyond this world.

'Bravo!' Lewis clapped, startling her, and Mr Hardcastle joined him enthusiastically. 'Amazing. You ought to be a professional.'

'Ha ha, very funny.' Putting away her violin, Stella shot her boyfriend a teasing look. They had only recently become lovers, but she already knew instinctively that she could trust Lewis, that he would always be there for her. 'I could say the same for you. Call yourself a bodyguard? I was nearly toast that night.'

'Yes, sorry about that. I've no memory of what happened after we crashed into the folly. I guess it was the Rohypnol that did it.'

Lewis stood up and walked to the window of the music room, gazing out across the frosty lawn. It was six weeks since he'd been shot on the beach and he was almost completely recovered. Though he still had the old twinge of pain, usually when he and Stella were in bed together...

As if he could read her thoughts, Lewis turned at that instant and their eyes met. His slow smile made heat rise in her cheeks.

'All right, Hardcastle,' he drawled, 'I'm sure you didn't drive all the way over from Bude to admire Stella's bowing, magnificent violinist though she is. What have you got for us?'

Stella pulled up a chair, her eyes on the solicitor's face. 'Yes,' she said eagerly. 'I know you've been keeping in touch with the police. Have forensics identified the body in the folly yet?'

'They have.' Hardcastle waited for Lewis to return to his seat before continuing, 'It's Jeffrey Dunn.'

Lewis pulled a face. '*Who*?'

But Stella's eyes had widened. 'Jeffrey Dunn... He was the cook's son,' she reminded Lewis quickly. 'The servant who swore my great-uncle was locked in his room all evening on the night of the murders. His testimony saved Maurice's life.

But, in giving it, he probably condemned his own mother to the gallows.'

'That's the man,' Hardcastle agreed sombrely. 'It seems Jeffrey was walled up while he was still alive. A nasty way to go. Immurement. Very popular in the Middle Ages, apparently. You die of thirst, not hunger. Takes a good long while too. Anything up to a week, I believe.' Hardcastle picked up his briefcase and extracted a sheet of paper from it. 'And here's why. It's a copy of what was found on the body. A signed confession.'

The copy showed deep indentations from having been folded, while the spidery writing held many spelling mistakes and crossings out, the paper stained in places, some of the writing faded almost to nothing. But the police had provided a clean, corrected transcript below the photocopy, which Stella read out loud.

To Whom It May Concern

I, Jeffery Dunn, in service at Black Rock Hall of West Pol, North Cornwall, to the Cossentine family, do hereby confess that on the thirteenth day of July, 1939, I did murder the entire Cossentine family – barring Master Maurice and Miss Celeste, who were not present at the dinner table – by poisoning of the soup with strychnine, which I did obtain from a man I knew in the army, whose job was to handle such substances.

I did this because Mr Sebastian took advantage

of my little sister Becky, only fifteen years of age, causing her much grief, and admitted as much in front of witnesses. Despite this, his father refused to punish him and even encouraged Mr Sebastian to beat Master Maurice for bringing the matter to his attention, which was a wicked thing to do. Nor did any other member of the family, save for Master Maurice, take my family's part against Mr Sebastian.

Neither my sister Becky, nor my mother Mrs Dunn, nor any other person, had prior knowledge of my decision to poison the soup, thereby killing so many persons. I also confess to having struck Miss Celeste that evening, rendering her unconscious, for I did not wish her to die at my hand that night. I do not know what happened to her after that. I accept that death must be my punishment for these heinous crimes and I forgive Master Maurice for being my executioner.

May God have mercy on my soul.

Jeffrey Dunn

'Oh God, that's horrible.' Stella looked at Lewis, thinking out loud. 'The building of the folly was completed in December 1939, the same year the murders took place. I guess Maurice must have lured Jeffrey there and walled him up alive soon after it was finished, doing the brickwork himself.' She swallowed. 'The ideal place for a murder. A long way from the main house, in the middle of woodlands... Nobody to hear him scream while he was dying.'

'Gruesome,' Lewis muttered.

'And at some point in the past,' she continued more slowly, 'Maurice must have realised that part of the folly wall was crumbling and shoddy, probably because of his amateurish brickwork, and that Jeffrey's body was in danger of exposure. But he couldn't risk bringing in workmen again, hence all the plastic sheeting and metal poles to shore it up.'

'Why take the law into his own hands, though?' Lewis took the confession to study it himself. 'Why not simply hand the real murderer over to the police? By not telling anyone, Maurice seems to have condemned Jeffrey's mother to death instead.'

'But the confession is undated,' she pointed out. 'Perhaps Jeffrey didn't admit what he'd done at first. Perhaps not even until after his mother had been condemned and hanged. Maybe guilt over her death was what drove him to confess.'

Hardcastle was nodding. 'That's a reasonable assumption.'

'Also,' she added, struck by a sudden memory, 'there was something interesting my grandmother wrote in one of her journal entries about her brother not being *the marrying kind*.'

Lewis narrowed his eyes at her. 'You think Maurice was gay?'

'Given this confession, it makes sense. I mean,

why would Jeffrey risk his neck by admitting to Maurice what he'd done, unless they were secretly lovers? Maybe they weren't lovers before the murders, but were attracted to each other, and it was only later, once Maurice had inherited everything and was master in his own household, that they had greater freedom to act on that attraction.' She nodded. 'It would also explain why Maurice chose to confront Sebastian over the housemaid's rape, despite knowing he'd get his teeth kicked in, because she was *Jeffrey's sister*.' She sat up straight, a new thought having occurred to her. 'And that's why Jeffrey was so angry when they beat Maurice... Because he was in love with him. But they could never openly have been lovers, not in those days. God, no wonder Jeffrey hated the Cossentines so much.'

'It could also be why Maurice got such a savage beating that day,' Lewis suggested, who'd become quite interested in the family history since moving into Black Rock Hall to keep her company. 'Because they guessed his motives for interfering and didn't approve. Especially given Jeffrey was a servant, not even his social equal.'

'God, yes, the class divide as well.' Stella gasped. 'And if Maurice *had* passed Jeffrey confession to the police later, he would have risked exposing his sexuality to the world. Homosexuality was still an offence then, punishable by law. Hard labour, imprisonment, even chemical castration... Maurice probably couldn't take a chance on Jeffrey keeping quiet once he was facing the noose.'

'He took a risk leaving the body walled up in the folly though,' Hardcastle pointed out.

'Maybe he half-hoped Jeffrey would be found,' Lewis suggested. 'He must have felt guilty about killing him.'

'Maybe,' Stella said dubiously. 'But I doubt his feelings for Jeffrey were strong enough for him to overlook the murder of his family... His mother and sisters, in particular. His sister Jolie was pregnant, don't forget. Maurice obviously put together that exhibition because he believed in justice and the truth. I don't imagine he would have been able to live with himself if he'd allowed their murderer to walk away. He had to make Jeffrey pay for their deaths somehow,' she said, adding quietly, 'and I suspect Jeffrey agreed to his own execution.'

'Out of love, you mean?' Lewis looked sceptical.

'An obsessive love, yes. On Jeffrey's part at least. Look at what he did for Maurice, after all. Cleared his whole family out of the way so he could be free of them. I'm not sure Maurice ever felt the same for him though, especially once he discovered what he'd done. But for Jeffrey, I imagine his was the kind of love you'd kill for...and die for, if necessary.'

'It's a pity Maurice couldn't have tracked down

Celeste while she was still alive and told her the truth,' Hardcastle said thoughtfully. 'Though he made a good effort to do so, especially after the letter she sent him just before she died.'

'What letter?' Stella was stunned.

'Your grandmother wrote to him on her death bed, apparently.'

'I had no idea.'

'I never saw it myself, but Maurice told me about it later. Apparently, it proved that he was right to keep looking for you, that a 'lost heir' to the estate was still out there.' He smiled at her astonished expression. 'You may find her letter somewhere among his papers, unless Walter destroyed it.'

'I wish I'd known Maurice,' Stella said wistfully, and then shuddered, remembering the withered skeleton she'd uncovered in the old folly. 'Then again, maybe not.'

'A bad business, all round.' Hardcastle stood and reached for his briefcase. 'But at least our statements about Walter and Allison's part in all this have cleared you of any suspicion in Mrs Hepley's death, and the police have found the same poison at Allison's place that was used to kill her. So that's something. But what about the exhibition space?' he asked cheerfully. 'Are you planning to do anything with it? There's not much left after the fire.'

'Well, we don't need it anymore,' Stella pointed

out, 'since we all know whodunnit. And I've put the London flat on the market and plan to apply for an arts grant. If I get it, I'll turn Black Rock Hall into a musical retreat. I'll teach violin and piano, and...' She glanced sideways at Lewis, a smile in her eyes. 'Well, I'm not terribly good at logistics and finance. I could really do with a partner for the business side of things.'

'And to keep the Brunos of this world at a distance?'

She grinned. Lewis had encouraged her to write a stiff letter to Bruno, warning him that she had passed his threatening texts to the police and would not hesitate to pursue him for stalking if he ever contacted her again.

She had never received a reply.

'If you fancy the job, yes.'

Lewis returned her smile lazily. 'Given I no longer come up to scratch as a bodyguard, I'm happy to volunteer my services in other departments.'

She held his gaze for a moment, her heart welling with a strange new emotion. She didn't dare call it love yet, but time would tell. 'Thank you,' she said. 'I was hoping you'd say that.'

Stella walked Hardcastle to the front door, slowly turning the silver ring on her finger, her gaze on the fighting serpents. She hoped there would be no more fighting in the Cossentine family. Not now she was planning to found a new dynasty here at Black Rock Hall. But still…

Amor aeternus. Love eternal. Yes, she liked the sound of that.

The solicitor stood on the steps for a moment, taking in the bracing wintry weather, the hint of grey ocean in the distance, before turning to shake her hand.

'Despite everything, coming here seems to have worked out rather well for you,' Hardcastle said, with the ghost of a laugh. 'I hope you'll be very happy here. You *and* Lewis.' He paused. 'Though it's a shame your grandmother couldn't have come home during her lifetime. I'm sure she'd enjoy seeing you make a proper go of this old place.'

'Oh, Celeste's still here, watching over us,' Stella told him softly, and stepped back inside Black Rock Hall, closing the door with a smile.

THE END

Printed in Great Britain
by Amazon

29898533R00261